PRINCE JODOS CAUGHT THE DEAD GUARD AS HE TOPPLED OVER. AFTER A MOMENT, THE CORPSE STIRRED AND PUSHED ITSELF ERECT.

"Are you in control?" Jodos whispered.

Rattling and whining came from the creature's mouth; it finally replied, "Yes, master!"

Jodos let go the thing's arms and stepped silently toward the bed where his twin brother lay. He looked down at his own face and wanted to smash it, to kill this horrible mockery of himself, and eat it, so that he would be the only one.

But that was not what he had been ordered to do. So, in a single, terrible thrust, he lunged into his brother's mind, gulping its total contents in a single bite....

Also by
PAUL EDWIN ZIMMER

The Dark Border Volume Two:
King Chondos' Ride

THE DARK BORDER
VOL. 1
THE LOST PRINCE
PAUL EDWIN ZIMMER

BERKLEY BOOKS, NEW YORK

THE DARK BORDER VOL. 1: THE LOST PRINCE

A Berkley Book / published by arrangement with
the author

PRINTING HISTORY
PBJ Books edition / September 1982
Berkley edition / April 1983
Fifth printing / April 1984

ISBN: 0-425-06552-9

For my daughter:
FIONA LYNN ZIMMER,
*who is almost exactly
as old as this book*

The Shadow

Sea of Ardren

Lutazema
Spoidia
Dontos
Ipazema

Port Cities

Oxena

Portu Taverna

ATSHNILON

TARENCIA

Kalascor

Uttar

Suklia Kimburzena

Drissia

Tarentia
Iskoda
Chantakar
Udapor
Karianadit
Mahapol
Mahavar

The Mardara

Hindrion R.
Kayurna R.
Nadesdia R.

Inagar
Ujaini
Agnasta

Rishipur

Elfakin
Tansripe

Vajrakota

Eidelborn

Ojakota
Mansipor

Kudrapor

Suknia
Damenco

Rashnagar

THE SHADOW

The Chosen

The Real Men   The Pure-in-Blood

━━ = 42 miles   ⌂ Hastur Tower   ⌂ Fortress   ● City
········ = Border of the Shadow

© Diana L. Paxson 1982

Chapter One

He had never known anything but fear. Like air, darkness, and ground underfoot, it was part of life. But there were few outward signs of the panic that washed over him every time he faced the twisted, black-robed form of the Master.

The squat shape stirred under the black cloth. The muffled, deep-timbred voice hissed at him: "It will be soon, Small Prince. Are you prepared?"

Jodos swallowed. "Yes, Master." In the half-darkness he could feel the terrible eyes behind the black hood. Pleasing the Master was the only way to avoid pain.

"When the King dies," the harsh voice went on, "the Children of Him We Do Not Name will crown your brother King. Then we move. If you fail, you know what will happen to you."

Jodos could become no more frightened than he was already. The fear of death and torture was drowned in the terror of the Master's presence. He had never known love, or friendship, or simple kindness. They were not even words to him. Even his Master's human servants knew nothing of such things. Fear he knew, and hunger and greed and hatred, but such other emotions as he had were warped imitations of the alien emotions of those he served.

He heard a sound in the dimness, and felt the Master's eyes leave him as someone entered the chamber. It was Emicos, his human master—or so Jodos called him, although strictly speaking he had not been human for some time now.

His face was bone-white, and there was dried blood on his chin. His burning eyes stared at Jodos' throat, but the young man always felt an obscure comfort in Emicos' presence, some memory from his childhood, of a time when that face had been different, when those eyes had not glared with that terrible suppressed hunger.

"Is it ready?" hissed the Master.

Emicos bowed, and held out a small box. "A gift for our Prince." There was no mockery in the soft, intensely weary voice. "I have worked hard to prepare it, to further the cause of the Great Ones." He turned to Jodos. "With this you will be able to take servants with you into the palace, protected from the burning, and hidden from the Blue-robes' prying minds. It has two compartments, and two openings."

"So . . ." The Master took the box and looked at it closely. "One to carry and one to bind. I shall place within it those who will serve him. We need only wait for news of the King's death."

Around them, the ancient royal city lay in the darkness that had covered it for a thousand years.

Martos of Onantuga watched as the Twin Suns sank slowly into the smoke and fumes that hid the mountains. He sighed, wishing for a real sunset.

It was hot. It was always hot here, even at night. He wiped the sweat from his forehead and ran his fingers through his carefully trimmed, golden-brown beard, remembering sunset at home, in Kadar, far beyond the inland sea to the north. The northern ramparts of the mountains had been a dim line of blackness on the western horizon, often hidden by nearer, cleaner clouds, and the sunset had been a mass of rainbow colours.

Here there would be only the faintest hint of colour at the very top of the looming wall of shadow, and then the screening vapours that sheltered the servants of the Evil Ones would cut away the light, and gradually the sky would darken overhead.

But long before the blue had faded from the sky, darkness would cover the castle of Lord Jagat. On three sides—west, south, and east—a wall of shadow rose. Only to the north was the sky clear above the barren, poisoned wasteland the Borderers had reclaimed from the Dark Things.

In the courtyard below, the women of the castle were covering the cooking mirrors and pulling the meal out of the great stone ovens at their focus. In the dimming light, the faded patterns of their loose gowns seemed deliberate, as though chosen to blend with this ashen wasteland.

He heard a voice singing, and had to smile as he recognised his own name. Martos of Kadar, they called him, as if he were a Prince of the royal blood of Ore, instead of the younger son of a younger son of the House of Raquio.

The singer's words roused memories of that wild ride through Demon-haunted darkness, of the confused struggle of men and nightmare shapes. It had been a mad enough scheme at that, to place himself with less than a hundred men directly in the path the horde of Night Things must take to return to the Shadow. No wonder men made songs of it!

He struggled to fight down his pride, remembering the words of the philosopher Atrion: *Take no pride in the praise of men, for thus you become a slave to the opinions of others, and will do evil if men will praise you for it.*

Even as his mouth moved with the line, he remembered shaking the kinks out of his arms, forcing himself to relax as he watched the scuttling figures racing down on his little command, and wondering if what they had told him were true, and his dwarf-forged sword of war was keen enough to cut troll-flesh.

And it had been. His fingers tightened on the hilt of the light court-sword he wore now.

The vast form striding towards him, looming above the chaos of battle, its eyes pits of flame, its club tall as a man.

The ground rushing towards him as a glancing blow from that club hurled him from his horse with an aching shoulder and a crumpled shield, even as his keen blade sheared through the huge arm that wielded it.

Staggering to his feet, hurling his ruined shield into the monster's face. Cutting out at shoulder level, the sword gripped with both hands, to shear through the stone-hard flesh behind the knee.

The giant falling like a tree, roaring. Valiros leaning from his horse, his blade glancing harmlessly from stony scales.

A huge hand fastened on the horse, tearing away a chunk of flesh large as a ham.

Valiros trapped under his screaming horse. Men running with axes, striking smashing blows that barely gashed the

*monster's hide as it crawled towards Valiros, dragging its
ponderous body with its single arm and single leg.*

*His curious pity for the poor crippled creature as he leaped to
shear off its head with the dwarf-forged blade . . .*

A good memory to have, whether men praised you for it or not!
He could not help it if men praised him, he decided, but he must
try to make himself more indifferent to that praise, even should he
become as famous as Birthran himself, make himself truly the
Self-Judged Man of whom Atrion had written, to whom praise
and blame were one.

He turned, and saw Kumari. Her eyes were very dark, and
gentle. The fading light accentuated her soft features. Her hair
was black, and her wine-red, clinging gown was cut deeply at the
neck to show the hollow between the firm, jutting breasts whose
softness his hands knew so well.

In the dying light of the sunset, she looked as she had when
they'd first met—and for a moment he was almost as tongue-tied
and silent as he'd been at that first meeting. Then he mastered
himself and stepped forward. Her arms wrapped tightly around
his neck, her body moved against his. Their tongues circled
passionately. She leaned back in his arms, and looked up at him,
smiling.

"Beautiful," he said, breathless, "there's a bed in that room
down the gallery . . ."

But she laughed, and pushed him away. "Not tonight," she
said. "Uncle wants you."

He let go of her. "He sent you for me?"

"He was going to send Pirthio, but I wanted to come." She took
his hand, and set off down the gallery, half dragging him behind
her. "And Pirthio, as the heir, is needed."

In the courtyard below, the guards had kindled tiny fires beside
the gigantic heaps of wood and bales of straw—more precious
than gold in this treeless country—that would be set alight if the
Night Things attacked. Fire was the chief weapon in the long war
against the Dark Ones.

"What does he want?" Martos asked. "Are we at war?"

She shook her head. "I don't think so. I'm not sure. Lord Hamir
and some of the others are there—Suktio, and Lord Saladio, I
think. Uncle wanted you to attend. It must be important. It may be
. . ." She hesitated. "It may be the King has died."

"From what men say, that would be a mercy. It's a wonder the poor old man has lived so long."

They turned into a corridor, and then went down the long staircase. Their feet clopped on hard stone. Witch-jewels glowed dimly from the walls.

"What will he be like?" asked Martos, after a moment. "The new King. Chondos?"

"The Prince of Manjipor?" She shot a sideways glance at him, with a mocking smile. "Uncle wants me to marry him."

"Will you?" he asked.

"Why not?" She laughed. "Just think, if I am carrying your child now, he could be raised among the Princes of the blood, and—"

"Don't joke about such things! If you were carrying my child—" He stopped as she swung to face him.

"I could be, you know. In fact . . ." She paused. "It's too soon to tell, really, but I think perhaps I am. Call it a premonition, if you like."

"But—but," he stuttered a moment, struggling with the lifeless thing his tongue had become. "What will your uncle say? Your kinsmen?"

She put a finger to his lips. "If I carry a child, and it is born alive," she said, her voice level, "people will be too busy rejoicing to ask about the father."

She turned, looked down the stairs. "This is not Kadar," she went on, low-voiced. "This near the Border, living children are rare, and precious. It is not often that a woman of our blood is brought to bed with a living child. That is why so many of our women leave. And if it is stillborn, nobody will blame me for trying." She glanced up then, saw the look on his face, and added quickly, "But really it's much more likely to live now than in the old days, and besides I don't really know yet. It may be just daydreaming."

"But will you not come away with me?" he asked. "Get away from the Border, and the Devils in the hills who attack the very babe in the womb? Marry me and come away, and I will at least find you a place where you can bear children in peace!"

Her head came up angrily, and she glared into his eyes. "Where? Where will you take me? Back to Kadar, to be the wife of a poor fencing-master with no reputation to bring him students? Or must I follow you from camp to camp, as you try to make a name for yourself as a mercenary in wars between men? Knowing always that I have betrayed my blood and run away from my kin? We discussed this before, I think!"

"And you would rather marry Prince Chondos and be Queen of Tarencia," he said bitterly—and instantly regretted it.

But, surprisingly, she smiled at him. "My uncle wishes that." Her face was beautiful in the dim glow of the witch-light set in the wall. "So does every nobleman with a daughter of marriageable age. For myself, I think that Prince Chondos is the most conceited and unpleasant man I have ever met!"

She turned away again, and started down the stairs. Confused, Martos followed.

Far to the north and east, where the Oda flows into the broad Pavana on its way to Portona Mouth, the Twin Suns vanished in rainbow splendour. The shadowed land was a faint smudge on the southern horizon, and not even that in the west.

Prince Chondos looked out over the royal city, his huge dark eyes fixed on the sunset—but what he saw was his father's face. Sometimes it was the strong, dark-bearded face he remembered from his boyhood; but it kept changing into a gaunt, wasted face, with a snow-white beard and burning eyes that struggled always. The face he saw day after day, as the dying King held to life by force of will, refusing to die until all was in order.

With his father gone, there would be no one to trust, no one to talk to. No more happy shared singing, or long peaceful silences where neither need speak. No more long nights analysing the problems of the kingdom. No more, even, of the deep and bitter quarrels . . . Even those he would miss.

Hunting in the jungle, and bright campfires after. Learning swordsmanship, his father passing on the elaborate training-dances and the tricks of a dozen styles of swordplay that he had learned from the world-famous warriors who were his cousins on the DiVega side. Never-ending lessons in statecraft, teasing laughter, family jokes—

Footsteps sounded behind him in the twilight and a young girl's voice broke rudely into precious memories.

"Lord Prince! You should not be alone!" The voice was soft, solicitous. "Will you not come with me, and have wine, and talk? What are you doing here all by yourself?"

"Waiting for my father to die, so I can take his throne, of course!" He did not even turn to see which one it was; they were all alike. "What did you *think* I was doing?"

There was a gasp, and the hurried sound of feet. The tips of his teeth pressed together savagely. The story would be all over the castle by morning; it usually was. Maybe now they would leave him alone for a while!

Let them whisper and talk behind his back! He knew about them! Because he was Prince they scrambled for his favour, but not one of them cared for him except as the source of power and gifts. The women were the worst. All they ever wanted was the precious royal seed, and the royal heir that would ensure the standing and prestige of their families.

He had almost fallen into that trap when he was fourteen. It had been a bitter lesson. He had not dared lie with a woman since, unless she was in her time of bleeding. Indeed, he scarcely dared avail himself of the usual courtesies between young men and women of his class, since that idiot Border girl had scooped up his seed from between her breasts, and started smearing it between her thighs, babbling that royal seed was too precious to waste.

He snorted. Precious indeed! An assured position as mother to a child who might someday be King; power and prestige returning to a minor Border family whose lands had been eaten away by the Shadow.

He almost wished that he had let one of them succeed, so that he need not hold himself back from the numerous lips, breasts, bodies, constantly offered him. But too much hung on the choice of a mother for that first child. The kingdom must be strengthened, not weakened. In order to be able to pick and choose among advantageous alliances, there must be no child with a previous claim that might be pressed.

For a time everything had seemed settled. His father had worked long and hard for the match with Vallauris to the east, but the growing power of Devonia had made that unwise. He could be bound to aid his father-in-law in a war his people could not afford to fight, with the Dark Ones always on the southern border. As for Ashnilon in the west, it was wary of such an alliance: its Princess had been quickly married elsewhere.

Within the kingdom there were only three matches worth considering. There was Monirana, daughter of the Prince of Mahapor—and if *that* marriage could be brought off it would end half the problems of the kingdom, by the next generation at any rate. But old Prince Hansio would rather see the whole kingdom in flames—or even eaten by the Dark Ones, perhaps—than see his daughter wed to the grandson of the man who had made the members of his proud House of Mandava bow their heads to the hated Lords of Tarencia. Then there was Kalascor: Prince Phillipos' sister, Aithra, was a nice little piece, if you liked thirteen-year-olds.

And then there was Pirthio's cousin, Kumari, but she didn't seem to like him much. They had lain together once but had quarrelled afterwards. Border girls were strange, everyone said so. Old Jagat, her uncle, would fall heir to the principality of Manjipé if Chondos could not get an heir *somewhere*. If he married her, he would never have to worry that Jagat's claim would be pressed—not that it was ever likely to be. Jagat was too fiercely honest, or at least seemed so, for his loyalty to be entirely a lie. And Pirthio was his friend, and seemed genuinely to want nothing from him. Though you could never tell. He had trusted people before . . .

His fist knotted, his arm trembled, and his face twisted in rage. Once his father died he would be able to trust *no one!* Politics! Always Politics. They poisoned his life, strangled his thoughts, crept insidiously into his grief for his father. That very morning a man had tried to turn him against one of his father's officials, obviously hoping to get the post himself. Every day the fools fawned on him, knowing he would soon be King.

He did not want to be King. He hadn't wanted to be King since he was twelve.

He brought his fist down on the hard stone, and the pain jarred some of the rage out of him. *Stupid thing to do*, he thought, shaking his hand. *I wonder if it's broken?*

He leaned over the wall of the parapet. Below, the muddy Pavana flowed past the castle wall, on to Portona and the landlocked Sea of Ardren. There seemed to be some excitement by the docks. A crowd of people swarmed there, and he saw messengers running towards the castle. The whole mass drifted towards Pavana Gate: curious spectators surrounding a little group of porters, carrying baggage for some important visitor.

The Prince bent over the parapet, his eyes fixed on the elegant, lordly figure in Seynyorean ruff and doublet, tiny in the distance, walking calmly ahead of the crowd. There was something familiar about that walk. As the procession neared the castle wall, all Chondos could see was the top of a head of grey-flecked hair, set on broad shoulders. But his mind flew back to his childhood, and he knew.

No one else walked quite like that, and even at such a distance, after all these years, there was no mistaking his famous kinsman, the man for whom his father waited, clinging grimly to life: Istvan DiVega, whom minstrels' songs named Istvan the Archer.

As Kumari pushed open the door of the Council Chamber, Lord Jagat's voice rang out angrily.

". . . free principality! And then what? Eat grain you raise yourselves and watch child after child die in the womb as the Dark Ones blight the fields? Starve, because there is no longer a King to make the midlands send us food?"

Martos and Kumari slipped quietly through the door. The Lord of Damenco stood in the centre of the room like a boar at bay, his face swarthy under his silver hair, his back to the long table at which his chair of state stood empty. The rich embroidery at neck and sleeves of his dark robe was frayed, but there was no doubt who was Lord here.

Facing him were six Bordermen, lean and dark, robed in the patched and faded silk passed down through generations of poverty and toil. In the corner Jagat's son Pirthio stood watching. Martos and Kumari made their way to his side.

"Better that," said a stocky young man in threadbare robes that had once been rich and brightly colored. "Better all you have said, under a true Prince of the Arthavan line, than to continue to bow to this upstart DiVega! We have stood alone before! We have our own wizards to guard our grain. We need not depend on the midlands."

"Wizards fail." Painful memories haunted Jagat's scowling eyes. "Fine words, fine words, Lord Hamir, but you speak of matters you are too young to remember! I have lived in a free principality, under a true Lord of the Arthavan line." The scorn in his voice was thick. "When you were still a child, our Princess' marriage saved us from that glorious state! The throne of Manjipé, as well as Tarencia, descends to her son, Chondos. *He* is your true Prince of the Arthavan line!"

"But Prince Singram had two sons," said another Lord, his patched robe bleached ash-grey, "and one was your great-grandfather. Your claim to the throne is better, for it comes through the male line."

"Why, whoever would have guessed?" Jagat walked around the table and dropped into the low chair of state. "Imagine my forgetting who my great-grandfather was! And now that you have produced this news, this startling piece of genealogy, I am to come over to your side, seize the throne of Manjipé, and we will all live happily in our free principality, merrily raising our own food as in days of yore. How sweet! I am overcome with noble feelings."

"We can dominate Massadessa, and most of Orissia," said Suktio, one of Jagat's vassals. Alone of the men in the room, he wore a rare shirt of the ring-mail that had come down from ancient times, from the great days of Takkarian glory: few had such an heirloom. "We can get grain enough from them! But you need not mock us because we want you instead of Chondos to rule us. We know you both, and know who we would rather serve."

"Not mock?" Jagat's white eyebrows rose. "Even after such an amusing statement about dominating Orissia, which took the Hinarion Valley away from us, fifty years ago? You deserve mockery. You are fools!" He rose from the chair. "But I fear you must find your true Prince of the Arthavan line somewhere else. I am King Olansos' man."

"And Chondos?" cried Lord Hamir, sweeping the air with the wing of his sleeve. "I have served Prince Chondos, ridden with him against the Night Things! What reward did I ever get for my service? Insults! Gibes! Should the descendents of the Takkars allow themselves to be taunted by the grandson of a northern mercenary?"

"Do you think you'll get better from me?" Jagat roared. "You deserve insult! Our King is dying, our great King, who has put this realm together with his own hands, his own sweat, his own blood! Who has made it possible to drive the Demons back from Manjipor and recover a little of our ancient land—the land on which we stand *now!* And while he yet lives, you dare to plot against his son, to tear down what he—and I, and mine—have striven for?

"You are my vassals or my kin. That alone saves you. Fools! Do you think I do not know of the emissaries from Portona who are gently stirring this pot? Do you not realise that all they wish is to stop paying the tax that buys our bread?" He glared at them, and his voice dropped to a growl. "You are my kinsmen, and so you need not fear that I will speak of this to any other. But if you dare act against your rightful King, in word or deed, you will answer to me. Now go."

None of them dared to speak. They shuffled from the room like children, staring at the floor. He glared at them until the last had passed beneath the stone arch, carven with flowers the Border had not seen for ages, then swung around to face Kumari.

"Took you long enough to bring him," he grunted. "Where was he, on top of Mount Acala?"

His eyes moved to Martos. "I want you to remember the names and faces of those men. We'll be at war with Portona, and probably Mahapor, before the end of the year. I want my commanders to know who they can and who they can't trust.

"The fat fool who did most of the talking was Hamir of Inagar. He controls the province on the other side of the Prince's domain, between the Marunka and the Yukota. If he didn't look so full-fed, I might have found less to mock, but he hasn't starved enough to be taken seriously." Martos could not help smiling. Only another Borderman would call Hamir of Inagar *fat*.

"The tall moron in grey—" Jagat went on, "the one instructing me on the mysteries of my own genealogy—that's Moklos, one of Hamir's vassals. The one in red, Bajio of Kaspor, is Lord of Kalgaviot. Did you see him nod when Suktio—the scar-faced fellow who holds Varakota for me, you know him—was spouting his nonsense about dominating Orissia? He nodded, and it was *his* grandfather who lost us our farmlands along the Hinarion! And Lord Saladio—"

Pirthio broke in angrily, his black eyes smouldering, unable to contain himself any longer. "He's hated the Prince ever since Chondos made Maldeo his Vicar and gave him Manjipor as a direct fief! He wanted the city himself, and he knows Maldeo will hold it as long as Chondos is on the throne. It's just jealousy and greed, that's all!"

"That would be Prince Chondos' side of the matter, I doubt not!" said Jagat, smiling at his son. "But you must remember, Pirthio, that every coin has two faces. They may be very different, but the value of the coin is in the metal between. You cannot take one face of a coin to market. Chondos' side of the tale may not be false, yet it is not the whole of the tale. There is much to be said on Lord Saladio's side as well. Our Prince is"—he sighed—"seldom tactful. Often he wounds those who might be his friends."

"He has no patience with fools and rogues!" said Pirthio. "No more than you have, Father. And his mind is quicker than other men's, and he has no patience—"

"I know," his father said. "I have felt the rage inside him when he feels another has been intentionally stupid. If Chondos could sense the stirring in other men's hearts, as I do, then perhaps he would learn to control that rage. But he thinks only of what Prince Chondos thinks and feels, and cares nothing for how another might interpret his actions."

But is that a fault? Martos wondered, remembering the words of Atrion.

"Now, as I was saying," Jagat continued, "there will be war when the King dies. All the coastal cities will rise, probably Orissia and Ipazema too. The whole north, with the Guild Council of Portona at its head. Mahapor province is waiting for just such an opportunity, whether there's any formal alliance with Portona or not. But if I know Hansio, the old fox will wait until we're fully engaged with Portona before he makes his move."

He sat down and shook his head. "The only thing that could hold the kingdom together—and I hate to say or even think it—would be another major assault by the Dark Ones." He frowned at the table, his eyes remote, then shook himself and leaned forward again. "In any case, everything's arranged. I'll be leading the Manjipé levies. You two will be my chief

aides, and will often find yourselves stuck with command—
Pirthio because he's the heir, and you, Martos, because you're
the Hero of Ukarakia." The old man sank back in his chair,
eyeing them thoughtfully. His eyes moved to Kumari, brooded
on her.

"We need more Seers," he muttered to himself, after a
moment. "We should mix more with the Seynyoreans—breed
into our blood and . . ." His fingers drummed on the table; then
he sat up with a jerk. "In the morning I must leave for the capital.
The King has summoned me. He cannot last much longer, and
wants to confer. What greeting should I bear him from you,
Kumari?"

The girl blushed and bit her lip, and Martos saw the old man
wince.

"What greetings do any of his subjects send him?" Her voice
was level, but there was an edge of strain. "Do I have to *say*
anything, Uncle?"

"No, child," Jagat said, wearily. He turned to Martos and
Pirthio. "You two will be in charge while I'm gone. When the
King dies—it cannot be long now—Pirthio must ride and join
me at once. You take over then, Martos. I want you to escort
Kumari to the Coronation. Put a man you can trust in charge of
the castle—Udio or Ymros, I would suggest, but as you
will—and plan to arrive the night before the Coronation. That
should be safe enough. Hamir and the rest will all be there.
Hmm—just to be sure, make Suktio a part of the escort." He
scowled.

"No telling what those fools will do next," said Jagat. "They
might even go to Prince Hansio and offer the throne to him. The
Mandavans have intermarried with our house often enough to
give him some claim. And, of course, his line comes from the
Takkarian Kings too—you should marry his daughter, Pirthio."

"I've thought about it."

Jagat yawned. "I want to get to bed. I've a hard ride
tomorrow, and there is no surety the King will be alive when I
get there." He sighed, and pushed himself out of his chair. "I
heard he's sent for his cousin—the famous one."

Martos looked up sharply. A stirring of glory pulsed through
him and sparked in his eyes. "Istvan DiVega? Istvan the
Archer?"

"Yes." Jagat laughed. "Don't call him that to his face, though. He hates the name."

"So my Swordmaster, Birthran, told me. Both Istvan and Raquel DiVega are old comrades of his."

"Yes, I remember Birthran. He was down here looking for the Lost Prince, twenty years or so ago, along with Istvan and Raquel DiVega, Tahion of the House of Halladin—all the great heroes, or nearly all. Demitrios Chalcondiel died here, you know. Ambushed by Demons while he was looking for little Prince Jodos." He pushed back the chair of state and rose.

"I was a young man, then," said Jagat. "I'm not now, though. I've a long journey in the morning, and I haven't eaten yet. Come along, children."

Istvan DiVega had travelled steadily for more than two months: by land as far as Paracosma, by ship the length of the Sea of Ardren, and finally by riverboat from Portona Mouth. It had been a long and tiring voyage, with no better reward at the end than the chance to see a friend die.

That Olansos was dying he had long known. But until he entered the sickroom and saw the thin, wasted face lying among richly embroidered pillows, it had been only a word. *Dying.* Cold upon him Istvan the Archer felt the blast of old age, the slow and creeping change that would soon turn hair and beard as white as the King's.

A frail and ghostly smile moved Olansos' lips, and the pale blue eyes brightened. "Cousin!" he cried, for the King, too, was a DiVega, his father a younger son of the great Seynyorean family, a mercenary who had won a wife with a throne for dowry. "Forgive me that I do not rise to greet you. The good Brothers of the Order have worked themselves sick keeping me alive until you came. Soon I will let them rest. Come, Cousin, sit beside me."

Shock and dismay struggled with Istvan's tongue. *How can he be so cheerful?*

"I saw Cousin Raquel in Kadar, on my way south," Istvan said, torn by the need to say *something.* "He and Birthran both send their greetings." The only other things he could think of to say sounded either silly or morbid, so he shut his mouth and sat down, adjusting the sling of his sword to let it lie neatly along his lap.

"Leave us." The King waved a weak hand at the red-robed Healer who hovered inconspicuously near the door. "I am sure that my kinsman can shout loudly enough if I begin to die. You too, Aratos, but first pour us wine."

The King's bodyservant, almost as frail and old as his master, busied himself in the corner. Istvan stared past the toe of his boot at the rioting colours of the Alferridan carpet. Old, yes, but *this* old? Age, old age, it crept on you so slowly, so surely . . .

Minstrels said that Istvan DiVega was a brave man. He knew better. He feared death as much as anyone did. It was his trust in his own skill that had brought him unflinching through battle after battle, confident he would still be alive when the fighting was over.

"You look worse than I do, Cousin!"

Startled, Istvan looked up. The King's eyes twinkled.

"Oh, I was thinking," Istvan said slowly. "I always thought I would be able to fight my way out of—well, almost anything. But . . ." He hesitated a moment then shrugged. "You cannot meet Time with a sword."

"No, you can't," said the King with a smile. Aratos brought goblets and a flagon on a tray, and bent to pour.

"I haven't much news from home—from Seynyor, I mean," said Istvan. He listened to the wine gurgle in the goblets. "I've been serving in Thorban the last few years. You already know, I suppose, that Raquel is Swordmaster to the House of Ore now, along with Birthran?"

Aratos, with a mournful glance at his master, slipped from the room.

"I had heard that," said Olansos. "The next King of Kadar will be well taught. But I must confess, Cousin, that I did not call you away from your profitable ventures in the north just to see your ugly face again, pleasant though that is. I have work for you."

Istvan grunted, not really surprised, and leaned forward to listen. The King's voice was growing steadily weaker as he spoke, as though the energy with which he had greeted his cousin was now used up.

"I must take thought for what will follow my death. Chondos is"—the King paused, and sipped at his wine— "not popular. He will be an able lawgiver. And a good general—and warrior. I've taught him all I could of what you've taught me. But"—he paused again, breathing hoarsely—"he uses his tongue as a lash. He will *not* learn tact. He makes enemies."

I warned you ten years ago, Istvan thought, but said nothing. A deathbed is no place to remind a man of his mistakes.

"I put this kingdom together with my own hands, Istvan." The old man's voice sunk almost to a whisper. "You know that. When Father came, there were a dozen squabbling little principalities and city-states. The Bordermen were cut off from the main trade routes, with their own poor lands barely able to feed them—and the Shadow gobbling that away. The coastal cities were rich, the midland farmers well-off, while the Bordermen were pushed back a little farther each year, a vanishing race, forgotten by people whose own land was safe only as long as the Bordermen stood between." He paused for breath, and sipped more wine.

"They're a proud people," Istvan muttered.

"They've reason to be!" said the King. "They claim descent from the ancient Takkarians, who once ruled all this part of the world. They've fought for every scrap of land the Dark Ones have taken from them. Did you know there was a time when the border was actually *inside* Manjipor? Half the city was under the Shadow—and people were *living* in the other half! Women and children, too! They stayed, and fought as best they could, with what help the Children of Hastur were able to give them, until the Shadow was driven back." His voice had grown shrill and rasping; he paused to drink wine and catch his breath.

"I'd heard stories about that," said Istvan, "but I'd always thought them some poet's lies."

"No," the King whispered. "When I was a boy I knew old men who had lived through it. Jagat's grandfather, for one. Even then, the Shadow was barely a mile south of the city. There are men living now in castles a few miles from the Border—castles where Night Things laired only ten years ago. All Damenco was under the Shadow when I married Tarani."

"I remember," said Istvan.

"Things could be that bad again," said Olansos.

Chapter Two

Forty miles north, the Pavana poured fresh water into the wide bay of Portona Mouth, to mingle with the salty currents of the Sea of Ardren. To either side the coast went curving up to the north like the toe of a sock.

A ship following the curving coast some one hundred and fifty miles to the north and east will reach the harbour of the lesser port city of Poidia. Two days' ride due east is the province of Ipazema.

At last the envoy entered the room where the Duke of Ipazema sat waiting impatiently.

"What word from the Council of Guilds?" the Duke demanded. The envoy bowed. The duke leaned back in his golden chair, and his thick black eyebrows were like thunder-clouds above his black beard.

"The Council has agreed that all is in order." The messenger from Portona was pudgy, clerkish-looking. He appeared ill-at-ease in the pleated tunic of gold brocade, which was doubtless richer than the garments he usually wore. "Our mercenary troops are being called in. Bribes have been set aside for the commanders of companies employed by the Crown. Once the King dies—"

Ipazema interrupted rudely. "I am starting to think that old man will outlive us all! What else?"

The envoy, flustered, stuttered a minute. "Once the King dies," he began lamely, "there will be a period of confusion—"

"I know that, you idiot!" the Duke snorted angrily. "Has the Council managed to set a date? Or are they still arguing?"

The messenger blinked owlishly, and wilted under the

Duke's angry glare. Nervously he licked his lips. "Only that it should be between the old King's death and the Coronation, probably the day before Chondos is to be crowned."

"Brilliant!" the sensuous lips moved in a sneer under the Duke's bristling black beard. "All that was settled months ago! What about the other cities?"

"The League is sound, Your Grace. All will rise when Portona rises."

"That's something!" The Duke's white teeth flashed. "All that's needed is for *Portona* to rise! Is there any word from Prince Hansio?"

"The message Prince Hansio sent to the council was . . . um, somewhat enigmatic, Lord, but it is the opinion of—"

"Wait!" the Duke barked. "*Somewhat* enigmatic? Just what *did* the message say?"

"The Prince said that he had no need of our gold—though he did *not*, Lord Duke, send the gold back—but that all the country looked to Portona to humble these upstart DiVegas."

"Somewhat enigmatic!" The Duke laughed. "The Old Fox is watching and waiting! You'll not get *him* to show his hand too soon! He knows that the Royal Army's waiting for him to move, and he's hoping that the rising will draw them off. Very clever."

"That was what the Council thought the message might mean, Lord Duke. Prince Hansio's hatred is well known."

"To think," the Duke said, "that this is the hero of all those ballads! A brave man, but a smart one, Prince Hansio! Mahapol" (the usual northern mispronunciation for *Mahapor*) "will rise, but only *after* Portona has led the way."

Cynically, he thought to himself, *A good thing for Hansio I'm behind these rabbits, pushing them, or he might wait forever*.

Eyes closed, the King lay very still and shrunken among his pillows. Istvan looked up from the map he had been studying, and for a heart-stopping moment thought the old man had died.

Then, as he filled his lungs to shout for the Healer, he saw the chest move under the white beard, and heard the sound of a snore. He laid the map on the bed and slid to his feet, meaning to slip from the room and summon the Healer; but as he moved, the King's eyes snapped open.

"I wasn't asleep!" The King rolled up onto one elbow. "Just

resting a moment. Where were we? Oh yes—if Chondos dies without an heir, then the throne will pass to Illissia, my daughter by my first wife, who married Phillipos of Kalascor. Jagat would be Prince of Manjipor, and his people would force . . ." He finally saw the confusion on Istvan's face and paused. "But I've wandered off the subject, haven't I? Let's see, I was talking about . . . the merchant cities, and their taxes . . ."

"And the mercenaries," said Istvan, helpfully.

"The mercenaries, yes. That's why you're here," said the King. "You must forgive an old man if his mind wanders sometimes." He let himself fall back and collapse against the pillows with a sigh.

"Yes, yes. We have so many mercenary troops—most of them," he rolled his head towards Istvan, and winked, "*Seynyorean* mercenaries, of course!—that the balance of power will depend on which side they take. Portona is secretly trying to hire them all. It can afford to, with all the wealth that flows through the city. But the mercenaries will take the side you're on, because you're Istvan DiVega, the greatest swordsman in the world."

"What nonsense!" Istvan snorted. "Both Raquel and Birthran are still alive!"

"But they're old now," said the King. "Almost as old as I am. And I hear Prince Tahion is dead, and Tugar of Thorban."

"Tugar's dead, true enough," said Istvan. "I was there. Demon got him. Wasn't pretty to watch. But there are *always* rumours of Tahion's death. He's hard to kill, and a lot younger than I am."

"Well," said the King, soothingly, "even if you're not the best swordsman alive, that's the reputation you have, and that's what counts. If it's known that you support Chondos, all the *Seynyorean* mercenaries, at least, will follow you. They're the largest single force. There are several dozen scattered around, some employed by the Bordermen, some paid directly by the Crown, a few in the pay of the coastal guilds. But they all know it's the taxes from Portona that allow the Crown and the Border nobles to pay them."

"All the more reason to put the revolt down quickly, then," Istvan said thoughtfully. "Several Seynyorean companies, you say? What are the rest?"

"Ahh, let me think," said the King. "There are three companies of Carrodian Axemen—two of them employed as marines by the Portona Shipping Guild, the other by Chondos' Vicar in Manjipé. That's Ironfist Arak's company, so you're not the only famous man in the area. The other two are led by someone named Gunnar, I think, and one of the Kung family. Nobody too well known."

"Probably Esrith Gunnar and either Asbiorn or Sigard Kung," said Istvan, as though to himself.

"Hamir of Inagar hired a troop of N'lantian Bowmen—the Farshooters, they call themselves. And Jagat has a company of Kadarin Cavalry led by Mar . . . let's see, Martos of Anataka, or something of the sort."

Istvan looked up sharply. "Martos? Martos of Onantuga?"

"Why, yes, yes, I think that was the name." The King's eyebrows rose. "You know him?"

"I know *of* him," said Istvan. "He's one of Birthran's students—his best, from the way Birthran brags about him."

"Hmm!" said the King. "He's built up a bit of a reputation locally, but I'd not heard of him before that. Birthran's best student," he mused, shaking his head, "right here in the kingdom all along. If I'd known, I'd have had him come and teach the boy. Chondos may need all his skill. *You'll* help the boy with his swordwork, won't you, Istvan?"

Istvan grunted in reply. The air in the room seemed choking, filled with the presence of death. He cursed himself for a coward. Had he not seen death often enough, on field after bloody field, to have gotten over his fear of it? But that was clean killing, where death had an understandable reason, because your head had come off, or there was a sword-point stuck in your heart. Or because a Demon had dissolved the flesh off your bones. But this horrible slow waiting, watching your body run down . . .

He was supposed to be cheering his cousin, not depressing himself!

"You said Martos had picked up something of a local reputation?" asked Istvan.

"Indeed yes! Quite a reputation. Some months back, a really big raiding party broke over the Border—ghouls, goblins, trolls, men from the Dark Kingdoms, a Demon or two—and attacked a small village called Ukarakia, near Jagat's castle. The Children of Hastur came from their towers, and drove the Night Things from the town with need-fire. They ran for the Border—and found Martos waiting for them. With less than a hundred men he held them there until Jagat could come up with his army. It's thought that none escaped. You can imagine the reaction of the Bordermen to *that!*"

"They must worship him," said Istvan. The King nodded.

"Yes. Is it true what they say, that the Kadarin Army is the best in the world?"

"It was true thirty years ago," said Istvan. "I should know—I fought at Ovimor Field, on the wrong side. But now . . . ?" He shrugged. "I'm not sure."

"I do wish I'd known about Martos before," said the King petulantly. "I've done the best I could for Chondos. I've probably made him the best swordsman in the kingdom, but . . . well, too late for a lot of things now. I hope you'll teach him a little. He's still so young. If he was just a few years younger I could appoint you Regent. Or Jagat. That would solve so many problems. But you will help the boy, won't you, Istvan?"

Control the breath and you control the mind, Istvan thought. Something in the King's voice sent a shiver of horror through him. He took a deep breath, held it, let it go.

"What is it, exactly, that you want me to do?" he asked.

"Promise me that you'll see Chondos securely on his throne. That you'll stay and support him until the danger of revolt is past. That you'll fight for him and counsel him, and use all your influence to strengthen his cause."

"I swear it," said Istvan, breathing slowly and deeply. "I swear it by the honour of our ancestors."

"Good," said the King. He closed his eyes. "Now I can die in peace. I'm grateful, Cousin, very grateful."

"But what arrangements have you made for me?" asked Istvan quickly. "Has Chondos agreed to follow my advice? What's my position at court? Official Pest?"

The King laughed. "I *have* discussed it with Chondos. You will be Supreme Commander of all mercenary forces, which gives you a place on his Council. The papers are all drawn up and signed. You needn't worry about any of it." He lay back with a yawn.

The King's face was so pale and drawn that Istvan felt ice trickling about his heart. "Shall I fetch the Healer, Cousin?" he asked. "You look . . ." He paused, and the old man shook his head.

"I'm just very tired, that's all. Help me with these cushions, if you would, so I can lie flat."

Istvan lifted the King and pulled the cushions away. The King smiled.

"I've been having an argument with the Healers, you know. They were telling me that since I was a wise and noble King in this life—they said it, not me—I had earned myself a higher birth next time, and would be born a great wizard or hero, or perhaps even a Hastur. *What?* I said to them, *you mean the reward for hard work is harder work? I'm going to be born a peasant next time! I deserve a rest!*" He smiled up at Istvan, who somehow managed to twist his face into what he hoped looked like an answering smile.

At least, with the blood of Hastur in your veins, you wouldn't have to worry about old age, he thought. It wasn't fair. Why could not men be like the Immortals—Hastur's descendents, the elf-folk of far Y'gora? Even the Sorcerers that served Dark Ones did not die unless they were killed. Indeed, only by serving the Dark Things could a mortal man hope for extended life. Even the greatest of the wizards that served the Hasturs would live little, if any, past the normal span.

"Jagat should be here in a few days," the King said. "You'll have to go over the timing of the invasion of Mahapor with him. Remember, it's *por*, not *pol*—you'll hear it wrong around the court often enough. I did tell you about the plans for countering the revolt in Mahapor, didn't I?"

"At length and in gruesome detail," Istvan assured him.

"Yes, I suppose I did," said the King. "What was the old joke they used to tell about me? Something about a discussion of strategy being the surest cure for insomnia?"

"They used to say," Istvan said, "that the reason you won all your battles was that your generals were always well rested from the strategy sessions the night before."

The King chuckled, then yawned again. "Next to you, I'm depending chiefly on Jagat. He's the most loyal man in the kingdom. He'll lead the forces of Manjipé and the Kantara across the Atvanadi from Kantakin. You and Phillipos should—" He broke off, yawning. "Perhaps you'd better fetch the Healer and leave now after all, Cousin. I'm so tired, I was starting to fall asleep in the middle of saying something. You should rest too, after travelling so far. We'll talk again. In the morning."

Istvan slid to his feet. "Tomorrow then. Sleep well, Cousin." He felt a horrid relief at leaving the sickroom, with its brooding presence of approaching death. It was his duty to sit with his cousin, to make his last days comfortable.

He was almost to the door, still cursing his guilty reluctance to go through this again, when he heard a gasp and rustling sound, and then Olansos' voice:

"Wait!"

Istvan whirled, certain the old man was going to die *now*. The King had pushed himself up on his elbow. His voice, shrill and thin, babbled excitedly.

"I forgot to tell you! Chondos has bad dreams!"

Istvan stared at him. Was the old man's mind gone then?

"Terrible recurring dreams. Always of the mountains, and the darkness. Lord Shachio and the Hasturs say that means Jodos is still alive."

Jodos? Istvan hunted for the name through his memories, then stiffened as he remembered. Jodos, twin brother to Chondos. Istvan had never had any hope that the child would ever be found alive, not even when he and Rafael had combed the edges of the Shadow nearly twenty years ago. Why, the child had still been a suckling. What on earth could the Dark Things have found for it to *eat?*

"It's not possible," Istvan said flatly. "And even if it was, he can hardly ride in with a horde of goblins at his back and claim the throne."

"No. Well, I thought you should know. Good night, Cousin."

"Good night, Olansos," said Istvan, but now he walked across the room and kissed the old wrinkled forehead. "Pleasant dreams."

So far from the Border, peaceful sleep and pleasant dreams were simple. South, along the great wall of shadow that hid the

Dark Things, sleep was rarely peaceful. Scarcely a night passed without something from the mountains creeping over the Border to feed. A troll might smash its way into a barn to carry off a cow, a vampire might take a careless guard from a castle wall. These things were normal, and expected; it was not these fears that haunted the sleep of the Bordermen. But all dreaded the breaking of the Border; the bursting forth of great raiding armies, or, worse still, the sporadic mass attacks by which the Dark Things strove to enlarge their realm.

Guards watched the wall of starless blackness, fingering weapons wizards had wrought for them, and keeping close to their tiny watch-fires and the piles of fuel ever ready to light. And always their eyes sought out the distant shapes of the glowing towers that rose against the very edge of the Shadow, fearing to see the need-fire leap up. Within those towers, Immortal minds watched the Border.

Before Hastur could people the world, he had first had to cleanse it of the deadly powers that Sorcerers of an extinct race had called down upon themselves from outside the Universe. That had become a legend among the descendents of the men Hastur brought into the world; a thousand years passed before they learned it was true. Then the barriers broke; the Eight Dark Lords stalked across the world, and ate up whole nations where they passed.

Only at great cost did the Children of Hastur hurl the Eight back to their own place. The Sword of Hastur was broken, and the Son of Hastur slain, before the Greatest of the Eight could be driven from the world, and on the spine of the mountain chain that spanned the continent from north to south, the track of the Dark One became a vast and barren waste. The servants that the Dark Lords had left behind covered with Shadow that great blot of poisoned earth, and the powers of the surviving Hastur-kindred were no longer great enough to drive them from it.

For more than nine thousand years the glowing towers raised by the Hastur-kin had ringed the Shadow, trying to hold it back from the lands of men. Each time the Shadow grew, new towers were needed.

From their citadel of Carcosa in Seynyor, the Hasturs ruled

the world. Mortal Kings were their vassals. No King was crowned save by their hands. But outside royal courts few mortals ever saw them. Seers, Healers, and wizards trained in Carcosa, and in the streets of the mortal city of Carcosa that spread below Hastur's citadel, it was not uncommon for them to mingle with men.

But the Borderers knew them. In peaceful times men might ride in daylight to the glowing towers, asking aid in reclaiming the land. Only the Hasturs could clean away the poisonous grey dust that the great Demons left; before anything could be grown on the land, it must be scoured down to bedrock, and new soil built up, with dung and garbage and the ashes of the dead. And when the Border blazed with need-fire and night-mare shapes raged through the land, the Children of Hastur appeared to aid the hard-pressed Bordermen.

But the Seynyorean mercenaries knew them best of all. For the nobles of the *Land of the Lords* counted the House of Hastur as the eldest of their list of noble houses; nor were Hasturs displeased that in the streets of Carcosa the Elduayens, the D'Oleves, DiFlaccas, DiArnacs, Vegas, and DiVegas greeted them as kinsmen and equals. On the far-flung battle-fields of the endless war against the Dark Things, the nobles of Seynyor had proved their worth.

None would dare war on the *Land of the Lords*, but the noble houses sent their sons out across the world, mercenaries, an elite soldiery who could command high prices from any they served. And the great families were rich with the loot from thousands of years of war.

Though they might serve anywhere when the Border was quiet, every great stirring of the Shadow found them flocking to the Border from all across the world.

For this the Hasturs had bred them.

Habit woke Istvan DiVega before dawn. His hand shot out at once to the low rack where his sword rested in easy reach. Donning a light dressing-robe, he descended to the grey mists of the garden, buckling his sword-belt tightly, and adjusting the sling until the scabbard hung nearly parallel to the ground. The grass was damp under his bare feet. There was a faint chill to the mist, delicious after the stifling heat of the night.

His mind hunted among the various ceremonial training-dances that were the basis of the School of the Three Swords. Years had passed since he had used either the needle-sword or the two-handed sword of war; his technique with court-sword had been refined and extended by contact with other styles from distant parts of the world. It was strange, he thought, that he still considered himself part of the school.

But that was the task of the Swordmaster; each new technique that he mastered, he passed on to Birthran and Raquel, to teach to their students. Thus the school had lived and grown, since Adonn of Leventosa had founded it in the last century . . .

His arms hung loose and relaxed at his sides. He stood casually, breathing deeply. Swift and sudden as a bird, his hand flew to the ivory hilt. He stepped forward, his blade whipping from the sheath, slashing the mist at the level of a human throat. Then he was spinning to the left, and the blade hissed down in the cut that could slice cleanly through a collarbone to reach the artery behind. The pommel dropped to the left hand waiting at his hip, and his knees straightened as he made a long, two-handed lunge.

Out of boyhood memories he seemed to hear old Adonn's voice: *The secret of true swordsmanship is the calm acceptance of death.*

He pivoted on the balls of his feet, the natural movement of his body freeing the blade from his imaginary opponent.

Raquel, Birthran, old Demitrios Chalcondiel, all said much the same thing.

The sword hissed down. His left hand released its hold. The sword passed in front of his eyes, rising to the guard above his head. His mind showed him the great practise hall of the school in Kadar—Birthran, lecturing his students: *You face death each time you touch the sword. Remember this, and in time Death will become an old and dear friend. You will smile when you meet him.*

Blade and arm stretched to the right in a long thrust.

Was he, alone among the Master Swordsmen, afraid of dying? Had he failed to find some basic and simple answer to the fear of death that all the others had discovered long ago, and assumed that he knew also?

Both hands brought the blade around in a looping arc that could take off a man's head. His bare feet moved swiftly over the grass.

Or were these phrases only empty words? He remembered old Demitrios Chalcondiel, the great hero of his father's generation: *Nothing is so futile as a life wasted in flight from death.*

His body shifted to the side as his blade dipped in the slash that ripped a man's guts out. It was Cousin Raquel's voice that he heard now: *Mortal men die when their time comes, today or ninety years from today.*

The sword lashed out in the final stroke of the dance, and hung poised in his hand. He shook it as he would to shake blood from the blade. With a fold of soft cloth he wiped the dampness of the mist carefully from the blade. Although its enchanted, Hastur-forged steel could not have rusted though it lay a thousand years on the ocean floor, habit wiped the blade, and habit would cleanse and oil it later, as carefully as a blade of common steel must be cleansed and oiled.

The golden moons of dawn hung in the east. He shivered, wet with sweat in the morning mists. The sword-guard clicked against the metal lip of the scabbard.

Before the grey had touched his hair, death had many times seemed certain, yet he had felt no terror. Did age make cowards of all men? *Perhaps the young never believe they can really die.*

The Twin Suns flared on the rim of the world. Time to be up and doing. He went back to his room, found a towel, and stepped into the dim candlelight of the corridor. He wondered if the bath attendants were awake yet.

By the half-open door of the King's room he saw the Red-robe asleep in a chair. The man stirred and looked up as Istvan approached.

Istvan stopped, and was suddenly ashamed to realise he had not thought of his cousin all morning. "How is the King, Healer?" he asked, low-voiced.

"Sleeping soundly." The Healer rubbed his eyes and blinked at the daylight that was slowly filtering into the palace. "But it is time I looked in on him again! A moment." He lurched to his feet and tiptoed through the door. Istvan waited, the towel over his shoulder. Perhaps the Healer could direct him to the bathing rooms . . .

He heard the Healer gasp sharply, and was through the door and inside the room instantly, already knowing what he would find there.

The Healer dropped the limp arm to the bed, and laid his palm on the still, white chest, his face blank with concentration. Sometime in the early hours of the morning, the old man's heart had stopped. There was a smile on the cold lips.

Seers spread the news across the kingdom in a flicker of thought. The Twin Suns crawled across the sky. Below, some men mourned, while others plotted treason.

The Duke of Ipazema's teeth flashed. *Now these rabbits will have to do something! Maybe they'll get things under way at last!*

Jagat had left his castle an hour before the news came, and for hours he rode unknowing over grey and barren land. Not until noon did he hear it. His face turned pale and grave, and he drove his horse on like a madman, galloping on towards Tarencia through the furious dust of the highway, as if the King could still be saved.

Pirthio followed at an easier pace. A plan was shaping itself in his head. Portona gold might stir up rebellion among the Bordermen, but it would buy neither lasting alliance nor lasting peace. Divided though the Bordermen were by the age-old feuds that had torn apart the remnants of ancient Takkaria, they all despised the coastal merchants.

Behind him mournful men laboured in the stone desert surrounding Jagat's castle, spreading dung and sand and clay over the bared bedrock to build soil where food might someday grow. Kings might die, but the land must live. The land was all.

Clover grew on new-made fields, clamping the soil with wiry roots. All about the castle, new fields lay fallow, waiting to be hallowed by the ashes of the dead. They seldom waited long, on the Border.

Martos and his men toiled alongside the Borderers, for farmwork was counted as honourable labour, suitable for Kadarin gentlemen—and in this case, it could be counted as work of war. For this was a war that never ended.

But Martos worked with one eye on the sky above, on the slow-moving suns. For after both Jagat and Pirthio had gone, Kumari had squeezed his hand and whispered in his ear: *"Tonight! The tower room!"*

Tonight! Would night never come? To him the day seemed endless. The Twin Suns crawled across the sky.

Chapter Three

Night came. At intervals of sixty miles or so, all along the Border that divided the Shadow from the lands of men, the Hastur-towers glowed dimly against the darkness.

In Agnasta Tower beside the Yukota, where strong spells purify the water of the river as it flows out of the Shadow, Elenius Hastur sensed a subtle tension. His powerful mind probed the wall of darkness. He felt forces building there, powerful sorceries of the Dark Ones. His companion in the watch, young Kisil, who had not yet grown out of his mortal years, was also testing the blackness, and even as the two called to their kin, Elenius touched the mind of his brother Earagon in the next tower, and knew that he, too, was threatened. Then old Narmasil Hastur was with them in the tower, in his mind the news that their mighty city of Idelbonn, in the volcano at the eastern end of the Shadow, was under attack.

There was no more time. A wave of cold magic surged against Agnasta, and barriers of blazing need-fire leaped, driving back deadly forces that could have shattered stone and dissolved men to grey dust. The lattice of crystal light that glittered in the waters of the Yukota was swept away, and the river ran foul into the lands beyond.

The minds of the Hasturs united grimly to the knitting of powerful spells, forces of burning light. A single thought wandered briefly through three linked minds: *They know King Olansos has died*. Then their thoughts became flowing forces and burning rays, lightning threads that wove a fabric of living power. Neither in Agnasta nor in any tower was there thought or energy to spare.

* * *

Kumari's dark eyes were wide and mysterious, and her skin was soft under his questing hands. All day Martos had lived a dream of anticipation, waiting for the day to end. Now, at last, with all the night before them, he could hardly believe he was not dreaming.

His lips found the tips of her breasts, then moved slowly down. Her hands moved frantically on his shoulders, tousled his hair. Her breath was loud and rapid . . .

The brazen tone of the alarm tolled through the castle. His head jerked up, her hand gripping him painfully. *No! Not now!*

But the bell clamoured on, and flickering bluish light from the window showed the pink buds of her nipples. She pushed him away and rolled off the bed, running to the window. Her crystal dagger glowed in the darkness. He pushed himself up and followed. Her nude body, outlined in the distant light, was maddening in soft curves of hips and firm rounded breasts. He shuddered with desire, his body bursting.

But there was no mistaking the meaning of that light, and as he reached the window he gasped at the extent of it. East, south, and west the whole horizon was lit with flickering sheets of flame. Sometimes it burned a steady, bright blue, shot with tiny yellow lines like lightning bolts. Then suddenly it would flare up, flashing in different places with rippling waves of crimson, purple, or green. The towers themselves flared bright enough to burn the eyes. A confused cockerel crowed from the rampart.

He put his arm around her, rejoicing in the sweet torture of her naked flesh against his, though he knew it was hopeless. She trembled against his arm.

"Perhaps they won't break through," he said, but his voice trailed away without conviction, and she shook her head wordlessly.

His hand sought her breast. She looked up at him, then gently but firmly moved his hand away. Suddenly she kissed him, but before his arms could close around her she was gone, searching for her dress beside the bed. Morosely he began to pick up his own scattered clothes.

Nets of energy flickered across the surface of the Shadow. Out of the darkness, halfway between Agnasta and the tower that guarded the waters of the Atvandi to the east, rode a little group of men, clad in homemade bone and leather armour of Border-make: fine-chiselled faces bore the signs of Takkarian blood. Their clothes were dark, and they rode wiry little Border ponies.

Prince Jodos gasped and his hair crackled with shock as he rode through the net of force. Behind them the power that shielded the mountains from the lights in the sky bulged far into the plain, covering a barren wilderness of dead tree-trunks. Before them, like a wall, rose the Forest of the Kantara.

Almost due north lay the royal city, and the castle of the King. The castle where the King lay dead. That was one fear gone. The body that had sent him forth could not reclaim him: his father would never eat him now.

They rode into the jungle. There was a sort of trail here, an old raiding route, that would take them before dawn to the great road that ran north from Ojaini to the capital. When they got farther from the Border, and the powers of the Blue-robes, he would have to check the precious box, and be sure that the beings the Master had placed inside had not been harmed crossing the Border. He had felt energies crackling and surging all around the box—forces too weak to harm coarse things of flesh and blood like himself, but deadly to those he carried.

Emicos had told him that the box would protect them. Without them he would be lost. And he dared not fail.

The lands of men were roused and alert before them. The men of the Pure-in-Blood, born and bred to the service of the Dark Ones, rode fearfully. All around them were the servants of the Lords of Ravening Fire, the Children of One Too Terrible To Name. Soon the lights that burned the eyes, which few of the tribe had ever seen, would brighten the sky. Only the horses, stolen from the herds of the Bordermen and preserved uneaten against this need, were happy. They galloped eagerly away from the place of fear.

All night the Hastur-towers flamed with rainbow light and need-fire burned along the Border. Towards dawn the focus of the attack shifted, moving away to the west, and then north, beyond Aldinor, to Creolandis and Kadar.

A little before dawn Martos and the men of Suknia watched

the Shadow in the east slowly darken as the attack there lessened, then ceased. But from the western wall they saw new towers flaring up, far in the north. The blazing lights in the south dimmed; they watched need-fire crawling north along the western sky. The nearby towers faded, but far to the north a fitful light showed where the battle raged, as the Dark Things' forces shifted in the Shadow.

Even after the attacks on their tower had ceased, the warders of Agnasta did not relax their vigilance. Their minds roamed swiftly along the Border, seeking the raiding parties they were certain must have slipped over the Border while mightier powers had occupied them.

Their thought followed the Yukota towards the sea, and found and destroyed one dreadful water-thing hiding in the mud of the Pavana, but that was all.

Martos woke drenched in sweat. It was late in the afternoon. Soft, feminine radiance warmed his back. He rolled over quietly and, propping his head on his elbow, looked down at Kumari sleeping beside him, her dark hair spreading out from delicate, fine-chiselled features. So beautiful! He lost himself in contemplation of the shape of her nose.

He had stood watch the entire night. But the castle had not been attacked, nor had there come any word that the Dark Ones had been able to make any major breach. Shortly after dawn they had fallen, exhausted, into bed, and after too-brief lovemaking, had fallen asleep in each other's arms. But the night had been spoiled.

He could see her body outlined under the thin sheet, and one small breast peeped out at him, its nipple a delicate rose on the soft golden-brown of her skin. Desire crawled in his loins—but there was work waiting for him.

Slowly, so as not to wake her, he swung his feet over the edge of the bed and sat up. He yawned, and shook the grogginess out of his head. But as he started to get up, a small brown hand closed over his wrist and pulled him back. Beautiful earth-brown eyes stared up at him. Her arms went around his neck and her open mouth met his, and he forgot all about the men and duties waiting downstairs.

* * *

The two horrible burning lights in the sky went down at last. But the darkness was ruined by thousands of tiny little sparks, some moving and some still.

Jodos was angry as he led his men out of the forest towards the trail, dragging their reluctant horses. They had seen a woman pass within a hundred yards of their hiding place. They could have caught her and enjoyed her and eaten her. It would have been a change from the dull, disgusting food they had been given. But they had not dared. If they brought attention on themselves, their mission would fail, and that would mean months of torture by the Master.

He frowned. He had had the dream again, during the day. Seeing the woman had reminded him. He had had that dream so often. It always puzzled him. It was all about a woman being prepared, and screaming as her skin was stripped away. That was ordinary enough. What he could never understand was why, in his dream, he was always disturbed about it, as though there were some reason why this particular slave-woman should not be eaten. It was all very strange.

They reached the trail. Jodos forced his horse to stand, and scrambled clumsily onto its back. He hated riding on these hideous, dangerous beasts. The ground was such a long way down. But it was necessary.

A hundred and fifty miles north, Chondos started out of sleep and sat up in bed, shuddering uncontrollably. He shook his head, trying to remember what had been so frightening. But all he could recall was riding through a dark forest at night, and something about someone screaming, but that wasn't clear at all.

He yawned, and lay down. He must sleep. Tomorrow . . .

Tomorrow would be another day without his father, another day of being pestered by idiot officials trying to prepare for the Coronation, or worrying about traitors or the Dark Ones. Men too stupid, too insensitive, to understand his grief. Why could they not decently wait out the week of mourning before bothering him with such nonsense? He hated them all.

In two weeks he would be King.

The red flare of the watch-fires pulsed in Martos' eyes. A smell of roasting meat made his mouth water. He wanted to sing and laugh and dance, because Kumari loved him. Kumari slept blissfully in the tower room, her black hair spread about her, the delicate veins of her eyelids hiding the earth-brown orbs he loved so well.

Precious stocks of fuel vanished crackling in the flames, and the women of the castle bustled around them. Months might pass before there was another chance to eat food cooked over an open fire. Once the rains came, and clouds shut away the rays of the Twin Suns, there might be no cooked food at all until spring. And it might be that none of them would live to eat another meal. Frantic gaiety covered the tension, the fear all felt that the Border would burst and vomit forth the nightmare hordes of the Shadow.

Swarms of tiny moons drifted among the stars. Beyond the walls, sterile, poisoned land stretched to the looming black bastion of the Shadow. Now no glimmering sheets of need-fire flamed between earth and sky. In the distance, the towers were slim stalks of dim light.

Bordermen in loose flowing clothes filled the courtyard. A very few glittered in the long shirts of light mail that came down from old times, but most wore dull armour of horsehide and felt. Among them Martos' men stood out in their form-fitting Kadarin clothing, firelight gleaming from the steel of their breastplates.

If no attack came by midnight, the small day watch would go off to sleep. Bordermen seemed able to sleep anytime, or to do without sleep for days. They were nearly as nocturnal as the things they fought. But this soon after an attack, no one slept. At any moment, the Border might flame out again, and force men into the haunted night to ride against the things from the mountains.

Men who knew they might not see the dawn were jesting and amusing themselves. Some fenced, wooden blades clicking musically. As Martos came into the firelight, he heard men shout his name, calling to him in mock challenge. Light bamboo canes from the Kantara were flourished like swords.

Martos laughed, drunk with youth and love. He unbuckled his sword-belt, and laid the long dwarf-forged blade carefully beside the fire. Someone pressed a length of bamboo into his hand. It was an old game. They all knew none of them could touch him. They worshipped him.

The hollow length whistled in the air. He lashed it up and down and shifted his grip from one end to the other several times before he nodded that he was ready. He did not even come on guard as a Borderman named Ymros advanced on him hesitantly, but stood casually, the cane dangling idly from his right hand.

After a moment's hesitation, and an encouraging nod from Martos, the Borderman lunged in. There was a sudden loud clash of bamboo, the tip of Ymros' weapon shot past Martos' shoulder as the Kadarin stepped aside, and as Ymros turned, the stick lashed down on his head. Ymros bowed ruefully, shaking his aching head.

Jests were hurled at him from the crowd, until Martos' voice drowned them:

"Who thinks he can do better? You, Bimsio?"

Some said Bimsio was the best swordsman on the Border, next to old Prince Hansio of Mahapor. He was big for a Borderman, though still smaller than Martos. Again Martos stood easy, waiting for an attack. Bimsio's teeth flashed, and his cane darted for Martos' chest. Martos' stick spun, and swept it sharply aside, then whipped at Bimsio's arm. Hollow tubes smacked musically as the Tarencian guarded.

"Very good!" called Martos. His cane blurred, and dipped under Bimsio's guard. The big man grunted as it slapped across his belly.

Men cheered. Martos grinned boyishly. Another was coming in already. Martos ran the tube through his left fist as though sheathing a sword, and walked with his left hand holding the cane like a scabbard at his hip.

The Borderman leaped shouting, the bamboo sang in the air like a flute. Martos' right hand was a blur. The sticks clashed as he drew from his fist, dancing to the side. As the Borderer whirled, the tip of Martos' cane caught him under the arm. The yells were deafening.

Martos' smile died on his face. Above the crowd, he heard in memory Birthran's voice: *You are not here to learn pride, but to study swordsmanship!*

The Self-Judged Man! Martos sneered at himself. Puffed up

in an orgy of vanity, revelling in petty victories over men who had never even seen a real swordsman, like Birthran, or Raquel DiVega . . .

Four of the Bordermen were spreading around him now. This too was an old game.

Do not seek any man's approval—not even mine! Birthran's voice whispered in his memory. *Let your sword move as a flowering of your inner self, free of all desire for outward things.*

Both hands raised the bamboo gently upward. His feet shifted in tiny graceful steps.

A line from the *Precepts* came to his mind: *Do you act out of a desire that those around you should speak well of you? Then you too are a merchant, and that which you barter for the coin you seek is your freedom of thought.*

The tip of his cane followed the sound of the man behind him. He lunged backward, his left hand flying open, and the tip rapped the man's chest. The man to the right was charging, and Martos' bamboo sighed in the air and whipped the Borderman's side.

"To desire praise is to fear censure," Atrion had written in his *Book of Freedom*. "If others than yourself sit in judgement over your actions, if praise or blame concerns you, in time you will begin to lie, lest others think ill of you."

A Borderman cried out as Martos' bamboo swished down on his shoulder with unexpected force.

It's true! I've been lying to Kumari all along! Bamboo clashed hollowly. *Or to myself . . .*

He rapped the fourth Borderman soundly across the chest, and threw the cane away. Men pressed around him, shouting for more, or clamouring for a turn. Ingrained courtesy made him smile as he shook his head and walked away. After a while his silence drove them back to their games.

He remembered that first night, towards dawn, when he had told her of Kadar—of the swarms of landless, penniless noblemen, younger sons, and the sons of younger sons. Of his hope for the future, of founding his own school when his fame in the wars would bring students flocking to learn, as they flocked to Birthran.

Why had he not told her that he had come here seeking war,

that as an honourable man he could be swayed by no thought of gain? That wandering forever would be more honourable than making a name as a Swordmaster and settling down? But to her he had said nothing of honourable self-fulfillment; he had spoken as the basest merchant might.

He tried to picture himself saying these things to her, and felt foolish. She would never understand! These things would not be important to her. For a noblewoman and a mercenary to amuse each other for a night, or a few nights, was a simple enough thing. But somehow it had not stopped there. He wanted her with him always. But she could not marry a landless mercenary . . . Or was he lying to himself even about that? Had he stressed the impossibility of going back to Kadar, for fear that he would lose his chance for battle and adventure? He *could* open his own school—Birthran would help—and it would be a lean time at first, perhaps. But with Birthran's recommendation . . .

There he was, thinking like a filthy merchant again! The noise in the courtyard annoyed him. He climbed the stairs to the parapet.

He *did* want to open his own school someday, to pass on the skills Birthran had taught him to a new generation of swordsmen. But that quiet peaceful life was in the future; this was the time to use his skills, and find adventure on the bloody fields of life. He had nothing to offer her now. Back in Kadar many young men of his class were turning to banditry, or even stooping to hire to merchants as bodyguards, just to keep themselves from starvation.

He leaned on the parapet and looked out across the barren wastes. He could see the watch-fires of other Border castles in the distance. The towers of the Hasturs burned with steady blue light against the blank blackness that blotted the stars from the southern sky.

He could not ask her to follow him from camp to camp, or to come with him to an uncertain future in Kadar. He could not hope for her, unless . . . unless he stayed here, and took up land along the Border. But he had been here long enough to know the effects of the blight the Dark Ones sent forth upon the women and children of the Bordermen. It was one thing for a man to risk life and sanity holding back the Dark Ones, but to have a wife and children, so close to the Shadow . . . He could not face that.

Horror crept over him. No, if they married, she must come away with him. No child of his should grow up with the Dark Border always in sight.

Soft flower-scents filled the garden, and in the mist before dawn all colours were muted, like a faded tapestry. *Alone at last,* Chondos thought. Then he heard the dull whistle of a blade slicing air. His fingers closed on his sword-hilt, then eyes found the sword and the man . . .

Graceful as a kitten playing among blown leaves, Istvan DiVega slashed the morning mist, his face serene and gentle. His blade darted to the side at the height of a man's throat, and on the other side of the poised figure a leg shot out, the foot barely skimming the ground. The sword dipped and turned like a swallow, the body following it.

Chondos stood entranced. He knew this training-dance—his father had taught him—but never had he dreamed of a sword that moved so swiftly, so surely. There was never a moment's hesitation, nor, he was certain, a hairbreadth of variance in the precision of the pattern. The sheer beauty and perfection of movement stilled his thoughts and held his breath.

DiVega spun and faced him across the garden, his wrists crossed before his throat, his face framed in his hands. Chondos saw the keen eyes focus on him. The hands shot out, the razor-keen blade whistling through the mist, and then the man had turned away, the blade dangling loosely down his back, both hands gripping the hilt behind his ear.

Each movement flowed naturally into the next, and the blade sang through the air in a continuous, shimmering blur. Slowly the Twin Suns lifted themselves over the castle wall, and in their beams steel flashed like lightning around the gracefully dancing figure. The long, gentle face with its pointed beard was calm, and Chondos envied the old man, so free from the fears and cares that troubled other men.

Then, at last, the final snap of the wrist to shake the blood from the blade, the click of the hilt against the scabbard, and the old man was walking towards him, smiling, as though nothing had happened.

"A pleasant dawn, Lord King!"

Chondos stared at him, his tongue fighting back a cheer, a compliment, or some other emotional, out-of-place remark.

"Do—do you do that every day?" he found himself stammering.

DiVega nodded. "Every day, Lord King. It's my trade."

The man talked as though he were a labourer hefting his shovel! Chondos had spent all his life among warriors; he thought himself a good swordsman, but he had never seen anything like that. No wonder minstrels sang of Istvan the Archer!

"Don't call me 'Lord King,' " he snapped brusquely, "I'm not crowned yet, and I don't like it!"

"Very well, Prince Chondos," said Istvan. "That will make things simpler. Your father asked me to advise you, and to see what I could do to improve your swordsmanship, but it seemed a difficult subject to raise with someone I had to address as 'Lord King.' " He smiled.

Chondos could barely breathe. More than anything else in the world, he realised, he wanted to learn from this incredible swordsman, to achieve that deadly grace, to develop that inner peace. That was worth more than all the crowns in the world. Had he not been born to be King, he could have become this man's disciple, to travel the world with him and study the art of the sword.

"Shall we begin now?" A sudden eagerness crept into his voice despite his best intentions, and Istvan looked at him in surprise. "I know the dance you just did—and the Close Quarters Dance, and the Dance of the Twelve Cuts, and—and several others! My father taught me! Let me show you!"

Istvan nodded and stepped back. Chondos cursed himself. Now he would have to reveal his meagre skill to those hawk-keen eyes. He had always been proud of his skill, but now he felt as awkward as a newborn foal. He set his mind grimly to the task of picturing the ring of opponents, closing his eyes, breathing deeply, trying to calm himself.

The sword hilt felt cool against his palm. His eyes snapped open; his blade flashed from his scabbard in a long slicing cut to the throat, as he stepped forward.

Perfect, he thought, intensely aware of the calm grey eyes that watched him. He let his weight settle back on his left leg, the right loose and relaxed while the sword's point drifted earthward. The finest swordsman in the world was watching. He must do it right . . . *lunge! Recover! Lunge! Recover!* He was too tense. He put too much strength into the following cut, and had to fight the sword all the way to the next position. And his feet were wrong.

His blade went too high on the next cut, and at the wrong angle. It would have hung up on the jawbone, instead of going cleanly through the throat. He hesitated, confused for a second, trying to remember the next move . . . *Spin!* The left hand rising as the right comes down. Both hands on the hilt. *Step! Thrust! Spin!* Not smooth enough, and the feet were at the wrong angle. He'd practised this a thousand times!

He froze a moment, realising he'd omitted a move, then went on. But he found himself hesitating at the end of each movement. That was wrong. Each step should flow from the last, like a river.

One technical flaw after another jarred his awareness. Here he stepped too high, there a stroke was imprecise. He kept on doggedly, shame and chagrin boiling within him, until he reached the final cut, and the sheathing of the sword. He stood sweating, his hands shaking. He turned to DiVega, expecting detailed, scathing criticism.

"You were trying too hard," said Istvan quietly. "You were nervous because I was watching. It's obvious that you're used to doing better than that. Your father taught you well."

"But—" Chondos shook his head, confused.

"You made a couple of technical mistakes," said Istvan. "But you recognised them as soon as you made them, which means you can correct them yourself. But your sword-arm was not working freely. You were too aware of being watched, and you let that awareness come between you and your sword."

Chondos frowned. It sounded suspiciously like the man was praising him. Wasn't he going to tell him how to improve? Teach him anything? Was he trying to gain something from flattery?

"Are you saying that I know it all already, and all I have to do is practise? That there's nothing you can teach me?"

"No, no!" laughed the Seynyorean. "I said you knew that

particular dance well. There are others that your father never knew, that I can teach you. But more to the point, I think, would be some work with—"

"Lord King!" It was old Lord Taticos' voice. Chondos turned around, and rage twisted his face as his Steward came panting up. *Fat old fool!* he thought.

"—work with wooden swords," finished Istvan, under his breath. "Looks like you'll be busy, though."

Chapter Four

The days that followed were filled with gruelling work for both of them. An ominous quiet brooded over the Border: subterranean currents of Portona gold hinted at a brisk traffic in treason. But the Coronation *must* be held, and that was no simple matter. Chondos, trapped in the wheels of ceremony, wondered if his officials were trying to drive him mad.

There were delicate points of precedence to be decided, costly robes of state to be fitted, arrangements made for lodging and feeding the crowds that would fill the city. Already, nobles from the nearer provinces were flocking in, to mourn the old King and crown the new. Lord Taticos, as Steward, must oversee it all, and court officials with work to do—for the usual business of the kingdom must go on—dreaded the appearance of his portly figure.

Istvan did not escape. It seemed that when Riccarho Di-Vega, after uniting the principalities of Tarencia, Kalascor, and Mahavara, had had himself crowned King of the new-forged realm, his helm-bearer for the ceremony had been his friend and second-in-command, Belos DiArnac. King Olansos had brought Raquel DiVega to fill the same role at his own Coronation, and decreed that at the crowning of all his successors in time to come, the post should be taken by a mercenary, as a reminder of the origins of the house. Lord Taticos handed Istvan a scroll to read—one of the great Scrolls of Ceremony—as though he thought DiVega had no other work to do.

Each day Istvan plunged into the mass of contracts and muster rolls for the companies employed by the Crown. He spent much time among the litter of maps and papers in Lord Zengio's office, trying to track down those companies in the pay of the guilds or of individual noblemen.

The task seemed endless. Fortunately, Firencio DiVega, a distant cousin, was in command of one of the companies quartered in the palace, and had for a time assisted Lord Zengio. With his help, Istvan began to make sense out of the confusion.

The Rivermen's Guild of Portona employed a Seynyorean company under the command of an old friend of Istvan's, Aurel Ciavedes. Istvan decided that a quiet drink with Ciavedes might be very useful. And while he was in Portona, he might stop for a talk with Asbiorn Kung, whom he knew slightly, the commander of the Carrodian marines employed by the Shipping Guild.

The commanders of some of the companies in the King's service had been approached by guild representatives with offers of higher pay. Some of them were old friends, too—Palos DiFlacca, Leonic Servara, Rupiros D'Ascoli . . .

He would be drinking with a lot of old friends over the next week or so, he thought.

On the fifth day of mourning, Lord Jagat of Damenco rode his tired horse into the city. He had ridden day and night, changing mounts regularly, eating in the saddle, sleeping hardly at all. He looked like a skeleton asleep on his feet. Rumour in the court claimed the old man had come bearing some desperate message of doom or glory. Few understood the depth of Jagat's love and loyalty to the dead King.

Chondos looked down at the white head, bowed in grief: there were tears on the dark face. This man, too, had loved his father. Or—suspicion whispered in a dim corner of his mind—he feigned it very well. But that was nonsense, he knew. Whatever Jagat's feeling towards the son might be, he had always been utterly loyal to the father.

Five days had slowly eroded Chondos' grief. But for Jagat, who had filled those days with gruelling travel few men could have borne, the sorrow was still raw.

"Have you any notion, Sire, why your father summoned me?" Jagat's voice was low and muffled. Chondos only shook his head. Jagat's face dipped. "I had hoped, perhaps, that—that it might have been about you and—and Kumari that he wished to speak."

Chondos stiffened. *Even Jagat!*

"He said nothing of it to me!" he snapped.

"She is like a daughter to me, Lord King," the old man went on. "It had been my dearest wish that she—" He stopped, suddenly aware of the boy's anger.

In Chondos' memory was Kumari's face as he had seen it when she had left his room that one night, so long ago—eyes flaming, lips drawn back in a cat's snarl.

"I do not think she desires to be Queen of Tarencia," Chondos said coldly. "You will have to marry her off to some lesser prize."

Jagat's face grew utterly still. Pain showed in his eyes, but he said nothing. Furious, Chondos rose. Disgust choked him. For Jagat, of all people, to prey on his sorrow merely to press that ridiculous marriage! That was all that any of them ever cared about!

"I am sorry I have angered you, Sire," Jagat said at last. "I did not—"

"Of course," said Chondos, pressing back the long, scathing speech that rose to his lips. "You did not understand. No one ever understands. But thank you for reminding me of my grief. It is not fitting that time should soften my pain. And I thank you for the offer of your niece; she is very beautiful. But not everyone can be Queen of Tarencia. Indeed, she deserves it more than most, since she does not seek it for herself. A lack of self-seeking is a great virtue, and rare, like honesty. Good night, Lord Jagat."

He stalked from the room, ignoring Jagat's clenched fists and set teeth.

Jodos pulled his pony to a halt and gestured at the others. The warriors of the Pure-in-Blood stopped behind him. He pointed to the lights of the little village in the distance.

"We must camp here," he said. "And sleep so we can go on in the morning."

There were mutters and curses. The day just past had been the first time most of them had ever been exposed to the full light of the Twin Suns. They did not like it. For a moment Jodos was afraid he would have to open his box to make them obey, but a sharp command from Hotar, who had led many such missions, and raiding-parties as well, silenced them.

He did not like travelling by day any more than they did, but the orders were very specific. They would be too conspicuous travelling at night; fear of the Masters kept most men indoors once the burning lights had left the sky. And the lands here were too thickly settled to allow them to avoid notice.

He clambered awkwardly off the sweating, trembling horse, and tied it firmly to a tree, being careful to stay out of the way of its hooves and teeth. He ducked to avoid branches and leaves. The grass was detestably soft under his feet.

The men pulled food out of their saddlebags, dull, hateful stuff, like the Sun People ate. One of the warriors caught a little lizard, and began to devour it with great relish, while the others watched, and laughed at its frenzied struggles. Jodos looked on, nibbling morosely at the tasteless, unresisting stuff he had been given, and after a while tried to catch a lizard for himself. But to do that he had to run his hands through the grass, and he found that frightening. He did not like the feel of it, and did not trust it not to attack him. Finally he snatched the remnants of the lizard—part of the back, with one leg and the tail still twitching feebly—out of the man's hand. The man snarled and reached for his sword, but Jodos caught him with his eyes, and let him go only when he was sure the other was sufficiently frightened. The rest of the men only laughed.

Martos staggered from bed cross as a springtime bear, stupid from lack of sleep. After standing night watches most of the week, he was not yet used to being awake during the day. He did not relish the thought of the long journey to the capital.

He snarled at Paidros when the little man tried to get instructions out of him, but Paidros only laughed, and brought him more of the herb tea. He knew his Captain well. Martos' gear was already packed and his clothes and armour laid out. He finally got himself dressed, and staggered into the courtyard, where Kumari laughed at him. Stung by that, he lined up the men of the escort, and bawled them out roughly, pouncing on the slightest flaw. Half an hour later, it was a very impressive guard—half Borderman, half Kadarin—that escorted the Lady of Damenco and her maids through the main gate of Suknia.

After they had been on the road awhile, riding between barren fields, the cobwebs finally cleared from his head. He let

Suktio take the lead—the Borderer was glaring like a wet cat—and dropped back to ride beside Kumari. She was maddeningly beautiful in her flowing dark blue gown. She grinned mischievously as he rode up.

"Are you going to lecture *me* on dress and deportment now?" Her laughter trilled, and then, forcing her voice as deep as it would go, she mimicked: *"This is a guard of honour, not a work detail! What did you clean those boots with? Milk?"* She laughed again at his expression. "If you could only have seen yourself this morning! Or heard yourself! Tell me, do you have any little pet-names for me like the ones you were calling your men this morning?"

"Um . . ." His face burned. "No. No, not like those. No." He licked his lips and tried to think of something to say, but as usual, his tongue seemed to be tied in a knot. "I—I'm sorry," he stammered. "I'm afraid I—wasn't awake yet. I'm sorry."

She laughed again. "Silly! After this past week, do you think I don't know what you're like when you first wake up?"

He had nothing to say to that. They rode on, knee to knee in the heat. Off to the left the Marunka bubbled noisily through its stony bed. Scattered willows fluttered pale green leaves above the swirling water: the only trees for miles. Here, large patches of undamaged soil had survived, islands in the sea of grey dust, covered with sun-dried grass. The Twin Suns, hanging above the distant black wall in the east, spread pitiless light over the barren ash.

Kumari muttered something under her breath that Martos could not quite catch, and turned to look around. Her maids had all dropped well back; there was no one in earshot. She turned to Martos.

"Do you remember the night before the King died?" she asked, very softly.

"Yes." He blinked at her. There were other nights more important, he was thinking.

"Do you remember me telling you . . ." She hesitated a moment, then started again. "Remember that I said I—thought that—that I might be carrying your child?"

Something happened in the centre of his chest, and he did not know whether it was shock or elation that gripped his heart.

"You mean—" he yelped. "Do you mean . . . ?"

"Not so loud!" she said. "No need to shout the news all over the countryside just yet. Later, if you want to. Yes, it's true."

"But—but," he stammered, his tongue trapped by strain, "what are you going to do?"

"Do? I'm going to have a baby, you big, dumb oaf! A little wrinkled red thing that drinks milk and squalls a lot. Your baby, if that means anything to you."

His tongue was totally useless to him now, even if he had been able to think of anything to say. He sat on his horse and stared at her. She stared back. After a moment an angry red blossomed on her cheeks.

"All right!" she said. "I'll forget whose child it is, if that's what you want! I thought you might like to know, but since you feel that way about it, fine. I never spoke to you, much less touched you. I have no idea—and don't care—which one of my uncle's soldiers it was. Is that what you want?"

Without waiting for an answer she kicked her horse's sides, and suddenly he was riding alone. He stared after her stupidly a moment, then prodded Warflame and caught up.

"I'm sorry," he said, "I didn't mean—I mean—" He shook his head. "You know I can't talk when—when . . . It's all I can do to give orders in battle. Usually Paidros has to. My tongue just—just sits there."

"Now everybody's staring at us," she hissed, unreasonably, as though it were his fault. "Well, are you happy about it?"

He'd managed to come up with something to say by now. "Will you come away with me?" he pleaded. "Come with me back to Kadar? I'm—I'm not famous, but I ought to be able to attract enough students to keep us fed. Birthran will help. And . . ." He hesitated, and then, in a rush, said, "And the Dark Things won't be able to—to hurt the baby . . ." He ran out of voice, and swallowed. She was looking at him, thoughtfully.

"I don't know," she said slowly. "I've always been taught to think of the women who run away from the Border as cowards, traitors, but—it's different when there's a baby in your own belly. I don't know yet. I'm thinking about it."

They rode on in silence, and did not speak of the matter again that day. Their trail led away from the Marunka now, and into vast wastelands of grey dust, north and east towards the ancient city of Manjipor. At noon they halted, cringing, in oven heat. Both suns glared mercilessly down. Kumari and her women slept under a hastily draped cloth. The Borderers drowsed in the sunlight. Martos and his men rested, roasting.

They rose and rode on through the afternoon. Manjipor reared shimmering out of the haze before them, surrounded by fields: blessed earth reclaimed by generations of toil; soil where plants could grow. They did not stop at the city, but rode around the great mound on which it stood to strike the road that ran east, to Ojaini in the Kantara. Caravans of carts bound for Manjipor passed them on the road: carts carrying food; carts laden with precious wood; cartloads of dung for the land. All paid for by the Crown with the taxes from the coastal cities.

Eight miles past Manjipor, the ponderous walls of the fortress of Ojakota reared invincible and ancient from the new-made soil. There they stopped for the night. Kumari seemed distant, thoughtful, and Martos feared to break the barriers of her reserve. Although he could easily have arranged to share her room with no one the wiser, he found himself alone and sleepless, his mind astir with Kumari's news—the baby that would change his world. Wildly giddy, he went wandering through the keep. Elation and worry chased each other through his thoughts.

"Hah! Kadarin!" a hearty voice called out. "Your employer find out you mispelled your nationality on your contract yet?"

A candle made a cheery oasis of light in the dark hall. Ironfist Arac and his son Alar sat beside the castle's stockpile of wood, stripped to the waist in the heat. Their shoulders were inhumanly broad, a heritage from the N'lantian blood of Ironfist's mother. Their legs were shapeless in the loose Carrodian trousers gathered at the ankle. Ironfist, a red-bearded bear of a man, came to his feet like a cat as Martos tried to find some clever answer to the inevitable wordplay on *Carrod* and *Kadar*.

"Warm enough?" Ironfist laughed. "There's plenty of wood here, if you'd like a fire!"

"I don't even want to get near your candle!" Martos retorted. The sultry air was smothering; his tight-fitting Kadarin breech-hose clung to his legs. "How can you *think* about fire, even as a jest?"

"Ah, you southerners have no appreciation for warmth and comfort," said Ironfist. Sweat jewelled his naked chest in the candlelight. "You can't imagine how good it is to get the icicles out of your beard! You should come up to the mountains! Why, back home, it gets so cold that the flames freeze, and turn into the prettiest icicles you ever saw, and you have to break a couple off and rub them together to get the fire going again! My Uncle Evard, now . . ."

Oh no! Martos thought. *Another one!*

". . . he fell asleep with his feet too close to the fire, and his boots caught. Anywhere else, he'd have burned to death! But he kept his head, and turned around and stuck his feet out in the middle of the room. Then he broke the flames off his boots and tossed them back in the fireplace. Gave him a terrible case of frostbite, though." He shook his head sadly, his face solemn.

Alar was fighting with the corners of his mouth. Martos wondered what it was like to have a legend for a father. Fighting to get his breath back, Martos wished he could top Ironfist's story with one of his own. But he never seemed able to come up with anything clever.

"Is the Border still quiet?" was all he finally thought of to say.

"Not a spark more than usual," Ironfist said. "They say the Dark Ones are busy up near Hali."

Hali? Something was kicking and struggling in his chest. "Where? Handor? Creolandis?" He could not bring himself to say *Kadar?*

Ironfist shook his head. "It's rumour. The people here don't know the difference—it's all 'far away' to them."

Martos sat stunned, picturing dark shapes stalking through Onantuga, the hills and fields covered with grey dust. His mother, his father. Surely the Dark Ones would be stopped before they got so far! Onantuga was miles from the Border; no one there was forced into the hideous life of the Bordermen. The thinly settled land west of Onantuga had been troubled with nothing worse than a raiding-party since Grandfather had been a little boy . . .

And he was trapped here! Even if he raced his horse to Portona, and found waiting there the fastest ship that ever crossed the Ardren, it would be months before he could get home. And what would happen to Kumari, and the baby?

"It's part of the trade, lad." Ironfist's voice sounded miles away. "I know how it is. The desert Gondurs raided my home province once, when I was in Y'gora, with the whole eastern ocean in the way. Word reached me, but there was nothing I could do. All my children were small then. You have to learn to bear it. It's part of the trade."

Martos closed his eyes. First the news from Kumari, now this! He pushed the breath from his lungs, trying to push out the tangled images of terror that swarmed in his mind. He must talk about something else, anything else!

"What news from—from the capital? Beside the Coronation and all that?"

Young Alar laughed. In sharp contrast to his father, he was dark-haired and slimly, almost delicately, built, except for the massive arms and shoulders. He had been one of Birthran's students for a time. Martos remembered him as a shy, quiet boy, very much in awe of the senior students like Martos.

"An agent from the Portona Sellers' Guild was here the other night," Alar said, "supposedly to sell armour, arrows, cheap swords, and the like. What he wanted to buy was more interesting than what he had to sell." Ironfist looked troubled, but the boy went on, grinning like a wolf. "He wanted to hire us away from Lord Maldeo—buy our loyalty for Portona. We listened to him talk for a long time before we threw him out."

Ironfist clucked disapprovingly, and Alar shut up. "Tell me, Martos," said Ironfist, very softly, "have *you* been approached by such an agent?" He seemed relieved when Martos shook his head. "Shows what a liar that man was! He said that all the other mercenaries in the country had already been bought up by the guilds. Doesn't solve our problem, though. Both of the other Carrodian companies are already in guild employ. Our contract's void, of course, if we find ourselves on the opposite side from our countrymen, but it's always a bad situation."

"I doubt if they have many Seynyoreans," said Alar. "Not with a half-dozen DiVegas in every company!"

"There aren't *that* many!" said his father. "Strange they haven't approached you, Martos."

"Perhaps they know better than to try to bribe a Kadarin

gentleman," said Martos, quite seriously. Ironfist laughed aloud.

"If they had the brains for *that,*" he said quickly, before Martos could take offence, "they'd be smart enough not to go stirring up treason while the Border's in such a state! It's insanity!"

"I thought you said the Border was quiet," said Martos.

"You haven't been on the Border long, have you, lad?" said Ironfist. Martos, feeling like an idiot, shook his head.

"Thought not. They shifted their attack north to—wherever it is—in a matter of hours. They can shift back just as quickly—and will, unless they break out somewhere else. I've seen it before. I remember a time in Norbath . . ." Unpleasant memories haunted his eyes. "We'd been out drinking. The Dark Things had been attacking Darna, but that was more than a thousand miles away! We barely had time to arm. There wasn't time to sober up.

"I'm getting too old for this life." He sighed, and shook himself like a bear. "If the contract goes, maybe I'll head home and settle down—let my sons take over the soldiering. Arn is almost old enough now, and Alar's not doing badly." He smiled at his son. Martos saw the father's pride, and Alar's pleasure in the praise.

"I'm sorry for the people who live here, though. Maldeo's a fine man, and"—bitterness filled his eyes and his voice— "many a man who came south with me is ashes, spread over the fields out there, to sanctify the land, as the Borderers say, and make it fertile again. I don't want the Dark Ones to get those fields back!"

Martos nodded. In his mind he saw the solemn fields of clover, the fields of ground nuts and beans. He remembered the labour, mixing dung and clay and gravel, laying it over the bared stone . . . but that brought back the picture of the hills near his own home covered with poisoned grey dust. He shivered. He would take Kumari to eastern Kadar, to Sardis or Ranikert, far from the Border. Their child would never know these horrors.

Could he be as fine a father as Ironfist, as close to Kumari's child? What if it should be a girl? How good a father could he be then? He wished he had a sister so he could know better what to do. A son he could teach all his swordsman's skills and watch him grow to a man. As Ironfist watched Alar, with pride glowing in his eyes. He glanced from Ironfist to Alar again, remembering the boy in Birthran's hall, among the mob of students.

"Have you been keeping in practise since you left us, Alar?" he asked.

"Has he!" Ironfist boomed. "You should see him! And his brother Arn! Hah! They keep *me* in shape, these days! Though I could still use a good workout with you, Martos. How about it?"

No! Martos hesitated, fearing to seem rude, then remembered gratefully that this time he had a legitimate excuse for refusing.

"Not tonight, I'm afraid. I've a long ride tomorrow, and all the week after, and I should have been in bed by now." He yawned and stretched ostentatiously as he rose, bidding them a cheerful good night.

He had grown up on romantic stories of Ironfist's youth exploits in Thernhelm, and when he had met the man, it had seemed as though he bathed in the glow of legend. But every time he had fenced with this hero of his childhood, he'd beaten him easily. And each time, a little of his boyhood had left him.

Aurel Ciavedes greeted Istvan like a long-lost brother. A great, black-bearded man, with shoulders like a bull, and bare pink scalp peeping out between the black strands of his hair, he filled Istvan's goblet with rich Nervian wine, and poured out another for Firencio.

Outside, hawkers called their wares on the busy Portona streets. Bullies and pickpockets made way for richly dressed, swaggering bravos they would have knifed in the meaner quarters by the docks. Portly merchants in elegant robes and their elaborately gowned women swept arrogantly through crowds of clerks and porters, surrounded by hired guards.

"Yes, we're all very busy here," said Ciavedes, sipping his wine. "The Guildmaster sent us word to prepare for war, but he forgot to say against whom. *I* think it's going to be against traitors to the Crown, though that may not be what the

Guildmasters have in mind." He grinned conspiratorially at Istvan over his drink.

"Then," said Istvan, "if you received orders to march against the King, you'd refuse?"

Aurel's feet thumped off the footstool as he sat up, his grin shifting to one of surprise. "Why, dear fellow! What choice do we have? There are thirty or forty of our brother companies employed directly by the Crown! There are only seven employed in all the harbour cities, three here in Portona! How can seven companies demand that thirty void *their* contracts, especially when we'd be cutting off the source of their pay if we fought for Portona and won? We'll fight for whichever side our brother companies elect to fight for. That's why you're here, I presume?"

Istvan nodded. "King Olansos was my cousin. I promised I'd stand by his son."

"I thought so," said Ciavedes, nodding sharply. He grinned. "Well, who am I to argue with the DiVegas?"

Between the frowning walls of the royal castle and the river, in the poorer merchant quarter of Tarencia City, Bordermen, though not unknown, were rare. Not a few eyes followed the little group of drab-armoured men making its way through the tangled streets; some wondering to see Bordermen that sat so poorly in the saddle, and to see Border ponies that had been mistreated, as these plainly had.

Jodos' eyes, by habit, were still slitted against the daylight, despite the shadow of the houses. He let Hotar lead the way, for Hotar had been here before. They threaded a maze of alleys, where ragged men eyed them speculatively, and dirty children darted away from the horses' hooves. At last they pulled up before a large, rundown wooden building. As Hotar, a little more agile than the other men, scrambled off his pony and pounded it on the nose as it tried to bite, a boy came running from the recessed doorway.

"Greetings, Noble Lords!" He took the reins from Hotar. "What is it you would have of the House of Jacopos?"

"Rooms," Hotar answered shortly, as Jodos and the others clumsily dismounted. "But first, take this to your master," he said, drawing from his pouch a small envelope sealed with wax. "If you get to him quickly you'll be rewarded. If the seals have been tampered with," he added with a glare, "you will suffer for it!"

As the boy hesitated, Hotar pulled a large gold coin from the pouch, tossed it idly into the air, and caught it. The boy grabbed the envelope and ran.

Hotar turned to Jodos and bared his teeth. "You see?" he mocked, carelessly. "Nothing to it!"

The boy came back with a number of men, who took charge of the horses. He bowed to Hotar, more deeply than before. "If my Lords will follow?" Hotar tossed him the coin, and he led them up the stairs and down long corridors, and at last threw open a heavy wooden door. Behind was a vast, dark space.

"The Master said to give you these," the boy said uncertainly. "Are you sure you don't want something with a little more light? There's only one window in the suite, and that has heavy drapes . . . ?"

"This will do," said Hotar gruffly.

The boy turned to go, and bumped into a plump, grey-haired little man, whose clothes hung on him loosely, as though he either had been or expected to be fatter still. He bobbed up in constant bows, rubbing his hands together. He was terrified, Jodos saw, torn between fear and greed. Behind him came the men who had taken the horses, loaded down with saddlebags. They dumped them on the floor and left. The grey-haired man waved irritably for them to hurry, his face frozen in the grimace of a smile. When they were all gone, the plump man turned to Hotar. The fixed smile vanished.

"How may I serve—" he began in a quavering voice, then shut up as Hotar grinned at him, nastily.

"See that we are left alone," said Hotar. "How long until the Coronation?"

"Eight days, Lord."

Jodos stiffened. All this hurry, only to hide here for so long, in constant danger.

"If you betray us, you betray yourself as well," Hotar snarled. "And we have our own ways of dealing with those who trouble us. Now get us some food—food like I had the last time I was here!" The man blinked, and trembled.

"Please, Lord, that is dangerous."

"What do I care about your risks?" sneered Hotar. "Results are all I care about! You'll get your price—"

"If it's risky, forget it!" Jodos interrupted. "The Master said to do nothing to draw attention!"

The fat man glanced at Jodos, and started, his mouth dropping open. He shut it again, and shook his head, tried to look away. But Jodos caught his eyes, held them.

"Sleep!" he said. The man's body slumped, and would have fallen had Hotar not reached out and caught him by the arm.

"Stand up. Look at me."

The man's body straightened, and the eyes opened again, locked on Jodos' eyes.

"Why did you act like that when you saw me?"

"I thought you were King Chondos." The quaver was gone; the voice was a monotone.

"Who do you think I am now?"

"You are Jodos, the Lost Prince."

"You will forget that. You will forget that you ever saw a man who looks like King Chondos. You will forget what Chondos looks like. You will forget that you ever heard of the Lost Prince. You will forget that I have spoken to you. When you wake, you will not know that anything has happened, and will go on talking to Hotar. Now wake!"

The man blinked stupidly, turned back to Hotar: "My Lord," he said, "I—" and stopped, confused, knowing he must talk to Hotar, not knowing what to say. Hotar laughed, bent down, and drew a large sack from a saddlebag. He shook it. It clinked.

"There will be more," he said. "For extra payment, take those horses we rode in on, and sell them for what you can get. Make sure we are fed and left alone. Now get out!"

With a frightened bob, the man darted out the door, clutching the bag tightly.

Jodos bared his teeth at Hotar. "You see?" he mimicked. "It's easy!"

Asbiorn Kung would not have to worry when *his* hair turned, thought Istvan; it was so pale a blond that no one would notice.

"I must admit," Kung said, leaning back in his chair, "with

you leading the Royal Forces, I have small inclination to be on the other side. I know what you can do. But our direct employer is the Shipping Guild. Supposedly we were hired to garrison the ships at sea, but there's nothing in our contract forbidding them to send us into a civil conflict on land. Of course, Ironfist is employed by some Border Lord down south—Manipol, or something like that. I don't know anything about local politics—it's not my concern—but if he turns up on the other side, one of us will have to void our contract. I could use that as an argument to convince the guild to keep us on the ships and out of the war. I'd prefer that. Civil wars get nasty."

"How many of your men are in port now?" Istvan asked.

A troubled look flitted across the Carrodian's face. "I'm afraid I can't tell you that. Obviously, I can't tell you that."

"Why not?" said Istvan. "Orders from the guilds? If so, that's proof enough of treason, and the Crown can arrest your employers, void your contracts, and deport you. If not, you are still employed by loyal subjects of King Chondos of Tarencia, and under my authority as Commander of Mercenaries."

"True," Asbiorn said, after a moment, and sighed. "Most of my men are in port. I don't remember the exact numbers."

"But more than half?" asked Istvan. Kung nodded. "Isn't that a little strange if you're supposed to guard the shipping?"

"I'll admit—" The Carrodian stopped. "No. I'll admit nothing. I don't know why my employers have cut down the number of men assigned to a ship. Things have been peaceful. But we've received no orders that would implicate the Shipping Guild in any kind of plot against the Crown."

But Istvan knew by the worry on his face that, although the man would not lie, he had heard or guessed something that made him very careful how much truth he told. "Very well. Thank you, Captain Kung." Istvan rose and bowed. "You have been very helpful. But—a word of advice." He paused, and put on his cloak. "If you truly wish to keep your men out of civil wars, I would suggest that you and Esrith Gunnar both study your contracts carefully, and either renegotiate them to keep your men on shipboard, or find some technicality allowing you to avoid them. Otherwise . . ." He shrugged, bowed again, and left.

* * *

In the shifting light of a dozen tiny moons, Pirthio rode through the gates of Tarencia Town, and through the cobbled streets to Jagat's house. Northward, the ominous storm clouds hovered above the Sea of Ardren, and tongues of lightning licked the sky.

He found Lord Jagat striding angrily back and forth. Harsh lines of rage faded from the old man's face as his son's voice brought him round with a smile of greeting. But when Pirthio asked after the new King, the anger was suddenly back.

"The young whelp's tongue is sharper than ever! I'm sorry." Jagat paused as he felt Pirthio's shock at the slight to his friend. "But I had forgotten how much easier it is to be loyal to our new Lord and King at a distance. He's striking out at everyone around him, as though that would bring his father back. The thought of what we will have to go through because of that tongue of his is maddening. And if he were not—" He stopped with a gasp of exasperation. "Ah well. But you have something on your mind too, have you not?"

"Yes," said Pirthio, nodding. "There are some men I need to find. Rinmull of Ojaini first, I think. Do you know if he's here?"

"Probably. Most of the Kantara Lords rode in yesterday."

"What about Mahapor?"

"Mahapor?" Jagat's eyebrows rose. "I don't know. But there is a rumour that Tunno is here—to represent his father, some say, but the most likely story has it that he defied Hansio to come, and that he's just here to drink and revel. I'm sure some of the minor nobility have drifted in. Why? You're up to something."

Pirthio grinned. "Tell me, Father, who do we Takkarians hate worse than we hate each other?"

Thunder boomed and frolicked above the Sea of Ardren, and rain fell on the road that ran south from Portona. A brief shift in the wind threw rain in Istvan's face, and then it went back to chattering on the back of his hood. He pulled the cloak tightly around him, and huddled down in the saddle.

"Captain Kung is a very disturbed man," said Firencio. He was riding close beside Istvan, and his strong ringing voice carried clearly over wind and rain and hoofbeats.

"Yes," said Istvan, "and soon, I hope, he'll have Esrith Gunnar a bit nervous too."

They'd not gone to see Esrith Gunnar; he was a stiff-necked, stubborn old soldier who'd only have argued. But with Asbiorn Kung worrying, Gunnar would take action, and Istvan thought he knew what it would be.

Boughs were writhing in the wind. The chill between his shoulder blades made him shiver, and he wrapped his cloak tightly around him. He was getting old. What then, give it up, go home and die? Watch as the body fails and your mind goes, until at last you sit talking to men forty years dead?

Istvan shivered again, but not from cold. He strove to turn his mind from this morbid path, to concentrate on business. For people who planned a war, the Portonans paid remarkably little heed to their city's defences. His memory moved again through the suburbs of the city, and the rich villas of the nobles . . .

"Here we are !" called Firencio. Istvan stirred and pulled his horse off the road, and a few moments later was scrambling onto a fresh horse. Cousin Firencio was a very efficient young man.

"Are you sure we need to be back in Tarencia tonight?" asked Firencio. He waved an arm at the lights of a building whose outlines were hidden by the rain. "We could spend the night here, and ride on in the morning."

"I'll go on!" said Istvan shortly, and turned the horse back to the road. One of his old wounds was aching fiercely, as it always did when it rained, and somehow he felt as if the rain had gotten into his joints and collected there in cold pools.

The Satragara was filled with scions of the Border nobility. Pirthio, bathed and changed into neatly patched and brightly embroidered garments of ancient cut, slipped in quietly, and hunted through the crowd with his eyes.

Scholars said that *Satragara* meant "Warrior's House" or "Gentlemen's House" in the ancient tongue that the ancestors of the Takkars had brought with them from another world. Once there had been a famous castle of that name, deep in the mountains described in old songs and stories with such glory and splendour; those same mountains that now crawled with the unclean servants of the Dark Ones, hidden from the Twin Suns' light.

But it was as a gentlemen's house that its owners meant it to be understood; their ancestors had been Bordermen who had fled the encroaching Shadow, and so lost caste and honour in the eyes of their kin. But the inn that they maintained had become the gathering place for the Bordermen of all three provinces, the one place in the city where their food and customs were never mocked.

Pirthio had hoped to find Rinmull of Ojaini here. Not only had the Kantaran one of the finest voices on the Border—and he could sing the wild "Ballad of Pertap's Ride," or the plaintive "Lament for the Fall of Rashnagar," better than any living man—but he was a scholar and antiquarian, and had found in neglected corners of his castle manuscripts of ancient ballads long forgotten, from the lost days of Takarian glory. One in particular that Pirthio wished to hear him sing, as publicly as possible, was a lament for a Lord of Mahapor, betrayed and slain by treachery of the merchant-princes of the coast.

But although more than half the men there were from the Kantara, Rinmull was not among them. A few Manjipéans and a handful of Massadessans mingled with the Kantarans on one side of the room, kneeling, Border-fashion, at the low tables. The men of Mahapor sat apart, however, as though an invisible dividing line ran through the room. Memories of old feuds walked that line. There was no open hostility, but the tension of an armed truce.

Among the men of Mahapor sat a large and powerful figure, richly dressed. Hardly daring to believe his luck, Pirthio studied the man carefully, comparing the fine, aquiline features with those in his memory. Certain at last it was indeed the right man, he ordered a whole flagon of the finest wine, and threaded his way carefully across the room, greeting the men he knew from Manjipé and the Kantara.

The conversation was suddenly muted as he crossed the empty space that marked off the Kantara men from those of Mahapor. The few Manjipéans rose suddenly to their feet; the men of Mahapor looked up, puzzled, trying to identify him. Pirthio ignored them all, and sat down with his flagon of wine beside Tunno, heir of Prince Hansio of Mahapor.

Trumpets sounded at noon the next day, as Phillipos, Prince of Kalascor, entered the city with his royal wife Illissia, daughter of Olansos and half-sister to the King. The Duke of Ipazema came riding into town behind Prince Phillipos. His beard was black, and he wore white clothing. Stocky and short, and a proven warrior, he sat his horse like a conqueror riding, and let himself sneer at the cheers not meant for him. And the eyes that he fixed on his Overlord were filled with hate.

Thoros of Ipazema had business in the city. Impatiently he waited for pageantry's ending. When they reined in at the palace at last, he watched while Chondos embraced his sister, and greeted Phillipos more formally. As the royal party vanished into the castle, he caught the eye of his chief retainer, then skillfully jerked his horse free from the mess as lesser Lords and their retainers began to break ranks and scatter.

He turned his horse and rode out of the gate, and maneouvred at a trot through crowded streets, demonstrating superb horsemanship and a calculated disregard for lesser folk. People scampered from his path as he rode through the Market District into the Merchant Quarter.

He stopped before a row of prosperous houses and dismounting, tied his horse to a lion-headed post of bronze, and quickly sprang up the marble staircase. A servant in the livery of one of the great merchant families recognised him, bowed, and led the way.

A dozen men sat arguing at a long table, in a vast chamber with gilded walls and ceiling. They fell silent as he entered.

"A good day to you, gentlemen!" He tried to hide the mockery he felt. "I trust that you have not been waiting too long, and that my delay has caused you no trouble." With calculated arrogance, he picked out a chair and sat down facing the Lords of the Guilds. Suddenly he dominated them all. "Is everything in readiness? Do you rise today, tomorrow, or the day after?"

"Everything has gone wrong!" snarled Andrios, Archon of Portona and head of the Council of Guilds, his voice edged with hysteria. "Everything! Our Seynyoreans won't budge! Our Carrodians have been gotten at somehow, and want to rework their contracts so that they can only be employed on our ships! The provinces won't rise! And now our allies from up the coast"—he gestured at representatives of the other harbour cities, sitting around the table among the heads of the Portona guilds—"tell us they want *us* to rise first, rather than having a single rising all along the coast!"

"That *is* foolish," said the Duke, frowning at the men from Poidia, Antonopol, Opuntopol, and the rest. "What's this about the provinces?"

"Orissia *will* rise, almost certainly," said the Master of the Rivermen's Guild, from down the table. "But we've made almost no progress at all in Kimburtia or Manjipé."

"I take it, then, that your mission to Prince Phillipos came to nothing?" Duke Thoros asked, in a carefully careless voice.

"He tried to capture our agent, and deliver him to the King!" said Andrios. "But our man had been warned to expect something of the sort, and managed to escape."

"Aah . . ." the Duke said, stroking his beard to hide a smirk behind his palm. Had he been able to implicate Prince Phillipos, tomorrow he'd have been the King's man and ruler of Kalascor the day after that! Then he'd be finished with these treacherous pigs! But with that hope gone, he'd have to put some heart into them.

"You told me before that you had half the mercenary companies in the country in your pocket! What happened?"

"It's this DiVega, this Istvan the Archer!" said the Lord of the Shipping Guild. "Our spies tell us he called on Asbiorn Kung last night, and he must have gotten to Esrith Gunnar too! This morning Gunnar came storming into the Guildhall, demanding to renegotiate both his contract and Kung's. He said his men were hired to guard the ships, not to fight in a civil war!"

"And our Seynyoreans have been skittish ever since DiVega arrived," said Lord Andrios. "He's been running around visiting all the Commanders."

"Kill him, then!" said Duke Thoros. "Surely among the sailors and riffraff in the Harbour District you can find some not averse to slitting a throat for profit?"

"I have a man in my employ who is very good at finding such

scum," said Lord Andrios, "and at arranging things so they don't know who they're working for. No doubt he can find a rogue or two."

"A rogue or two?" Duke Thoros jeered. "This fellow is the most notable swordsman alive! You'll have to do better than that!"

"True." Andrios nodded. "I'll have him hire five, then."

"The Duke or Ipazema started laughing. The envoy from Poidia piped up: "I saw Raquel DiVega kill ten men once, in Riovia. These men are trained to fight against odds like that!"

Eyes widened in disbelief, but Ipazema's voice was calm and flat. "Hire twenty. You may not be able to catch him alone."

"My Lords." A new voice drifted lazily into the discussion. Fat, cherubic, sleepy-looking Lord Demitrios, of the Suppliers' Guild, leaned far out over the table, half-reclined on one elbow. His lips and cheeks were girlish below his dark hair, and his free hand traced odd designs in wine spilled on the table.

"As you know, my agents have been busy in Manjipé and the other Border provinces these many months, trying to turn them to our cause. Because of the character of our beloved King, they have, by and large, succeeded. The greater part of the nobility of Manjipé—and even the Kantara—have no great love for Chondos, and to turn them against him was child's play. Yet, as reported, Manjipé will not move. And why? Because of the respect and awe in which men hold Lord Jagat.

"It seems to me, my Lords, that the support of the throne rests upon three men: a tripod, you might say—Lord Jagat, Prince Phillipos, and this Istvan the Archer. Take away those three props, and—" His hand shot out suddenly, clenched in the air, and opened slowly, palm down.

Chapter Five

Istvan set down his goblet, then covered it with his hand as Leonic Servara raised the wine jug. Servara laughed.

"I swear, you carry moderation to excess, DiVega!" The slender, black-bearded man tilted the jug over his own goblet instead. "Why you had hardly enough to wet your meal—and you eat like a bird, at that! Twenty years I've known you now, and in all that time, I've never seen you drunk! Have you, D'Ascoli?"

"Never." The red-haired man shook his head.

Istvan chuckled. "Neither of you is old enough to have seen me drunk. I had to go into battle with a hangover once. That cured me."

"Do you expect war in the morning?" asked D'Ascoli.

Istvan shrugged his shoulders. "I wouldn't be surprised. Not many more days left before the Coronation. They're fools if they wait for that! I've been expecting Mahapor to rise for the past week. Can't see what they're waiting for."

"Portona!" Servara laughed. "Old Hansio wants *them* to start things, and get the Royal Forces thoroughly engaged in the north, before he moves. He's a canny old devil. But the Portona guilds are trying to bribe all the opposition first, and don't realise how delay weakens their position. Their leaders are merchants, not soldiers. If they'd acted a day or so after the King died, they might have succeeded. Instead they sit around offering money to everybody, and—are you listening?"

Istvan flicked his eyes back to Servara's face. "Oh yes," he said mildly, "go on."

Over Servara's shoulder Istvan could see a flabby, dark-haired man in the red robe of a Healer. He had seen that man before, and recently. There was something disturbing about the man's manner, and he seemed to be listening.

"Well," Servara was saying, "now Portona has lost all chance of buying up a majority of the mercenaries, and is afraid to move. So Hansio will probably wait forever."

"I hope you're right," said Istvan, and yawned. "I'm afraid I must ask you gentlemen to pardon me now. The King has finally consented to allow the Council to meet, and I have to get my plan ready to present." He left the chair in a fluid blur of motion.

"You'll not have another glass before you go?" asked Servara. Istvan shook his head. "Ah well, all the more for the rest of us, eh, D'Ascoli? A pleasant night to you, DiVega!"

"And to you, Servara! And you, D'Ascoli!" He bowed. Ruperos D'Ascoli bade him good night, and reached for the wine jug.

The night was warm and foggy. Istvan had no need for a cloak. Habit adjusted the sling of his sword to hang a degree from the horizontal. The air was laden with ill-smelling reminders of the city. He sighed, homesick for Carcosa, where such odours would be hidden by the fragrance of a thousand growing things. He walked softly by habit, and his feet made little sound on the cobbles. Now his ears picked up the sound of other feet behind him.

Many feet.

He ignored the sound at first, until something in their rhythm told him that this was not just a large band of late-night strollers. His ears told him the men behind were spreading out in a half-circle. What did they want? Robbery? He doubted it! Steel scraped softly against leather, against wood. He heard the tension of their breath. He did not turn. His left hand settled gently on his scabbard. He let the right dangle loosely at his side, and shook it gently to relax the fingers.

Feet pounded towards him. He spun to face them, his fingers folding over his hilt. The nearest man's sword was lifted to cut. Istvan's blade left the scabbard, its tip flicking through the attacker's throat. Before the corpse could fall, the Hastur-blade darted over his shoulder, into the throat of the man behind, then out again as Istvan spun to the right, his sword drawn up above his head. His left hand floated to the pommel.

The man running in from the right had his sword low, to stab. Istvan's blade whipped down, slicing bone and brain, then snapped up to rest on Istvan's shoulder as he whirled again. The corpse flopped on the cobbles, and a ragged man jumped back with a yelp of terror, guarding frantically. They were spread all around in a circle now, but somehow none of them wanted to be the next one to come within reach of his sword.

Istvan bared his teeth in a wolf's smile. He held the light blade with both hands, knees bent and ready to spring. There were a lot of them, fifteen or twenty, he guessed. He heard a faint shuffle behind him, and pivoted on his toes, his blade flashing above his head. A sheepish-looking man reeled back. Istvan laughed. These were the sweepings of Tarencia's gutters—thieves, boatmen, dock workers, not swordsmen!

"Get him!" a voice shouted. "He's only one man!"

"You first!" someone muttered.

"Close in on him! Slowly!" the first voice yelled again. Now Istvan picked him out, a dark, lean man, who looked to have a trace of Border blood. "Come on, he can't kill us all!"

Istvan was privately minded to agree with him, but it didn't look as if he'd have to. Some of them were ready to run now.

Step by step, they edged towards him. Istvan marked the man who had spoken, and deliberately turned his back on that part of the line. They had no sword-room. When they attacked, they'd be crowding themselves, getting in each other's way. He could sense their tension building like a wave, as they gathered their nerve for the final rush.

In the instant before that rush came, Istvan whirled and leaped. The lean man went down, blood spurting from the artery behind his cloven collarbone. Some scrambled back, as Istvan thought they would, while others bunched together. Istvan ducked a hissing cut, and drove his point up through a man's belly and on into his heart. As he pulled it free, he had to spin wildly to dodge another sword. Death was far too near. His blade came around in a circling cut. A head bounced on the cobbles.

A sword-edge shrieked for his eyes. His own blade crossed it with a deafening peal, then dipped, slicing through cloth and flesh, and a man screamed and clutched at his falling bowels.

He went on screaming. Istvan's heart contracted with pity. He'd not wanted that. He hated to cause pain. When he killed a man, he wanted it to be quick. His sword rang as he guarded a cut to his head, and lashed out under the striking arm to find the artery in the armpit.

At his feet the disemboweled man was writhing and moaning hopelessly. In an agony of guilt, Istvan sidestepped a thrust, and whipped his blade down behind the dying man's ear. That was quick, and merciful, and nearly cost him his life. He managed to sway to the right and the sword that would have spitted him tore through the cloth of his doublet and grated along his ribs. He felt a warm ooze flow down his side, and that put extra savagery into his last whirling cut as he vaulted the piled-up bodies and ran down the street.

Shouts behind him, and drumming feet. He cursed under his breath. Running had been a mistake. The sight of his back gave them courage. And wounded, he could not hope to outrun them.

One had almost caught up with him now. Istvan spun and stepped, his blade sweeping up under the other's chin. He sidestepped the falling corpse, and wondered if he should run again. He did not want to kill any more of them than he had to. He decided to stand his ground. That would take the heart out of them faster. They came cautiously over the blood-smeared cobbles, stalking like wolves past the bodies of their dead friends.

Had he run towards the tavern, or away from it, when he broke through their ring? If the tavern was somewhere behind him . . .

He began to back down the street. The others quickened their pace. He stopped. He had already run a greater distance than he had walked from the tavern. If he'd gone past it, D'Ascoli and Servara would be here. Blood was drooling down his skin, soaking into his doublet. Only a scratch, but loss of blood would weaken him, slow him down.

There were about ten of them left. Why didn't they go away and leave him alone? He didn't want to kill any more!

A man was running at him, screaming curses, and as his blade fell, Istvan slipped out from under it and slashed up through the shoulder. Without a cry the body dived onto its face.

He didn't want to kill, and he didn't want to die. He hated

death. These men, worthless as they were, must have women who loved them, kinsmen, parents, children . . .

Three of them rushed him at once, others coming up fast behind them. His blade sliced through a man's temple, dropped to turn one thrust as he sidestepped a second. He stabbed to the left, cut to the right; his blade hissing from eyesocket to throat. A fourth man ran around the falling bodies and his sword flailed at Istvan's head. Istvan jumped aside, slashed the man's gut open, and raised his sword to face the rest.

The others stopped, skidding on the cobbles, bumping into one another. The dying man moaned with terror and pain. His blood-dripping sword brandished over his head, Istvan glided towards them. They ran, shouting, throwing down their weapons. Istvan leaned on his sword and watched them go, his hand pressed to the cut over his ribs. *Alive!* he thought, *It's over, and I'm alive.* The cloth of his doublet was wet under his fingers. The dying man was calling for his mother. He couldn't let the man lie there and suffer. He turned towards the sound.

Wait! In the tavern, the red-robed man, the Healer— perhaps, if he could get him there in time, this fellow could still be saved. He wiped his sword, sheathed it, and knelt down to lift the man in his arms. A tide of blood poured over the cobblestones. He tore a large piece of cloth from his doublet, and stuffed it into the wound after pushing the looping entrails back where they belonged. The man screamed and screamed. Istvan held him in his arms like a frightened child, murmuring to him soothingly as he staggered to his feet and lurched down the street, past the piled corpses.

The cut in Istvan's side was a throb of tearing pain. It must have ripped wider under the strain. Istvan set his teeth and trudged on.

He set one stubborn foot in front of the other. The screams were weaker now, dying away to choked moans. He felt his grip loosening. His breath was coming in short, quick gasps, and he felt his knees begin to buckle. The man kicked and struggled. Istvan almost dropped him.

"DiVega!" Through the fog he heard Servara's voice. "DiVega! Where are you, DiVega? Are you alive?"

He braced his legs, and tried to gather breath enough to

answer. The man moaned and struggled in his arms. Far off in the fog were running feet, and ghostly voices calling out his name.

"DiVega! DiVega! Are you alive?"

"Here!" His voice was weak in his own ears, but D'Ascoli and Servara heard.

"We're coming, DiVega! We hear you!" Feet pounded in the fog. What if more assassins were waiting out there? He swayed dizzily. He'd have to put the man down to draw his sword . . .

Two figures burst running from the mist, naked swords in their hands. Istvan almost dropped the man, then recognised Servara and D'Ascoli.

The injured man kicked again, and this time Istvan could not quite keep his grip, but he managed to slide the man gently to the pavement, letting his own knees buckle under him.

"DiVega?" It was Servara looming above him. "I thought that was you screaming! You're covered with blood."

"Mostly his—and other peoples'." Istvan's voice was a croak. His side throbbed. "Help me get him to the Healer in the tavern. He's dying, but if the Healer's skilled enough . . ."

"I'm not sure even a full Adept could save this one," D'Ascoli said through the dying man's moans. "He's pretty far gone. Who is he, Istvan?"

"Just . . . a man. You two carry him." It was hard to talk. "Nothing wrong with me. Only a scratch." He pushed himself to his feet and stood swaying. The street was littered with bodies. So many dead men! For what?

He heard the wounded man cry out as Servara and D'Ascoli lifted him. Rupiros was muttering under his breath, something about the idiots who were supposed to be patrolling this district.

He staggered after his friends, concentrating on keeping his feet moving, on keeping himself steady. The cut in his side throbbed. It wasn't as bad, now that he wasn't carrying anybody. The others were out of sight ahead, though he could still hear their footsteps in the fog. He felt sick. He heard a challenge in the mists ahead. D'Ascoli's voice answered.

Dark shapes on the cobblestones. The first of the men he had killed tonight. He shook his head. So many men, dead, their limbs cold and stiffening. He shouldn't have fought so passively, so defensively. If he had not tried to escape, if he had attacked more fiercely, he might have scared them off without killing so many.

He felt his knees tremble. His head was spinning round. He stopped, breathing deeply, planting his feet. He *would not* keel over! Not from a silly little scratch like that.

Servara came running back. "Met the watch on their rounds. About time they got here! They're taking your friend to the tavern. We've sent for the company's Healer in case the fellow in the tavern's gone. Here, let me help you."

Istvan threw an arm around Servara's shoulders, glad enough to lean on the younger man. He let his head drop, and watched his feet stagger on the cobbles. This was stupid! He wasn't hurt that bad! He saw the bottom of the door. It opened, and he was inside. Candlelight hurt his eyes. He heard the injured man moaning. There was a chair, and he slid into it gratefully. Servara helped him with his doublet, and examined the wound in his side.

"Only a scratch, eh? What kind of cats did you play with as a child, DiVega? Snow tigers?" Wine was poured down his throat. Servara shouted for the Healer.

"No!" Istvan shook himself awake. "Not until he's finished with the other man! He's in pain, and probably dying, but if he can be saved, I want him saved! Too many men have died tonight!"

The Healer came over, but Istvan waved him back. He could still hear the suffering man moaning across the room. Servara scowled, and tried to protest, but D'Ascoli shut him up, and began to wash Istvan's wound with liquor. It stung. Istvan found himself blinking at a room that was once more real. The little pain was good; it reminded him that he was alive.

"How did you find me?" he asked after a moment.

D'Ascoli laughed. "What other swordsman in this part of the world would leave a trail of corpses like that? We leave the tavern happily drunk, and find ten or fifteen men laid out, a few others bolting past like rabbits, and somebody screaming up the street. My men are supposed to be patrolling this area anyway, so—"

"At last!" Servara's voice broke in. A tall, red-robed man

pushed through the door and glanced quickly around. The other Red-robe was busy over the dying man.

Servara gestured and the Healer came over to Istvan. His hands were calm and professional. Istvan felt his mind delicately brushing the fringes of consciousness as the Red-robe probed the cut.

The wounded man's moaning had stopped, but that did not mean anything by itself. The Healer had drugged him, of course. How much had he aggravated his own wound carrying the man? All wasted if the man died.

His hands were shaking. He was shaking all over, in fact. Nothing to be ashamed of. It had happened before. But he'd nearly died tonight. If he'd been a shade slower, or if he'd been looking a little more to the right . . .

He shivered. What had they said? Ten of fifteen men? And all so he could go on living the few years left him. At his age, it was hardly worth it. And if he hadn't dodged that one stroke, he would have killed five or six men for *nothing!* And they, in turn, had rushed out to die in the street because someone had paid—or maybe just promised—some paltry bit of gold, that they would have thrown away on wine or women in a few days.

The Healer packed salve in the wound, and began to sew it up.

What foolish things man found to pass away the time between birth and death! He, too, caught up in all this nonsense because of a promise to a dead man. Sooner or later he must learn the truth behind all the empty words that covered the reality of death. Rebirth or nothingness, he could not hold it off forever. He loved life, and had lived it to the hilt, in battle and love and child-raising. He'd seen more of the world than most men ever saw, and gotten more than his share of glory—

The Healer's voice broke into his thoughts. A potion was pressed into Istvan's hand.

"We're going to take you back to the palace now, with an escort so you won't have to rip that cut open again chopping up assassins. A week should heal it up, but I want you to get some sleep. You're exhausted, and you're not a young man anymore. You lost a lot of blood, too—except for that, the scratch would be nothing. Stay out of street fights, and you ought to live to be a hundred."

Who wanted to live *that* long, he wondered. Just that much longer to watch the approach of death . . .

The face of the other Healer swam out of the confusion of the room.

"I did all I could, Lord, but he was too far gone. The man is dead."

"Fifteen men!" Lord Andrios gasped in shock.

Duke Thoros smiled and stroked his black beard. "All of them died without talking, I trust?"

"Yes, Lord," said the man in the red Healer's robe. "I saw to that myself. DiVega had brought one man back—Orandos the boatman—with his guts ripped out, and wanted him healed up enough to talk. I made sure he died without speaking."

"I warned you," Enricos of Poidia was babbling. "I warned you these Seynyoreans couldn't be trifled with! I told you that man was dangerous!"

The Duke of Ipazema leaned back and sipped his wine, while he studied the man in the Healer's robe. *So you kept him from talking, and made sure he died, did you?* The Duke's eyes glittered ironically. Not too hard, he thought. A Healer might be able to make an eye or hand grow back, but—

"You say the other five ran away?" sputtered Andrios, indignant. "The cowards!"

Ipazema smiled maliciously. "Ah, you'd have stayed and fought, I see?" He laughed at the Portonan's glare.

"We'd already paid them half! All that gold—for nothing! If any of them had had the courage to keep on and kill him, they'd have had all the others' pay!" He turned sharply to the Healer as another thought struck him. "None of the ones who ran away were identified or caught, were they?"

"I told you, only one was brought back," the red-robed man snapped, "and he died. The rest were either killed outright or got clean away. None of them knew anything about you, anyway. Most of them never even saw me; the man who paid them is dead. The worst that can happen is that they might start looking for a man in a Healer's robe. I'll get rid of the robe—it's dangerous anyway—and nobody will be able to trace me. As long as I'm safe, you're safe."

The Duke of Ipazema smiled to himself. "Why don't you wait and get rid of the robe after you've recruited men to go after Phillipos and Lord Jagat?" he said.

Andrios looked up, startled and angry. The Duke's lips twitched. He didn't mind spending Portonan money. He enjoyed the way they stared at him.

"You mean to go on with—with *that* plan? After *this!*" Andrios' voice broke with a little squeal.

Duke Thoros laughed. "Why not? Neither Phillipos nor Jagat was trained in the northern schools. They're good swordsmen, but ordinary. Send the same number of men after them, and then there'll only be DiVega. He can't keep the throne up single-handed! Without Manjipé and Kalascor, the King is doomed. And we may still be able to take care of DiVega—" He broke off, and sipped his wine.

As the words left his mouth he regretted saying them. Andrios and Enricos looked at him quizzically, but he only poured himself more wine. Sandor was far too valuable a secret to reveal to these rabbits.

> The lamb runs to its Master's call, and leans its throat
>   against the knife:
> 'Twas even so the Lion Prince rode trustingly to yield his
>   life.
> Never back to Mahapor on his noble fleet steed rode he;
> The merchants count their shining gold: royal blood
>   pours into the sea.

Rinmull of Ojaini's voice wailed out the last line of his song and died away. For a moment, the painted and woven figures of ancient Takkarian heroes on the walls of the Satragara gazed upon their descendents in silence. Then wine cups clanged and hammered on tables, and the voices of Bordermen roared in wild applause. Pirthio shouted with the rest of them. A part of his mind smiled with hazy knowledge that his plan was working, but even that was drowned in the surge of emotion.

On the walls about them, tapestries and paintings showed

scenes from ancient stories that the men gathered here knew by heart. Here in paint and embroidery the Shadowed Mountains rose pristine and sunlit, living trees and grass upon their slopes, their peaks bright with snow. Here, too, the painted towers of Rashnagar swarmed with silk-clad, brown-skinned folk: nobles of a realm that spanned the mountains and spread south across the desert.

Drunken Bordermen would stare at these paintings for hours with undisguised burning hunger of the soul. Here was their stolen heritage, and whether they had been born in the blasted grey wastes of Manjipé, or the still-fertile uplands of Mahavara, or among the great trees of the Kantara, here was the true home of their youth, the land of childhood story.

Drinking vessels pounded on tables, shouting drunken voices filled the room. Pirthio tried to speak above the babble, but his words were lost. Yet at last the hammering and shouting of applause faded to a murmur of conversation, and out of it lifted the voice of Tunno of Mahapor, thick with drink, but still a bull-rumble, menacing and dangerous:

"They fear us yet, those fat, money-counting toads! 'Fisheaters,' they call us, and 'Scarecrows'—but set hand to hilt and they remember that we Takkarians ruled all this land once!" The Heir to Mahapor flexed powerful muscles, and plucked at the moustache above his sneer. "And when there's a war to be fought, then they forget about 'Fisheater' and 'Starveling'— then it's 'Noble Descendent of the Takkarian Kings,' as they crawl on their fat bellies, begging you to take their filthy gold!"

Pirthio blinked and sat up, and carefully raised his voice as he answered, so it sliced open the curtain of talk around them. "So they seek to buy us now, these swine of the ports, to buy our swords and our honour that is beyond price?" He heard lower voices stop, knew men were sitting up to listen. "To what end? That by paying us now they may rid themselves of us, and cease to pay the tribute that buys our bread?

"What have the Sons of the Takkars to do with the sea-folk's gold?" Pirthio's voice was a trumpet now, and in the hearts of his listeners it echoed from the fancied walls of Rashnagar. "Is it not ours by right? Do we not shelter them from the Demons of the Shadow? Should not we 'Men of the Hills' take tribute from the merchant-folk, just as our forefathers did?"

The room around them had grown hushed. Tunno, dazed with drink, plucked at his moustache. "The toads mock us," he growled. "They mock us because our clothing is worn and plain, and because we have not a ring on every fat finger. And because we do not stuff ourselves as they do, 'Starvelings,' they call us, and 'Scarecrows,' but show them a blade and watch them quake! Big bellies they have, but not for fighting! But they were traitor dogs always. *We* remember. They betrayed King Mahadev to his death on the field of Klordri! Fat peddlers and moneylenders! We will loot Portona, one of these days . . ." He gulped down wine like a man in the desert, and another voice spoke up from across the room, where the men of the Kantara were sitting.

"One of the dogs wished to dispute my right to walk the streets," the Kantaran snarled. Pirthio recognised the speaker as Ajesio of Kantakin. Rumour said he was in love with a girl in Mahapor; certainly he had been the first Kantaran to cross the invisible barrier that had divided the Satragara.

"A fat slug in a litter, with a dozen hired bullies clearing folk from his path. One tried to push *me* aside, then changed his mind when he saw my sword at his throat. They went around, while the mound of fat they carried shouted at me, and swore he would see me jailed—that no ragged vagabond out of the woods could threaten his men on the streets and go unpunished! I kicked one of his guards, and hurried another along with a prick of my point. But there is no fight in those street ruffians they hire to bully weaker men. None, to my sorrow, dared to turn and argue with me."

"One mocked my clothing yesterday, on the street," snarled another. "All I possess has been eaten in war with the Dark Things, so I had no jewels for my fingers. But they fit well upon a sword-hilt!" He raised a hand, showing the long, delicate fingers that result from generations of breeding for the sword.

Pirthio leaned back smiling, as other voices were raised, complaining no longer of misdeeds of merchants long dead, but of the slights that living merchants had put upon the tender Border pride. In some ways it was going better than he had hoped. Few among the Bordermen had no grievance, either real or fancied. Men who valued worth by wealth were natural enemies of men to whom not only wealth but life itself was fuel to be burned to drive back the darkness.

The ancient Takkars pictured on the walls were dressed in gorgeous finery, and old stories told of pride that would hide poverty and maintain an outward show of wealth by fantastic stratagems. Those days were long gone. The Borderers' land was their only treasure, and they squandered all else to hold it. Yet to be mocked for their poverty and their worn raiment rankled deeply, and many a fat fool, without the sense to close his mouth, had made himself the focus of a secret, long-held grudge.

A man burst in from the street. "Have you heard the news?" he babbled excitedly to men who turned to look, hands dropping automatically to their swords. "Istvan the Archer was attacked by thirty or forty men, down in the River District, and killed them *all!* Bodies all over the street!"

If there was more to his story it was lost, as voices rose in a riot of questions. The very name of Istvan DiVega was enough to rouse awe; it had echoed in so many hero-tales in their youth—more modern, perhaps, than the legends of ancient Rashnagar, but no less wonderful. No story that contained that name was beyond belief. Had he said it was a thousand men DiVega had killed, more sober men than any in the Satragara would have believed him.

Save perhaps for the landlord, no one in the Satragara was sober; more, they had all been revelling in the golden glory of ancient tales for hours. Pirthio recovered his wits more quickly than any, and by sheer bravado and use of rank, got through the crowd and brought the fellow to Tunno's table. As the clamour slowly sank around them, they got the rest of the story. At least thirty men, the man said, and Istvan the Archer had killed them all without a scratch himself. The bodies were all over the River District—he'd seen ten of them himself. Gutter-rats, sailors, petty thieves, pickpockets, and the like. Typical hirelings.

Tunno rose importantly and announced the news to the room. Eyes turned glittering towards him. The glory of old tales had invaded the room: the paintings on the walls were windows that opened on fabled Rashnagar; spilled wine on the table was a map of faery seas.

"Hired killers—but who hired them?" someone asked.

Pirthio leaped to his feet. "Who hired them? Do warriors hire ruffians to do their killing for them? There are many who *might* have hired them—but most of them, surely, live in one city! Need I name it?"

"No!" men shouted back at him, but others muttered, "Portona!"

"Who would rather spend their gold to see a warrior dead than spend it that the land might live?" His eyes blazed and his voice was a trumpet. On the tapestry behind him, woven elephants marched solemnly between the towers of ancient Rashnagar.

"Pity the poor fools who took wages from Portona to bring back a hero's head!" Pirthio's voice began to fall into the cadences and the language of the old tales of his folk. "Even had they lived to earn their pay, they would have been cheated of their hire! That was always the merchant's way—to risk nothing except a little gold, and then to safeguard that as best he might, after the deed he dare not face himself is done."

His eyes raked his audience, and he paused, struggling against the wine he had drunk, strongly tempted to spell out the lesson. But thoughtful expressions on several faces told him that the point had not been missed, and to press the matter further was to risk touching the tender Border pride.

Instead, "It is time we dealt with these fat swine," he went on, "who think that gold makes up for the lack of courage and breeding, and that a full purse makes a coward the equal of a Takkar Lord—or his better!"

In the streets outside, men were startled by the sound of many voices, roaring with rage, from the Satragara, and wondered if there would be a riot.

Birds sang at sunrise in the Kantara. After months on the blasted wastelands of Damenco, Martos had almost forgotten how sweet a bird's song could be, how restful was the colour green to the eyes.

When the green wall of the Kantara had reared up beyond the Yukota, some of the Bordermen had dismounted and knelt down, then dropped their foreheads almost to the earth, while others had merely bowed from their saddles and made archaic gestures of respect. Martos, like all the Kadarins, had stared at them, but now he understood.

There had been fruit trees in one or two of the oldest fields around Suknia; there were orchards around Manjipor. Willows grew along the Marunka and some of the smaller streams that ran into it. There were no other trees for miles, and there were no birds at all, anywhere along the Border. No wonder, then, that the Borderers worshipped trees; no wonder that they bowed to this remnant of the ancient forest.

Martos, wakened by birdsong, rising to look out upon green clouds of leaves, began to worship the forest himself. Sunbeams slipped between branches to find the castle where they had stopped for the night, and strike sudden brilliant needles of light from the armour of the escort as they bustled about. The branches swayed as birds flitted through them.

Kumari had not yet come down. Martos looked up at the slim tower that loomed above them, and then turned back to the men. Horses lashed the air with their tails as men tightened saddle girths and prepared to mount. Warflame stamped, and shook his head with a soft jingle of harness.

Leaves glowed soft green in the east. Martos stretched and yawned, and then took a deep breath as a cooling breeze played across his face. Men were swinging themselves up onto the horses. He turned back to the tower. Still no sign of Kumari. He sighed, and then wondered at his own reluctance, the fear that kept him from breaking the reserve with which she had surrounded herself since leaving Suknia. Even in bed . . .

The tower reared above the trees, its tiled roof a red glow in open sunlight. He walked under the arch of its door, into the cool stony gloom. He met her women on the spiral stair, but she was not with them. He gestured them down and went on to her room. Her window faced west and was curtained. She knelt, Border-fashion, in the dimness, staring at something in her hand.

"Martos, look!" she said. "The blade is clear and—and— empty! We are so far from the Shadow there is not even a flicker in the blade, even at night!"

He stared at her a moment, and then realised that her crystal dagger lay across her palm, and remembered the way it had glowed at night beside her bed. Nearness to the Dark Things kindled need-fire in the blade.

He stepped forward to look over her shoulder, and saw the curve of one breast almost bared where the neck of her dress stood out from her body. Something caught him by the throat then, and he was only able to spare the briefest glance at the weapon. Only twice had they been together, in all the time they had been on the road! And both times she had been withdrawn, apart, cut off from him—now, of all times, with her flesh and his blending in her womb!

With an effort he drew his eyes away from the honey-brown sweet mound in its nest of blue cloth, and made himself look at the dagger. Always before, a tiny white moon had glowed in the centre of the blade, surrounded, when the Border was quiet, by tiny glittering sparks, and the little red jewels in the hilt had glowed like live coals in the darkness. Now the flesh of her palm showed through the glass-clear blade. The moon disk was only a distorting blur. The rubies in the hilt were merely stones, with no light of their own.

He remembered the rainbow flare that had filled the crystal the night of the attack, when she'd snatched it up as she leaped from the bed, from his arms . . . And his eyes were pulled irresistibly back to the fold where the neck of her gown bowed out from her skin. He ached with the need for her.

"I'd forgotten this happened," she whispered. "I haven't been this far from the Border for so long that—it's strange. I'm so used to it glowing—just a little, just enough to remind you that the Dark Things are there, just across the Border. It's almost frightening!"

He wanted desperately to slide his hand under the errant fold of cloth, along the soft skin. He could almost feel her nipple against the palm of his cupped hand. He licked his lips, forced words past them.

"My Lady's escort waits."

The cloth stirred, and curtained her breast as she moved. Words of love cascaded through his mind, and stumbled over the lump of dead flesh that his tongue had become. It was maddening! He would never be able to tell her how he loved her. He would only stutter and look foolish.

Why am I afraid to look foolish? he wondered as he followed her down the stairs. It had been so long, so long . . .

They walked into the tree-filtred daylight. Men snapped straight in their saddles with a rattle of steel. Swarthy Bordermen in lacquered horsehide armour sat on their rugged little rough-coated ponies, while the Kadarins in their glittering steel breastplates and morions towered above them on their powerful war-horses. A step from the tower door, he felt her fingers close on his arm.

"Do you still want me to go away with you?" Her whispering voice shook.

He swallowed hard. Words would not come. They never would when it was important. He wanted to sing, to dance, to laugh; but the whole escort was watching them, her ladies were watching them, and his tongue was crippled, worthless. He turned to her and nodded, dumbly.

She sighed. "If only Pirthio were married, or had gotten an heir somewhere," she said, "I could go happily, with a clear conscience. But—sad or happy, right or wrong, I—I will come to Kadar with you, Martos, if—if you want me . . ."

Martos saw tears on her lashes, remembered the scorn with which she had spoken of the women who fled the Border. He touched the tips of her fingers.

"Give me a little time," she whispered. "Uncle must not be hurt. I have been a daughter to him, after all. Let me tell him in my own time, and in my own way. Remember that for . . ." She paused, and teeth worried her lower lip. "Remember that to my people, this will seem a thing of shame, that I would run away from the land that we—that my people have struggled so long to gain. Do not make it hard for me, Martos!"

He mastered his tongue at last. "I will not," he said softly. He wanted to take her in his arms and comfort her, but the whole escort was watching them. "We—we'd better be going," he stammered.

She looked at him sharply, hurt. "Is that all you have to say? Doesn't it mean any more than that to you?" Tears accused him from the wide, dark eyes.

His nervous fingers combed his sun-gilded hair, tugged at the shadowed brown beard. "I—I—love you!" he stammered. "I—I don't have—I can't think of anything else to say that matters. I could—I want to laugh or sing or—but half the province is watching us! What do you want me to do? I—I thought—"

Then her arms were around his neck and the soft cloth of her gown rustled against the unyielding steel of his breastplate. Her lips closed his.

"Foolish man!" she whispered a long moment later. "What is there to hide *now?*"

Word of the attack on Istvan the Archer spread through the city on a thousand tongues: rumour doubled and trebled the numbers he had slain; said he was untouched; said he was dying. Among the mercenaries, the stories brought scowls, but little wonder. They knew what Istvan was capable of. They wasted no time in speculation.

Leonic Servara put the matter quite simply: "I do not believe that the King is trying to stop DiVega from binding us to his cause."

Shortly after the news reached Portona, Esrith Gunnar and Asbiorn Kung made a second—more forceful—demand for a new contract.

"Prince Phillipos keeps to the palace, but Lord Jagat goes back and forth from his town house unattended. The men I've hired will gather there this evening."

The speaker no longer wore his Healer's robe; Duke Thoros smiled to realise that he would never have recognised the man on the street. A thousand men must have faces like that.

"If you have all your men there just at sunset, you're certain to catch him," said the Duke. "There's a Council meeting tonight; he'll have to go."

"They'll be there by nightfall. This time, we're taking no chances. I found a couple of trained swordsmen—Bordermen from Mahapol who'd been thrown out of the city guard."

The Guildmasters murmured approval. And the Duke could barely keep from laughing. As though any native-bred swordsman—even in a mob—would be of any use against DiVega! Sandor, of course, was another matter . . .

"Probably more than you need for Jagat, if he has no guards," said the Duke. "DiVega is a special case—you don't get songs sung about you from here to the Northern Deserts if you're only an ordinary man. Jagat is a good fighting man, but not in that class."

He poured himself more wine. He could afford to be patient.

A few hours later, Lord Demitrios of the Suppliers' Guild lounged in his litter while his bodyguard cleared a path before him through the thick crowds that filled the street with frantic gaiety in anticipation of the approaching Coronation. Suddenly, shouting voices raged around him, and he found himself tumbled rudely out of the litter to sit, a pile of jewels and offended dignity, listening to the laughter and insults of a group of drunken Bordermen. Someone spat on him.

Their sword-hilts jutted arrogantly from the sashes of thread-bare robes their grandfathers might have worn to court. Demitrios' guards cowered back against the buildings, afraid to draw blade against these proven warriors who had spent their lives in constant combat against the Dark Things.

They laughed as they moved away, leaving Demitrios sprawled on the cobbles, glaring at his hapless guards. At that he was lucky. A merchant-prince of Armadopol, forcing his way through a crowd on his horse, shouted something about "Dung-hoarding scarecrows" at a group of Bordermen who blocked his way. He was dragged from his horse and beaten; he tried to draw his sword, but it was taken away from him and snapped over someone's knee. He staggered into the Guild-hall, hours later, the flesh under his robe covered with bruises made by the flat of a sword.

Chapter Six

Martos heard strange rumours on the crowded road. Folk said that Istvan the Archer lay dying after a battle with some vast number of men: some said a hundred; others said more. Some said there had been an attempt on the life of the King. One story had it that Hansio of Mahapor had smuggled an army into the city, to attack the palace, and that Istvan the Archer had slaughtered them single-handed. That was ridiculous, of course.

Whatever had happened, it did not affect the festival spirit of the crowd. Tumblers and jugglers performed beside the road, and minstrels wandered singing through a flood of smiling faces. It was as though the whole world shared Martos' happiness. Surely, Martos thought, all this merriment could spring from no such common event as the crowning of a King! No, surely the road and the world rejoiced because Kumari loved him!

Off to the left, the river Yukota, widening, had become the Pavana, and on the right they could see, beyond fields and farms, the Atvanadi, and the Oda beyond that, rushing to join with the Pavana north of the city. Ahead, at the point of the arrowhead formed by the meeting rivers, the Rock of Tarencia loomed above the city, the castle crouched on its back. It had been a robber's hold once, men said. Tents sprouted about the walls, as though the city were under seige. The rich pavilions of late-coming nobles mingled with crude makeshifts of sticks and blankets.

Tarencia overflowed with people. At its gates a river of flesh poured past guards who stood like rocks in the stream, while thousands pushed past. The horses, nervous and snorting, moved at a slow walk, though even in a crowd such as this, people tried to get out of the huge beasts' way.

Slowly the heavy Kadarin war-steeds bluffed their way

through the choked streets, towards Jagat's town house, while the Borderers' ponies followed in the bigger horses' wake. As they got off the main street, the crowds thinned, until a shout would open a path and they could move at a trot. Martos let Suktio take the lead then, and dropped back to ride by Kumari.

"What shall I say to your uncle?" he asked, just loud enough for her to hear above the hooves.

"Nothing, tonight," she said. "Let me tell him—after the Coronation. He has enough on his mind now."

"You'd better tie up Suktio, then," said Martos, "maybe drop him down a well. He looks like he'd like to do something of the sort to me! And they all saw—"

She laughed. "I will take care of Suktio. As for the rest—I've had lovers before. And Uncle isn't blind, you know!"

He blinked, confused. In Kadar, a duenna would have been watching like a hawk, to be sure that whatever might pass between them, her charge would still be a virgin afterward.

Over his left shoulder the Twin Suns settled behind the roofs. He watched. Sunset had become for him an important ritual: every day the Shadow had dwindled behind them, shrinking at last to a black line on the horizon, then vanishing. Martos gazed a moment, delighted by the distant loveliness, at pearl-bright clouds streaked with rainbow light, with gold, pink, and burgundy clouds lower in the sky.

The column halted. Brilliant colours glowed above Jagat's roof. Jagat's crest—the "Sword Wheel," an eight-pointed star of swords, their pommels touching—was carved in wood above the oaken door at the head of the stairs. The wall was all plain wood—but for a Borderman, that was incalculable wealth.

Even here were crowds. Across the street several small groups of passersby had stopped to watch their arrival, lounging against the walls. One or two seemed to be Bordermen, but most were the sort of riffraff he would have expected to see down by the docks. Jagat himself was coming down the stairs to greet them, his white hair dyed by sunset, his teeth gleaming in his dark old face. Kumari ran to him with a glad cry, and the old man wrapped her in a close embrace.

"I was afraid I'd have to leave for the castle before you

arrived," Martos heard him say. "The Council meets tonight, and I must be there."

Martos blinked back sudden homesickness, thinking of his own family, so far away. He only dimly heard Jagat formally thank Suktio for escorting his kinswoman, and was puzzled when Jagat caught his eye and winked.

"You'll both be staying here, of course," Jagat went on. "I've arranged for rooms for your men and stable-space for your horses down the street at the Brown Boar."

"My thanks, Lord," said Suktio, with a stiff formality Martos thought odd, "but I had already decided to stay at the Satragara."

"Good luck to you!" Pirthio laughed from the stair. "Every room is crammed. You'll be lucky to find yourself sleeping ten in a bed—and all men, too!" Pirthio sprang down the steps, teasing Suktio, kissing Kumari, bonging Martos's armour with a friendly fist. "Fortunately, they had the sense to lay in a good supply of Massadessan wine. We'll all go down and drink some later. You come too, Martos. I remember you complaining about being shut up in Suknia!"

Even Suktio's frown was fading before Pirthio. It was a standing joke among Jagat's men that no one could dislike Pirthio, and they pointed to his friendship with Prince Chondos as proof.

Martos wondered if he really wanted to go drinking that night. It was doubtful if anything this little kingdom had to offer could match the civilised elegance of the night life in Erthi or Almahar, but it would be a change, and this was the capital city, after all. But at the moment, he wanted nothing so much as a bath.

So it was an hour later, bathed and refreshed and dressed in his second-best court clothes, that Martos descended the stairs from his room, buckling his light court-sword over his short wine-red tunic. His white breeches clung like skin. Pirthio and Kumari stared at him. He was a long way from the Kadarin court.

"Father's outside," said Pirthio, "waiting for our horses to be brought round. He has to attend a Council meeting tonight, but he said he wanted a chance to talk to both of us."

"You go ahead," said Martos. "I—I'll be with you in a moment."

But Pirthio seemed in no hurry, and he wanted to talk. "I've kept myself busy since I got here." He leaned back against the door, smiling as though pleased with himself. "Not that it hasn't been enjoyable work! But you'll see the change. Hamir of Inagar may not be ready to drink the King's health yet, but mention Portona in front of him, and watch!" He laughed. Martos wondered what he was talking about. Hamir of . . . ? He searched his memory, then saw Jagat facing a group of men. Yes, the one Jagat had called *fat*.

"Portona will probably lose all its support, after last night!" Pirthio went on. "Maybe they've learned some respect for the DiVega name, too! But I've done well, and I may have averted the danger entirely. We all know Portona will never move on its own!"

Kumari's arm came around Martos. His own slipped around her waist, and moved, caressingly, where Pirthio would not see. Looking up, Pirthio suddenly realised that he was not wanted. As the door closed behind him, Kumari laughed, and turned to press her yielding breasts against the claret of Martos' tunic.

"What should—"

She stopped his words with a kiss. "Get along with you now, if you really *must* go and get drunk!" she said, when he raised his head at last. "I'll go to sleep, and dream about the beautiful baby we're going to have! You go celebrate." She pushed him—puzzled, wordless—towards the door.

He stood looking back a long moment at her body's curves in the clinging gown. The oaken door blotted her from view, leaving his eyes full of lamplight, and full of her.

"Father!" a voice behind him shouted. *"Look out!"*

He whirled, left hand lifting the scabbard, right fingers brushing the hilt. Blinking house-light from his eyes, he saw Pirthio run into the night, ghostly sword waving. Beyond, dim shapes surged and twisted in darkness. Was that Jagat, winged sleeves flapping, arms thrust up like two black branches to grasp a third? Where the three hands met, starlight rippled on steel.

Martos bounded down the stairs. Harsh voices shouted. Boot-soles slapped on the dark street's stones, and Pirthio vanished among vague figures swarming in the deep blue night. Clanging metal echoed down the canyon of the street. Martos vaulted the last steps; hard cobbles hurt his pounding feet.

Squared cloth flapping, a shape in jagged Border robes hurled another figure staggering. There was a sudden faint glimmer like starlit water rising waist-high. Rushing dark figures blotted both shapes from sight. Harsh chimes echoed.

Martos shouted, wordless. Four, turning, ran to meet him, spreading out, dim phantom swords carefully spaced. Martos dodged to the right, his hand hovering, open, above his hilt. A sword-edge shrilled. Martos' hand clamped his hilt as he sprang from under the falling black wedge, and darted under the arm that held it. Beyond, a startled man opened his mouth to shout as Martos' blade lashed out and stroked his throat.

Behind him a sword was rising to cut at his back. He whirled on the pivot of supple knee and ankle, his sword twirling up to guard. The thin steel sliver quivered in his hand as it pitched the pealing blade aside. His arm snapped straight, drew back, feeling flesh collapse around his point. Breath and blood gurgled in a punctured throat.

Two others were turning to rush him. He did not wait for them. Heaving air from his lungs in another wordless shout, he ran across the street, towards the surging, clattering mob. Boots hammered behind him. Steel stabbed out of the crowd ahead. He dinged it aside as he heaved a foot into another man's back, toppling him forward, sending a dozen men staggering. Faces turned in fear. Flesh parted under his edge, and he bounded into the crowd, another faceless shape in the dark.

Through a gap in the milling mob he glimpsed two figures fighting back-to-back against the wall. A moon slipped past the edge of a roof, frosting speed-blurred steel. Jagat's parrying blade chimed and sparked; dark blood dyed his sleeve. Martos shouted and rushed. His sword-arm thrashed in a looping curve, and he felt flesh tug his edge. Men scattered before him.

A sword-point drove at Jagat. Martos' sweeping blade plunged down on it, and belled as it bounced. His wrist rolled; steel twirled and dipped; a cutthroat screamed as its tip ripped entrails free. Wheeling, Martos swept aside steel that dived at his back. His point hissed inches from the eyes of a cringing man.

"Run!" someone shouted. "It's Istvan the Archer!"

A sudden loud shuffle made room all around. Jagat and Pirthio leaned gasping against the wall, their clothes dappled with blood. A dying man screamed and flopped on slick wet cobbles at their feet. A wedge of moons sailed free of the rooftops. flooding the bloodied street with light.

"That's not DiVega!" a hoarse voice shouted. "DiVega's old! This one's young! Kill him!"

Leather slapped stone. Moonlight rippled over steel. Behind him Martos heard a rush of running feet. He spun and sprang, and a shape cascading blood dropped inert. He danced away from a glitter of swirling light, and his own edge swooped through flesh. A long lunge plunged his point between ribs. He ripped the blade free, up into the path of a flailing cut.

Again he felt the thin steel tremble. Would it break? He wished for his dwarf-forged sword of war, but it was packed away. He would not have feared *its* breaking! He ducked, hearing the air whine over his head as the shaved wind stirred his hair. His point sank into softness.

Dying men moaned. Feet shuffled back. Sweat oozed through his hair. He gulped sweet air into thirsty lungs, both hands gripping the hilt above his head. They were drawing back . . . All but two. Something in their walk alerted him. These were not gutter-rats like the others. They moved like trained warriors. Like Bordermen.

Taut senses thrilled. His soul was a thin line of steel. His left hand caressed the pommel. The Bordermen checked, staring.

"Rush him!" a voice rasped. "All together!"

Both Borderers charged, and behind them the scum of the wharves waved swords and daggers. Mirrored moonlight stabbed from left and right. A two-handed hammer-blow drove one blade before him while he stepped from the path of the other, in between the two Bordermen. His wrists slapped together, spinning hands flipping his point from right to left. A throat vanished in bloody mist.

A ripple of moonlight keened for his flesh. A heave of his shoulders crossed clanging edges. Steel rasped as his body uncoiled in a lunge; then he sprang between the toppling bodies, into the crowd.

His edge flew to a shoulder, slicing an artery; his point

plunged through an eye to the brain behind. His left hand dropped from his pommel like a striking hawk to grip the wrist above a dagger that spiked at his side. The flat of his blade brushed the back of his neck as he stabbed over his shoulder.

Feet drummed on cobbles. The cowardly murderers were running, those that were left, and in his rage he was running too, chasing them.

One turned, sword raised. Martos dodged plummeting steel, his own sword dipping to scythe across the hollow belly. The man screamed, clutching at falling slimy coils as Martos ran past. He caught up with the others and darted ahead, sword's weight poised. One cowered screaming against the wall; the other three backed slowly away behind the hedge of their raised swords, towards dying men's wails and the approaching footsteps of Pirthio and Jagat.

Sudden light poured from a gate, dappled with the tense shadows of armed men standing, trying to decide whose side to take. Desperation broke the hedge of steel: Martos slipped easily from under a wildly flailing sword, felt his edge tear cloth and flesh as the man ran past him, racing down the street screaming until his feet tangled in his gut and tripped him. The other two hesitated, but the fear-ridden creature that gibbered by the wall tried to run, and ran his throat onto the sudden spike of Martos' point. Panic writhed on the faces of the last two as Martos glided towards them with tiny, dancing steps, sword poised above his head. Beyond, Jagat came limping up, while Pirthio paused beside a dying man thrashing in a mire of blood.

One dived, sword-first, at Martos. The other, terror tempered, perhaps, by some memory of promised gold, whirled and rushed at Lord Jagat. Far behind the streak of mirrored moonlight that arrowed at his breast, Martos saw Jagat hurl his blade up to guard. Steel belled, and the old Borderman went down, his feet slipping on the bloody cobbles.

Martos danced like a windblown leaf. A watery shimmer stabbed past. His edge reached under the man's ear and caressed soft skin. A dark fountain blossomed in the moonlight. He ran over bruising stone. He saw a blade stabbing down at Jagat, but the old man rolled on his back, sweeping the thrusting steel aside with his own.

Pirthio came running up with whirling sword and dagger. The assassin turned to run. His terror-filled eyes met Martos' gaze. Martos stepped. His blade swept under the man's chin.

Up the street, a dying man cried hopelessly. Jagat climbed slowly to his feet. Pirthio looked down at the still body of the last of the killers, and his knuckles were white on his sword-hilt. A bitter snort of laughter burst from his lips, and he shook his head back and forth.

"Earth's breasts, Martos! You could have left that one for me!" His voice was angry, despite the laugh. "It was my own father they were trying to kill, after all!"

The dying man wailed like a lonely child.

"Where is Lord Jagat?"

Age had made Lord Taticos' voice harsh and shrill, but it could still fill a larger chamber than this Council room. Istvan's head jerked up, and he found himself glancing at the door as though expecting Jagat to appear at that summons. But all he saw was Lord Taticos himself, arms folded behind his back as he looked down the long corridor. After a long, silent moment the Lord Steward shook his white hair and, turning back to them, strode purposefully towards the King.

"Everyone else is here, Lord King," said Taticos. "I would suggest, Sire, that Lord Jagat will not mind if we begin without him. I am sure he will be here soon, but we have much work before us, and a hard day tomorrow—harder for Your Highness, I fear, than for any of us."

The young King frowned, and worried his lip between his teeth. "I did not wish to begin until all nine Councillors were here. But—" he sighed, "I suppose you have the right of it, Lord Steward. It will be late soon enough, and we shall all lose sleep as it is. You have my permission to sit, gentles." He dropped back in the chair at the head of the long table, and blond, big-boned Prince Phillipos took a seat beside him.

A fine flock of greybeards, we! Istvan thought wryly, as he watched the other old men take their places according to some well-established order. *How long, I wonder, before he tires of our white hair and wise expressions, and finds younger men to replace us all?*

He waited for someone to show him where to sit. Shachio, the King's Herald and Seer, looked up. Istvan could remember when that dark-skinned, white-haired old man—half Seyn-yorean, half Borderman—had been called the Red Seer, because his copper hair had been nearly the same colour as his Borderman's skin. He motioned Istvan into an empty chair near the King. The place opposite was also empty—doubtless Jagat's seat.

Chondos cleared his throat. "Well, Lord Taticos?" he asked. "It was you who badgered me to hold this Council meeting. I trust you have something to consider?"

"Yes, Lord King," said Taticos, but he hesitated, fidgeting, while the King glared at him.

"Well?" snapped the King, caustically. "Shall we get to it, then? I suppose the main subject is going to be the usual problem: how to preserve the kingdom from my normal tactlessness, ineptness, and stupidity. Or have you managed to think of something different to discuss?"

Not a muscle moved in the Lord Steward's face, but a rush of blood stained the transparent skin above the white beard. Yet his voice, when he spoke, was so gentle that Istvan could only marvel at his self-control.

"A great many matters demand our attention, Lord. Lord Zengio has something to report, and our most pressing business is to be sure that all details of the Coronation—"

"What!" Chondos roared. "Are we to lose sleep for that! There is a ritual, after all! What is tradition for?"

"There are delicate questions of precedence involved," said Taticos, his voice still level. "Any confusion tomorrow could lead to grave consequences—even to war. Or, again, action decided on tonight might avert war and bring unforeseen benefits. For instance, it has been reliably reported to me that although Prince Hansio of Mahavara has sent a barely polite refusal of the invitation to attend, his son, Lord Tunno, is in the city."

"Against his father's express order," Lord Zengio said. "I'd not expect too much—he's here to drink, and that's all."

"But if he attends," said Prince Phillipos, sitting up sharply, "might he not be persuaded to join the rest of us in swearing fealty?"

"I doubt if he'll drink that much." Zengio laughed.

"But did not your informants tell you, Lord Zengio, that he

has been seen in company with Lord Jagat's son?" said Taticos.

"Pirthio?" said Chondos, surprised. He sat forward, blinking. "I wonder . . ." But then he closed his mouth and sat back, his wide eyes thoughtful.

"Pirthio, yes," answered Taticos. "And have I not heard it said that Lord Jagat's son can make a friend of—of anyone?" And Istvan, watching, saw the perfect mask of the Steward's face almost crack, and men's hands covering their faces all around the table. He glanced curiously at Chondos, but the young King seemed to be studying the table before him. Istvan frowned, then remembered hearing that Chondos, too, was Pirthio's friend.

"It might even be," Tacticos went on, after an odd pause, "that through his son, Lord Jagat may be able to turn the heir of Mahavara from an enemy into an ally. We must ask Lord Jagat—"

"If he ever gets here!" snorted Zengio.

Duke Thoros, roused from sleep, was like a drunken bull. His bleared eyes blinked surprise at the men he found waiting for him.

"What is it?" he growled, rubbing his eyes. "What do you want at this time of night? Has anything happened?"

"Disaster!" squealed the Lord of the Guilds. "Every man we sent after Jagat—killed! Some of them may have talked!"

"Not likely," said the man in the Healer's robe, quickly. "It was just like before—except this time, no one escaped. Jagat *may* be wounded, but I am not sure."

"What?" the Duke said muzzily, shaking his head. "Did you say *Jagat* killed all your assassins? How many this time?"

"Twenty!" Lord Andrios wailed. "And we paid each man in advance! Fifty gold pieces! All that money gone, and that dung-hoarding fisheater is still alive! Two men helped him!"

"Two?" Duke Thoros' eyebrows rose. He seated himself in his ducal chair. "Your wharf-rats must have been inept."

"One of his Kadarin mercenaries was with him," said the red-robed man. "He killed most of them, I think."

"A Kadarin?" The Duke laughed. "I suppose that explains it! Ah, these dreadful northern swordsmen, scattering bodies all over the street! Makes you sorry for the men who have to clean up!"

"Be serious!" Lord Andrios yelped. "This is no laughing matter! If they trace us, our cause is in danger!"

"If what you've told me is true," the Duke purred, "the only way we could be traced is through this excellent servant, Luijos."

The red-robed man was suddenly pale. Lord Andrios looked away, avoiding his eyes. The Duke laughed.

"And so, it is greatly to our advantage to get you safely out of the city, Luijos! I will write you a letter, to give to the captain of a certain ship anchored in Portona Mouth. It waits only my word to sail. You may read the letter—and watch me write it!" He lifted a bell, rang it. "With your Healer's robe, could you not have managed to treat Jagat's wounds?" He broke off as a servant entered. "Paper and pen, and something to drink! Quickly now!" He turned back to Luijos. "Well? Why didn't you? If Jagat died of his wounds, you'd have'd earned your pay!"

"Too dangerous, Lord!" Luijos muttered. "Any Healer would have been able to tell—and if I'm caught in this robe, they'll search my mind."

Teeth flashed in the Duke's black beard. The servant returned with paper and quill.

"The arena, or—worse?" the Duke said, smiling. Luijos looked no happier. The Duke dipped the quill in ink. "That robe has outlived its usefulness!"

When the Duke had finished the letter, he handed it to Luijos to read, and turned to the waiting servant. "Find some other clothes that will fit this man, and burn that Healer's robe," he ordered. "Send a messenger to Lord Enricos of Poidia, to bid him attend my presence. Then, when he's arrived, summon Sandor."

"That's more than Istvan DiVega killed!" Rinmull of Ojaini exclaimed. Martos started, and nearly choked on his wine, then shifted uncomfortably. He'd never gotten the Border knack for sitting on the floor, and there were no chairs on the Satragara.

Rinmull snorted as a murmur of protest rose around them.

"Those stories are all nonsense!" he shouted above the other voices. "I went down to the palace myself, and talked to men who'd been there, men of the Seynyorean Guard that were patrolling the street that night. DiVega only killed about fifteen men! There were more, but they ran away."

"They would!" sneered the man Pirthio had introduced as Tunno of Mahapor.

Martos gulped the rest of his wine, and reached out with a hand that was already unsteady to pour another glass with exaggerated care. Pirthio, gloriously drunk, finished reporting the fight in the street, then went on to a highly coloured account of Martos' exploits at Ukarakia. Martos stared into his wine, and wondered if his ears really were red.

Slowly he sipped the sweet blue wine, trying to ignore the conversation around him, trying to pretend to himself that he was above it all. Surely a Kadarin gentleman should not be moved by the praise of his deed! The Self-Judged Man should never feel pride.

They had given him a bottle of the fine blue wine of Paracosma, the kind he drank at home. He'd hoped to get some decent food, too, but that had been a vain hope; all the Satragara served was the same highly spiced chicken, fish, and venison he'd gotten so tired of in Damenco. Every day there'd been some variant of it, except for an occasional rabbit, and the day the horse had died and they'd eaten that. Ironfist had told him they might eat beef if a cow died, but that had never happened since he'd been there.

At least the wine was a change. Most of the Bordermen were swilling the sour, watery stuff that the Massadessans made from rice, and that was a curious matter: rice, for some reason, was considered by the Bordermen "woman's food," and no man there would have touched the grain in any other form— might, in fact, kill anyone who suggested he did. They made coarse and sometimes obscure jokes about the Massadessan "wine" but drank it anyway.

> *They set their backs to the Shadow's wall*
> *And raised their sharp swords high . . .*

He tried to fight back the pride that swelled through him.

While the Dark things raced across the plain
To feast on men who die.

Why should he not feel pride? Had he not killed more men tonight than Istvan DiVega?

That might or might not be true, but when they heard that in Kadar . . . He blinked suddenly, and sat up straight. When they heard that in Kadar—and they would, they would! Such tales spread among fighting men like wildfire: the mercenaries would carry the story all through the elite community of warriors! And his name, linked thus with the great, would bring students flocking to his school. Kumari would be happy. Now he could keep her and the child well fed and content.

Merchant! he mocked himself. *What price for the Self-Judged Man? Gold and glory are tempting, are they not?*

He gulped the rest of his wine quickly and poured more. The song had stopped now. Pirthio had launched into a furious diatribe against the treachery of merchants. Martos' head jerked in agreement as he thumped the table with his fist. That was right! There was only one way to deal with merchants! They'd learned that in Kadar long ago! Tax them mercilessly, and keep them in their place, so their greed could not control the state!

The smile faded from his lips. Was he himself any better than a merchant, ready to abandon this ideal, heroic life for the comfortable existence of a rich Swordmaster? Was he not about to betray everything he believed in, and go back to Kadar, seeking fame as a Swordmaster?

That was an honourable profession, but did he not dishonour it by his motives? It was all for the child, though, all for Kumari and the child. It was *not* mere greed, he thought, either for fame or for the wealth it would bring. He must protect his child, surely! And the child was in danger, even now!

His knees were hurting, and he had to change position. Thousands of tiny prickles ran through his leg. The low table rocked as his knee bumped against it. Why didn't they have any chairs? Down by the Border there was no wood, of course, but *here* they didn't have to sit on the floor—they could sit up like civilised people.

Rinmull of Ojaini began to sing. Other voices joined him.

Soon they were all singing, a familiar tune, the wild and pulsing "Ballad of Pertap's Ride":

> *Where is the light of Hastur's Tower?*
> *Why are there no stars in the sky?*
> *The Shadow covers Kudrapor*
> *And all within its walls must die.*

His knees bumped the table again as he moved, and night-blue liquor slopped over the edge of his cup. He shook his head. No, this was not much like the night life in Erthi! For one thing, you could sit in a chair in Erthi. And the Bordermen were boastful savages, who cared nothing for philosophy, and thought that fame in the eyes of men was a proper goal!

He sighed. He should try to enjoy himself: this carefree life would end soon. When he took up the duties of father and husband, the noble life of high adventure would be gone forever.

> *But no man can ride from Kudrapor*
> *Through all the armies of the foe.*
> *"Saddle my horse!" young Pertap cried,*
> *"Saddle my horse and let me go!"*

Lord Taticos' voice faltered. A stick tapped on stone.

"Lord Jagat!" cried Prince Phillipos. "What happened?" Istvan looked up quickly.

Leaning on a stick, Lord Jagat limped into the room, his shoulder thick with bandaging under the torn, bloodstained sleeve of his robe.

"I cry pardon from my King that I am late," said Jagat, bowing Border-fashion from the waist. "I was attacked on my way here, outside my house, and the Healers kept me for a time afterwards. I came when they would let me."

"Attacked?" Chondos stiffened in his chair. "By whom? Where?"

"In the street outside my house, Lord King," Jagat's deep voice answered, "by twenty ruffians. Gutter-rats, like the ones that attacked Lord Istvan." He shot a quick smile at DiVega. "Fortunately, my son and the captain of my mercenaries were both within call. Martos of Kadar killed them—*all* of them! Twenty men—if you call gutter-rats men."

"Hired killers, then," Chondos mused. His eyes moved to search the faces around the table. "Now who, I wonder, wished to keep Lord Jagat from this Council tonight?"

"The same, most likely, that wish Lord Istvan dead," said old Lord Zengio, the Constable. "Perhaps they think Manjipé will revolt if he is no longer alive to control them."

"Nonsense!" snorted Jagat—too loudly, Istvan thought. "Manjipé is loyal! Even had I died, Pirthio would hold Damenco after me—for the King!" Envy stabbed Istvan with the sudden memory of his own son, the dead son he had hardly known.

"It seems my Coronation is to be celebrated with murder and rioting," said Chondos, sombrely. Then, unexpectedly, he laughed. "That reminds me," he said, in a voice tinged with bitter irony. "The Guildmasters of Portona, and some others of the merchant-nobility, have appealed to me for"—his lip curled—"protection." Teeth flashed all around the table, with the low snorts of laughter.

"They complain of lawless behaviour. Cousin Istvan, will you assign guards from one of your companies—a hundred will do, I'm sure—to stand guard at the various Guildhalls tomorrow and the day after?" He yawned, ostentatiously. "And now, my Lords, if you have all had time to gawk at Lord Jagat's bandages, perhaps we might return to this so-pressing business that keeps us from our sleep?"

Jagat slid awkwardly into the chair opposite Istvan.

Lord Taticos ruffled a sheaf of papers nervously. "Yes. Well, here we are. Lord Berrisos of Kimburtia. A delicate problem. In the last war, as you know—"

Lord Zengio stirred at Istvan's side. "We need lose no sleep over that question, Lord Taticos!" Zengio called out. "Lord Berrisos has sent his excuses and will not attend the Coronation. As you would know had you allowed me to speak earlier."

"Ah! Well then!" Lord Taticos smiled, and ruffled his papers once more. Nodding to himself, he straightened. "So! I thank you all for your patience, then. That is all of *my* business. I know many of you have other matters on your minds. Lord Zengio has questions of the gravest concern to bring before this Council. So if it is the King's will . . . ?"

Chondos waved a hand, irritably.

"Yes, yes! Let's get on with it! Speak, Zengio!"

The white-bearded Constable pushed himself to his feet. "For much of this information we must thank my son, Mario, who has become increasingly active in Your Majesty's service as age has weakened me. I beg Your Majesty to remember this when the time comes—as it soon must—when age forces me from the post of Constable."

Chondos' lip curled, but he said nothing.

"I must ask," the old man went on, "that what this Council is about to hear be kept secret. We do not wish to move until we have indisputable proof against all parties. Some of these proofs will be difficult to obtain, and for all I will need the support and assistance of this Council.

"But were it not likely to imperil the investigation and cause the culprits to take flight, I should bring now charges of High Treason and Conspiracy against Andrios, Archon of Portona, Lord Dimetrios of the Suppliers' Guild, and more than a dozen members of the Portona guilds. There is also evidence—not unshakable as yet—implicating the Archon of Armadapol and several of his Guildmasters, several Lords of Poidia, Oponto-pol, Thusipol, Antonpol, and Idroclor, the Duke of Ipazema—"

"Aha!" Prince Phillipos' voice clapped through Zengio's, and echoed like a fanfare from the walls. "We must compare notes, Lord Zengio! I've been watching that weasel myself!"

Zengio bowed, and went on. "It is a tangle, and we have yet to unravel it all. Many Lords in many provinces are involved, and as Lord Istvan knows, agents of various guilds have been trying to hire mercenary companies away from the Crown . . ."

"Unsuccessfully," Istvan pointed out.

"Due to Lord Istvan," said Zengio. "And that, I am sure, was the reason for the attempt on his life last night."

"Unsuccessfully," remarked Phillipos, in a tone that brought laughter from all the Councillors.

Zengio changed his laugh into a cough. "When the time comes for us to act," he went on, "I must warn Your Majesty to take great care in replacing these treacherous Lords. It will be hard to find a reliable man in such a hotbed of rebellion. I doubt, myself, that there is a loyal man in Portona.

"Large amounts of gold have been sent from Portona into the various provinces, and agents from the Rivermasters' Guild have been very busy these last few months. A great deal of Portonan gold has turned up in Kimburtia and Orissia."

"So you think those provinces will rise, then?" asked Taticos.

"There is a strong faction of young fools in Kimburtia, who wish to regain independence, and many of those young fools are suddenly far richer than they were," said Zengio. "Still the guilds may have wasted their money this time. The people of Kimburtia are well aware of the strength of Manjipé, and they also know that there is only a narrow strip of Border land to protect them from the Dark Things. You will remember, when the Border was broken a few years back, Night Walkers penetrated far into Kimburtia, and the aid by the Bordermen is still remembered. And many of the nobles of southern Kimburtia are from Takkarian stock, and some have married Border women. So I do not think there is like to be any rising in Kimburtia as long as Manjipé stays loyal." Zengio turned to Lord Jagat, and his face was troubled. "But," he added, "I have learned that messengers from the guilds have been busy in Manjipé as well."

Lord Jagat cleared his throat ominously, and Zengio stopped talking.

"I have news as to that," said Jagat. "Portonan emissaries have been active in Manjipé, yes, trying to stir up rebellion. But they have failed! Manjipé remains loyal, both to the Crown and to its own lawful Prince." He bowed to Chondos.

"You sound very certain, Lord Jagat," said the King, and there was a hint of mockery in his tone.

"You are our Overlord, rightful Prince of Manjipé," said Jagat. "You *know* our loyalty, Lord King!"

"I do not know *anyone's* loyalty," snapped Chondos, his wide eyes burning. "I will not trust *anyone!*"

Jagat was suddenly pale. He bowed and sat down, and his face was set and grim. Zengio cast him an apologetic look, and went on hastily.

"Orissia, I fear, may react to Manjipé's unquestionable

loyalty quite differently. Traditions of the old wars between Orissia and Manjipé are still strong, and too many young hotheads have been brought up on those stories. I fear they will join Portona just to fight the Manjipéans."

"What about Hansio?" Prince Phillipos asked.

"My son's informants report that Hansio has sworn he will die rather than renew his fealty," said Zengio. "He is only waiting to see what Portona will do. But whatever happens, Mahavara *will* rise, have no doubt of that."

"I have never doubted that!" snapped Chondos. His dark eyes were insolent. "I wish I could be as certain of others' love for me as I am of Hansio's hatred!"

Istvan saw Jagat's scowl, and straightened. He had made a promise to the boy's father, after all . . . "If your Highness could forbear the pleasure of insulting your servants, I am sure that they will love you more, and serve you better."

Dark eyes glared into grey: Chondos' face darkened with rage. "You dare question the justice of my words?" the King snarled.

"I have nothing to lose," said Istvan with a shrug. "If you dismiss me from your service, I can simply go home, back to Seynyor. These men must fear your anger because they have others dependent on them." His eyes were calm under Chondos' glare. "I am here only because of a promise to your father."

Chondos blinked, then turned away, his face thoughtful. "Is that all your report, Lord Zengio?"

"Why—well—almost all, Lord. There is . . . " Zengio seemed confused. He shuffled the papers before him. "There is . . . I have information that the Duke of Ipazema has been meeting with the Guildmasters here in Portona regularly these past few days. And he has been seen in the company of a man wearing Prince Phillipos' livery."

"What!" Prince Phillipos leaped up, his chair clattering to the floor behind him. "That worries me! If Ipazema has corrupted my guard . . ." He picked up the fallen chair. "That man has plotted against me for years. He has some claim to Kalascor, though a thin one. He might be content to see Ipazema an independent duchy again—especially if he can grab Lutazema and Poidia. I'm told his father was the same."

He shook his head and sat down in the chair. "My apologies, Lords. I do not trust that man out of my sight at all."

Chondos stared into space over Lord Zengio's head. He seemed to take no notice of the Prince's outburst.

"You say that you wish your son to be your successor in office, Lord Zengio," Chondos said slowly, stroking his chin, looking at the old man thoughtfully. "Do you wish him confirmed tomorrow at the Coronation?"

Lord Zengio blinked and stared, and sat stupidly for a moment. Slowly a smile spread over his face, and he said, "It—it would please me to lay down the cares of this office, Lord King. And it may be that I have become a feeble prop to lean upon. And yet . . ." He paused, and wrinkles writhed. "Yet to speak my mind plainly, it might seem wisest to wait until this time of crisis is past. I would not deprive my King of such knowledge as my experience has taught me, if this may serve in such troubled times."

Chondos was silent, considering, and before he spoke, his eyes sought Istvan's, as though seeking his approval. Then he spoke: "Your son, surely, may still come to you for advice and help? And if you learn of matters needing your experience, surely you may come to your King?" he hesitated. Istvan nodded vigorous approval. "Why do we not invest him with the title, then, tomorrow, but make clear to him beforehand that he is to seek your advice? In this way, most of the burden will be taken from you, but we will not be deprived of your wisdom and knowledge."

Well done, Istvan thought, nodding again. Perhaps the boy had the makings of Kingship after all. And perhaps not. As Zengio thanked the King, Istvan wondered if Zengio's son were, in truth, the best man for the position. That, only time would show.

Zengio and his son, Jagat and Pirthio. Envy ached. He had barely known his own son, had wandered over the world while Rafayel had grown to manhood—and to war and death . . . He drove the thought from his mind, as he had so often before, and brought himself sharply to the present.

". . . others among you have matters to bring before me?" Chondos was saying.

Istvan slid smoothly to his feet. "I have a plan to present, Your Majesty."

Chondos gestured for him to speak.

"No man could wish for the Dark Things to come," Istvan began, "yet that is the one thing which would resolve all the hatreds that divide this kingdom. And which is worse: to fight them now, while we are still strong—or to wait until the kingdom has been weakened by dissention and war?

"If they attacked now, this week, Tarencia might be united. But we cannot hope they will be so obliging. They know all that passes in the lands of men. And, although the Dark Things do not think as men think, and we cannot know their minds, yet we do know they always attack weakness. I believe that they will wait to attack until they are certain of finding us divided. We cannot wait for that. We must go to them." Men gasped.

"We must cross the Border ourselves. We must prepare to move *now!*" The chart he had brought crackled as he unrolled it across the table. His finger traced the line of the Atvanadi that runs between Mahavara and the Kantara, and settled on the Border.

"We must enter the Shadow here, at Rishipor, and follow the Atvanadi south, during the day, when the Dark Ones are weakest. The forest covered all this land before the Shadow came, and there will be much dead wood to burn, but we must carry in more fuel with us, wagonloads of it. When night comes we must stand and fight, with fire and with steel, and with such magic as the Hasturs may lend us."

"Listen to him!" Jagat boomed. "Thus we won Damenco!"

"We must fight by night and march by day," Istvan went on, "and force our way slowly south and east, towards Idelbonn. And from Idelbonn a second force must march to meet us."

Excited Lords leaned over the table, studying the map.

"The Hasturs will aid us," Istvan said. "As we drive to meet each other, the Dark Ones' spell will loosen, and the suns break through the Shadow." His finger made a half-circle on the map. "The Border will have been driven back."

Then Chondos' voice rose in excitement. "We need not stop there! After the new Border is established, we can strike west, to the Yukota. And a force from Damenco marching east! The Border could be at the edge of the mountains once more!"

Jagat was frowning. When he spoke, his voice was bitter. "I

do not wish to speak against this plan. It is a good plan, not only because it may hold the kingdom together, but because it is *right* for us to do this, soon or late. But Lord Istvan makes it sound too easy.

"We can do it, yes! We *have* done it! My own land of Damenco was carved out of the Shadow thus. Some of you were there and fought within the Shadow yourselves." His eyes turned to Chondos. "You are too young to remember, Lord King, what such a war is like. Lord Istvan speaks of this as though it were a matter of weeks or days. We old men understand him. But it will be a long time before those two forces meet. And if an army then marches from Damenco, it will be Pirthio who leads it, and not I. I will be dead most likely, or if not, too old to be of use.

"Out of every ten men that enter the Shadow, fewer than five will return. Many will be slain by Demons, so that even their bones are lost to the land. And"—he hesitated—"many of the Dark Things will flee, as we drive into the Shadow, north into Mahavara and the southern Kantara. And it will be Mahavara and the Kantara that supply most of the men. Women and children will suffer for this thing, and many men will be returned to the land. Mahavara will suffer most of all. And I do not like that."

"Why?" asked Chondos. "Have you some special love for these traitors?"

"It is because I bear them no love," said Jagat, "that I dislike sending men to their deaths for our own purposes. In some sense, it is a very evil thing Lord Istvan wishes us to do."

Istvan's Hastur-blade slid from its sheath, and he laid it naked across the table.

"The brunt of the first fighting will be borne by my own people," he said, and the terrible Seynyorean pride rang in his voice. "This sword will be among the foremost. I am not sending men to their deaths, Lord Jagat, I am leading them!

"And yet . . ." His voice softened. "What Lord Jagat says is true. I cannot deny that it is my hope that Mahapor will be too busy to rebel. Many men will die because of it." He shrugged. "But, if they are not kept too busy to rebel, many of the same men will die by my own hand." He lifted the sword from the table, and sheathed it.

"The men of Mahavara will be better off if the Shadow is

driven back. What will they gain by destroying the kingdom?" He shrugged. "Yet this plan has a flaw which Lord Jagat has not seen. It may fail. Prince Hansio, whatever else men may say of him, has never been called a fool. He may count the dead in Mahavara, and place the blame squarely where it belongs—upon us, and upon the King. We may start a war instead of stopping one.

"And the plan may have other flaws that I have not seen. I ask you, my Lords, if any of you see such flaws—speak! Advise the King not to follow it! It is he who will be blamed if matters go ill."

No one spoke. Istvan waited through a moment's silence before continuing: "It would be well if you all took thought about this. My own immediate task is the same, whether we war against rebels or Dark Ones. I must gather the mercenary companies and have them ready to march. Your Majesty's decision," he said, bowing to Chondos, "can wait for the next meeting of the Council."

"No, my mind is made up. We will try your plan, Lord DiVega. And that is enough for tonight! If any of you have other matters for me to consider, tell Lord Taticos, and we will discuss them later! This Council is closed!" The King rose and strode from the room, leaving them blinking behind him.

"Well!" gasped the fat man who was the Royal Exchequer, and then they were all talking at once. Istvan, rising, rolled up his chart and headed for the door. The rest of them all seemed to be converging on Lord Taticos.

A swordsman's instinct told Istvan there was someone behind him, and turning he found Lord Jagat following him from the room.

"I wanted to thank you," said the old Borderman quietly, as the door behind them closed on the babble.

"For what?" Istvan asked. Jagat's teeth flashed in a smile.

"For being yourself, I suppose!" Then, more soberly, "For standing up to the boy. I had forgotten, you see, how much easier it is, to be loyal to our new King at a distance."

Istvan nodded, and the two walked in silence for a moment before Jagat spoke again. "Will he be a good King, do you think?"

Istvan considered, weighing the boy's actions and words.

Finally he shook his head. "No. But what other choice do you have?"

The Duke of Ipazema sat reading indolently, the rustle of paper loud in the room. Andrios and Enricos fidgeted. Luijos had left, in his borrowed garments, long ago. The Duke could hear clearly their nervous whispers. He smiled maliciously. It amused him to keep them waiting so. If he could not sleep, they would not sleep! The Duke yawned. He would sleep late tomorrow, and only bother with the end of the Coronation. That was the important part.

At last his servant returned, followed by Sandor's tall, big-boned figure, shrouded in his dark cloak, his hood shadowing his face. Duke Thoros sat up yawning, and laid his book casually aside. He turned to the merchant-lords.

"I told you I had a plan," he said, "a method of redeeming this disaster. The time has come to reveal it now."

He watched their faces, contemptuously. He must take the lead now, or watch the port cities bolt like frightened rabbits! And he needed them—their wealth, at least!

"What is our goal?" he asked, gesturing grandly.

"To rid ourselves of this tyranny," snarled Andrios, "that taxes away our hard-earned profits to feed the black-faced Border rabble! To return to the old ways, to free cities ruling themselves under rightfully elected Guildmasters."

The Duke grinned, cynically. "Well, the attempts to remove the props and pillars from under the throne have failed," he said. "I have a bolder plan. Show them your livery, Sandor!"

The big man threw back his cloak. The blue and scarlet and gold of Kalascor was unmistakable. The two city Lords caught their breath. The Duke smiled.

"A man in Prince Phillipos' livery is hardly likely to be questioned. The Prince brought a large retinue with him, and all his men do not know each other by sight. Sandor has mingled with them many times, so that his face is familiar to them. No one questions his presence. His entry to the castle is assured."

"But what do you mean to do?" asked Andrios.

The Duke smiled at him as at a lack-wit child. "My first thought many years ago, when I schemed to put a man of my own in the Prince's guard, was to kill Prince Phillipos. But when I found Sandor I realised that such a perfect tool had better uses. If Prince Phillipos dies, I will be pleased. But first Sandor will kill the King." They gaped at him.

"But they say the King himself is a deadly swordsman, trained by his kin among the DiVegas!" Lord Andrios squealed.

"And by his father," said Enricos. "I've heard that old Olansos was a better swordsman than any hereabout, better even than Prince Hansio!"

Sandor chuckled in a deep bass voice.

"Sandor is himself a dangerous man," said the Duke with a mocking smile. "Take off that cloak, Sandor."

Slowly, the big, long-fingered, fine-boned hands undid the clasp. The cloak fell. The face the hood had shadowed was dark, aquiline. A lock of black hair fell to cover the forehead. The body under the face was powerful, and bigger-boned than was common among the people who dwell near the Sea of Ardren.

"Did you think I had hired one of your wharf-rats?" mocked the Duke. "Sandor is from the north, and trained in the style of sword which is called the Seagull School, said to be the chief rival of the School of the Three Swords. Istvan DiVega may be a match for him, but no other!"

"But the King will be guarded!" said Enricos.

"Closely enough that Sandor cannot reach him? Not likely. To kill the King we need a man with access to the palace, able to cut his way out if he has to. In Sandor we have that man." He laughed and walked over to stand beside Sandor.

"What if he's taken alive?" cried Andrios. "He has seen our faces, and he knows you—"

"Sandor will not be taken alive," the Duke said. "He is as deadly as DiVega, or this—Kadarin, was it?—who cost you so dearly in hired killers. The guard around the King is never that heavy. But Sandor will wait for his chance to strike down the King when he is alone, or with Prince Phillipos, and there is an escape route open. Even if there were too many guards for him to cut his way free, there would never be enough to take him alive!"

"If he was faced with death, would he not surrender and betray us all?"

The Duke, standing beside Sandor, suddenly turned. His

hand shot out, pushing the hair from the forehead, rubbing hard against the curiously discoloured skin beneath. Cursing, Sandor hurled the Duke staggering away, and whipped out his sword.

The Duke laughed, and pointed. "Surrender? Betray us? With *that* on his forehead?"

Above the blazing eyes they saw plainly, where the stain had been wiped away, the Sign of Hastur, perfectly drawn, a line piercing a circle, and they knew that neither hot iron nor inked needle had drawn it there. They knew what crimes could condemn a man to wear that mark and, ruthless as they thought themselves, they shuddered.

"I tell you," Duke Thoros shouted, "Sandor will fight to the death! And only DiVega himself could kill him. Tomorrow they will crown the King, and after that, any rebellion will be futile that does not begin with Chondos' death! But once the King is dead, no force in all the world can hold this realm together! Not even the Hasturs themselves!"

Chapter Seven

The day of the Coronation dawned like any day. Over the mountains of Vallauris, a pale light cleansed the sky. The Twin Suns rose in a rainbow blaze. The voices of birds filled the countryside.

In his special stall in the royal stables, the single elephant belonging to the Crown of Tarencia, brought over the mountains from Devonia at great cost to revive the vanished glories of Takkarian courts, raised his trunk and trumpeted a shrill salute to the dawn, and in another part of the stable, panic-stricken horses plunged in their stalls, their heels pounding rhythmically as they tried to kick themselvs loose.

Members of the royal household, up long before, were bustling about on a thousand frenzied errands through the streets; and jugglers and musicians entertained those idle folk who had risen early for this holiday. Thousands of pleasure-seekers lay long abed; some, stupefied by drink, would miss the great day altogether.

Vendors of fruits and sweets and wine were already hawking their wares. Sellers of more substantial foods were waiting for hunger to grow; though one enterprising seller of sausage did a brisk breakfast trade that would keep him happily drunk for the rest of the day without even denting his immense profits.

In the palace the young man whom courtesy had named King for weeks, but who this morning, by immemorial tradition, was again "Prince Chondos" for the last time in his life, was rubbing his eyes and cursing the servants whose duty and toil it was to disturb his too-brief slumber.

The men of the night watch, filing wearily back to their quarters, their halberds on their shoulders, were reckoning how much of their sleep they would have to forgo to attend the festivities in the afternoon, and how much of their free time the next day would be spent making up for it. Those of the city guard who would be privileged to march in the procession were polishing their boots and their armour, while those fated to stand guard in parts of the city far from the festivities grumbled at their luck.

Istvan DiVega slid his blade into its scabbard with a sharp click, his lips pressed tight to suppress a grunt as the pain in his side throbbed angrily. He had worked very carefully to avoid placing any strain on the cut, not doing any single training-dance in its entirety, but instead splicing together various moves, avoiding those that would flex these particular muscles overmuch.

Pain does not hurt, he told himself. *Only fear hurts*. Then he smiled as he tried to convince himself of it. Grimly ignoring the pain, he strode from the garden. He must bathe and dress—and the sooner he got to it, the more attention he would have from the attendants. The baths would doubtless be crowded early this morning.

They were. Through the curling steam, nude bodies moved anonymously, their outlines vague, undefined. Istvan heard Lord Zengio's voice, and moved towards it through the steam.

". . . up near Hali? Suppose they are too hard-pressed? What would happen? And what should we do?"

"I assure you, Lord Zengio, that they will contrive for one to be free." It was the clear, ringing voice of Shachio the Seer that answered. "The crowning of a King, even in the smallest realm, is an important matter to them. No, the Hastur will come, at the proper time."

"But suppose the procession is delayed?" asked Zengio querulously. "Suppose he arrives in the hall and no one is there? Or suppose we time it wrong, and arrive in the hall early? Will we have to stand there waiting, at the steps of the throne, until he arrives to continue the ceremony?"

"We would," said Shachio with a chuckle, "but it won't happen. You'll see. They'll take the trouble to look at us every so often, to time the procession."

Istvan could see them now, two old men naked on a bench, thick steam around them. Zengio had a pot belly. The sight made him aware of the increasing gauntness of his own frame. He glanced down at himself, self-consciously. To his own eyes, his body still looked young, with muscles like whipcord, still graceful and well-proportioned; but he might be fooling himself. *A dying fire burns the hottest,* he thought.

They looked up as he approached, and Lord Shachio's voice greeted him: "Lord DiVega! Perhaps you can reassure my Lord Zengio. You come from the Land of the Lords, and should know a great deal of the Hasturs. Lord Zengio is afraid that they will be so busy with the struggle in the north that they will be unable to send one to examine and crown the King; or that they will not arrive at the right time."

Istvan shook his head and smiled. "If this were the coronation of a King of Messentia, or Verterre, or some other little land that was far from the Shadow, there might be some cause for such concern," he said. "There *is* a story—though I don't know whether it's true or not—that an Emperor of Kadar was once kept waiting at the foot of his throne for a full hour—some say a half-hour—because the Border had been broken by one of the Greater Powers, and no Hastur was free to come. But Tarencia is a Border country, and therefore important. The Hasturs are very punctual. And it is not a hard task for one of them to look into your streets and see where the procession is.

"They certainly will not have time to spare—whoever comes will probably examine the King, crown him, and vanish—but I think the situation on the Border would have to be bad indeed—worse than it has been for a hundred years—for them not to be able to spare one man for the Coronation. Though it may well be one of the younger Hasturs. Just how bad *is* it, Shachio?"

The old Seer scratched his head before replying, "Good enough in Creolandis and Handor. In Creolandis, in fact, they appear to have restored the Border, and driven them back. Kadar doesn't seem so well off. One Demon got as far west as Erthi last night, and another one went south and killed a hundred people or so in Paracosma. The Kadarins aren't giving the Hasturs the support they need; they've been at peace too long. Also, there was heavy pressure on the Border of Norbath last night—some on Orovia as well."

Istvan frowned, and nodded. "Bad, but not that serious. So far the Border's been pierced in only one place, and of course the attack will have slacked off at dawn. Most of the Hasturs will be resting. But one will wake up to crown the King."

One of the bath-girls appeared out of the steam, her breasts large and firm, their tips vividly red; the soft mist made the girl a thousand times more alluring. The white cloth about her hips was wet, and clung tightly.

Istvan felt desire stir, and looked guiltily away, wishing he were twenty years younger. Or thirty years younger. The girl couldn't be more than eighteen. What would she want with an old man? She probably had to deal with dozens of them, all day; and she could, of course, have her pick of any number of younger men, and doubtless did.

It was very lonely, being old.

That Kingship was a prison, that power was a toil and a burden, none knew better than Chondos. The Prince of Manjipé, who would soon be King of Tarencia, protector of Orissia . . . After today he would be always alone, shut away from the fellowship of men by a golden crown and a high throne. Upon him would rest the weighty matters that would mean peace or war, life or death, prosperity of suffering, for his subjects. To him would come the blame for all. If his ministers made mistakes it was because he chose them unwisely; if disaster came unforeseen it was his fault for not having the vision to prepare against it.

All he could think of this morning was his father, everything reminded him, and by nightfall he would wear his father's crown and sit in his father's place . . . He did not want the throne. His sister was first-born; if he could only resign the throne to her—but they would not accept that. If only there were some other man to hold the realm together—but there was not. Duty hemmed him in, bound him as tightly as a fly trapped in a web. He would not mind losing the throne, but he could not bear to see his father's and grandfather's work wasted.

And he was not fit; he knew that he was not fit! They all knew it! He could not still his cursed tongue, could not smile and lie and flatter the fawning dogs who sought his favour for their own ends; and now in mockery, his enemies would cheer his enthronement today, that they might snatch it from under him tomorrow. He might well lose his own life in the process. He did not care much; his life now would scarce be worth living.

Humble men surely had friends who loved them for their own sake and not for what they could give? A common man, doubtless, could lie with a woman confident that she desired him, and not the power and prestige that such a liaison could bring? Bitterly he envied the simpler lives of his subjects. He would never know such pleasures. Nor again, the relative freedom he had enjoyed as a Prince.

Jodos was awake, and Hotar, but they did not leave their darkened room. Later Jodos would have to go out, hidden where the crowd was thickest, as he made his way to the castle. But this was the most dangerous part of their mission. For now the eyes of the Blue-robes were upon the city. Jodos hoped that his masters, in the mountains, would do their part.

He was afraid. He knew what power the accursed Blue-robes could wield. Were it not for the greater fear of his masters, and his knowledge of the penalty for failure, he would long ago have fled back to the familiar darkness.

Carefully he wrapped in silk the little box that was now his greatest danger, and concealed it in his clothing. Emicos had designed the box to hide as well as protect, but if the Blue-robes sensed the slightest hint of his hidden allies, it would all be over. Neither he nor those he carried could stand before the power of a Child of the Nameless One.

He tried to get a little sleep before he had to go out, but fear kept him awake.

Istvan came up out of icy water, and the bath-girl in attendance wrapped him in a great towel and rubbed down his limbs fiercely. A bare breast brushed against his arm; he closed his eyes and began to breathe deeply, thankful that the shock of the icy water was still strong enough to keep his rising excitement from becoming obvious.

Relax and enjoy it, he thought. *It's the best you're likely to get at your age.* Down the pool came a chorus of giggles where one of the younger men was being dried off. Istvan pressed his eyelids down more tightly, trying to forget that he had ever been young. And still was, in some essential but unfortunate ways.

Shachio the Seer spoke at his elbow, and Istvan turned, glad of the distraction. "I'll tell you what worries *me*, my Lord DiVega," said Shachio. The Seer was seated on the edge of one of the massage tables, gratefully stretching the muscles which had been caressed into health. "The Border is too quiet. There hasn't been a single raid since the King died—nothing! No Night Walker has shown its nose over the Border since the night of the big attack, after the King died! That's not natural. Even one week without a Night Walker being reported would be strange enough. For nothing to happen in all this time . . ." He shook his head.

Istvan knew what he meant. The lesser creatures of the Shadow—the goblins, the trolls, the ghouls—were savage and rapacious; human flesh was their favoured diet. An absence of organised raiding was one thing, and there could be many explanations for that. But for a complete lack of solitary foraging, there could be only one: that the Dark Things were holding their servants in check, deliberately keeping them on their side of the Border.

"They're hoping we'll forget about them," he said. "They're keeping the Border quiet so that we can concentrate on destroying ourselves."

Shachio agreed. "That is what I fear. And it may work. We are devoting far too much of our time and attention to treason and internal problems. We are forgetting all about the menace from the hills while we try to keep the realm from coming apart. And they're just waiting to sweep down on us. That's why your plan is so important."

Istvan nodded. But before he could say anything more, the girl who had been attending him spoke: "My Lord? You're dry now. If you'd lie down on the table?" He smiled and thanked her, and as Shachio jumped off the table to make room, he laid himself down on his stomach, and she began to knead the muscles of his back.

It felt good. *See,* he told himself, as she pressed and prodded at the aching muscles between his shoulder blades. *Pain does not hurt. It's only a sensation like any other. As hard as she's rubbing, this should be painful—but it's pleasant. It's all in the mind.* He started to detach himself and drift into meditation, but the girl wanted to talk.

"Are you *really* Istvan the Archer? I heard the Lord Seer call you DiVega—"

He stiffened with irritation, and for a moment the smoothly rubbing hands really did hurt. But then he forced himself to relax, suppressing his anger. The girl had no way of knowing. There was no way to rid himself of that name, or of the memory that went with it.

"Some call me that," he admitted.

"The poets say that you're the greatest swordsman in the world!" she said, her voice high with excitement.

"Poets," he said, wearily, "tell a great many lies."

The Twin Suns climbed higher and higher in their journey across the sky. The crowds in the street grew thicker, their excitement stronger.

Servants brought Chondos food, but he would not eat. He was not hungry. His stomach shuddered with tension and baffled rage, and the very thought of food was hateful. According to the ceremony, as his father had reworked it, he must wear the coronet of Manjipé. But nothing else in his raiment was princely. His tunic and doublet were no finer, and they were less costly, than many of those worn by the poorest of his nobles, although the colours were carefully chosen to match the glorious robes that would be placed upon him later in the ceremony.

Ritual demanded that he walk in procession about the city before his crowning, that the people might see him. This part of the ceremony had come when there was no kingdom, and only the Prince of the city had been crowned. His servants urged him to eat. It would be a long walk. Nervousness tore at his innards, and he ordered the food from his sight. Pacing irritably, he waited for the Lords to assemble, that the procession might begin. The sooner it was all over with, the better.

Martos awoke with a splitting headache, and a soft hand caressing his shoulder. Warm lips came down on his mouth.

When he got his eyes all the way open, he saw Kumari sitting on the edge of his bed, smiling at him. His mouth tasted foul, and someone inside his head was swinging a heavy hammer back and forth, back and forth, pounding against the walls of his skull.

He made the mistake of trying to sit up, which must have angered the fellow with the hammer. The room decided it wanted to dance, and he lay back with a groan. The light that came through the draperies over the windows was *much* too bright.

"You're a hero," she said, her eyes great and dark. "And you're mine."

Her robe slid down, over glorious curves of breast and hip and thigh, and rustled softly on the floor. She pulled the covers back, and then her warmth was beside him.

"Jagat?" he asked, getting the single word out with great difficulty.

She laughed, a low silvery sound. "Uncle has gone to the palace for the Coronation. Pirthio, too . . ." She laughed again. "If he can make it in *his* condition! Anyway, Uncle did say I was to wake you up in time for the ceremony, so you can see it. And I can't really think of any other way to make waking up attractive to you . . ." She giggled again, and her hands moved caressingly over him.

The blood that had been pounding in his head was going somewhere else now, and he was beginning to feel almost alive. He rolled up on one arm so he could look down on the wonder of her body. He laid his hand gently on her belly, thinking of the little life within. His child! How long, he wondered, before it would begin to show? Before it would make the little kicks and struggles that would be its first signals to the great world outside? Ahead of him lay a lifetime of watching this little creature under his hand grow up.

He smiled down at her, and suddenly found that he was blinking back tears. He looked into her eyes, his hand resting gently above her womb, and then, deliberately, with a smile that was almost cruel, moved his hand lower, and watched as her eyes grew slowly round and misty.

Those who sold food and wine were in a delirium of happiness as gold found its way into their coffers. Music filled the streets, and here and there wide circles were formed in the middle of the slowly moving crowd, where people danced, or watched jugglers, fire-eaters, sword-swallowers, or acrobats.

Inside the castle the procession was forming at last. Minor nobles snarled at each other over precedence—for however just the decision, not everyone would agree with it. Trumpeters assembled, banner-bearers tried to find their places in the confusion.

Istvan DiVega slid through the crowded hall with a swordsman's trained ease of movement, easily dodging through small openings in the crowd where another man would have had to push and shove his way. He sidestepped a long banner-pole moving through the crowd like a spear, slipped around a little knot of guardsmen who were leaning on their halberds and talking in low tones, and found himself face-to-face with Lord Taticos, gorgeous in silver and crimson, with a gold rod of office in his hand.

"Good, good, Lord Istvan!" Taticos said, quickly and fussily. "Go over by Lord Zengio and wait with him. We'll get everything straightened out here in a minute." He rushed off, officiously, and Istvan could not suppress a smile, even though he understood the strain the man was under.

Lord Zengio, his rich robes of purple and black trimmed with gold, was standing by a low table on which the royal regalia were piled. Near him Prince Phillipos sat easily on the floor, his coronet pushed back, his richly brocaded sleeves in his lap, an amused smile on his boyish face, blue eyes twinkling. Lord Jagat, resplendent in blue and scarlet edged in black and gold, paced like a nervous lion back and forth in the little clear space surrounding the great Lords of State.

As Istvan made for the table, Lord Shachio, in his full yellow ceremonial robes, came up. "Bad news from the north since I talked to you," he said. "A daylight attack."

Istvan pursed his lips in a soundless whistle. That was rare. That was bad.

"They don't really know yet what the Things are, but they can stand daylight, and are very powerful," the Seer went on. "They're driving straight into Kadar. And the Shadow is beginning to bulge out behind them."

Istvan frowned. If a Hastur could not come to crown the King . . .

"Make way! Make way!" voices shouted. The crowds began to part.

"The King at last!" said Shachio. "I must go. I'll talk to you later, DiVega."

He hurried off, and Istvan went to join the others beside the table. He made a strange contrast, among their gorgeous robes, in his ordinary court doublet and hose. He had carefully chosen the colours, indigo and black, to match the symbolism of the others' robes, as well as he understood it. He felt very uncomfortable, but Lord Taticos had assured him that the Scrolls of Ceremony deliberately made no provision for the garments of the helm-bearer.

A path opened through the crowded hall as Chondos came in, and the masses of men began to find their places. It began to look a little more like a procession, and less like a mob.

Contempt boiling in his soul, Chondos allowed Lord Taticos to conduct him to his place in line. It was all so stupid. A silly show to impress the populace. Yet within his rage he could dimly perceive that half his sudden hatred of ceremony was a new way of biting his lip to distract himself from the pain of his father's loss, as circumstances tore that wound wide open.

And the other half was fear of what lay ahead. Today the secrecy of his mind was to be violated. Not entirely for the first time: twice in his childhood, Hasturs had looked briefly, through a window, as it were, into his mind to investigate those curious dreams which they linked with his mysterious brother; and many times, during his long if superficial training in the Arts Magical, the surface of his mind had brushed briefly with that of old Shachio the Seer, and once or twice with Thulipe Hastur. But this would be a different thing. He knew just enough to understand that. The inmost citadels of his soul, the darkest rooms at the back of his brain, would be ransacked, searched thoroughly, to test his fitness to rule.

He almost hoped that he would fail that test. Surely they would be able to see that he *was* unfit, that he would make, as everyone said, a bad King? Then, suddenly, he would be plain Chondos DiVega. He would be free. He could go away then; perhaps his famous cousin would take him into his service. He had a vivid picture of himself tramping the roads of the world with Istvan DiVega, learning the secrets of the sword, making a name for himself in the elite of fighting men . . .

He had come to his place now, and they were gathering about him, the regalia in their hands. Behind him was DiVega, bearing the royal helm; and next to DiVega was Zengio, carrying the heavy shield painted with the royal device—a hand holding the crown.

Jagat came, bearing the sword of the King, the enchanted blade that Eldemir Hastur had forged for Chondos' grand-father, and took up his post at Chondos' right hand. The white and gold of Phillipos' long robe swirled before the Prince's eyes. A trumpet sounded. The background of quiet talk stopped, and tension gathered up and down the line.

Chondos remembered an old legend about a coronation somewhere. The Hastur that looked into a Prince's mind, instead of crowning him, had reached out a finger and drawn the Mark of Hastur on his forehead, making him an outlaw and an outcast, condemned to wander the world, his life forfeit to any who cared to take it.

But it was all nonsense, he knew deep inside; he had committed no great crimes, had never broken the Law of Hastur nor consorted with the Creatures of Darkness. And that was all they were interested in. Many Kings who were unfit to rule had been crowned by the Hasturs, many less fit than he . . .

Lord Taticos came rushing up, gesturing frantically, and had barely taken his place when a trumpet sounded at the head of the procession. It was the signal to march.

Music began, and Chondos saw the figures ahead stirring, the soldiers at the front of the procession passing through the great door. He wanted to shout, to make them stop, to tell them that he would not go on with it, that he would *not* be crowned King.

He saw the backs of the men in front of Lord Taticos moving away, saw Taticos stiffen, waiting until they had reached the proper distance, and then stride grandly after them. Phillipos and Jagat tensed and took a stride forward . . . And now it was his turn, and he found himself walking in the midst of his nobles with his heart racing as though he had just run up the spiral staircase to the top of the West Tower.

I don't want to, said a voice inside his head. Yet a part of his mind suddenly betrayed him, caught up in the pageantry and wonder, and brought out from his childhood treasure of dreams, visions of the Takkarian Kings of vanished ages, and glorious tales of the Hero-Kings of old.

A wave of heat struck him as they passed into the streets.

Martos looked in the mirror again, making sure that his hair was properly arranged, and his beard combed to his satisfaction.

"Will you never finish fussing with your hair?" said Kumari laughingly. "You men! Hurry, or we'll miss the Coronation!"

He chuckled, and caught her in his arms.

She kissed him, then pulled away. "Come along!" she said. "We'll miss the procession!" She threw her long cloak about her shoulders. He caught up his own cape, and could not forebear another quick glance in the mirror. The short, rose-pink tunic was magnificent, and the skin-tight white breech-hose beneath showed well the fine muscles of his legs. He followed her out the door. Even at the Kadarin court, he would have looked dashing, an elegant figure. Here, he would outshine them all in grandeur.

With the Heir of Mahapor at his side, Pirthio shouldered his way through the crowd, and behind came more than a score of the young nobles of the Border. The street was lined with people, waiting for the passing of the procession. There were still a dozen places where the Bordermen could have stopped to wait, but with deliberate assurance they searched through the crowd for the area occupied by a party of the richest merchants of Portona and Armadopol, with their hired bullies about them.

As they drew near they cocked their swords jauntily forward on their hips, swaggering, openly inviting provocation with every aggressive step, daring anyone to bar their way. No one did. The bodyguards turned pale, the merchants scowled petulantly, but as the Bordermen elbowed their way into the middle of the reserved space, merchants and hirelings split left and right to make room. The Borderers were too obviously drunk enough to be dangerous, too obviously willing to draw steel at the slightest excuse.

The merchants may have remembered that many of these were the sons of men who were desired as political allies; or perhaps they simply did not wish fighting so close to their carriages. And after the events of the last few days, the hired bravos of the ports had no stomach for facing these trained veterans of the Border raids.

The music of the procession throbbed ever stronger along the echoing canyon of the street, and the sound of cheering grew louder. Necks craned as the head of the procession came into view: two carefully picked halberdeers, the largest and heaviest of the city guard, flanking Lord Shachio and a pair of trumpeters. Those foolish enough to rush into the street to see, blocking the advance of the procession, might expect to be jostled rudely to the side by massive shoulders, or pushed carefully but quickly out of the way by the skillful sweep of a halberd shaft. This was business, and these were men trained to force their way through crowds while maintaining a steady marching speed; and apologies would not be offered—not to commoners or nobles, the poorest of beggars or the richest of merchant-princes.

A row of banners, with the night-blue pennant of the King, silver hand and golden crown, exalted in the centre between the devices of the subject states, flapped above the heads of trumpeters and guards; a row of brawny banner-bearers, likewise braced to shoulder aside the crowd when necessary, held up the long poles with their heraldic burdens.

Behind them marched the first consort, and the music echoed loudly from the walls of the houses, drowning out the growing murmur of the crowd. A block of soldiery of the city guard followed, swinging along with their halberds on their shoulders, sunlight glinting on polished cuirasses and morions. And behind them, their left hands on their scabbards and their right swinging in unison, came the small, proud body of Kantara Lords who acted as the royal guard, leading the Prince to his throne.

Now Pirthio gestured excitedly as Chondos marched by in the midst of his nobles. The cheering grew to a thunderous roar. And the merchant-nobles about them were treated to the spectacle of Tunno, the heir of the rebellious Prince Hansio of Mahapor, standing shoulder-to-shoulder with Lord Jagat's son, leading the young warriors of Mahapol and Manjipol in cheer after deafening cheer.

Pirthio smiled to himself. The young Lords of Mahapor cheered for Jagat, and roared for Istvan DiVega. What cared they that they might also seem to cheer the Prince of Manjipé? The greatest swordsman in the world was walking by, with the man who had reclaimed part of the ancient land from the Shadow! But the merchants about them could not know that.

Chondos' feet hurt. At least, in the traditional procession *after* the crowning, he would ride the elephant. The rhythms of their feet on cobblestones, with the muted thunder of drums that was all he could hear of the music, beat in his head above the roar of the crowd. He was sure that his heart was pounding to the rhythm, and he could not help feeling that when the drums stopped, his heart would stop, too.

The heat from the cobblestones smothered him. The air he drew into his lungs dried mouth and throat, and he would not be able to get a drink until after the crowning. He felt he could drink the Pavana dry. His clothes were drenched with sweat, and the constant roar hurt his ears.

And all to impress a mob of stupid tradesmen and merchants and farmers. Some of these idiots probably envied him. What a pity he could not change places with them! What nonsense! His feet burned, and he began to regret his earlier refusal of food. He could feel his empty stomach trying to dissolve itself.

Behind the rank of soldiery that followed Chondos and the regalia, the greater nobles of the King marched according to a delicate order of precedence that had been worked out with long effort.

There was a place near the front for the Duke of Ipazema, but he was not in it. Cynically, he sat his horse not far from the great doors through which the procession must eventually pass, and yawned. If they were to crown *him* King, then it might be worth walking the cobbled streets around the city. But for the crowning of *this* young fool . . . ! After all, was a King who would die the first time Sandor found him far from his guards, worth wearing out one's feet for?

The assassination would probably be within the week, too.

He was ready. The ship awaiting his orders in the harbour at Portona could leave at a moment's notice, with him and Luijos, and, if he lived through it, with Sandor. But it was unlikely, he thought, that Sandor would live to claim his reward. DiVega would probably get to him before he could escape. For that matter, some of the other Seynyoreans quartered in the palace were quite efficient. A pity. But if Sandor managed to kill the King, it would all come tumbling down. And if he could kill Prince Phillipos as well, that would be even better.

Still, the man was very useful, and could be again, if he did manage to cut his way out of the palace and down to the ship. A swordsman like that was a rare and precious treasure—and one who was utterly ruthless, willing to stop at nothing, that was something to have in one's service! Luijos now—perhaps he could find a use for him. If not, it would be easy enough to push him over the side on the way to Poidia. Soon Ipazema would be independent again—yes, but now with Lutazema and Poidia and Thusipol—ah, and then Kalascor. Even if Sandor didn't get Phillipos, sooner or later . . .

Thoros, Prince of Kalascor, he thought of himself. There was a definite nobility to that! And a Prince was not nearly as likely to be bothered by the Hasturs as a King. Even so—he'd heard that it was possible to doctor a man's mind so he would forget all about any evil he had done, so that not even the Hasturs could find it; if one was able to persuade a wizard to do it. And if that could be done, then he could be crowned King, facing the Hasturs with a clean conscience.

He laughed at himself. There'd be time for that later. Kalascor first! And all the coastal cities. When they were in his grasp, then perhaps there might be time to worry about Kingship.

The vendors of food were out at last among the hungry crowd, making merry by enjoying their favorite pastime, a game called fill-the-purse. Many in the crowd greeted them enthusiastically, and set to work to recover from long fasting. Others, fortified by early-morning sausage, took note of the prices, and decided they could hold out until evening, when free food would top off the glories of the day. Some, wise in the ways of merchants, realised that the food would cheapen as the day wore on, when stocks must be disposed of before they spoiled.

Martos and Kumari picked their way through the crowded streets. The odours of fresh fruit, roast meats, and a million different ways of cooking vegetables, filled the air. Voices babbled all about them; happy, excited, serious, wheedling:

"... Fine! ... Melons! ... Sweet ... Juicy ... Melons! ... Fresh ... Tender ... Melons! ..."

"... Did he really? ..."

"... Come on! We'll miss the ..."

Somewhere beyond the crying of the hawkers and the chatter of the crowd, faint drumbeats hinted the progress of the procession. But that was confused by odd bits of music from various street musicians who had set themselves up on corners here and there, and were gathering crowds of listeners or dancers. As they made their way through the crowd, Martos sometimes found his ear beguiled by some exotic instrument, and would gladly have stopped to listen, but Kumari hurried him on.

She led him away from a strange, many-stringed instrument playing a slow, dreamy melody, and as it faded behind them it mingled strangely with a merry dance tune played by a number of horns and reed pipes, and sung by three young girls. His ears caught familiar words from "Pertap's Ride."

They passed a man juggling knives and torches, a man who made a snake rise out of a basket and dance to music, and a man with a talking bird. They passed young men and young women intent on rituals that were older than coronations or Kings.

They sought a gap in a solid wall of people that lined the street of the procession. When they found it, Martos picked a way through for Kumari, sliding easily into the crowd and then reaching back to draw her to his side. Once or twice he was met by the challenging stares of young men as he cleared a space for her; but when he met their eyes, they found something disconcerting in his carriage and in the casual way his sword lounged on his hip. After a time, he worked his way to the front, and drew her before him so that he could look over her head at the still-empty street.

Somewhere he could hear distant drums. He lowered his face into the perfume of her hair, feeling the warmth of her all down his body. He thought of her back, as he had watched that morning, bared when she pulled her long, glossy black hair over her shoulder to brush it, the soft skin rippling with the wingbeat movement of her shoulder blades as she brushed and brushed, and the enticing glimpse of her breast under her raised arm. And then she had tossed the hair back again, a dusky curtain between her rounded shoulders.

Strange that the sight of her naked back should so move him, when they had been lovers for so long. He had even felt an odd sense of loss when she turned back to face him, even as he had gloried in the wonders of her breasts and hips . . .

The arrival of the procession was an unwelcome distraction.

"There's Lord Shachio," she whispered. "The old, white-bearded man in the Seer's robes."

While the musicians and soldiery marched past, he sniffed at the perfume of her hair, and tightened his arms around her waist. What did he care for the Lords of Tarencia, for the crowning of Tarencia's King? Kumari loved him; they would go away together, and then let this damned little Border Kingdom fall to pieces behind them!

Let the stupid fools squabble! He would take Kumari to Kadar, and she could have her child far away from the mountains and the Dark Things. They would go to the eastern part of the Empire, to Sardis or Estepay, and he would open a school of the sword that would bring men flocking from Seynyor and Nydor and Leonterre to study with him.

"Here comes the King now!" said Kumari. "The Prince, I mean, there behind Uncle. Is that Istvan the Archer, carrying his helm? That's Prince Phillipos with the crown, and Lord Zengio . . ."

Martos came out of his daydream, and a faint memory of rivalry made him study the Prince's face as he strode by. It was a memorable face, with those large, liquid eyes and handsome features; a strong face, despite a hint of petulance in the set of the mouth.

And Istvan the Archer! He had seen him once before, at Birthran's school. The Archer's face was gaunter now, hair and beard turning grey. In Birthran's hall the man had walked in a mist of romance that had blurred boyish vision. Now Martos felt oddly disappointed. That skinny, dried-up old man, the greatest swordsman in the world?

His clothing was of a cut that had been out of fashion at the Kadarin court for nearly ten years now, his hair in a style badly outmoded. He looked like an elderly provincial gentleman, come to court to try and find his son a post in the Imperial Guard. Yet he walked with a swordsman's poise and grace. As disillusion died away, Martos found himself fascinated by the way the man moved, by the way the little court-sword at his hip seemed to grow there, a part of him. The man's whole being seemed to revolve about his sword.

You could tell a trained swordsman by the way he moved: Birthran had taught him to recognise the school, by subtle nuances of behaviour, and to make a good guess at the general level of skill. And after a moment's study Martos had no doubts. Birthran himself moved with that same fluid grace . . .

The thought brought his eyes back to Chondos, and he saw that the next King of Tarencia walked with a style that had the School of the Three Swords written all over it. Not as good as DiVega or Martos himself, by any means; but an apt pupil, certainly. Had DiVega trained the lad? He was a cousin or something to the royal family here, Martos remembered. One of the DiVegas had married into the House of the—Achillas, wasn't it? The old Princely House . . .

The procession moved on, and the Prince and his attendants swept out of Martos' vision; the soldiery that followed held no interest for him, nor did the long line of marching nobles. He tightened his arms around Kumari, pulling her back against him.

"Tonight?" he whispered in her ear. She shook her head.

"Not until after I've talked to Uncle. He'll be home tonight."

"You're not going to tell him?" His voice showed surprise.

"Not until tomorrow, at least." Her voice was sad. "Perhaps not then. He has so much on his mind."

"So you're sleeping in your own bed tonight?" He pressed himself up against her, hard. "And I have to sleep in mine? I can be very quiet, you know."

"Silly!" she whispered back. "My room is right between

Pirthio's and Uncle's—and as you'll remember, *I'm* often quite noisy. But . . ." She rubbed against him, tantalisingly. "Since you're stallion-mad, I think I'll send Mirrha in to visit you."

"Mirrha? The little girl?"

"Little! She'll be fifteen in a few months!" She laughed. "And she's mad for you—watching you all the time, mooning about. She's still a virgin, poor thing."

"I don't want Mirrha. I want you!" He squeezed her tighter against him. She laughed softly.

"Once she's in bed with you, I think you'll find you want her. You be gentle, now! The poor little thing dotes on you, and it's always better for a girl to start off with a man she adores." She leaned back against him. "I've been very selfish. I've been going to bring her in with us for some time now. But I kept putting it off, keeping you all to myself."

He kissed her. He wanted to protest once more that he desired her rather than Mirrha, but that was no longer quite true. He'd never taken a virgin—the idea excited him.

The consort that brought up the end of the procession had passed; its music went blaring down the street away from them. The crowds were beginning to straggle into the road, surging behind the parade.

"We'd better go to the hall," she said. "If we cross the street here and go right, then cut through the alley over there, we should be able to get to our seats before the King comes in. But we must hurry!"

The smell of food was maddening. Chondos saw the people in the crowd eating, and his empty stomach burned with hunger. He felt that he would faint before he ever reached the throne. His feet tortured him, and the heat was terrible. That he should be forced to suffer this merely to appease the populace's hunger for pageantry enraged him. The people, munching away on meat and delicious-smelling pastries and fruit, were having the time of their lives; *they* weren't starving, or pounding their feet flat on the cobblestones at this preposterous quick-march. Suffering for his people was one thing, when it was necessary, but to walk his feet off and broil—the starving was his own fault—only that they might be amused, did not seem a reasonable sacrifice.

But at last he saw the great archway before him, with the

soldiers passing under it, and the music from the leading consort echoing hollowly from inside. The guardsmen split off to left and right, forming a long corridor; the chosen nobles of the escort did the same, deeper in the hall. He passed in out of the heat and glare, and cooling shade covered him.

There was carpet under his feet. The great Coronation Hall, in normal times the Greater Chamber of Audience, stretched about him, lofty arches hidden in darkness above high windows, which cast slanting beams through dimness to the floor. The nobles were assembled in their galleries. As he walked up the long carpet towards the stairs of the throne, those nobles who had marched behind him were scattering to join their families.

The music stopped, and in the deep hush he could hear the rustling of many people. Someone coughed. Chairs creaked. A scabbard clattered against a railing. Only Lord Taticos and the bearers of the regalia were with him as he walked towards the throne. The others had all moved to their places: guards to their posts; musicians to the stands provided for them; nobles to the gallery. Lord Shachio was by the steps of the throne, leaning on his staff. Two trumpeters stood at attention to either side, their clarions ready.

They had reached the steps, and above them he saw the old throne, carved in his grandfather's time, out of oak from the Kantara, inlaid with hammered gold along the front of arms and legs. There was a murmur of shuffling feet and rustling cloth as everyone in the hall leaned forward to look, a multiple hiss of indrawn breath as Lord Shachio turned and set his foot on the lowest step. Phillipos and Jagat moved forward with the crown and the sword, their robes rustling. Somewhere people would be waiting with the robe and mantle. Shachio and Taticos stepped up the stairs together.

A blue-robed figure materialised out of the air in front of the throne, hand upraised. "Halt! Who comes to be crowned with the Crown of the Kings of Tarencia?" The voice was deep, and echoed through the hall like a trumpet.

Even when you expected it, it was still a shock. Chondos had thought himself thoroughly prepared, yet now he stood with one foot raised, staring at the red-haired man who had appeared from nowhere.

"Chondos, Prince of Manjipor, Heir to the Throne of Tarencia, is here, my Lord Hastur," Lord Shachio's voice rose in answer. "He has come to lay claim to his father's throne."

"Let him come forward!" came the ringing voice.

Chondos swallowed, and stepped towards the stairs. As he set his foot on the bottom step, he heard Lord Taticos' voice in a low hiss, and the snapping of fingers. Glancing at the old man in incomprehension, he saw him gesturing wildly. He blinked, and Taticos tapped his head and held out his hands. Chondos stared, and then, remembering, reached up and pulled off his coronet, and, bowing, set it in the seneschal's hands. Taticos smiled and bowed.

Chondos started up the stairs. Only seven steps, but the ascent seemed endless. *Very impressive,* he thought, struggling for his composure. *Fine theatre. Awe the populace.*

But it had startled him, too, even though he had known what was coming. Now he must face that which all Kings must face. He braced himself, and pushed back the fear that gripped him. He knew and understood the necessity behind this part of the ritual, at least.

He raised his head and met the steady grey eyes of the Hastur calmly, almost challengingly. The Hastur would see the fear that was inside him, but there was no point in showing it off to all. And in truth, there was nothing to fear.

"I am Miron Hastur." The voice was calm, gentle now.

At least, the Hasturs need have no fear of hypocrisy; in the blending of minds, honesty would be automatic, unavoidable. If mortals could do it, the world would be a better place . . . What was it like, to know what another was thinking? If only I could see the Hastur's mind as well . . .

. . . But you can . . .

And while he stood puzzled, trying to decide whether that had really been an alien thought or whether he had imagined it, the Coronation Hall vanished from around him, and he found himself surrounded and engulfed by the mind of Miron Hastur.

There before him, as in a mirror, was his own mind reflected. But beyond that were vastnesses of thought, gulfs he could not bridge, heights he could not climb, depths he could not plumb. For only a tiny portion of that stupendous mind was needed to completely examine and understand his own: this mind that could, when necessary, concentrate itself totally and absolutely upon a single subject without a trace of irrelevant thought, was compartmented as though it were the minds of many men.

The visualisation of his own mind, so tiny, in a corner of this awesome intellect, shocked him, and he felt himself (and saw himself, mirrored in the other's mind) cringe away from this terrible self-knowledge, from this vision of his own weakness. But he forced himself to remain steady, holding himself firmly in hand, studying the mind of which he had always been so foolishly vain.

There it was, not only that tiny part which handled his normal thinking, but the depths beneath, where lay buried all the things he had forgotten: all the resentments and evil thoughts he had not allowed himself to cherish, instincts, memories from lives not his own, dreams, symbols, strange insanities—he forced himself to face it all squarely, and then lifted his "eyes" to the vastness beyond, to immensities in which he was so hopelessly lost. He stretched himself to understand the greatness that surrounded him; but although he could see his mirrored mind stretch and grow from the effort, it was hopeless.

Beneath their feet, whirling sparks made up the dais on which they stood, swirling in eternal dance; by changing the figures of the dance, the marble of the dais could change to gold. The air swirled about him; each breath he took into his lungs was a cloud of sparkling, living particles. And as casually and thoughtlessly as a man might drum his fingers on a table, Miron could strengthen himself by imbuing the rudimentary minds of those tiny sparks with a single essence, and then breathe that essence.

A thousand miles to the north, his kinsmen struggled with deadly, invisible creatures (multilegged and misshapen) which could stand the light of day, and strove to drive the Hasturs and their mortal allies away from the Border. If they succeeded, that night, when the full host of the Dark Ones would be free to move, the Border would advance, and the Shadow would cover a little more of the lands of men. He could speak instantly to any of the seven hundred or so Hasturs in the Universe, or to any of thousands of Seers, Healers, and Wizards . . .

The scope and power of Miron's mind was beyond his comprehension, and Chondos could no more have stuffed its contents into his own than he could have swallowed the ocean. A thought came to him out of the vastness: *It is good that you have not failed to face yourself. Most mortals do. This is the true Ordeal of Kings. Many are offered this opportunity for growth, but few dare to take it up. Many do not dare even to remember that it was offered, but bury it away in the depths of their souls to hide from themselves.*

Pride stirred at that, but it was short-lived, for Miron's laughter was plain to see. It hurt Chondos, and he saw that total honesty had its drawbacks after all—saw, too, the reason for the common politeness which he had always seen as hypocrisy; saw why most mortals cringed away from this pitiless exposure to superior intellect, and the treasure that they lost thereby.

Among the confusing immensities of that incredible void of spirit he could observe the beating heart and watch blood flow through a body whose every cell was monitored and understood; the fantastic bodily control which enabled the Hasturs to live for many lives of men.

Somewhere in that vast mind he could hear the voices of Hasturs speaking silently a thousand miles away—to which Miron paid no heed unless one addressed him, or called for help—and there was a blurred murmur of unformed thought that echoed from the minds of the thousands of mortals nearby.

Chondos was enchanted by shimmering patterns of energy that were the foundations of powerful spells; arrested by visions of life upon the greater moons and upon far worlds of which he had never dreamed; fascinated by insights into the life of wild beasts and plants. Complex and profound secrets of magic floated there, ready for use; incredible elucidations of symbols and philosophies; experiences undreamed of by the greatest of mortal wizards.

He was stunned by memories of minds which had surrounded this one as easily as it surrounded his: minds whose memories contained history; faces of men who had died when the Takkarian Empire still throve; daily life in kingdoms that were now ancient legends. A childhood spent in contemplations of things mortal wizards found hard to grasp and other men never learned at all; years of training in visualisation and clairvoyance and . . . At sixteen, Miron Hastur had been expected to demonstrate knowledge and powers that a mortal wizard might spend a lifetime acquiring.

Chondos' mind was being lifted, guided through that vast, incomprehensible storehouse of mind, shown those things that would do him the most good. He had already learned much to expand his sketchy magical training, and for the first time Chondos realised how sketchy that training had been. It was not his fault, of course . . . But he saw from the Hastur's mind that it was. Too much time spent on envy and self-pity, and pride in his intellect; too much pride to seriously try to learn.

No part of Miron's mind was hidden away. It was all consciousness. And now Miron's mind was speaking to him and he could watch the words as they formed out of understanding, could watch them shape themselves into sentences. He could see the thoughts in their raw form, but could not interpret them: *Your greatest weakness is distrust. Look a moment upon these, your Councillors, through my eyes, and learn. You are too harsh in judging your fellow-men. Look!*

Chondos was looking out at the throne room. In front of him was his own body, but the eyes were not concerned with that. Instead, they peered over Chondos' shoulder at the assembled Lords below. The Hasturs did not read the minds of men without their permission, except upon rare and important occasions, when the need was great. Yet to their vast powers, some things were obvious and could not be ignored . . .

Chondos saw Lord Jagat wreathed in brilliant colors, and as Miron's mind interpreted those colors, Chondos *saw* Jagat's loyalty, his fierce pride and quiet wisdom glowing in beauty around him, and knew unquestioningly that this was a man who could be trusted. Knew, too, that he had hurt him deeply.

The eyes of the Hastur dwelt briefly on the others of Chondos' escort: the sorrow and courage of Istvan DiVega; the trained calm of Lord Shachio; the weary sacrifice of Taticos, and Zengio . . .

Then Miron drew Chondos' attention elsewhere. A radiating net of possibilities spread out before him, the future fanning out in all directions. Ominously, he saw, many of them showed Tarencia covered by the Shadow.

Surprise flickered in Miron's mind. *There are unknown factors at work here,* he thought, and Chondos saw a grim worry cloud the tranquil wisdom. Visions came of the intense struggle to the north upon which the Hasturs must focus so much of their attention, and of other struggles in distant lands. Chondos saw that the Hastur was well aware of the delicate political situation here.

The Hasturs had been weakened by a battle in Y'Gora, beyond the sea, with a monstrous creature called the Nualdoel, in which some of the greatest of the Hasturs had died. The Hastur-Lord himself had been forced to go to Y'Gora to deal with the menace. There were signs of further trouble there. Forces were building in Noria which must be watched; there were dangers in distant lands of which Chondos had never heard. This near to Idelbonn, it seemed impossible that there should be such danger as he saw.

But there was one major danger in Chondos himself. His mind was still vulnerable to the mind of his twin, Jodos. Their bodies were built on the same pattern, and it would be a simple act to control Chondos' mind through that of his brother—unless Chondos' mind were shielded.

Chondos could watch, in the mirror of Miron's mind, as the Hastur reached into the hidden sector of his brain and built there a shield of considerable power. Some words, a diagram—these were the keys that would bring that shield leaping from the depths of Chondos' mind. All Chondos need do was picture the diagram clearly in his head and speak or think the words at the same time, and his mind would be safe. Another set of words would release the block again.

Miron showed what to look for, taught him how to detect foreign influences in his mind, even in sleep; then let Chondos watch while he installed a reflex which would bring those symbols leaping into his mind at any time such indications were noted. Only if he were knocked unconscious would it be possible for his mind to be tampered with.

Now, test it, came Miron's thought, and Chondos said the words, pictured the symbol in his mind . . .

And found himself standing on the dais before the throne, face-to-face with Miron Hastur.

The young Hastur nodded, satisfied. "I could break it, by sheer force," he said in a low voice, "but only because I built it myself, and know how, and know your mind intimately. No other Hastur could, save perhaps the Hastur-Lord himself, or some few others of the Empowered. But not easily. And the minds of the Dark Ones are so different from ours that they could never pass it."

He smiled at Chondos, and turned to Phillipos, farther down the steps. The Crown of Tarencia lifted form the cushion, floating through the air, and settled into Miron's hands.

Miron Hastur lifted the crown, and his voice echoed through the hall: "I have examined him and found him free from all evil taint. All hail Chondos, King of Tarencia!"

As he lowered the crown onto Chondos' head, a bell rang out far above them, and trumpets sang at the foot of the stairs. A roar of cheering filled the air. Throughout the city, bells began to ring.

Miron Hastur caught Chondos' eyes and smiled again. "You know why I must leave. Good fortune to you, King Chondos!" And he vanished like a blown-out flame.

As the bells echoing through the city signalled that his brother had been crowned, Jodos slipped quietly out of the house of Jacopos and moved towards the palace, mingling with the thickest of the crowds.

People were shouting and dancing in the streets. Their senseless noise irritated and frightened him. It grew as the crowds thickened. He saw a great grey monster with four massive legs and a single tentacle beneath its wicked little eyes, and wondered if this was one of the Lords here, some ally of the Nameless Ones, and if the noise the people were making was part of some sacrifice they were to make to it.

The crowd split right and left before the beast, but it walked among the people docilely enough. He wondered how many of them it would take to appease its hunger. He stayed well away from it. He had seen its likeness sculpted in the deserted cities of the mountains. He hoped it did not have the power to sense him.

Outside the great hall, the revelry was at its height. The happily drunken sausage-seller was one of those actually lucky enough to have made his way inside the hall, near the front of the crowd.

As he came out, someone stopped him and asked if the Lord

Hastur was gone, and after answering, he was puzzled by a curious feeling that he knew the speaker. There was something extremely familiar about the handsome young face with its wide, dark eyes, and for a second he realised that it looked just like . . .

Then those eyes fixed on him, and he could not remember.

Chapter Eight

The castle on the hill was dark, as tired officials sought rest. But in the city the lights of revelry still blazed, though now mostly indoors: in the taverns, in the homes of citizens and nobles, and in the great guildhalls.

In the hall of the Rivermasters' Guild, the greatest of the merchant-nobility of the coastal cities were honoured guests. Wine flowed freely, the food was good, and the women that circulated among the tables were shapely and properly impressed by the power of wealth.

As the night wore on towards dawn, the Seynyorean guards, told by Istvan DiVega to provide protection for the richest men in the kingdom, grew bored and irritable. To be forced to stand watch while others were happily eating, drinking, and ogling women was bad enough; to be forced to stand and watch them doing it was torture.

In the palace, the guard Tonios felt a delicious drowsiness steal over him, and set himself grimly to fight it off. His eyes kept trying to close—but he must *not* sleep! He was guarding the corridor that led to the King's bedchambers! If they found him asleep they'd—they'd . . .

He shook his head to clear it. He was too groggy to remember what his punishment would be. The corridor whirled, and he almost fell. This would never do! He was guarding the King himself! He leaned on his halberd, holding himself erect. After a moment, he realised he was leaning partly on the shaft and partly against the wall. His eyelids felt sticky, and his feet didn't seem to be there at all. The strip of carpet before his eyes grew narrower and narrower . . .

His eyes closed. What nonsense! He'd been dreaming that he was falling asleep on guard, and here he was, safe in his own bed! He snuggled into the warm covers. There was a pretty girl looking at him. Leaves rustled in the forest . . .

The sound of a step in the corridor brought him instantly awake, halberd level. "Halt!" he shouted, and then his eyes focussed on the face before him, and he saw the King.

For a moment he was struck dumb. The dark eyes fixed on his.

"Who am I?" said the other, and Tonios fell to one knee.

"You are the King." His voice trembled. "Your pardon, Sire."

"Rise," said the other, his voice very soft. "Are you sure? Look at me closely. Look at my eyes. Am I the King?" Tonios, obedient, came to his feet, and looked earnestly on the King's face. The King was very pale. And his eyes—the eyes were so huge and dark . . .

"You are the King, Sire."

"Good. Now leave your post and come with me. I have a special mission for you. Come. Walk quietly. Do not make a sound."

Surely he must still be dreaming! He had expected punishment. But perhaps the King had not seen him sleeping . . . There was something very wrong here, but he could not think what it was.

The King gestured again for him to follow, but even when he had turned away, those great dark eyes still seemed to hang in Tonios' vision, and the hall about him was dim and vague. He followed the King as in a dream. After a time they stopped. A dim glow came from a small cluster of gems set in the wall. Tonios knew that these, and the others like them in the castle, were part of a spell protecting the palace from the Dark Ones.

The King stepped to the wall, and his back hid the gems from Tonios' sight. He could not see what the King was doing, but there was a faint sound of scraping metal. He stood waiting, silent. His head felt as though it were stuffed with cotton. He closed his eyes . . .

When he opened them again, the King had stepped back from the wall and was surveying the star-shaped pattern of the gems critically. Their light seemed dimmer somehow. The centre stone was not as bright.

"Lead the way to my sleeping chamber," the King said, and

Tonios obeyed without a thought, walking down the hall to the door, and opening it.

"Quiet!" hissed the King, as Tonios stepped aside to let him enter. Wondering, Tonios closed the door behind them.

He had never actually been inside the royal bedchamber before. He felt soft carpeting under his feet. Great windows opened on one side, and the light of the brilliant moons flooded the room with a dim, shifting radiance. Between him and the windows was the great canopied bed, its soft hangings pushed up against the post.

But there was someone in the bed. The moonlight fell upon the sleeper's face—and it was the King's face! Tonios' eyes moved helplessly from the face in the bed to the face beside him. The one in the bed seemed darker, more tanned. Otherwise, they were identical.

"That is not the King," the soft voice whispered. "That is my brother, Jodos, who was stolen away as a child. He has come back to pass himself off as me, and take the throne. You and I, Tonios, must stop him."

Jodos? Yes, that explained it. Dimly, he remembered the story now: how Queen Tarani had borne twins, and, shortly after their birth, before they were weaned, had insisted on going to one of her castles near the Border in Manjipé. One night, the tale went, they had found the guard unconscious and one of the Princes gone from his cradle. The guard had gone mad, and the Hasturs had had to take him away to be healed. One of the King's Seers, Emicos, had vanished that same night. Some said he had studied Forbidden Powers.

The greatest heroes in the world had searched for the missing Prince: Tahion, the Aldinorian pretender, Birthran the Kadarin, Raquel DiVega and his younger kinsman Istvan, and others. But no trace of the baby had ever been found, and men said that he had been carried away by the Dark Ones. But even the Hasturs could not say how, or why.

The King had drawn a small box made of some dead-black material from his garments. He stepped closer to Tonios, and slightly behind him. "Hush!" the King said. "Do not move!" Out of the corner of his eye, Tonios saw him open the box, whispering words that Tonios could not understand.

The King seemed to take something very small out of the

box, but Tonios could not see what it was. Then the King stepped behind Tonios, and the guard felt a hand touch him lightly on the shoulder. He started to turn, but the King hissed, "Hold still!" and then stepped in front of him, and looked into his eyes.

It was all very strange. Perhaps he was still dreaming. The King's eyes filled all his vision. He felt something crawling on the back of his neck, like some kind of insect, and started to raise his hand, but the King touched his wrist and the arm would not obey him, falling to his side again. The King's eyes were so huge . . .

The insect crawled up the back of his neck, into his hair. There was something desperately wrong, but he could not think clearly. His mind was numb, he could do nothing but stare into those terrible eyes . . . Searing pain pierced the back of his head. Tonios tried to scream, but only a choked rattle came from his throat.

Prince Jodos caught the dead man as he toppled into his arms. After a moment the body stirred, the muscles moved convulsively, and the corpse pushed itself up and stood awkwardly erect. A dull croak came from its throat.

"Are you in control?" Jodos whispered.

Rattling and whining came from the creature's mouth, and then a soft, croaked, "Yes, Master!"

Jodos let go the thing's arms then, and stepped silently towards the bed where his brother lay. He looked down at the creature in the bed, the thing that had his own face, and wanted to smash that face, kill this horrible mockery of himself, and eat it, so that he would be the only one. But that was not what he had been ordered to do.

So far he had laid only the lightest compulsion on the sleeper, only enough to keep Chondos from waking. But he knew, from that slight touch, that this mind was protected and strengthened. He must strike quickly, and smash all resistance with a single blow.

He gathered in his powers, withdrawing from other contacts. All through the castle, guards would soon be waking. Slowly, in absolute silence, he leaned over the bed. Chondos tossed uneasily on the pillow. Jodos' eyes blazed with concentration. In a single, terrible thrust, he smashed into his brother's mind, gulping its total contents in a single bite. Chondos sat up convulsively, his eyes rolling back in his head, mouth opened in a silent scream. Then he crashed back, senseless from shock.

Jodos smiled, and stripped away the light coverlet. The King lay in a thin white night-robe, and Jodos' lips curled in a cruel smile as he thought of the cold of the mountains.

The windows were open. He looked out into the night, his thought searching the courtyard and the land around the castle. There was almost no one awake. It was unlikely that any would see the winged one.

He opened the other compartment of his box. *"Sjawg!"* he whispered, "Yizjoth and Lyghoth have bound you to serve me! Obey! Lest Uoght deliver you for punishment!"

He set down the box and stepped back. What seemed at first a thin smoke rose from the box in the light of the shifting moons, and then the box was hidden. The sourceless shadow grew. Looking closely he saw something solid rise from the box, something that looked like a folded packet of cloth. It unfolded, and the shadow draped itself about it as it spread itself into membranous wings. Powerful as it was, he could feel the creature quail before him, before the names on which he had called.

He gestured towards the senseless figure on the bed. "Bear this living and unharmed to the Master, in *Rajinagara* in the mountains. If it is not living, you know what suffering will come to you. When you reach the Barrier of Light, call out, and a path will be made. Go now, or suffer!"

A thin wail came in answer, and the shadow lifted into the air, hovering by the bed. Thin filaments, stronger than steel, stretched from the tiny body between the wings and wrapped themselves around King Chondos' arms and legs and body. Beating its wings, it lifted him and swept through the window, vanishing in the night.

Jodos shut the window. He needed time now, time to examine the contents of this mind he had eaten. He turned to the corpse which his servant rode. "Go take up your post in the hall," he said. "Use the rest of the watch to study the mind you have taken. In the morning you must convince them that you are human and alive, and that nothing has happened."

"I burn!" the thing stammered, mouth and tongue under better control now, but still not right. "Here is fire in the air. If I stay long I will be destroyed!"

A curious emotion, which he did not recognise, swept over Jodos. This weak creature would indeed die if it remained here long; for although the net of energies that had protected the castle was broken, there remained a powerful residue which could only be lifted by removing all the gems—a residue he dared not dispel, for that would be all too noticeable.

This creature would die if he took one of the gems he had pried loose from the walls and dropped it into the corpse's hand. It would die if it were to brush against any of the jewels that remained. Why that should affect Jodos thus, he did not know; but if it died, he would have lost an important servant.

"Stand watch tonight, and then go to the barracks. Then, after a time, go to his commander. Tell him you are ill and wish to be excused from duty. Then go to the house of Jacopos, and wait with Hotar until I summon you!"

The creature stumbled awkwardly to the door, and out into the corridor. Jodos began to strip off the clothes he had worn, absently, while he began to sort out his brother's mind. He had never probed a human mind so deeply before. There was much that was disturbing and incomprehensible. He found a name for the strange emotion. It was pity.

In the Satragara, wine cups filled and emptied. Loud, drunken chatter rang merrily, and the ancient Takkarian Kings and heroes gazed down from painted walls at their descendents.

Around Pirthio, the room swam in a pleasant haze of wine. The dark wood of the old table before him seemed to crawl slightly, and when he raised his arm so he could lean his head on his hand, his elbow thumped on the table.

Tunno heaved his great bulk down next to him. "Haw!" he rumbled. "Did you notice the way those fat pigs stepped aside for us? Hah, I bet if anybody'd pulled a sword they'd be running yet!"

Pirthio made a muffled sound of assent, and burped noisily. He cradled his head in his elbow, reached for the wine jug and shook it. There seemed to be some left, so he poured it into his cup, and when he saw that it was spilling on the table, poured some for Tunno.

"Would've been something to see!" Tunno's thick voice mumbled on. "Show 'em a few inches of steel and watch 'em run! Hey! Why didn't we do that, huh?"

No one answered him, so he picked up his cup and gulped his wine. "Next time," he muttered. "Next time—I wonder how fast they can run? What does a fat man look like running? Hey! I'm talking to you! What do they look like when they run, hey?"

Pirthio opened a bleared eye and tried to remember whether he'd ever seen a merchant running. He poured the rest of his cup down his throat. "I don'no if they can run with all that weight," he said. "Maybe their guards would have had to carry 'em. If their guards waited for 'em. Only one way we'll ever find out, though."

Something fell over with a loud crash, and then a young man was leaning against the table. After a moment, Pirthio recognised Ajesio of Kantakin, a young Lord of the Kantara—who, Pirthio knew, was arranging a marriage with a girl in Mahapor.

"What's all this? Who's running?"

"We're talking about putting a scare into those pigs from the coast," said Tunno thickly. "Flash steel at them and see how fast they run."

"Hey!" The Kantarin straightened up, blinking. "There's a big feast at the Rivermasters' Guildhall. All the fat ones will be there—the really fat ones, the big important rich ones. Why don't we pay them a visit?"

Pirthio shook the bottle again. It seemed to be really empty this time. He upended it over his cup, and a few pale drops dribbled out. "More wine!" he shouted, and then looked up at the others. "Musn't—" He hiccoughed. "Mustn't start a fight. Mustn't have a riot on the evening of the Coronation. Not right after Chondos' Coronation. It would be very bad manners!"

"This is the morning after, not the evening after," Ajesio pointed out. "Besides, we aren't going to fight them, are we?"

"No!" said Tunno. "We aren't going to fight them. Just scare them a little. Watch them run. Maybe chase them a little. But we aren't going to *catch* them!"

"Certainly not!" said Ajesio. "That would be beneath our dignity as Takkarian gentlemen. Gentlemen only fight other gentlemen." Tunno nodded agreement.

The innkeeper came hurrying up, a bottle of wine in his hands. "The Massadessan vintage is all gone, gentles," he said regretfully. "Perhaps you might find this satisfactory? It is real Onporfay, all the way from Virtera." He opened the bottle and poured some into Tunno's cup.

Tunno sniffed at it suspiciously, took a tentative sip and rolled it around in his mouth for a while, considering, then swallowed. "Stinks!" he snorted, and drained the rest of the goblet. "Maybe the pigs at the Guildhall have good wine." He grabbed the bottle out of the startled innkeeper's hand, and jumped up on the table, swaying.

"Hey! Listen everybody!" His voice roared above the chatter. "Those fat merchant pigs are feasting and drinking over in the Rivermasters' Hall. We're going to give them a good scare. Teach 'em a little respect for gentlemen!" He paused, and took a long pull from the bottle. "And we're going to get ourselves some decent wine." He took another swig. "Everybody come along, now! We're going to see how fast merchants can run!"

The Warders at Agnasta and Rishipur had only a moment's warning before the wave of dark power was upon them. The screens about the towers blazed up, and their cries for aid echoed from mind to mind along the Border.

Miron Hastur leaped at once the hundred-odd miles from Idelbonn, and appeared in Agnasta in the blink of an eye. His mind uniting with those of the other Hasturs in the tower, he braced himself against the blasting, freezing assault that swept out of the mountains. In the lands to the north, alarm bells were ringing in the fortresses of the Kantara Lords. The towers flamed in the darkness as they fought back the Shadow.

The towers held. And as flickering need-fire beat the terrible forces back, Miron hurled his mind across the gap to the next tower like a rope, and linked with the mind of Amivahan Hastur in Rishipur. United they strove to reestablish the shattered net between the two towers. A burning ray sprang into being, pulsing between Agnasta and Rishipur.

As suddenly as it had begun, the attack ceased. The darkness was still, empty. The Hasturs launched bolt after bolt of raw power into the sudden void. But the air which a moment since had seethed with the terrible powers of the Dark Things was now silent, untroubled.

Tensed and waiting, they braced themselves for another attack. Still as statues their bodies, but their minds were busy, testing and priming the defenses of the towers; probing the darkness beyond for some sign of malign activity. They waited and waited.

Still no attack came.

Gradually tension lessened. They forced themselves to relax, without reducing their alertness. After a time they set themselves to strengthening the net between the towers, and to searching the land for creatures that had crossed the frontier during the attack; still watching the darkness, expecting at any moment the deadly, blasting force of the Dark Things. Moments stretched on and no attack came.

At least things are back to normal, thought Angiro Hastur. *There'll be something out raiding.*

What got out? thought Miron in answer.

The voice of old Elnar Hastur rang through all their minds. *Nothing got out. Something went in.*

Young Baernarho DiVega, a distant cousin to the famed Istvan, was struggling to fight off boredom through meditation. He was not used to meditating in the middle of quite so much noise and confusion, however. Nor with quite so many fleshly pleasures to distract his attention. But he had been set to guard the Guildhall.

Again and again he would clear his mind laboriously of thought, only to find himself listening to the words of some rowdy song; or else his mouth was watering at the smell of food; or his eyes moving over some particularly luscious figure. And as he struggled to clear these things from his mind once more, he would find himself growing sleepy, and have to jar himself sharply back to a state of alertness. Then irritation would set in, and he would have to cleanse his emotions once more. The state of alert empty-mindedness he sought was not easy to attain . . .

Below the wide Guildhall window by which he stood, the feast went on, though there were far fewer at the boards now, and the food had long since been devoured. Now the feasting was only wine and women, and—after the fashion of drunken men—song, if one could so dignify their off-key croakings.

Many of the serving-women who remained had lost portions of their clothing, and some, on the knees of their drunken patrons, were in the process of losing more. A few of the guests, asleep or dead drunk, had resisted all efforts to get them on their feet and off to bed, and lay with their heads on the table; others were on the floor beneath. Their comrades were too drunk to care.

It was almost dawn. The sky to the east was slowly fading to a paler blue, and black stars stood out in relief. Aldebaran and the Hyades glowed like pearls, and far to the north, Hastur glinted with crystalline splendour. Three golden moons lifted slowly above the walls of the city—the moons that men call the Heralds of Dawn. Somewhere a rooster crowed.

Pirthio followed Tunno through the shadowed street, his senses blurred and his mind muzzy with wine. He had a strong feeling that there was something wrong with what they were doing, that he should stop it somehow; but he was not sure why, and could think of no argument that would dissuade Tunno. He staggered along behind Tunno. The King's Peace. That was it. They should not break the King's Peace. But you couldn't say that to Tunno. Besides, they weren't going to hurt anybody! Just throw a good scare into some fat fools who were probably traitors anyway. There would be no fight in merchants, certainly!

Worse yet, if he backed out now, he might undo all his work with Tunno and the others. This was another step in the uniting of Mahapor and Manjipor, and the cutting off of Portona from her allies. It could all be for the best after all, he decided, and hiccoughed. Here were men of Mahavara and Manjipé, together at last, blocking the street as they followed him and Tunno.

They made a fair amount of noise, until Tunno turned and hushed them, several times, gesturing at the Guildhall which lay just ahead. At last, with Pirthio's help, he got them quieted down, and they began to creep towards the building.

"What are we going to do?" someone whispered. "Just march in the front door?"

Tunno shook his head, and gestured vaguely around to the right of the Guildhall. "Windows," he whispered thickly. "Around the side. Saw 'em once when I came here to—to discuss business for my father."

Pirthio found himself giggling at that—*We know what kind of business that was*—and struggled madly against laughter. Fortunately, Tunno was too drunk to notice.

They crossed the street in a swarm, drifting around to the side, where great windows that were almost doors opened onto the gardens. They crouched down in the shrubbery. A thrill of adventure raised goosebumps all up Pirthio's arms, but something troubled him, and he puzzled over it while the others drew their swords and readied themselves for a dash through the windows.

"Remember, we don't want to hurt anybody," he said after a moment, drawing his own blade and taking his place beside Tunno. "Wave your swords and yell a lot, but don't hurt anybody."

"That's right!" said Tunno. "Just scare 'em. Make 'em run a little. Everybody ready?"

What a wasted night, Baernarho thought. *What do they think they need guards for? I almost wish something would happen . . .*

He emptied his lungs of air, let them rest a moment, and then breathed in slowly and deeply, driving away his discontent, driving from his mind the images of the women below. He held the breath, and slowly and calmly began to breathe out. *I have no mind . . .*

A shout echoed behind him. As he came around, he saw a lifted sword, and his blade left its scabbard in a sweeping cut. A chorus of yells hurt his ears.

Pirthio fell without a cry, blood gushing from his throat. Tunno shouted as he saw his friend fall, and drew back his sword to cut. It clattered on the floor as the Seynyorean's point found his heart.

A dozen more men jammed in through the window, confused, those behind running into those ahead of them.

Behind him, Baernarho heard the screams of women, the babbling of drunken men, and the clatter of feet as his fellow-guards rushed to his aid. His sword went up to block another cut, but this one jumped back from his return and blundered into his fellows in the window. They were all drunk, he saw. He leaped towards the window, and his blade swept across another throat. Zumio and Troel were beside him now, hurling themselves on the clustered men, and pride brought a smile to his lips.

"Young fool! *Stupid* young fool!" Old Palos DiFlacca went running past. He had caught up a halberd from somewhere, and his sword was still in its sheath. "Get back!" He pushed Troel out of his way, knocked down one of the attackers with the butt of his halberd, and then hurled himself at the mob in the window.

Baernarho had never seen anything like it. With the halberd horizontal before his body, old Palos evaded and blocked a dozen swords, and suddenly swept almost the whole mob back through the window. A man thrust at him from the side and Baernarho leaped in and took off the Borderer's head.

"Get back, I said!" DiFlacca roared, and swept the butt of the halberd in Baernarho's direction. "No more killing! Danel! Bernal! D'Ascoli!" He whipped the halberd expertly between the legs of an attacker. "Valanos! Here! Help me, and keep these idiots back!"

Baernarho fell back puzzled and aggrieved, as the senior members of the company came running up. He'd have thought the Old Man would be pleased . . .

Aurel D'Ascoli had another halberd, and Valanos DiVega and Bernal DiFlacca had found long poles; Danel DiFlacca had a wooden stool. The rest of the guards stood back, ready to fling themselves into the battle if needed, watching as the older warriors expertly disarmed and knocked out nearly a dozen of the attackers.

The Bordermen, surprisingly, did not put up much of a fight. Vallanos was run through the shoulder and Danel was cut across the face, but the enemy seemed confused. They fell back and vanished in the dawn mist.

Then it was over, and Palos was looking down at the bodies of the dead.

"Young fools! *Crazy* young fools! Why did they . . . ?" He wept.

"They were drunk, sir," said Baernarho. "They—"

"I know they were drunk!" roared Palos. "And what makes you think I was talking about *them?* You dim-witted, brainless, dung-headed ass! If you knew they were drunk, why did you have to kill them?"

Baernarho blinked. "But they *attacked* me, sir, they were—"

"I saw what they did! I saw it all! You could have drawn and blocked, you could have stepped back and laid your hand on your hilt and looked menacing, you could have disarmed him a dozen ways! You were supposed to *prevent* bloodshed, not start it! Those idiots weren't trying to kill anybody! They were probably going to take the flats of their swords to some merchants who'd stepped on their aristocratic toes!"

"But I thought—"

"You *didn't* think. You just started cutting." He looked down at the bodies on the floor and shook his head sadly. "No reason for it at all. Well, if these men are who I think they are, you'll get your bellyful of killing, soon enough."

Jodos carefully practised forging his brother's name again and again, following the figures laid out in his mind, forcing his unwilling reflexes to move in the correct patterns. He examined the seal very slowly, remembering the way it was used.

Carefully, he wrote out the order he had decided on, taking a long time to shape each letter. Finally it was done. He examined it critically, comparing it with bits of his brother's handwriting he had found, and with his brother's memories.

The Guard Tonios, bearer of this note, is assigned to special duty and is to be relieved of all other duties at once. Below, he had laboriously copied Chondos' careless scrawl.

He poured wax and set Chondos' seal to it, and then leaned back to study the result. This would work far better than his original plan. They might have called in the Healer, who would know at once that Tonios was dead, and recognise the creature for what it was.

Chondos' memory of palace routine told him that it was

nearly time for the guard to be changed. Birds were making noise outside, and sunlight was beginning to come through the window.

Jodos was tired. He had been too frightened to sleep the day before, and the night's work had left him exhausted, drained of strength. And now he must stay awake the whole day, keep up this dangerous disguise; and until the masters came and covered this land with soothing darkness he must live and work in the glaring light of the Twin Suns.

One more thing to do; and then, perhaps, he might sleep a little before the others came to wake him. He gathered up the sheets he had used to practise Chondos' signature, and stuffed them into an envelope, first writing on the top: BURN THIS. Afterwards he wondered why he had done that; it was highly doubtful that Hotar could read this script, but perhaps the spider could; certainly he could if the guard had ever learned to read. In any case, he could send verbal instructions. He sealed the envelope with the royal seal, and smiled at his own cleverness. Now his creature would be able to leave the palace without question. Nor would he have any difficulty in arranging to meet him later.

He slipped out of the room and down the hall to where the dead man stood at his post. "Show this to your commander and you'll have no trouble getting out of the castle," he said. "Don't tell them you're sick. Burn the envelope when you get to the house of Jacopos. It should be—" He started, and looked up. Men of the palace guard were marching down the corridor. Tonios' relief had arrived. For a panic-stricken moment he wanted to run, but then he thought and stood his ground as the men came up. This was even better.

"Captain!" he said, as the soldiers came up to them. "I have just assigned this man—Tonios—to a special mission. See to it that he is relieved from all other duties."

"Sire!" The man saluted, blinking to hide surprise. Jodos caught a quick flash of the man's thoughts: *Tonios? Lucky beggar. Hardly the best man for a delicate job. Don't argue with the King. What's it about? What's the King doing up this early? Special mission? Something to do with Portona most likely, or Mahapol. The King is on the job . . .*

"See to it that the hall is kept quiet so I can sleep," said

Jodos. "I've been missing sleep trying to get the problems of the kingdom under control. And I didn't get to rest much yesterday."

As he turned back to his room, he could read in the Captain's mind a certain grudging respect that swallowed up any doubts he might have had, and a determination that the hard-working King should get his rest—coupled with a healthy fear of Chondos' well-known temper.

Jodos smiled as he slipped back into his room, and began to strip off his robe. He crawled into bed and soon drifted off to sleep.

Pain lanced Istvan's side as his blade flickered through a sunbeam. He pressed his lips tight to stifle a gasp, and went on to the next motion without a break. He was doing one of the simpler training-dances from one of the old Capiero schools—all one-handed stuff, which he had expected would spare his injured side.

He tried to clear the pain and irritation from his mind, to let nothing come between him and his sword. Each stroke should be a meditation. The blade glittered in the sunlight as it lifted over his head in a guard and then whistled around in the counter-cut. The smell of garden flowers was sweet in his nostrils.

I want to greet the morning for another hundred years . . .

You'd be awfully old, he told himself mockingly. *Go look for immortality in the marketplace and see what the going price is like.*

I don't want to die, or grow old.

A little late to keep from growing old, he thought. *The only cure for old age is death.*

His blade whispered ceaselessly in the air. *Each stroke should be a meditation.* A fresh breeze blew the scent of the sea from the north. The mind came between the soul and the sword, and the two must be one. Fear of death, most of all, cut one off from one's sword, made one hesitate at the wrong time and lose . . .

But that was the wrong approach, for once again that made staying alive important. Where, in fact, the important thing was not to care whether you lived or died. *The secret of true swordsmanship is the calm acceptance of death.*

To try to conquer fear of death that one might fight better and thus live longer was foolish and self-defeating. To strive to live was to fear death. And he had striven for too long. His skill as a swordsman had been bent to keeping himself alive, and his fame had come because he had gotten so good at staying alive. Hence, what he was famous for was his cowardice.

The thought amused him; he had early decided that fame was a worthless attainment. But spiritual surety in the face of death . . . His blade drove out a long lunge, and pain again ripped his side as he recovered. He hissed through his teeth and swore silently.

Pain only hurts if you fear it, he thought, and then it was only another sensation, one which vanished quickly. The conquest of pain and fear: that was the true mastery. That was more important than just staying alive.

Someone shouted his name, and he whirled, sword ready. Cousin Firencio was running towards him. Habit wiped the blade and sheathed it while Istvan waited for his cousin's approach.

"Fight between the guards at the Rivermasters' Guild and a bunch of Bordermen . . ." Firencio was breathing hard, out of breath. "Jagat's son was killed. Hansio's too. They just brought in the bodies . . ."

Jodos had almost dropped off to sleep when there came a pounding at his door. He did not have to feign anger or look into his brother's mind for suitable insults.

Lord Taticos was at the door, still in his night-robe, wringing his hands. "Lord King, a terrible thing has happened!" he began, his voice trembling. "There was a fight between the guards you ordered set over the merchants' feast and—a group of Bordermen got drunk and tried to break in—some of them were killed and one of them was Prince Hansio's son, which will mean war for certain, and one—one of the others was Pirthio. I'm sorry . . ."

Jodos stood silent, trying to learn from his brother's mind what his reaction should be. Taticos misread his silence. "I wish I hadn't had to tell you. I know he was your friend. It must be a shock—"

Jodos was confused by the reactions he saw. He did not understand. But as Chondos' mind told him what this could mean to the kingdom, he had to repress a savage smile of triumph. This was better than anything he had dared hope for!

"Lord Jagat will be . . ." Taticos shook his head. "He worshipped the boy. His only heir, too, except for that niece of his. The bodies are in the South Chamber. You must send a particularly nice message of—of—sorrow, to—to poor Lord Jagat."

"Lead on," said Jodos.

He followed Taticos down the hall, his head spinning as he tried to absorb the incredible things he found in Chondos' mind.

He could not believe it. Why should Jagat be sorry that this outgrowth of his body, escaped from his control, had died? It seemed he would not even eat the body! It made no sense! It must be some monstrous game they played with each other, an agreed-on false front to hide their true feelings.

Yet, there it was, undeniable, unfeigned, in his brother's mind: Chondos had *grieved* for his father's death.

He let that grief flow into the front of his mind, to make an effective screen for his thoughts, trying to understand the situation fate had thrown him. If what his brother's memories told him of human reactions was true, this was a great chance . . . But it *could not be* true!

He was very frightened! This was a chance he could not allow to pass; yet, here also was a terrible trial of his ability to fool them into thinking he was Chondos. If he failed, if he let them realise his true identity, the Blue-robes would come, the Hasturs would put fire on him, he would burn . . . But his mission must not fail. He must accomplish it quickly, while the Great Ones kept the Blue-robes occupied elsewhere, or they would find out about him anyway.

Haste! He buried himself in his brother's mind, attempting to discover a way he might accomplish his end without giving them reason to suspect he was not Chondos.

He followed Lord Taticos into the South Chamber, and there were the corpses, waxen-skinned and cold. They reminded him that he was hungry. He let Chondos' remembered grief for his father shape the movements of his face, as he picked out the body of Pirthio.

"Who are the others?" he asked. There were seven.

"We don't know yet, Sire," one of the soldiers nearby answered. "Prince Hansio's son and Lord Jagat's are the ones we recognised; none of the others is so well known, though someone said that one there"—he pointed—"looks like the son of one of the Lords of western Manjipé. Maybe some of the prisoners will be able to tell us who the rest of them are."

"You took prisoners?"

"Yes, Sire. Old DiFlacca and some of his men managed to knock out several of them—"

"Good. Lock them up. Make them talk. Have them—" He stopped, suddenly aware that if he ordered the prisoners beaten or flayed, they would know him at once. That would be against the Blue-robes' laws. "Have them questioned very carefully. I want to know what this was all about," he said, and then wisely shut his mouth and stood gazing down at Pirthio's body, feigning grief.

"Sire?" One of the soldiers was beside him suddenly. "We were about to take Lord Pirthio's body to his father. Do you wish us to deliver a message from you?"

"Yes, Lord King," came Taticos' voice from behind him, "you must help Lord Jagat in his sorrow. He was ever your good and faithful servant."

Jodos came to a decision. This grief for cells that escaped from control was still too new, but Chondos' distrust of Lord Jagat was a thing he understood. He let his brother's sneer come onto his face, and chose his words carefully from Chondos' stock.

"Good and faithful servants," he said, "see that the King's Peace is kept! Tell Lord Jagat *this* from me—" He turned to the soldier, his strange eyes dark and terrible. "Your son has died in open defiance of the Crown. Let this be a lesson to all who might endanger the peace of this kingdom. Let Lord Jagat remember it well—"

Taticos gasped in horror.

"And let him beware of a like fate! I charge you deliver that message, in just those words!"

The soldier had gone pale as the corpse by which he stood. "But Lord King!" he whispered. "That is no message for a grieving father! Surely—"

"You will deliver the message in exactly those words!" said

Jodos, his brother's voice coming firm and kingly from his lips. He fixed the man's eyes with his own. "Exactly those words, do you understand?" For a moment, from habit, he began to lay a compulsion upon the man; then, remembering that there might be Seers about who could tell what he was doing, he stopped. But the man would obey him.

"But—but Lord!" came Taticos' whimpering voice, and Jodos whirled to face him. In his brother's memories, he had found the exact phrase for this occasion, a line Chondos had rehearsed over and over in his head during his bad moods, awaiting the day to use it.

"I will not argue with a dotard! I am King here, not you! I will be obeyed, not chided!"

Lord Taticos shrank back before him, and Jodos' lips curled in Chondos' sneer. Suddenly he froze, panic shooting through him. A man had entered the room, who wore at his side a sword of living flame. Jodos fought down the shuddering terror that could have betrayed him, searching his stolen mind for clues to guide his action.

So—this was Istvan DiVega, his father's cousin. A great warrior with a Hastur-blade at his side. He knew that he had nothing to fear from the blade unless it was unsheathed against him; he differed from his masters in his ability to approach and survive that terrible power. But he did not yet feel ready for that test.

He turned back to the soldier. "Well, what are you waiting for? Get on with it! Take the body away! Go!" He watched the men and his companions move towards the body of Pirthio, then swung on Lord Taticos again.

"I am going back to my room, to sleep and to . . . grieve." *Was that right? Would Chondos have said that?* "Do not disturb me. I must be alone." He hesitated, examining his stolen mind for things to say, to make the illusion perfect. "Later, we will decide what message to send Prince Hansio." But there was no more time, for that burning terror was coming closer and closer. He turned abruptly and strode out of the room, keeping himself from running by force of will.

"He said *what?*" DiVega's voice was strained, incredulous.
"He said the boy had died in defiance of the Crown. That it

should be a lesson for Jagat to remember and beware. Lord Istvan, I fear that the King has gone mad—that his grief for his friend has turned his mind! This message . . ." But Istvan had already turned away.

"You there!" Istvan shouted, gesturing. The tall soldier to whom he pointed came to attention, and as Istvan gestured impatiently, hurried over.

"Go after those men, the ones who just left with the body. Catch up with them and tell their commander he is *not* to deliver that message. Do you understand? On my authority! Hurry!"

The man saluted and was gone, running rapidly out the door. Istvan thought of the King as he had seen him a few moments before, pale and agitated. Then he turned back to Taticos, and said, "Firencio told me that Prince Hansio's son was also killed. Which one is he?"

He followed Taticos to where the body of a big-boned man lay, caked blood from the wound in his chest covering the front of his tunic.

"You're sure this is the one?" Istvan asked sharply. "No mistake?"

Taticos nodded. "I've met him myself. And five other men have recognised him since he was brought in. That's Tunno of Mahapor."

Istvan shook his head sadly, and stood silent, but his mind was busy. He knew the signs of war when he saw them. He must speak to Lord Shachio, and quickly; must get messages to the commander of every Seynyorean force in the Border country. That meant Shachio would have to contact the Seers of Manjipor and Mahapor, Ekakin, Udapor, Inagar, Anutapor . . . His head swam as he tried to remember them all.

Turning to Firencio, he said, "I'll need information from the records. The location of every company in the Border provinces. Everything south of the Oda and Hinarion."

"It's war, then?" the young man asked.

"War?" Istvan laughed grimly. "When this news reaches the Border, Seynyoreans will suddenly be very unpopular with these poor dead boys' friends and kinsmen."

"Revenge?" Firencio was still very young.

Istvan sighed. "I don't care how many sermons you've

heard about the virtues of forgiveness and the futility of revenge. If you had a son, and his body was in front of you, you'd find every word had vanished from your head."

"So you want all our men out of Mahapor."

"Manjipé too. Even Lord Jagat is not likely to have any strong love for Seynyoreans after this; especially if any hint of that *stupid* message . . ." He broke off, wondering exactly what it was that idiot boy had said—Taticos *must* have garbled it, somehow—and what he had really meant.

Chondos and Jagat's boy had been very close. He had looked very pale and upset, and had almost run out of the room as Istvan had come in. On the heels of his father's death, and with all the strain of yesterday . . .

"Lord Istvan?" It was Taticos, at his elbow. "Do you think we should go talk with the King? Perhaps—"

"Let the boy rest," said Istvan. "If we put any more strain on him, he may really go mad. And then who would hold this mess together?" *Not that the boy's done a very good job so far.*

He would have to contact the more distant forces first, get them all out fast. Have them assemble at Ojaini—that should be safe enough, and it was a strong strategic point, useful if the borderers did rise. Once they'd joined up, it would take quite an army to tackle all the companies in the south. And after he had all the companies marching, perhaps it would be best if *he* sent the message to notify Prince Hansio. *We regret to inform you . . . We join in your sorrow . . . We have sad news . . . Your son and heir, Tunno . . . killed by the guards at a feast of the Rivermasters' Guild . . .*

Yes, that was it! *Killed by the guards of merchants from Portona and other cities*—not mentioning the nationalities of the guards, nor specifying that they were employed by the Crown. If nothing else, it would gain time, time to get his men out, avert a massacre. And at best, it would strain and weaken whatever ties existed between Mahapor and the Portona faction. It might even avert the war entirely. But he had little hope of that.

"Where is Palos DiFlacca? I want to hear *exactly* what happened?"

"Did you hear? It's all over the palace. There was a fight at the Guildhall last night and a lot of the Border nobility got

killed. Somebody named DiVega got both Jagat's son and Prince Hansio's son . . ."

Jodos lay rigid on his bed. He must sleep, if only for a little while. He must sort out his brother's mind, find out how he should speak, how he should act . . .

Sleep crept over him in spite of his fear, and he found himself having the dream again. There was the woman, screaming as the skin was stripped away from her belly and breasts, and he was trying to stop them, but there were men all around him—giants, big men more than twice as tall as he was, men whose hands covered his whole face as they hurled him back, and he went on fighting them (*why?*), hitting out with his little fists but having no effect; there was water in his eyes and he struggled and struggled and his heart was choked up and hurting . . . (*Grief!* The mysterious emotion these Sun People felt! He was feeling it in his dream, had always, but had never known what it was before!) . . . and they carried him away where he could no longer see the woman, and someone brought him a piece of meat . . . it was good, raw and bloody . . . the screaming was dying away . . .

A part of his mind that was somehow outside of the dream recognised the shape of the piece of meat, concluded that it must be a piece of one of the woman's breasts. It had been good. There had still been milk in it.

"It must have been part of some plot. I reckon Prince Hansio's son got a bunch of men together to try and kill DiVega, and somehow got Jagat's son to join in with them. They've been very close the last few weeks—I've seen them together all over the city. So they jumped DiVega, and of course he killed them. He's the greatest swordsman in the world, you know . . ."

Duke Thoros heard the rumour soon after he rode into the castle that morning, and smiled. Rioting already? Fortuitous, and a good omen, perhaps. But nothing to change his plans about. His retainers all wore great cloaks over their livery, and as they entered the palace they began to remove them. The corridor being deserted for a moment, except for a guard whose vision was quickly obstructed by retainers, Sandor removed his cloak, revealing Prince Phillipos' livery beneath.

"Remember," the Duke whispered, taking the cloak and throwing it over his arm, "the King frequently goes to the garden alone. But sometimes Istvan the Archer is with him. Stay away from him."

Sandor's lip curled. "I can handle DiVega!" he hissed.

The Duke schooled himself to patience. "Maybe, maybe not," he answered softly. "But not DiVega and the King both. The King himself is a fine swordsman, by all accounts. And it's *him* you've got to kill, not DiVega! Now, the horse will be ready in the courtyard. The moment it's done, head for the docks."

Sandor snorted. "I know what to do. Never fear."

He walked in the opposite direction, through the clustered ranks of the Duke's attendants. The guard, looking up, saw a man in Phillipos' livery walk out of the mob of retainers Ipazema had brought with him today, and assumed without a thought that the man had come down from the far end of the hall on some business of his master's. The man nodded and smiled as he passed, and since the face was familiar, the guard nodded back.

"Lord Tunno is dead!"

"No! It cannot be true! How . . . ?"

"Istvan DiVega killed him. Istvan the Archer. A whole lot of other men, too: young Rutnos and Jal of Ojadom and Ditar . . ."

"We'd better get out of the city. We've got to tell the Prince."

Jodos woke trembling, covered with sweat, and shuddered for a time. It did not seem that he could sleep—he didn't *want* to sleep anymore. He had work to do, anyway. He began to dig into his brother's mind, but somehow the dream kept disturbing him. He remembered—and it puzzled him—his discovery of the emotion of grief, coupled with the more familiar one of fear. But he did not understand why he should feel grief at a woman's coming to her fate. And she *had* tasted good.

His brother's memories must have intruded into the dream, he decided. The dream must have changed. Surely *he* could not have felt any such emotion! He had never in his life felt sorry for anyone—certainly not for food! And what else were women good for? He strove to bury himself in his brother's memories. He must be seen to be up and stirring during the day.

Chapter Nine

Martos was slowly and happily pulling on his clothes, while Mirrha stripped ruined sheets from the bed. They heard excited voices and a clatter of feet, and then a pounding on the door.

Kumari's voice shouted Martos' name. She threw herself through the opening door into his arms; he saw her face wet with tears before it vanished against his chest.

"Suktio came—and Hamir of Inagar. They say—they say there's been a fight—" Kumari's voice broke in a kind of squeal. "Pirthio—they say—Pirthio's *dead!*"

He pulled her closer, and she burrowed her face into the cloth of his tunic like a frightened child. Mirrha gasped behind him.

"How can it be true?" Kumari sobbed. "How could this happen so far from the Border? There are no Dark Things *here!* Just *people!*" she babbled, wildly. "Why would *they* hurt Pirthio?"

They hired men to kill Jagat, he thought, but he could not speak. His palm thumped awkwardly on her back. A numb lump in his chest made it hard to breathe.

The floor below echoed with a drumming on the door. Voices stopped. She stiffened in his arms; tear-filled eyes met his. He stretched away from her, to lift his sword from the floor by the bed. Mirrha sat crying, a blanket draped around her.

With one arm Martos held Kumari close as they walked to the stair; his other hand held the scabbarded sword, ready to fling the sheath off in a moment. The only sound on the floor below was footsteps, and then the creaking of the door.

At the head of the stairs Kumari huddled shuddering in the crook of Martos' arm. Four men were marching through the door below, carrying a long, cloth-wrapped burden. Two more men followed. They all wore sombre Seynyorean doublets. Martos saw Suktio and Hamir of Inagar seize the hilts of their swords, crouching tensely.

The Seynyoreans removed their hats. Jagat came into sight, walking towards the long bundle the men had laid on the floor. His arm stretched out, stopped, hesitant, then twitched back the cloth. Pirthio's face stared up empty-eyed, a long gash under his chin. Dried blood coated his face and shoulders. Martos felt Kumari shiver under his arm, but she did not look away.

Jagat reached out to touch the dead boy's face. "My little son!" His voice was shrill and broken. "Only a few years ago you were so proud of your first toy sword." Tears rained down the weathered face as he spoke. He was not talking to anyone, Martos realised, but the old man must do something with his mouth, or he would scream.

Suktio was glaring like a snake about to strike. Jagat's grey head lifted. "Who . . . ?" He shook his head. His voice was lifeless. "Tell me how my son died."

"It was a mistake, an accident!" a tall, anxious Seynyorean answered shrilly. "No one meant it to happen. Guards at the Guildhall thought they were attacked, and nobody knows how it . . ." The voice died away before Jagat's stare.

But as Jagat looked down again, one of the others, a dark, burly man, straightened like a puppet on strings, staring glassy-eyed, and spoke. "There was a message . . ." His voice was strange and strained, as though he spoke against his will. "A message from—the King."

Martos saw the tall man who had spoken before whirl as if struck, gesturing emphatically, but Jagat was looking into the dead face, and did not see.

"Earth must be fed," Jagat's voice quavered. "Tell me. What message does—my son's friend, who is my King, send to me?"

The tall soldier seized the other, as though to silence him by force, but the strained voice rose unheeding. "The King says—tell Lord Jagat—your son has died in open defiance of the Crown. Let this be a lesson to all who might endanger the peace of this kingdom! Let Lord Jagat remember it well—"

The voice broke oddly, then went on: "And let him beware of a like fate!" The speaker stood stupidly, while his companion shook him.

All stood in shocked silence. Martos heard Suktio's breath hiss through his teeth, saw Hamir's fingers whiten on his sword-hilt. With a strangled cry Jagat leaped to his feet, hauling out his sword.

The burly man stood blinking stupidly at the sharp steel swinging at his head. The man who had been shaking him heaved him out from under the falling edge and pushed him towards the door.

"No!" the tall man shouted, as other Seynyoreans tugged at their swords, "Don't fight! Just get out!"

They ran, Jagat close behind, hewing clumsily, as though he held an axe instead of a sword. Suktio and Hamir followed Jagat, swords drawn.

The last Seynyorean dodged through the door under a slash that buried Jagat's blade deep in the wood of the doorpost. Jagat wrenched the weapon free, but stopped at the threshold. Suktio and Hamir rammed into his back, but he stood staring out into the street, blocking the door. Slowly he turned, and the two gave way before his terrible stare. He strode to Pirthio's bier, and hurled his sword the length of the room. Jagat fell to his knees. His hand trembled as he pushed a lock of hair from the cold forehead. "My son, my little boy," he said—horribly, Martos thought, as though Pirthio were still alive, and a little child again, a child needing comfort. "Pay them no heed. Do not let their words grieve you." A shriek began to build in his voice. "I shall take such a vengeance that men shall shudder to remember, a thousand years from now! A river of blood shall pay for that wound!"

"Do you have *any* idea what started it?" Istvan asked.

"Drink!" Palos DiFlacca snorted. "They were all as drunk as magpies! Too much wine and pride, that's all! They never thought anyone would dare fight *them*. If that fool cousin of yours had been posted somewhere else, those—"

"Lord DiFlacca!"

Turning, they saw, rushing from the room where the dead men lay, a young man whose faded red Border robes were less threadbare than most. Strings of wooden beads—priceless on the Border—were looped around his throat; his dark face was troubled.

"I came to see if it was true," he said as he caught up with them. "Fire Immortal! Poor Tunno! And they tell me Pirthio, too, was killed. Flesh of the Earth! And to think, I could have stopped them!"

Istvan stared, and DiFlacca, seeing that look, quickly stepped to the Borderman's side. "My Lord DiVega, let me present Rinmull, the Lord of Ojaini. That is the Kantara's big city, down near the Border."

"I know where Ojaini is," said Istvan. "I've been there. Long ago. The Lord of the City back then was named . . ." He paused a moment, then remembered. "Purunos. Your father?"

Rinmull shook his head. "My grandfather." He turned to DiFlacca. "Some of my men were with them, and have not returned. I did not find them"—he gestured—"in there. Has anyone besides Pirthio been taken away?"

"No," said DiFlacca. "The rest are all there. Except for the prisoners. There were some we captured."

"Come with us, Lord Rinmull," said Istvan, quickly. "We are on our way to speak with them, now." *And with you there, they may answer,* he hoped silently.

The woven eyes of ancient warriors on the tapestries watched out of history as they marched down the long dim corridors.

"What did you mean back there," said Istvan, after a few moments, "when you said you could have stopped them? Can you tell us what they were doing?"

"No, not really," said Rinmull, slowly. "I was visiting a lady. When I came back to the Satragara, only the Kantara men were there. They said the others had all gone with Prince Tunno to fetch more wine."

"What?" exclaimed DiFlacca.

"It all sounded very foolish," said Rinmull. "The Massadessan wine had run out. Prince Tunno said they were going to get more wine at the Guildhall. My men—only a few went. Most were sensible enough to see there would be trouble, but . . ." His voice and his hands jumped. "No one expected anything like *this!* They didn't expect to fight! They were too drunk to fight! Too drunk to walk, almost!"

Istvan nodded, frowning, and they continued in silence until guards from DiFlacca's company passed them into the large, bare room, where a dozen young men lay moaning on mats.

"There's one of them, anyway!" Rinmull said.

They followed him to the side of a thin youth whose brown robes, though patched and worn, seemed of newer if plainer fabric than those of the men on either side. As they came up, a handsome dark face lifted, with a clicking of beads, from the cradling hands.

"Ajesio!" Rinmull said. "What are you doing here? What happened?"

"Don't shout!" the unhappy Borderer said, wincing. "I don't remember. Oh, Mother Earth! No!" he gasped, and his face changed. He stared at Rinmull in shock. "Prince Tunno is dead, isn't he? He was going to help me marry Sumitri! Pirthio too . . . Oh, Blessed Earth!" He hid his face in his hands again, and rocked back and forth.

"But what was it all about?" asked Rinmull. Ajesio raised his head, and twined his fingers together.

"It was . . ." he shrugged. "It was a joke! We were just—the wine ran out. And Tunno said—he'd been wondering how a merchant could run with so much lard, and—and what they looked like when they did. So we were going to give those fat traitors a good scare, and then—and then I saw Pirthio and Tunno, lying there, bleeding and—and—I was going to fight and—somebody hit me over the head." His bloodshot eyes suddenly focussed on DiFlacca. "You! It was you!"

He tried to heave himself up, but Rinmull wrestled him down. "That's enough, Ajesio!" The Lord of Ojaini's voice was firm. "This idiocy has broken the King's Peace. Now you must await the King's mercy!"

Ajesio subsided. Rinmull rose scowling, and began to search the room for his other missing men.

"A prank!" Istvan heard DiFlacca mutter under his breath. "A stupid, drunken prank!"

"I won't stay here!" Jagat's voice had changed again. He sounded like a petulant child. "I want to go home!"

"Yes, Uncle," Martos heard Kumari's voice answer from beside him, "but first Earth must be fed. First we must—"

"No!" he snarled. "We'll take him home first!"

"Uncle, we *can't!*" cried Kumari, and other voices rose around them. But Jagat's drowned them all.

"We'll take him home!"

Martos shuddered at the thought of the long ride, and in this heat . . .

"Of course we'll take the ashes back to the land, Uncle," said Kumari. "But we must perform the rites here!"

"No!" said Jagat. "I'll take my boy home! We'll buy a box from the Suppliers' Guild. It *can* be done! I'm not mad! Not yet! But I'll *not* stay to burn my boy in the city of the ungrateful dog for whom he gave his life! The dog who calls him traitor! I'll serve that dog no more, nor spend again the lives of my people to hold for that dog a throne he does not deserve!"

Hamir's and Suktio's eyes met. Jagat did not see that look; but Martos did, and icy rage knotted the muscles of his jaw.

Has that made it worthwhile to you now? he thought. *Is an old man's agony justified if it leads him to your so-noble cause?*

Lord Andrios was exultant: Duke Thoros heard his voice far down the hall. Outside the door, the Duke stopped and waited, listening.

". . . and we'll see action at last!" he heard Andrios say. "Old Hansio won't sit still now! The days of tyranny are over! We rise—all the cities rise—the moment Hansio moves! Then we'll throw the tax-gatherers out, and the Guild-Council will rule over free Portona, as in our fathers' time!"

"Rise? Throw the tax-gatherers out? *With what?*" Lord Dimetrios answered. Duke Thoros had to listen more carefully; Dimetrios' voice was not as loud. "Our Seynyoreans have turned against us; our Carrodians want to cancel their contracts! What do we have left, now, to rise *with?*"

"The people, of course! The folk of the towns will drive out the servants of the tyrant! What's wrong with you?"

"The people," sneered Dimetrios. "Of course! Wild mobs *always* defeat trained soldiery—in children's tales! What's the matter with *me?* I think you're out of your mind! As well as too pleased over Hansio's son being killed! If Hansio could hear you gloating like that—"

"Well, he can't! I don't understand you! The tyrant is

doomed! he's lost Jagat's support, and with Hansio after his blood—"

"I suppose it hasn't occurred to you that it may be *our* blood Hansio comes after?"

"What are you talking about?" Andrios sounded confused.

"It was at *our* feast that the fight took place. Tunno was leading an attack on *us!* Once word of *that* reaches his father, he may forget the King, and come after us instead! Then what?"

"Then it will be the King's duty to protect us!"

Duke Thoros smiled. He heard Dimetrios laugh.

"And what if Ipazema's pet swordsman kills the King? Who will protect us then against Hansio and his Bordermen?"

"We'll hire mercenaries."

"With the money we've saved in taxes? What is the difference between hiring outlanders to protect us, and paying the same amount to the King?"

"Lord Dimetrios! I am surprised at you!" Andrios' voice was indignant now. "Mercenaries will not presume to tell us how to run our city! And the taxes to pay them will be levied by the rightful heads of the guilds. Why—"

Duke Thoros coughed loudly, and stepped into the room. He scowled at them as they turned and stared. Deliberately, he curled his lip. "Fine conspirators you make!" he snarled. "Shouting treason at the top of your lungs, naming names and giving details of plots so loudly I could hear you all the way down the hall! I'd drop the whole lot of you fools right now, but you'd get caught and give me away!"

They shrank back from his glaring eyes, and he had to hide a cynical smile. They were in the palm of his hand.

"I gather you've heard the news about Jagat's son," he said, "but you may not have heard—though the palace is buzzing with it—that the message Chondos sent to Jagat lacked even his usual tact. Called Jagat a traitor, or something. The rumour has grown, of course, but one third of Lord Dimetrios' tripod is gone. The other rumour that is all over the city is that Istvan the Archer killed those young idiots!"

"DiVega?" Andrios exclaimed. "He wasn't even there!"

"I didn't say I believed it! But if I were you, I'd spread that story as far as I could, and be *sure* the story reaches Mahapor!"

* * *

Sad men rode from the city behind Lord Jagat. Four horses bore the supply box, airtight and watertight, of the kind used for shipping food and wine. Martos marvelled at the speed and efficiency with which the Borderers had moved. He had not had time to unpack his big sword or the rest of his war gear, except for the needle-sword, whose hilt rose from the saddle-scabbard by his right thigh.

Hamir of Inagar and his men had joined them, making a force of fifty fighting men. They did not take the Ojaini road, but followed a narrow street to the docks, and were poled across the broad Pavana's waters. On the Orissian bank they turned south: a straighter route, but rougher, and seldom travelled.

Martos worried. As they had packed, he had come up to Kumari and put his arm around her, meaning only to comfort her, and she had torn herself away with an exasperated *Not now!* that left him confused and hurt, not understanding.

Jodos, bathed and dressed, moved through the alien life of the castle, controlling his panic with the ease of long practise, listening to his brother's ghost in his brain as it told him how to act.

He smiled at the right times and places, gave appropriate ritual answers to greetings, and avoided talking to anyone for too long. He studied the minds around him, trying to judge his performance. Most, he saw, thought him exhausted from the Coronation, or distressed by Pirthio's death. All thought he acted strange—he carefully noted why, in order to perfect his role—but none suspected the truth.

Fear subsided. The idea never entered their minds; they were all too stupid to even imagine the substitution! But he avoided scrupulously the castle Healers and Lord Shachio.

The sheer numbers of people became terrifying. He remembered that his brother had often fled to the solitude of the garden, and made his way there. It was filled with detestable life. His brother's mind assured him it was all harmless, but the wariness which had kept him alive through long years in the Shadow made him keep a cautious eye on grass and leaf, bird, insect, and flower.

The light was much too bright. He sat fastidiously on a

bench in the shade, and studied his brother's mind. Lord Shachio was his chief danger. He must find a way to take over the Seer's mind—carefully, tracelessly . . .

He was suddenly aware of hostile eyes. Without turning, he studied the thoughts of the man coming up behind him. Coming close, to kill him. Booted feet moved unhurriedly over the grass, on a course carefully chosen to pass the bench—just close enough. The man's mind revealed a leap, a turn, a cut—it was all very prettily planned.

Jodos considered. He would have to kill the man. A pity, in a way; this Sandor could have been useful. It had been three years since the Blue-robe's finger had reached out to trace that mark on his forehead *(blood, screaming, a headless woman's body . . .)*, and this man, surviving by his wits and his sword, had had much time to build hatred since he'd abandoned the faint hope that he might redeem himself fighting on the Border . . .

Sandor had almost reached his goal. Another step and he would jump and draw, his steel spinning out across the throat of the unsuspecting figure on the bench. And no one was in sight! There would be time to escape unseen, perhaps even time to find Prince Phillipos, earn a little extra . . . He tensed for the jump.

Jodos rose, turning, and seized the man's eyes with his own. Sandor staggered, his hand locked to the sword-hilt. Jodos smiled, studying the image of the Duke of Ipazema in Sandor's mind, guessing the Duke's plans from Sandor's memories of things the Duke had said.   Sandor's sword pulled free with a desperate jerk. His gaze still trapped in those huge, dark eyes, he lurched forward one stumbling step, and then another, knowing he must kill to get free. Jodos enjoyed his struggles, and pulled his own sword, watching the trapped mind closely. He allowed Sandor to raise his sword. That would fit his plan. He would let his prey aim one stroke, and then . . .

When it came, the cut was so sudden and swift that Jodos barely stumbled aside. The trained sword-arm was almost free of the mind. Jodos pushed his blade out, set it between the ribs under Sandor's arm, and leaned against it.

Sandor's scream brought men running from all over the castle, to see the King pull his bloody sword from the body on the grass. The Captain of the Royal Guard expected a tongue-lashing, and Jodos gave him one, picking it almost word for word out of his mind. The Captain turned slowly red, then white, while Jodos watched his mind with great curiosity. When he had finished, he ordered the man to place Prince Phillipos under arrest. Lord Taticos, who stood wringing his hands behind him, started to protest.

"Whose livery is that?" said Jodos angrily, pointing the bloody sword at the corpse.

"It is the Prince's, Sire, but—"

"Prince Phillipos first—*then* we look for others!" He glanced quickly around, picked out a Seynyorean officer who stood nearby.

"You! Take your men and arrest Lord Jagat." Unspoken protests whirled half-formed in the man's mind, but he saluted and left.

Taticos made a small, strangled sound.

Istvan DiVega breathed out a long sigh.

"Why," he asked, resignedly, "did you deliver that message?"

"I—I don't know, sir." Lucarrho D'Estarras shook his dark head. "I—I couldn't disobey the King, sir! I meant to, I was standing there with my mouth shut and then—then it was just as though he was standing there watching me, and—and—I'm sorry, sir!"

"Inability to disobey orders when the circumstances require," said Istvan, slowly, "is a great weakness." Breath hissed explosively from his throat. "I suppose it shows the boy has *some* talent for ruling. What *was* the message exactly? Word for word?"

D'Estarras' eyes widened in a stare. "Your son has died in open defiance of the Crown," he said, his voice harsh. "Let this be a lesson to all who might endanger the peace of this kingdom! Let Lord Jagat remember it well . . ." He paused a moment. "And let him beware of a like fate!"

Istvan blinked. The man must have gotten it wrong; surely even Chondos could not be so heartless, so stupid! There was something strange about D'Estarras' eyes. Was the man under a compulsion? Did Chondos have *that* power? DiVega blood,

with Border blood on the other side. He would have to talk to
Lord Shachio—

Firencio DiVega burst into the room. "The King killed an
assassin in the garden! A man in Prince Phillipos' livery.
He's ordered the Prince arrested."

"I'll be right with you!" said Istvan. "D'Estarras! I'll need to
talk to you again, later."

"D'Estarras?" said Firencio, snapping his fingers. "Lucarrho
D'Estarras, of DiFlacca's company?"

"Sir!"

"Fernan DiGarsa was looking for you," said Firencio. "He's
in a hurry."

Duke Thoros was calmly enjoying his wine when the man he
had left to keep watch at the castle came bursting in. The Duke
set down his cup. "You have news," he said, reaching for the
bell on the table before him. If the King was dead . . .

"King Chondos has killed an assassin, Lord!" The man's
voice was shocked. "In the castle garden."

Duke Thoros' hand froze halfway to his bell. "An assassin?
What—" *Sandor?* Impossible! "How was he dressed?"

"Men say he wore Prince Phillipos' livery. Lord, the Prince
has been placed under arrest. I also heard that men have been
sent to the house of Lord Jagat."

The Duke's hand seized his bell, shook it furiously, then
groped for his goblet. Chondos could not have killed Sandor!
Even Olansos in his prime could not have matched the big
northerner! Phillipos under arrest! That would not last long.
But in the meantime, the north would be ripe and ready. And if
Jagat were placed under arrest . . .

The time for plotting, waiting for someone else to act, was
ended. Lutazema and Poidia would rise at his word. His stroke
had failed, but it had created a situation which a bold man
might seize. This was the time to dare and to do.

"Order my horse brought!" he said to the man summoned by
his bell. "Then give orders for the whole household to pack
and leave today. Everyone on board the ship by sundown!"

He poured himself more wine as the man departed,
schooling his nerves. There was no way to trace Sandor back
to him—but still, it would be well to be gone. His flight could

be taken as a sign of guilt, but the city was full of departing
nobles, and he had been deliberately vague about his plans.

He took a quick look around the room. He might never come
here again . . . Poidia. He snatched his riding cloak on the way
to the door. He should take Lord Enricos with him. The man
would be invaluable in making Poidia rise on time . . .

Lord Enricos, and then to Portona, and his ship!

Istvan stared at the dead face, amazed. "Heaven and Earth!"
he gasped. "That's—" He turned to one of the nearby guards.
"Fetch me a wet cloth."

The man blinked questioningly, but went. Istvan turned
back to the body, examining the face closely, pushing the hair
back from the forehead.

"You know him?" asked Firencio. "Who is it?"

Istvan tugged his beard, thoughtfully. "If I'm not mistaken,
that's Sandor Agloress. We'll know in a minute."

Firencio looked puzzled as the guard came back with a
dripping towel. "The Agloress family is pretty large," Firencio
said.

"You never heard about Sandor of Anganvar?" asked Istvan.
He took the cloth, and bending down began to rub the corpse's
forehead with it. When he lifted the towel away, the Sign of
Hastur stood plain on the skin.

Firencio whistled. "Anganvar! Yes! I remember now! Killed
a woman, didn't he? During that stupid feud between the
Agloress and the Levengur?"

Istvan nodded. "Wasn't content to kill his enemy—killed
the wife and had started after the children when his men
grabbed him. The best sword in Chilebinor, some said.
Chondos is better than I thought."

He examined the wound critically. "Unusual angle there—
must have sidestepped a cut and lunged under it. I'd have cut,
myself. Must have been a pretty fight."

"I sail tonight!" Duke Thoros said dramatically. "Join me on
my ship. The time has come!"

"You mean the King is dead?" Enricos looked startled.

"The kingdom is splitting in pieces," the Duke answered.
"Jagat and Phillipos have been blamed. The north is leaderless!

But delay may spoil all! Ride with me to my ship! Leave your servants to pack!" Watching Enricos closely, he saw his hesitation.

"Why?" said Enricos. "If things are going well—"

"Are you coming or not?" the Duke said. "I, at least, am ready to move! Lutazema, too, will rise; and if you join us, then success is sure. But if Phillipos frees himself and reaches the north before we do, or if your Councillors hem and haw, then Kalascor may keep you, for all I care! If you are coming, change your clothing and order your horse brought round! I sail at sunset, and wait for no man!"

"I am coming," said Enricos, and hurried off. The Duke drew a relieved, deep breath, and began to consider what words to use to explain the truth.

All day Jagat's party rode south through the broad wheat fields of Orissia at a gruelling pace. Martos guessed that they might well reach Massadessa by sundown, if the horses held out. Thrice Jagat had bartered for new horses to replace those that carried precious burden, but he could not arrange new mounts for so numerous a company. Martos hoped the horses could hold up.

When they had to dismount to walk the horses, Kumari and her women trudged through the heat with the rest, uncomplaining. Martos, worried, worked his way to her side, to ask if the pace was too hard.

"I'm fine," she said. "Worry about Mirrha, poor thing. She's still sore from last night."

"But—but—with the baby coming?"

She laughed at him. In the midst of mourning, laughter was strange, and good to hear. "Martos, the baby isn't coming for a long time yet! And it's pampered women who lie around that have a hard time!"

But the laughter left her face before long, and he saw the tears for Pirthio gathering again. He wanted to speak, but his tongue was up to its old tricks. They trudged in silence for a little while, and then she turned to him with a brave, forced smile.

"Go talk to Mirrha," she said, "You've hardly looked at her since this morning, and I'm sure she's suffering from all this walking and riding—last night's riding was hard enough!"

Guiltily Martos dropped back to where Mirrha limped beside her own horse. She did not complain. Border women never complained. He saw her bite her lip, and the tracks of tears were on her face. He wondered if she hated him for putting her through all this, for one night's pleasure.

She smiled at him. "My Lord?"

The surge of happiness in her voice shocked him. He swallowed, and cast about for something to say. Anything he said would be wrong. And his tongue was useless.

"My Lord?" she said again. "Is something wrong?" Her tone was worried; he realised she had seen his distress in his eyes.

He stuttered, trying to answer, but could not. But if he could not speak, he could act. He reached out, lifted her, and carefully swung her, sidesaddle, onto Warflame's back. The big horse tossed his head, but calmed as Martos thumped his shoulder and hummed soothingly. He caught her horse's rein and led both. She couldn't be more than half his weight, and Warflame was used to full armour. She sat, small and a little frightened, holding the saddle tightly.

"How can you think such a thing, Chondos? Even if Phillipos *wanted* the crown, he knows—and *you* know—that he could never hold it!" Princess Illissia was furious. Chondos' memory told Jodos why, but these peculiar attachments between humans made no sense. Even among the Pure-in-Blood, such aberrations were unknown.

"You always were a nasty, suspicious boy," she went on, "but to distrust your own sister! And do you really think him so foolish as to dress an assassin in his own livery?"

"People are always doing foolish things," said Jodos, seizing a phrase from Chondos' memory. Chondos' distrust of Phillipos was something he understood, but Chondos' feeling for this female—his *sister*—made no sense at all. *Sister!* It was a disgusting thought. He would have to eat her, of course, to bring matters into proper balance. But that must wait until the Great Ones came.

Had they both been of the Pure-in-Blood, custom would have demanded he spawn in her, because of the preposterous brevity of human life. But that shed no light on Chondos' curious softness for this creature. Nor did it explain why the

Sun People's custom demanded that he listen to her instead of having her beaten or killed. Chondos would never have resisted her this long.

"Forgive me, Sister," he said, pulling words from Chondos' mind. "In this confusion, I cannot tell which way to turn! Who is my enemy?"

"You *know* it is not Phillipos!"

He saw in her mind the intention to demand trial before the Blue-robes. That would reveal all.

"You are right, Sister." He hung his head. "I will order his release." *In my own good time,* he thought. It would be so useful to keep Phillipos locked away! But . . .

He felt need-fire singe the fringes of his mind. Illissia looked at him as he started, but he regained control instantly. For a second he'd thought the Blue-robes had found him, but it was only the fire of that terrible sword.

Istvan DiVega was striding towards him now, need-fire throbbing in the sheath at his side, a bright pain that hid his thoughts from Jodos' probing mind.

The Twin Suns dipped towards the thin black line that edged the far horizon. Martos watched. Ahead, water glimmered in the sunset rays: the Marunka at last. Beyond lay Massadessa, which was friendly soil. Its people came of Takkarian stock, and still had many ties with the Bordermen. Riding through Orissia, Martos had seen half-veiled hatred in many eyes. But perhaps in Massadessa they could rest.

Warflame was weary. Accustomed as he was to long rides, the powerful horse knew it was time to rest now, for grazing and grain, and his temper was short. Martos checked his hooves carefully at every brief halt. So far, Kadarin war-horses and tough Border ponies alike seemed to be holding up, but Martos knew they could not take too much more. Nor could the women. He looked back at Kumari, and poor Mirrha, and the others, and then at the thread of water ahead. The tiled roof of a large building glowed beyond a fringe of trees. At least the deadly heat was lessening.

He saw a stocky figure spur to Jagat's side, and heard Hamir's voice: "Where do we stop for the night, my Lord? At Acarsica?"

Jagat shook his head. "We do not stop until we reach Utasitra."

Martos saw Hamir straighten, and tried to remember where Utasitra was, and how far they had yet to go. Jagat had already driven them to cover twenty miles more than most people would count a day's journey. He frowned at the remembered map in his mind. He must be wrong! That would be nearly another half-day's journey! And with the horses so tired . . .

Jagat was nearly out of his mind with grief, he thought. He glanced again quickly at the women. Then, as he struggled with the thought, he heard hoofbeats drum in the distance. Turning, he saw horsemen behind them. Sunset sparked on mail.

Jodos wanted to run, to hide, as he felt power crackle at the edges of his mind. He forced himself to sit still, to remember that the blade could not harm him unless it was unsheathed, that he was in no danger as long as its owner did not guess what he was.

"Do you know who you killed out there?" Excitement filled Istvan's voice. "Sandor Agloress of Anganvar—a swordsman I would have taken thought before facing myself!"

"My brother has always been a good swordsman," said Princess Illissia, her eyes sparkling.

"An excellent swordsman, Lady," said Istvan, bowing, "out of all expectation!" He turned back to Jodos. "The poor fool was under Hastur's Ban—covered the mark with paint. He could have redeemed himself by service along the Border as other men have. Instead he seems to have gone further into crime. I imagine he was hired by the same people who sent the assassins to Jagat and me."

"Andrios and the Guildmasters of Portona," said the Princess, "and the Duke of Ipazema. Put *them* under arrest, Brother, and you'll be on the right track! Most likely it was Ipazema who dressed that man in our livery. He hates Phillipos, and wants Kalascor!"

"I don't want to stir up the coast any more than I have to," Jodos said. "Lord Mario is investigating the Guildmasters, and if we place Andrios under arrest—"

"You should worry less about offending your enemies and more about offending your friends, Brother!" Illissia snapped.

She swept out, and Jodos was alone with the flame of the sword. He groped uneasily through the dazzle of blinding power for the surface of Istvan's mind.

"I heard that you had Prince Phillipos arrested," DiVega said, looking after the departing Princess with a sigh. "I think, Sire, that perhaps—"

"I've ordered him released," Jodos lied.

"Good!" said Istvan with an emphatic nod. "It made sense to be cautious, but it isn't likely that whoever hired the assassin would dress him in his own livery. I remember, at the Council, that Lord Zengio reported that this Duke of Ipazema had been seen with a man in the Prince's livery. I think that may be important."

Jodos nodded, hoping the Duke was safe aboard his ship. His mind groped blindly through the fire of the sword.

"One other matter, Lord King," Istvan said; and through the veil of fire, Jodos glimpsed a bare room where men were moaning and holding their heads. "I've been talking to the prisoners Palos DiFlacca took. From what they say, it all started as a drunken joke, and they blundered into the guards without any intention or expectation of a fight. They thought the merchants would run like sheep." Now, through the blinding blaze, Jodos sensed the pulse of a question Istvan was hesitant to ask: the meaning of the message to Jagat. "They said that Pirthio was drunk as the rest," Istvan continued, "but that this was only one more of a series of pranks. I believe, my Lord, that Pirthio, your true friend from all that men have said, was trying for your sake to make trouble between Portona and the Border. I advise, Lord King, that we let these young men go. They are guilty of nothing beyond gross stupidity, and holding them, I fear, will only make matters worse between the Border and the Crown."

Jodos hesitated, wanting to refuse, then smiled. The story those young men would tell would not make the Crown any friends on the Border!

"Very well," he said. "Do as you see fit, Lord DiVega." He smirked to himself, and then Lord Taticos was standing in the door.

"Lord King? Is it true that you have ordered the release of Prince Phillipos? The Lady Illissia said—"

Jodos felt himself trapped. "Why, yes, yes!" He waved a hand, hiding the rage that filled him.

Jagat threw up his arm to signal the halt, and all sat waiting for the coming horsemen. There were not many, but they were riding fast. Martos wondered why his heart was pounding. Bandits would not bother this large a company of armed men . . .

Horses drew up, rearing. "We seek for Jagat, Lord of Damenco, in the King's name!" The voice that shouted had a Seynyorean accent.

"I am here!" Jagat shouted in answer. "What do you want of me?"

One horseman rode a little ahead of the rest. "In the King's name, Lord Jagat, I call upon you to ride back with us. These others may go their way, but we are under royal command to bring you before the King."

"Who are you?" Hamir shouted.

"Fernan DiGarsa, of Palos DiFlacca's company."

"I will not go," said Jagat.

Martos was counting the horsemen clumped in the twilight; he guessed there might be twenty, but could not be sure.

"The King has ordered you to return," said the Seynyorean, sighing. "If you do not come willingly, you will leave me no choice but to bring you by force." His voice did not sound happy.

Jagat's sword slid from its sheath. "Come, then, and take me."

Forty swords unsheathing made a sound like wind.

"Lord Jagat, this is treason," DiGarsa said; but he sat his horse calmly, and neither he nor any of his men reached for a weapon. "You are two for each of us, and it would be folly for us to attack. But my orders—and I will admit freely that I do not like them—require me to bring you before the King, and so we shall be back. If you then come peacefully with us, much bloodshed will be saved—" Shouted insults from the Border-men interrupted him, but he sat stolidly while voice drowned voice, and as the shouting died down, said only, "Think well what I have said, Lord Jagat," and turned to ride back to his men.

A fresh chorus of insult followed him, but his erect back never flinched. In a moment all of his men were in motion, riding towards the west.

"They'll get reinforcements at Karion!" exclaimed Lord Hamir, standing in his stirrups.

"Let them!" Suktio shouted. "We're ready for them!"

Martos turned quickly to Valiros, his tongue struggling for the words of the order he must give. They must stop now, unpack their war-gear, prepare to fight.

"Ride on!" said Lord Jagat.

"It's getting late," said Enricos, with a glance at the darkening sky. The Duke of Ipazema nodded, stifling the rage that boiled within him. His eyes kept scanning the wharves for signs of soldiery.

He told himself he was not afraid; that it was only war-horse eagerness that drove him to impatience. They could not trace him! Once those fools arrived with the baggage, he could cast off and laugh at them all. He paced the deck of his ship, and watched the sky.

"Ipazema," said Enricos, "you could talk a stone to your point of view! Every one of your plans has gone awry! Yet here I am, ready to sail with you—staking my fortune and that of my city on a hazard of your choosing." The Duke glared at him dourly, and the merchant shrugged. "Well, treason is always a risk. I wish you'd told me your plot had failed."

"Would you have come if I had?" said the Duke. "I had no time to stand and argue. But my plot did not fail. There was always that chance that the King would live; but for Phillipos to be blamed serves us as well. And now, with Hansio out for blood, maybe Jagat too, he'll have no time for—ah! There they are! At last!"

The baggage barges were drifting downstream, black against the water.

"Captain!" he shouted. "Captain Eissos!" The captain appeared at the rail. "Prepare to cast off. As soon as the baggage from those barges is loaded!" He turned to Enricos. "North at last!" he said exultantly.

North, his thoughts ran on, *and an end to all this scheming! Action at last, all cast to hazard on the great board of war!*

Chapter Ten

Martos worried: his men were dressed for courtly escort, not for war. Needle-swords jutted from their saddles, and bow-cases from under their stirrups, but their shields and heavy war-swords were safely packed away. And Jagat would not stop—not even after they had splashed across the Marunka into Massadessa. Martos tried to comfort himself with the thought that many men in Kadar now scorned the shield as worthless in the new style of war, but he had heard Birthran snort contempt for these ideas of men too young to remember Ovimor Field.

Sunset's afterglow had faded from the sky; white stars and pearly moons glinted. It would be too dark for arrows, he thought, and thinking of Mirrha and Kumari and the other women, hoped he was right. He listened. Insects sang in the warm air, and the tired hooves of their horses thumped dully on the ground. He became aware that men were dropping back; that Jagat, with Kumari and her women, rode now beside the casket at the head of them all. The march was slowing, as each man sought to be rear-guard.

He was opening his mouth to order his men to close up and let Hamir's followers squabble for the glory of being last, when his ear caught the clatter of hooves on the road. They were coming fast. He turned in the saddle, and saw Hamir's men spreading out in a crescent.

Hooves drummed, louder. Martos spurred Warflame to Jagat's side. Lord Jagat sat huddled on his plodding horse, chin on chest, and seemed to have heard nothing.

"They are coming, Lord," said Martos. "Do you wish us to fight, or . . ."

The white hair moved. The old man's voice was very faint.

"I—I do not know. Why do they not leave me in peace, to take my boy to the land? Earth must be fed."

Voices shouted in the dark behind them. Martos raised his hand for the halt, and heard Valiros' voice behind him give the order. He sat, waiting for Jagat to speak.

Beyond Hamir's men he glimpsed a phantom shimmer of moonlit mail. Men shouted. Horses neighed. Had the Seynyoreans gotten fresh mounts as well as extra men? Warflame and the others were stumbling with weariness.

Something flashed in the dark. He turned, and cold chills ran through him to see Kumari's crystal dagger glitter in her hand. He knew the Border women often had to defend themselves against Night Things, and Kumari had told him she had once killed a goblin with her own hand. But this was war between men. Sick with horror, he pulled Warflame around, his tongue struggling with the orders he must give.

He heard Jagat's voice, utterly weary. "Perhaps if I talk to—"

Hamir's voice shouted in the night. Hooves crashed like surf on a shore. Steel belled harshly on steel. Martos' spurs drove cruelly into Warflame's flanks. Whatever the cost, the battle must not reach Kumari or her women. Ordinary women would be safe enough; to kill a woman was to face the Law of Hastur. But what would a man do if she came at him with a knife?

He tried to shout a command, but his numb tongue would only form a wordless roar. That was enough for his men, however. On either hand, he heard the sudden rush of hooves. His needle-sword's hilt was rough against his palm. Ahead, mirrored moonlight laced moving steel. He saw flapping Border armour fall, and riderless ponies scatter. Mail-clad men glimmered like water pouring through a broken dam.

On his right, an armoured rider loomed out of the night on a shadowy horse, his sword-edge swooping for the kill. Martos' arm stabbed out. The needle-sword, nearly invisible in the dark, thrummed like a harp string in his hand. The glancing broadsword veered, skimming overhead, and the needle-sword's point darted above the shield-rim. He felt it pierce softness, and heard a cry of pain, but the horses passed so quickly he couldn't tell whether he had killed or only wounded his man—and already another horseman was charging from his right.

All around he heard the booming and the ringing of war. He tossed the needle-sword to his left hand, and ripping out the longer court-sword, crossed the blades before him, guiding Warflame with his knees. Seynyorean steel shrieked down, crashing on his crossed blades with a wrist-jolting *clang!* He rasped his court-sword free, lashing at the throat, but the Seynyorean twisted his shield-rim, heaving up the broadsword for a second cut. The needle-sword plunged under the raised shield.

"Martos!" Valiros shouted. "Behind you!"

Hoofbeats hammered on his left. Air whistled under a sword-edge. He hurled the needle-sword up to guard. On his right, too, steel was falling. He thrust under it, at the armpit, feeling the needle-sword shaken and his left arm tossed like a branch in a storm. A sword blow glanced off his head and his helmet rang like a beaten bell. He reeled in the saddle, trying to shake the ache from his head. Something dragged on his court-sword, almost pulling it from his hand. He tightened his grip, pulling it free.

Hooves on the left, and a dark shape looming, and moonlight glimmering on a lifted sword . . . Warflame stumbled as another horse pushed him, and Valiros was there with a clanging of steel.

On either side he saw men fighting, whirling blades flickering in and out of silver light. Swords crashed on shields; men cursed and shrieked. Warflame staggered again as a long-legged horse cut across his path, and the blank wall of its rider's shield rushed at him, eyes glaring above it, and a dim sword soaring above, diving to strike.

Martos' crossed blades shuddered from the blow. His needle-sword lunged at the eyes, and grated on the steel of the leaping shield. The Seynyorean's steed swerved, his shoulder crashing into Warflame's side. The big horse fell to his knees. Martos kicked his feet free from the stirrups, ducked as a blade lashed from behind the shield, and vaulted from the saddle. He landed, knees bent, in the path of a rushing horse. It reared and balked. Martos danced to the side. His head ached.

The Seynyorean pulled his horse down and spurred it to run, racing at Martos with heavy sword drawn back, leaning from the saddle for a scything cut. Martos' needle-sword snapped up, lifting sailing steel. He stepped under it, his longer court-sword driving through mail-rings under the arm. Blood ran down the blade; the hilt was nearly torn from his hand. As the horse dashed past, Martos clenched his fist and the blade pulled free; the corpse toppled jingling to the ground.

Vague shapes of horsemen battled all around him, shouting in the darkness. He stretched out the court-sword, raised his needle-sword to his ear. Hooves drumming, a second shape came leaping, and the court-sword drove the gliding blade up. He whirled underneath the rasping steel, his left hand driving the long spike through a mail-ring into blood. He spun away. Another horseman loomed, his sword slashing down from the sky. Again the court-sword met it while Martos came spinning in, stabbing with the shorter needle-blade.

Bad technique, Martos thought. *Same move twice in a row.* But already the court-sword was rising again, as another cut came down; again he pivoted under grinding steel. He felt his point glance harmlessly over moving mail. He ducked, his shoulder hitting the horse's belly. Mail-rings grated the court-sword's edge, and then he was dodging away from the horse's heels.

A horse head loomed over him. His blade came up for the cut to its neck, but instead he stumbled aside. He lashed his court-sword at the rider's back as they pounded past, and the blade rang on armour. He heard Jagat's war-shout, saw the little Border pony in front of the tall Seynyorean horse, and then whirling steel rippled in the moonlight and he heard the thunder of sword on shield.

Where were Kumari and her women?

He dodged to the right as hooves trampled towards him. His needle-sword darted up under a shield, grated on steel as the shield dropped, and his court-sword slashed across the eyes above it.

"Inagar! Inagar!" Hamir's men were shouting, all mixed with whooping laughter. He ran towards a horseman, blade ready to strike, and recognised one of his own men.

"Carcosa!" A man on foot came running up to him: a

Seynyorean, dismounted. Martos pointed his needle-sword at the face above the shield, his court-sword poised above his head. Left toe pointed to left toe as the two circled.

The Seynyorean was whistling a merry tune; his sword-edge lashed at Martos' eyes. Martos dipped the point of his court-sword into the way and lunged, left-handed. The court-sword rang and trembled; the needle-sword scraped harmlessly across the face of the shield. He whirled the court-sword down. The Seynyorean leaped back with a laugh, his shield dipping to guard his thigh, his heavy blade whipping straight down at Martos' head.

Martos sprang aside, cutting at the wrist, but the other was too quick. The Seynyorean was humming under his breath. As needle-sword darted at his throat, he spun his shield into the way, and suddenly began to sing:

> *There was a Lord of Heyleu Town,*
> *A Captain great and bold . . .*

Martos had always admired men who could do that; he himself had always been a silent fighter, unable to jar his concentration with even a simple war-cry. The singer's blade swept at his leg. The needle-sword's point dipped to meet it, while the court-sword leaped at the exposed arm.

> *In war he won him great renown,*
> *And mighty wealth of gold . . .*

The court-sword crashed on the shield. The Seynyorean blade circled, shrieking towards his shoulder. Martos crossed his blades to catch it, twisting his body. The wall of the shield leaped forward, pressing against both blades, pushing them down as the sword swooped above them.

Martos lunged back, stretching his arms to rip the court-sword free. Steel belled and quivered inches from his head. He slashed at the eyes above the shield, and as the shield rose, he dropped the point of the needle-sword into the man's thigh and lunged. The song ended in a grunt.

Martos jerked the needle-sword free just in time to catch the sharp edge reaching to embrace his back, and lunged with court-sword at a flash of exposed shoulder; but the shield rolled into the way, and the sword whirled swooping for his eyes.

"Victory! Victory!" someone was shouting.

Martos danced back. The wounded man hobbled after him, stumbled and dropped to one knee behind his shield. The sound of battle around them had ceased. Martos paused. If the battle was over, there was no need to kill . . .

But the wounded man slashed at his side. Martos reacted without thought, watching the needle-sword meet the cut, while his other hand drove the court-sword over the edge of the shield, between neck and shoulder. Bright blood spurted. He blinked. The man toppled on his face. Dim shapes of horsemen stood all around. Had he killed the man to find himself surrounded by Seynyoreans? Sweat burned his eyes. He held his blades up to guard, and then quickly drew one sleeve across his eyes.

"Well done, Martos!" It was Suktio's voice. Martos let his blades drop, feeling breath rushing from his lungs.

"Was that the last of them?" Jagat asked from the darkness.

"No!" Someone laughed. "The rest are still racing each other back to Karion!"

Loud laughter drowned the groans of the wounded. Martos closed his eyes. He could have asked the man to surrender. He wiped his court-sword and sheathed it, shaking all over.

"It was the Orissians that ran," Lord Hamir said. His voice was calmer than Martos had ever heard it. "I think we'll find all the Seynyoreans dead."

"How many of our men?" Jagat asked. Martos heard wounded men moaning in the darkness.

"Many, I fear," said Hamir.

"Earth is the Bride of the Warrior," Jagat said, sadly.

Martos shook himself. With the needle-sword dangling from his hand, he set off to find Warflame and his men. He stepped over many bodies. Pirthio would have an escort on his final road.

"Martos!" Looking up, Martos saw Valiros riding towards him, leading Warflame. "How badly are you hurt?" Valiros asked, sliding from the saddle.

"Not hurt at all. Just tired."

"You're the only one, then!" said Valiros. "When I saw Warflame with his saddle empty, I was sure you were dead."

"What about the rest of the men? And how badly are *you* wounded?"

"Scratches." Valiros laughed, gesturing at a gash on his cheek, and a blood-crusted tear in his sleeve. His face sobered. "But Ristobal is gone. Maybe Pavlos, too. I don't know about the others. Lost sight of them in the confusion."

"And not a Healer for miles!" Martos said, suddenly sick.

"No," said Valiros. "See there? With the torches? They brought Healers with them. They knew there would be a fight."

Red robes showed in the torchlight, where Hamir had made his stand. Martos heaved a sigh of relief. "Well, let's see how bad it is."

It was bad. Not only Ristobal but Etharto and Velanton were dead, and Pavlos and Aterion likely dying. Every man in Martos' command was wounded, some seriously. Even so, they were better off than the Bordermen. Half of Hamir's men were down, and only six of Jagat's were whole enough to ride.

They found twenty Seynyoreans, all but one dead. The single unconscious survivor, swathed in bandages, was loaded into the Healer's cart. Not one had fled with the Orissians.

Jodos woke, sweating horror. This dream had been different. The woman had been holding him in her arms . . . arms longer than his whole body! A giant woman, each breast larger than his head. He had been chewing on her breasts, drinking her blood—no, not her blood. Something else, sweeter. He shivered. The sickening *emotions!* This must be a part of Chondos' memory. He could never feel any such—

Sudden fear seized him. Had he eaten a mind too strong? Would Chondos' memory grow to master and devour him? His feet hit the hateful wood as he sprang in terror from the bed. Diving into himself, he grappled and bit at the stolen mind while his body prowled the dark room.

He shrank back from his brother's memory of the Blue-robe, feeling himself swallowed in vastness of alien thought. Yet his brother had emerged unscathed from that mind. Puzzled, he saw that whatever mysterious half-memory was behind the dream was in his own mind, not in Chondos'. Hunting, he found a small web-spider hiding in a corner. Its fear as he ate it helped reassure him that he was still himself.

A few hours before dawn, Lord Jagat's sad party trudged wearily into Kalasima. Lord Hamir had connections here, and had at last persuaded Lord Jagat to stop. This was peaceful, thickly settled country, well away from the Border. Not for fifty years had Dark Things raided so far. A prosperous village of carelessly fortified houses clustered under the castle wall.

Martos' eyes drooped as he led Warflame through the gate, the need for sleep driving all else from his mind.

After Martos had seen Warflame to the stable, and was sure the grooms were taking proper care of the exhausted horses, he followed the others to the main hall. Hamir and Jagat were talking to the Lord of the castle, a swarthy black-bearded man who might have been a Borderman but for his girth and the rich new cloth of his robes. Nearby, men were stuffing themselves at a table.

As he strode, starving, towards the food, he saw Kumari, sitting at the foot of a stairway at the back of the room, not far from where Hamir and Jagat talked to the Lord of Kalasima. He had hoped she would be in bed. Her face was white and strained. He started to turn away from the table, to go to her, but changed his mind. There was not much—bread, cheese, porridge, and milk—but never in his life had he smelled anything so delicious. He cut huge slices of both bread and cheese, and took them to her.

She smiled wanly as he approached. He had last seen her tending the wounded with the competence of long practise that was a part of life on the Border.

"Are you well?" he asked hesitantly, sinking down to the step beside her. "You look tired. Have you eaten?"

She accepted the cheese he held out, and smiled. "I am a little tired." She bit into the cheese, and chewed. "And I did eat, a little." She took another bite, then handed it back. "You eat the rest. I had some when I came in."

"Why aren't you in bed? And where are your women?"

"They wanted to sleep. I didn't. I want to hear what Hamir and Lord Balos are saying. And Uncle."

"You should rest. What about the baby?"

"What about the baby?" she mimicked. *"He's* certainly sleeping, dunderhead! Now be quiet and let me listen."

Puzzled and hurt, Martos turned his attention to the cheese. He had never in his life tasted anything so good. The bread was poor, coarsely ground stuff, but it, too, tasted magnificent. It was all gone far sooner than he liked, leaving him still famished, but too tired to walk back to the table.

Hamir and Jagat were still talking to their host. A fat, richly dressed woman had joined them, the Lady of the castle, he supposed. Something about her puzzled Martos. After a moment he decided that she must be Border-bred, despite her girth, and remembered Hamir saying the Lord had married one of Hamir's kin.

His eyes could not stay open. He moved closer to Kumari, put his arm around her, and laid his head on her shoulder. The scent of her flooded his nostrils. He loved her so! In Kadar they would be so happy . . .

His fencing hall was magnificent; his students, properly deferential. He began to teach them the various postures, but as he started to show them how to use court-sword and needle-sword together, the great door sprang open, and men on horseback were charging in, cutting at him, and he was killing them. Pavlos screamed as they tried to lift him into the cart. Birthran shook his shoulder, saying a famous Swordmaster does not fall asleep while teaching . . .

"Don't fall asleep here!" Kumari said. "They have rooms for us. Wake up!"

He tried to shake his eyes open, still hearing Pavlos' scream in his head.

"Suktio," he heard her saying, "help me get him upstairs."

They were trying to lift him! He pushed himself up.

"No," he said. "You're wounded!" He looked down at Suktio; the Borderer was nearly a head shorter than he. "I—I just need sleep."

"We all need sleep." Suktio grinned. "Come along. There are beds upstairs." Arm in arm they climbed the steps.

* * *

Istvan DiVega's sword slashed the morning mist as it had every dawn for forty years, from the Isles of the West to Y'Gora beyond the Eastern Sea.

Birds chanted a melody to the graceful steps of the dance; sunbeams leaped from blurred steel as from the dewdrops on grass and leaf. *Yesterday, I was a young man, roaming the great world, seeking glory, adventure. Forty years. Inconceivably long, to the young: time enough for anything. But it goes by so fast.*

Whipcord muscles moved in continuous, flowing grace, sword welded perfectly to hand. *Now that I'm old, what shall I do, to pass the time waiting for death?*

A whirling slash ended in a guard that changed to a long thrust. *Yet, inside, still young! A stranger in the mirror, with wrinkled face and greying hair. That's not me!*

The last step. The last whirling cut. Ignore the pain nagging in the side, the pounding heart, the oozing sweat. Wipe the blade. *Forty years. Such a little time: a lifetime. So quickly gone.*

Birds singing. How long will the ear hear them? Dawn lights the sky, but the eyes cannot go on seeing forever. Dew and grass under bare feet—but even touch goes at the end. Even the pain of the half-healed cut is a part of life: if life is good, pain, too, must be cherished.

I've seen men die; killed many of them. I've studied death for forty years. What have I learned? I've killed, but never died—or don't remember dying . . .

What's it like?

You'll find out, he mocked himself.

Palos DiFlacca was coming towards him, and there was urgency in his walk.

Forty years. He had a sudden, vivid image of himself dueling with a skeleton figure, and smiled in self-mockery. *And Death himself shall perish by this hand, and that grim skeleton shall walk no more. . .*

He laughed. Palos DiFlacca looked at him strangely.

"They said you'd be here."

"Trouble?"

"Might be." Worry creased DiFlacca's face with furrows like a new-ploughed field. "The King sent off some of my boys, late last night, to arrest Lord Jagat."

"Jagat?" Istvan's eyes widened in shock.

"After the King killed that fellow in the garden, I think he must have ordered half the nobles in the city arrested. But Jagat had already left."

"And you've heard nothing?"

DiFlacca shook his head, and Istvan swore. "Stupid to send Seynyoreans. You'd think the young fool was *trying* to start a war!"

"We're going to wind up right in the middle of this mess!" DiFlacca exclaimed, angrily. "Bad enough for Jagat's son to be killed, but this—!"

"Well, if it's war, it's war," said Istvan. "We'd have been caught in it anyway. But I wish that idiot would trust people. Or at least *pretend* to!" He closed his eyes, and shook his head. "I told Olansos I'd see the boy secure on the throne, but . . . I've never broken my word, but I've never sworn to do anything impossible before!" He sighed. "I'll have to talk with him."

"Martos! Wake up!" the voice said again.

"Go away!" He buried himself under the blanket. The voice nagged. After a time his eyes dragged open.

Valiros sat on the bed, dressed for riding. "Are you awake enough to talk? The Borderers are up already, the suns have been up for hours, and Jagat is ready to ride."

"Oh," said Martos, and began to curse. Valiros laughed.

"Now," said Valiros, after Martos had finished, "it occurs to me that we are about to be involved in a war. Or are we in one already?"

Martos considered, through the fog in his brain. "It's war. We fought the first battle last night. Now that blood's been spilled, on both sides, I doubt if anyone can stop it."

"That's what I thought," said Valiros with a nod. He leaned forward. "For war between men, shouldn't we get the horses? The Jumpers? We haven't needed them for Border work, but—"

Martos, beginning to wake now, sat up sharply in bed. "You're right!" he said. "And there'll be no better time to get them!"

"I'm glad to hear you say that!" said Valiros with a twinkle in his eyes. "Now I can explain that to Lord Jagat. Otherwise, I'd have to have you dressed and in the saddle in five minutes, and I don't beleive that that's humanly possible."

"DiVega!" Istvan recognised Lord Shachio's voice. Turning, he saw the Seer striding quickly towards him. "I am bringing news to the King, but you are the one man who should hear it first." Istvan looked at him sharply.

"There has been a battle," Shachio went on. "Some of your Seynyoreans were killed. Word reached the Seer at Erithra twenty minutes ago."

Istvan felt a stone on his heart. "Where?" he asked.

"South of the Marunka, in Massadessa, near Acarsica."

"That will be DiGarsa and his men," said Istvan dully.

"Nobody knows their names, or what company they were with. At least, Persios, the Seer at Erithra, doesn't. There were twenty of them. They rode up to Karyon a little after sunset, and told Lord Santhos that they were on business of the Crown, and demanded his aid in the King's name. They needed reinforcements, and Lord Santhos lent them thirty of his men." Shachio coughed. "It would seem that most of Lord Santhos' men fled, and it was their account of the battle that was sent to Erithra. They said the Seynyoreans had all been killed, by a party of Bordermen—Manjipéans, I presume. There may be a second messenger with more details; this one was rather vague. But I take it you know something about these men?"

"Yes," said Istvan, but did not go on. They had reached the anteroom by now, and a servant conveyed their requests for audience.

After a moment the servant returned, bearing a silver ewer and a goblet on a tray. "The King will see you first, Lord Istvan," he said, bowing low. "He sends this wine to Lord Shachio, in hope that he may enjoy it while he waits." He poured wine from the ewer. Lord Sachio, with a small shrug of resignation, accepted the goblet and began to drink.

Jodos, listening behind the door, hardly dared breathe until he sensed that Lord Shachio had taken the cup. He had made his plans as well as he could without examining the mind on which he would have to work—and Lord Shachio's mind would be trained to recognise the lightest probe. If the Seer called upon the Blue-robes, the fire would be upon Jodos before he could flee. But the wine would hide the taste of the drug he had prepared so carefully, and he had a perfect excuse for keeping Shachio waiting until it took effect.

He felt the burning sword through the door, drawing nearer and nearer . . . He held his brother's memory as a shield over his own thoughts. Chondos had believed implicitly that the Seers never looked into men's minds without their consent, but that was ridiculous. No creature with such power could fail to use it for his own advantage. He sat very still as DiVega entered, wrapped in the blinding magic of his sword.

"You have some pressing business, my Lord Istvan?"

"I have, Lord King." DiVega's eyes rose to challenge the King's. "I have just learned that you sent twenty of the men under my command—my countrymen—to almost certain death."

Jodos looked away, suddenly frightened. "What do you mean?" This man might be even more of a danger than Shachio. He must reach past the blurring radiance of the sword, find out what was in DiVega's mind!

"You ordered a Seynyorean officer—a man named Di-Garsa—to arrest Lord Jagat. If you had sent men of your own guard, Lord Jagat might have come peacefully. But you sent a Seynyorean instead."

"Why should it have made any difference?" Jodos asked, his mind flinching as he tried to insert a delicate probe through the hot crackle of energy that flickered from DiVega's scabbard. "Why should I not have sent Seynyoreans?"

"Because a Seynyorean killed Jagat's son," DiVega said. "Because, after that—that message . . ."

That stupid message, Jodos, his probe through at last, heard above the fire of the sword: *The boy can't be that blind!*

"What exactly *did* you say in your message to Lord Jagat?" DiVega asked. "The message had been—twisted—by the time I heard it. And I am afraid Lord Jagat heard a twisted version as well."

Jodos felt carefully the surface thoughts of Istvan's mind as he answered. "I sent my regrets that Pirthio had died under such circumstances. I was surprised that he had broken the King's Peace, and I said that while I knew of Jagat's loyalty, I feared that others might accuse him—that he must beware of accusations that might arise from Pirthio's actions."

I thought as much, he heard Istvan think through the sword's roar of power. *He was so shaken it all came out wrong, and then D'Estarras made it worse . . .*

"I thought you must have said something like that," DiVega said. "But by the time it reached Jagat it had become insulting. Threatening." Jodos let Chondos' memory drape shock across his face. "Jagat attacked the men who brought the message," DiVega went on. "And the men sent to arrest him were attacked. I fear you have not only lost a loyal supporter, but have plunged the kingdom into war."

Carefully, delicately, Jodos probed deeper. The sword burned his mind. As long as DiVega wore that sword, he could not be controlled, and this would be a dangerous mind to tamper with. But there must be weaknesses to play on, to distract him . . .

"I made a promise to your father," DiVega said slowly, "that I would see you secure on your throne. I mean to fulfill that promise, but—" He breathed a sharp sigh of exasperation. "I didn't realise I had sworn to grow old and die here, tied to an impossible task! You'll never be secure on the throne if you persist in making enemies of the men who must serve you!" And Jodos heard DiVega's mind raging on, *You offend your friends and turn loyal men against you. Did you mean to start this war? Are you trying to tear the kingdom apart?*

But Jodos had found what he wanted: fear, something he could understand, and work with . . . And just in time. DiVega was studying his face, noting how pale he looked, wondering if the King was ill, if he should summon a Healer, and, floating unformed, the notion that Chondos did not look like the same man . . .

"Yes," said Jodos, with a sigh, "at your age . . . so you fear to die of old age, before I learn sense?" He laughed. "You old men always say the same things! Always caution. So I can die safe in my bed!"

He laughed again, and changed his tone, satisfied at the sudden stir in DiVega's thoughts. "If I listen to you, I'll wind up afraid to do anything! I *have* enemies! I faced death yesterday!" He watched DiVega's mind carefully. "That man came very close to killing me! I could be dead now! Dead and rotting! Do *you* know who sent that man?"

DiVega blinked, distracted, as the carefully chosen words directed his attention to his own fear of age and death, until he saw the King waiting for an answer, and shook his head. "No," he said, "but I suspect—"

"I, too, have my suspicions!" Jodos interrupted. "But by your word, I must not act on them! Must I sit helpless, hopeless, waiting for death? Unable to act, unable to move? Should I let the next man who tries to kill me succeed, lest I offend him?"

"But you cannot just strike out blindly!" said Istvan, raging from the shame of his own fear that Jodos' words stirred in his mind. "You had no cause to suspect Lord Jagat!"

"No cause? How do you know? What was Pirthio doing with the son of my worst enemy, Hansio, stirring up trouble, attacking my soldiers with swords in their hands? Is there nothing suspicious in that? Must I trust Jagat because of his white hairs—because he is old, and will soon be dead? We will *all* be dead unless I take some action! You, too, may die!" DiVega blinked.

"You can only kill assassins for so long," said Jodos. "Your sword-arm will tire. Or doesn't your arm tire?" He watched the growing turmoil in DiVega's mind. "Trustworthy, white-haired Jagat leaves the city just after a man dies trying to kill me, but I must not suspect him. Now you tell me the men sent after him are dead! A strange way to show his loyalty, surely?"

"Lord Jagat is not himself!" Istvan exclaimed. "His son is *dead!* You cannot expect—" He sighed and shook his head. "It may be too late to do anything about Jagat now, but to send men of the same race as those who killed his son . . . !"

"I did not think of that," Jodos lied. "I sent the nearest soldier. That it happened to be a Seynyorean was a mistake, I admit that, but I don't see why I'm expected to keep my head but cannot expect the same of others!" Chondos' words.

"Because you are King," sighed Istvan. "Well, it's done, and we are all stuck with it. But try to think about what the effects of your words and actions will be. Try to see the thoughts and feelings of others, and act accordingly."

"I will try," said the King contritely; but inside, Jodos laughed. *I will indeed! I shall take great care to understand the effect of my words, and choose them well!*

Lord Julanos of the Vintners' Guild was not happy. In the absence of Lord Andrios he presided over the Council of Guilds, and Andrios had been taken to the castle. So it was to Julanos that the Seer for Portona brought the message from Prince Hansio. The message that swore that the hosts of Mahavara would raze Portona to the ground.

"The Seynyoreans all seem to have been killed; some of the Orissians escaped back to Karyon. Lord Santhos wants to know what he should do." Lord Shachio's voice grew solemn. "It would seem, Lord King, that we are at war."

"So it would seem," Jodos agreed, hiding cruel glee behind a sorrowful face, as he reached out with the faintest and softest of probes, brushing gently the surface of Lord Shachio's mind. He dropped away instantly as he felt the other react.

"A moment, Sire—another message," said the Seer, closing his eyes. After a moment he opened them. "I don't understand, Sire. I—there was no message. Your pardon."

"Do you feel ill?" Jodos asked. The old man shook his head.

"No, Sire, just very tired. Perhaps I have had too much wine. I usually drink only with meals. This is the first wine I've had on an empty stomach since—oh, since I was your age, I suppose." He smiled at the King, and the wide eyes fixed on his.

"Tired? Did you get enough sleep? Perhaps you need more sleep?"

Delicately Jodos reached again to the old Seer's mind, ready to drop away if noticed. There must be no struggle, no trace in Shachio's memory that another might see.

"Sleepy . . ." Shachio yawned. "Yes. I woke early. And I worked hard yesterday, sending all those messages for Lord Istvan, and got to bed late. What word should I send Lord Santhos, Sire? If you will tell me what to say, I could return to my chambers . . ."

"I must think on the matter," said Jodos, reaching out.

His probe met no resistance now. Softly he slid into the

Seer's mind. "Sleep!" he said aloud. Lord Sachio's eyes closed.

Time passed while he hunted through the maze of Shachio's mind, altering, adjusting, changing. Shachio had believed Chondos hopeless as far as any training in the psychic skills went; Jodos strengthened that belief until it became unshakable faith, until the old man was deaf and blind to any fact that did not fit his image: whatever Jodos might do, the Seer would not notice or believe. Nor would he notice the touch of Jodos' mind twisting his unborn thoughts. Jodos created a few false memories, and strengthened the taboo against looking unbidden into another's mind. But he was puzzled. Chondos had been right. Lord Shachio would no more spy on another's mind—except in rare and strictly defined emergencies—than he would have done any number of other things Jodos found curiously forbidden, like eating children.

He allowed Shachio to wake. The old eyes blinked.

"Sire? I . . . Have I slept? What . . . ?"

"You need your rest," said Jodos, smiling. "But now, send word to Erithra that Lord Santhos, and the other Lords, should gather their armies, and be ready to invade Manjipé if I give the order."

War! All day the thought throbbed like drums in Martos' mind as he rode from Kalasima to Urjvut. His two-handed dwarf-sword hung from his baldric.

They rode south along the Yukota for a time, passing the high walls of Acarsica, following the track of Lord Jagat. Then they turned from that road, into the Massadessan heartland. In the west the Twin Suns dipped ever nearer the dark edge of the horizon. At last the distant wall of darkness cut into the suns, and still they rode south.

Grain fields and orchards were replaced by grazing land dotted with horses and cattle. Much of this land was rented to Kantaran and Manjipéan Lords for the stock they could not feed and dared not breed on their own Demon-blasted lands.

A dozen moons were weaving through the sky, casting strange patterns of moving shadow, when at last they came to the gates of Urjvut and were reluctantly admitted by the sleepy watchman. Even so far from the Border, men did not travel at night except in cases of great need, and the watchman glared at them suspiciously.

A thousand miles to the north, beyond the far end of the Sea of Ardren, need-fire raged where Handor, Kadar, and Creolandis border three sides of the great bulge in the Shadow that covers the Lake of Cloud, and dread shapes prowl through the ruins of Thendara. Deadly Demons crawled and flew in Kadar, blighting all they touched. Burning beams and balls of need-fire surged about them. Men fought goblins in the dark.

Another thousand miles north, mortal men slept in peace, and the beasts of the field grazed, unconcerned, while the Hastur-towers blazed against the dark wall in the south, until a vast shape of Shadow rose about one tower.

Before its defenders could react, their defenses were quenched, and the tower shattered in molten fragments. Towers to either side rocked, as they, too, came under attack. Their wardens' cries for aid brought Hasturs flocking from all over the world. But already Dark Things poured into the lands of men, and the gathering Hasturs sensed, lurking in the Shadow, the malignant presence of dragon-headed Uoght, Regent of the Dark Lords who rule beyond the world.

In the dim half-light before the Twin Suns rose, Martos, still stupid with sleep, went with his men to get the horses. A thick fog hid the world, and the reluctant Urjvut men who guided them carried lanterns and were ill at ease, for the Border was little more than fifty miles away. The walls of the castle faded behind them, and they strode over empty moors. The tops of occasional rare trees were hidden, and ten feet away on every side a blank grey wall hid the world.

Martos found the faint chill of the mist a welcome change from stifling heat, and he did not share the Massadessans' nervousness. Yet his fingers tightened on the rough grip of his heavy dwarf-sword as a white shape came hurtling out of the fog, bounding like a deer, soaring like a bird. It whirled, and vanished again. Valiros whistled. A soft whinny answered him: a horse came trotting out of the mist.

Much as Martos loved horses, he was glad to leave these to Valiros. To his eye, they did not look like horses at all; too lean, ungainly, with legs too thin, hooves too small, necks too short, haunches too powerful. They were more like whippets, or strange, misshapen antelopes, and only in the air were they graceful. They made him nervous.

Only in the last fifty years had centuries of breeding produced its end. Martos watched nervously as others came flying out of the mist, hoping the smell of his nervousness would not send them bounding off. For the Jumping Breed did not have the calm for which the great Kadarin war-horses had been bred. Long inbreeding had produced an excitable beast likely to burst into fury or flight at any moment. And these were some of the worst, which was why Valiros had been allowed to take them from his uncle's estate.

He himself was glad to ride in the heavy force, with a good war-horse and solid ground under him. Soaring above his enemies' heads was not his style of fighting. Paidros, he knew, hated the beasts, and had left his secure post in the Royal Army rather than ride one.

A narrow muzzle dropped into Valiros' hands. He scratched the ugly jaw and the pricked-up ears, and ran questing hands over the lithe body.

"Well, Windracer's in good condition, at least," Valiros said in a soothing tone. Erivar and Rafael, too, had found their horses. Valiros talked soothingly to Windracer, and slipped the bridle over the ugly head that always made Martos think of a snake. The beast seemed willing to permit it, though Martos twice saw the pointed ears snap back. Erivar soon had Arrowflight ready as well, but when Rafael tried to slip a bridle over the head of his little mare, Greydoe, she snorted and bounced away, and as he stepped after her she whirled, ears flat to her skull, and kicked. Rafael dodged, and Greydoe rocketed into the mist with a shrill scream. A dozen other horses shot off like rabbits, and Erivar and Valiros had to hold their steeds down as they kicked and bucked.

"Let her go!" Valiros called to Rafael. "She'll follow, They'll all follow."

Valiros got Windracer under control first, and once Arrow-flight had quieted, they turned back towards the castle. But it was easy to lose direction in the fog, and they found themselves beside the wall, thirty feet high, that had been built in days when the Border was even closer, to baffle night-prowling goblins and trolls. It swept out from the side of the castle to enclose a large acreage, more than enough for the little herd. It was the wall which had caused Martos to choose Urjvut as a safe haven for the excitable beasts that could easily have leaped a lesser barrier. They followed it back to the castle. Martos smiled at the looks of the Urjvut grooms as the horses followed, a few plodding awkwardly behind, others appearing and disappearing, bounding like deer through the fog.

The east glowed brilliant white, shot with streaks of gold and tiny rainbow glints. The horses snorted and neighed as light grew. The wall met with the outer wall of the castle, and soon Valiros and Erivar were tying their horses to the posts by the gate. Rounding up the rest, they found only seven horses fit to ride in battle; many of the mares were either nursing or great with foal.

They saddled Arrowflight and Windracer, and put lead ropes on the other five, not without some difficulty. Valiros, Erivar, and Rafael would have to herd them all the way to Inagar; no ordinary horse could catch them if they chose to scatter. Then they had to drive the remaining mares back to pasture, so they could get the seven through the gate—a difficult task, for the Kadarin Jumping Breed was clannish; Windracer and the others did not wish to be separated.

Jodos had not had his usual dreams that night. Instead he'd dreamed of men and women Chondos knew, and of sensual, fleshly desires new to him . . . He opened his eyes in the royal bedchamber, and that seemed ordinary enough. He thought to himself that he had been having strange dreams, about Jodos and the Dark Ones . . .

Badly frightened, Jodos came all the way awake. *He had thought he was Chondos!* The overwhelming fear of all who serve the Dark Lords rose in him: fear that he had devoured something more powerful than he, that was absorbing him. And added to it, another fear erupted in that part of his mind which held Chondos' memories—that part of his mind *was* Chondos, and the thing that he feared was Jodos.

Twin fears swayed in his mind: Chondos' horror at the life

in the Shadow swept over him, and warred with fear of absorption and disgust for the Sun People.

He found himself muttering the words Chondos had learned from Miron Hastur, and a barrier rose around his mind, a barrier against Jodos . . . But he *was* Jodos!

Pirthio is dead! he thought. *What have I done to Lord Jagat? What have I done to the kingdom?*

Lie down, you mouldering yeast! No mere human will can be strong enough to absorb mine!

News of Pirthio's death and of the battle at the Marunka had not arrived before them, but at breakfast Martos heard other news.

"All the Seynyorean companies are on the move," the Lord of Urjvut told him. "No one knows why. Headed for Ojaini, I think. All very orderly. Sandor DiArnac and his men left Ekakin, and as they marched east, the Seynyorean garrison of every fort they passed marched out to join them. A mystery."

"When did this start?" Martos asked.

"Yesterday."

Someone is being very smart, Martos thought. *Probably DiVega.* Aloud, he said, "Then only the companies in the western part of the province have actually moved? The others are still waiting?"

"That's what they say," the Massadessan answered. "They'll be camping in Kaligaviot now."

If Hamir and Jagat choose, then, Martos thought, *we could cut the Seynyoreans off from Ojaini.* He felt a sudden keen pity for these men of his own profession, their blood and heritage closely akin, trapped in a suddenly hostile land.

Jodos sensed Lord Taticos' stare, and reached for the man's mind, to find out what he knew or suspected. Others, too, were staring at him.

"Sire, your sword!" Taticos' voice was a shocked whisper. *"Where is your sword?"*

He had forgotten it, the silly strip of steel the Sun People placed such faith in! He had been too frightened of the ghost of his brother's mind to take proper thought while he dressed this morning! It was trying to trap him!

He saw in their minds that they would never forget their swords. He cast about for something to say, while panic surged inside him. Then he saw the way out, and laughed aloud.

"What!" he cried, "are my guards so careless, my ministers so disloyal, I dare not face my own Council unarmed? Then perhaps I am better dead. Do *you* plan to stab me, Lord Taticos? Or you, my Lord Zengio?"

Taticos stammered, but Lord Zengio chuckled dryly, and Jodos saw in his mind admiration for the defiant gesture. It had worked. The twisted logic was in keeping with Chondos' manner.

"No one ever said the King lacked courage!" said Zengio. "Good sense, maybe!" He laughed, then waved at the young man who stood at his shoulder. "My son and I have been talking to Lord Andrios of Portona, and with Lord Dimetrios." He rubbed his hands together, gleefully. "Those are two frightened gentlemen. They're in separate rooms—quite comfortable, really—and we've been trotting from one to another, asking questions, comparing answers, and then asking them why their answers are different. They deny everything, of course. They've even denied some things we didn't know about. Andrios, for instance, denied knowing anything about someone he calls 'this Sandor fellow.' That was when we asked him about the attempt on Your Majesty's life. So we asked Lord Dimetrios who Sandor was. He said he heard that was the name of the big northerner in the pay of—and then he started to call Prince Phillipos a Duke! I asked him if he didn't mean the Duke of Ipazema. He denied that very fervently!"

Impatiently, Jodos listened, while he studied the minds of the men around him, as well as he could with that blazing sword in the room. He could sense something of the jealousies and tensions between them. Lord Mario, for example, Zengio's son, was ruffled that his father was still acting as though he were only an underling. Jodos smiled. He would have them all at each other's throats, soon enough! Then, when he had completed his mission, and the Dark Lords had drawn the shadow across the sky until it reached the sea, he would rule here, and feast, and grow in power. Those people who remained would be his slaves, to eat or torture as he saw fit. It would be good to have real food again, living, bloody food. His mouth watered at the thought.

"Sire." DiVega was speaking to him. "Have you mentioned the name Sandor to anyone? Or had you ever heard it before?"

"No," he said.

"Then, unless my cousin Firencio talked"—DiVega paused, snapped his fingers—"or the Princess Illissia. She was present when I spoke to the King. But unless Andrios heard from someone they might have spoken to—and that would be easy to trace—he must have heard the name from someone who knew of the plot."

"I'd like to know more of this," said Zengio. "I had not heard that name myself, except from Lord Andrios' lips. Was that the assassin's name?" DiVega nodded.

Two thousand miles to the north, Miron Hastur sat cross-legged on grass, his eyes closed but his mind alert and watching as warriors of Kathor combed the nearby forest for the goblins that were known to have taken refuge there. He was weary. Daylight permitted him to hoard his dwindling power for the struggle that would come with the night, unless the mortals in his charge should encounter something more dangerous than goblins.

Where the shattered tower had stood, murk oozed onto the plain, and Demons clustered. Miron's kinsman, clothed in flame, tried to drive the Dark Things back and seal the Border once more. But the real struggle would not begin until the Twin Suns sank.

Eyes closed, Miron watched blond-haired warriors in leather armour as they advanced cautiously through the underbrush. He could sense the twisted creatures that skulked ahead of them, trying to hide, or when cornered, leaping out with ratlike ferocity, stabbing with crudely hammered iron. From time to time Miron touched the mortal Seer who guided the men, showing him where to hunt, where to beware of ambush. But mortals could handle this, and he must save his strength for the night.

A sudden ripple of blackness welled out of the ground. Instantly he was gone from the hillside, and stood, wrapped in flame, in the path of the Demon as it hurled itself upon the mortals. The shapeless darkness recoiled, withering grass and trees to grey dust as it moved. His need-fire glanced back from its barriers.

A man shouted behind him, but he paid no heed, his mind locked on the tension of the forces between the Demon and himself. His shield-fire blazed against the cold power surging around him. A crude, iron-tipped spear drove into his back. He cried out; the flame about him flickered, and the black phantom rolled towards him. Miron hurled all his fadir.g energy into a bolt of flame that hurled the Demon back. A warped figure leaped at him, iron sword raised. He summoned a second bolt from somewhere. A scorched goblin body fell to earth. Then blackness flowed towards him again, and he had no more power to raise. But his pain had not gone unnoticed. Suddenly Elenius Hastur stood blazing between Miron and the Demon, and then Earagon and Herstes appeared. Miron let the flames fade from around him, and stood swaying, rapt in concentration while the blood poured from his back. His mind moved up and down the spear shaft, down into the wound itself, lingering over cruel hooked barbs on the spearhead, and the smeared poison that was slowly oozing into his blood.

A little to the right and the spear would have killed him at once. Walling away the agony, he changed the poison first, and sealed the severed blood vessels. His mind fixed on the spear shaft. Slowly, carefully, the spear began to pull out from the wound. Dispassionately he watched it wiggle back along the path of entry, carefully guiding it past an artery that could lose blood faster than he could seal it, until at last the point slid free of the wound. He let the spear fall, and pressed the wound closed.

Stench and rocking air told him that his kinsmen had defeated the Demon. He became aware of shouting and clashing steel, of men and goblins fighting all around him. He pulled his severed blood vessels together, and strove to make them whole, to knit the torn flesh. But he felt his strength fading . . .

Then another mind clasped his. The skilled thoughts of Elenius moved over the wound, and Miron let himself relax into gentle sleep.

Chapter Eleven

Chondos struggled to open his eyes, to escape the grip of nightmare. He lay in darkness. Water dripped somewhere. He knew he must still be dreaming, and forced himself to sit up. At least he was lying on a couch this time, instead of cold stone; no wet things crawled over him.

But he was not in the royal bedchamber. Ancient cloth tore under his fingers as he pushed himself up. Dust filled his nose, and he sneezed. *Do people sneeze in dreams?* he wondered. But they must, since he had just done so, and this could not be real.

He shivered. It was cold in this dream. He wore only a thin nightgown, and that cold draft on his neck must mean a window somewhere. He turned his head. His neck was stiff and sore; his throat was dry. Somewhere there was a sickening smell. He was thirsty. His bare feet brushed icy stone as he sat up.

His eyes began to pick out vague shapes in the darkness around him. A black oblong nearby must be a low bench or a long box of some kind. Surely that was a table in the middle of the room? His head hurt. Yes, a table, and a chair by the table.

A wide archway in blackness opened onto a starless sky. Dim shapes might have been crumbling towers. The chill barely disturbed the stagnant mustiness. At the side of the arch, tattered strips of hanging cloth made faint scraping sounds.

He closed his eyes again, and shook his head to clear it. Grogginess ebbed. But he was not in his bed in the castle, so he could not be awake. He must still be dreaming, another in the long series of hideous dreams that had gone on and on, until surely the night must be over; yet dust tickled his nose and his bare feet cringed from cold stone. He could not be anywhere but asleep in his bed, but here he was, freezing and thirsty on an ancient couch that was coming to pieces as he moved.

He sneezed again, and blinked. If he was awake, where was he? And how could he have gotten there? He had gone to bed at last after the Coronation, his head swimming and his back aching from the long day, and sleep had come quickly between the cool sheets. But sometime in the middle of the night, the dreams had begun. Dark Things had hunted him, haunted him: rough dark fingers probed his brain. And all through the night, as he had striven again and again to awaken, he had felt something *watching* him. That feeling was with him still.

He sneezed again. The couch creaked under him as he staggered to his feet, dizzy and reeling. He swayed unsteadily, his eyes struggling with the dark. There were low mounds all around the edge of the room, and he guessed them to be piles of cloth fallen from tapestries that had rotted on the walls and ceiling.

Chairs were set along the wall, covered with mounds of decaying cloth. One held a dark mass that, for a heart-stopping moment, he almost took for a human figure. But no, it was too lumpish, too rounded, too shapeless. It was only an odd pile of cloth . . .

It moved. It spoke. It said, in a curious hissing voice: "Welcome, O King, to the halls of your fathers! Welcome, King Chondos, to Rajinagara!"

And as the King stood frozen, peal after peal of awful laughter rang in his ears.

Night had come by the time Martos reached Inagar with his precious horses. In the twilight, the little dark people of the city watched, aloof and sullen, as the Kadarins rode down the long streets, until someone recognised Martos. The whispers of "the Hero of Ukarakia" grew to muted cheers.

Outside the walls they had ridden through fertile farmland and grazing pastures. The great Demons seldom came this far north, so there were few of the patches of poisoned dust that had destroyed the land farther south, although the crops were still liable to blights cast by the Dark Ones. Gardens behind the ancient houses were protected by strong spells. Grass and trees surrounded the citadel in the heart of the city, the dwelling of Inagar's Lord.

Legend said Inagar had once been the winter capital of the Takkarian Kings, and that the last of those had reigned here for a time, after the fall of Rashnagar a thousand years ago. But that was only legend: the annals of that time had long been lost in frantic wars with the Dark Things.

But the city was nearly as large as Manjipor, and only Mahapor, in all the Border country, was bigger than that; if the ancient Kings had never ruled there, the Princes of Manjipé had many times moved their seat here in the past thousand years, when the fluctuating Border had swallowed Manjipor.

In the square before the citadel, a pall of smoke still hung: Pirthio's pyre and—others. Ashes were being gathered for the blessing of the fields. Martos felt relief that it was over, yet he should have been here to say farewell. There would be empty places in their family tombs, he thought. But you could not bury men along the Border; bodies would not stay in the grave. And he knew that the Bordermen took as good care of foreign dead—of mercenary dead—as of their own. And nineteen Seynyoreans, too, were here, although the dead Orissians had been sent back with the Healers' carts to the care of their disgraced comrades.

The people of the city were still gathered near the square, but the crowds were small. He became aware of the emptiness of the city. There was room here for thousands more than lived in all the Border country. Many houses stood deserted, staring with empty windows like the eyes of skulls. At the gate of the citadel, huge figures bulked among the lean and ragged Bordermen, leaning on their bows: N'lantian mercenaries, not as tall as Martos, but with naked chests and shoulders broad as a bear's. Nearly half the women of the province lived here; they stood in silent groups around the square, and their hungry eyes followed Martos' men to the gate.

Lord Taticos looked uncomfortable, and Jodos could see vivid images of burning castles and marching armies in his mind.

"It is war, Lord King, or looks that way." Taticos paused and wet his lips with his tongue. "Hamir of Inagar has called in his vassals, and Lord Jagat is meeting with them now." He paused again. Jodos had already gotten everything from his mind, and did not care to hear it again in words. He sensed Lord Zengio's impatience; a simple touch on the old Constable's mind brought his voice bursting over Taticos' hesitation.

"I've started gathering my men, Lord King!" And Jodos noted the flash of irritation in Zengio's son, the new Constable, whose job this was. "Prince Phillipos has sent for men from the Iskoda garrison, and we can have an army marching within two days!"

Jodos laughed—

Horror swept through him. That had been Chondos laughing, not he! Chondos' memory of a war-horse hearing a trumpet, champing at the bit; Chondos' memory, trying to rule him.

"Aye, Lord King," said Zengio, misinterpreting the shock on his face. "It is tragic: Lord Jagat was always your father's right hand, and a good friend to me. We've all worked hard to avoid this war. But it's too late now."

"It is *not!*" snapped Taticos. "War with Mahapol, maybe, but now that Lord Jagat has completed his son's rites, I think he will come to his senses and renew his fealty."

"We must be prepared both for peace and war," said Jodos smoothly, knowing that was what they wanted to hear. He had hidden his shock and fear, but it still seethed under his mask of calm. How could he ever hope to eat the Master, if he could not even absorb his brother's thoughts—not even his living mind, but merely his memories? How could he ever hope to digest the countless lives needed to make himself immortal?

Rashnagar! The ancient capital! Chondos' mind reeled as the hideous laughter echoed around him.

"A thousand years ago the last of the Arthavan Kings fled this city in terror," the hissing voice said. The black-robed figure rose from its chair. "A thousand years have passed since a King of your blood walked these old stones; but the cycles have rolled, and once again an Arthavan walks in the halls of his ancestors. The very stones of the city rejoice in your coming, O King."

Childhood dreams stirred in the back of Chondos' mind. *King in Rashnagar . . .*

Suddenly Chondos laughed, his voice echoing merrily through deserted halls. King? King of what? Of spiders and bats, if any such wholesome creatures yet survived, hiding in corners of the dusty rooms? Surely not, save in mockery, King of the ghouls and goblins who haunted ancient ruins; King never to the Demons or their dreaded masters.

And now his mind took note of the bindings hooked in his childhood dreams of the ancient Empire. Men said that terror and greed were all the Dark Things understood of human emotion. Here was proof: to sit so, waiting to frighten him, and then to follow that with such a bribe, of rule in this ancient ruin!

"Interesting," he said, his voice scornful. "Strange I've heard no cheering! If I am King here, give me that ugly robe to keep me warm, and bring a torch to light my way out!"

"If you saw what this robe hides, O King," mockery hissed, "you would flee as swiftly as did the last ruler of Rajinagara! Then my servants would have to bring you back. They might harm you! That would be sad. But you would not go far. Be sure, you will not leave until I send you away!"

A threat may conceal fear, Chondos thought. The shapeless robe seemed hung on a frail framework: limbs like sticks under the cloth. Perhaps it feared him with reason . . .

"Then you'd best send me away now!" he said, watching for any sign of fear. "I will leave *now!* Stand aside or I'll break you like rotten sticks!"

Hissing laughter answered, as he feared it would. "Would you pit your strength against mine?" the deadly voice asked. With one impossibly long stride it closed the distance between them. "You who live at my whim, and sleep at my command? *Sleep*, then!"

A dark sleeve waved. Chondos' body was numb, and darkness spun around him. The black figure was gone, and instead he saw the couch rushing up to meet him. With a crash the ancient wood crumbled under him, and weights dragged his eyelids shut.

Jodos suppressed a cruel smile.

". . . unfortunately, all depended on the loyalty of Lord Jagat!" Lord Mario was saying. "We expected that the Manjipéan forces would do most of the fighting in the south, leaving the Royal Forces free to deal with Orissia and the coastal cities. But now there are only the Kantara Lords and the mercenary companies in the south, and to reinforce them, we must strip the capital of all defense, and run the risk of losing the north."

DiVega stirred, his flaming sword burning Jodos' mind, hiding thought. Jodos did not even try to reach for the Seynyorean's mind, contenting himself with studying the others in the room. He remembered the Master, terrible and stern, teaching him with pain and fear to rule the minds of men.

"When the mercenary companies here are united with those now gathering at Ojaini," DiVega said, "I will have more than nine thousand men ready to serve you, Lord King. And the greater part is already in the south. If I march with the companies in my command, I would think you need send no more." He smiled, an odd, self-mocking smile. "You know the reputation we Seynyoreans have."

That would do to shatter the Bordermen, he thought. Then he could summon them north again, to fight the rising here, leaving the Border defenseless.

"My Lord King and Brother," Prince Phillipos said, "I have now, in this city, ready to march, four hundred men. By tomorrow I should have a thousand foot. That will still leave a large force along the Oda, ready to move into Mahavara at the first sign of rebellion. But the thousand will follow wherever you lead."

Lead? He had forgotten: the Sun People expected their masters to risk themselves as they did, instead of driving them from the rear. More madness.

"It would be folly, my Lords, for me to leave the capital," he said, slowly, trying to sound reluctant. "While I sit here, in control of the north, my very presence will serve to quell rebellion, and the symbolic unity of the kingdom is preserved. But if the city were seized while I fought in the south—or even if an army were to move between me and my throne—the throne would be a laughingstock!" He saw the hesitation in their minds, and rushed on, not giving them time to think: "Lord Istvan, you will march south with your mercenaries and take command at Ojaini. Prince Phillipos will accompany you with his—a thousand men, you said, Prince? With the forces of the Kantara Lords, you should have enough men to crush the rebellion."

In his mind Jodos saw the Border castles in ruins, and slain

Bordermen lying in bloody heaps. Then he saw the Dark Things raging through the land, heard the screaming of women and children as sharp fangs ripped their flesh. Food in plenty! They must be getting hungry now, beyond the Border. The Master had forbidden raiding here and in Ashnilon: only in the desert country on the other side of the mountains could they hunt or feed.

"But we must also strive for peace, Sire!" Taticos exclaimed. "We must try to treat with Lord Jagat, and persuade him to return to his proper loyalties! And we do not yet know what he plans to do!"

"We will learn that soon," said Shachio. "He meets with his vassals now, and that meeting will soon be over."

When Martos had seen to the stabling of the precious mounts, he made his way through the old stone pile, following directions to the Council Chamber. Some corridors were dim and drafty, with torches fluttering on stone walls. In others, the crystal light of witch-globes glimmered on panelled and inlaid floors. Centuries had linked chambers of great magnificence, now faded with age, to crude, hastily finished work. The old palace had long been a fortress; the land had claimed the ancient wealth. He climbed a marble staircase that changed to rough stone. Muffled voices guided him.

". . . this nonsense of the male line!" That was Jagat's voice, surely, loud and scornful. "Once, in this land, men knew . . ." Fading tones hid the words, as Martos climbed several steps, then again the voice rang out: ". . . of us know or cares who his father was? Only through our women are these bloodlines preserved at all! Death is the Warrior's Bride, and women must get childen where they can. It is time we . . ." Again the voice dropped from hearing. Other, lower, voices answered. Martos moved quickly towards the sounds.

"No!" Jagat's voice was strong and firm. "We will not do that! We *must* not do it!"

Martos found himself facing a curtain of rough-woven, ancient cloth. He thought Jagat's voice had come from behind it, but there was only silence now. Then he heard Lord Hamir's voice, speaking in a low, shocked tone:

"You cannot mean to defy the Law?"

"When one state declares war on another state," Jagat's

voice answered, "they must first seek permission from the Hasturs. But this, also, is the Law of Hastur: the people of a state have the right to overthrow a tyrant, and the Hasturs deny themselves the power to forbid."

Martos slipped unobtrusively through the curtain, into a large, barren room, lit only by candles on a long, low table. Around it men knelt on the floor, Border-fashion.

"In strictest legality, my Lord," said a man Martos did not know, who wore the yellow robe of a Seer.

"I know," said Jagat, "in strictest legality it is questionable. Yet, if we send a full formal defiance, as I intend, we shall be within the law.

"But that would mean that we accept the claim of sovereignty!" Hamir's fist came down hard on the table. "If we ask Hastur's permission, we declare ourselves as a free principality."

"And the Hasturs will accept our claim, and refuse permission to make war!" Jagat snarled. "Then each part of the kingdom will do the same, and then the Dark Ones will eat us all, bit by bit! Fool! I told you before—we *cannot* survive as a free principality. Do you think that has changed?" Pain was in his harsh, quavering voice. "Do you think I act only from grief for my son? Do you think my mind so far wounded that I seek to break up this realm and bring destruction on us all? What monument would that be for my son?"

Martos slipped quietly to a place against the wall where he could watch Jagat's face.

"No, my Lords, there is reason yet in this old head. Manjipé *cannot* stand alone. We must preserve the kingdom, not destroy it! We must have a King to regulate the prices merchants set on goods we need to live! Only a King can tax the port cities' wealth to keep us from starving, and to hire mercenaries—" His voice broke; his fists knotted. "Mercenaries," he went on, "to replace our young men who"— another pause—"die."

White hair swayed as he shook his head. "You are all too young to remember!" His voice was jagged, harsh. "Look at the old maps, see how much land the Shadow has eaten! Then you will realise how weak we were, how weak we *are,* by ourselves."

"You mean to take the throne?" Saladio exclaimed. Jagat seemed not to have heard.

"Once I thought the kingdom could be preserved by defending the lawful succession of Olansos' son to the throne. Even when my son—" Again his voice broke. His face twisted as he clenched his eyes shut. "Chondos cannot preserve the realm." His eyes snapped open. "He is too great a fool to be King! The realm must be preserved despite him!

"We must have a new King, a King worthy of Olansos' crown! I have resolved that in this rebellion I must be first, and so control and shape it, to change it from this foolish squabbling to split the kingdom permanently, to make a single, unified revolt, to throw Chondos down from his father's throne and replace him with a King who can rule! After Chondos has fallen, let the Hasturs decide who shall sit in his place."

"But Princess Illissia is the nearest heir!" Hamir exclaimed. "Would you set us under the rule of Kalascor?"

"Yes," snapped Jagat. "Yes! Why not? Prince Phillipos will make a good King!"

"Mahapor will never accept him," someone muttered.

"Take the throne for yourself, Lord Jagat!" Saladio urged. But the old man shook his head.

"I shall—I must—lay formal claim to the throne, but I know, and you know, that any claim of mine is sheer folly." Then his face twisted, and a bitter laugh left his lips. "And you, who jabber on and on about the true male line of the Arthavans, wish to make *me* King? What will you do when I die? Now *my* only heir is a woman!"

An icy fist clutched Martos' heart.

". . . so, if Jagat wishes, he may cut them off from Ojaini," DiVega was saying. "I do not know how large a force he can raise at Inagar."

Jodos listened, but more and more his mind was turning inward. For more than an hour some dim fear had stirred at the back of his brain. It was almost as though he felt the Master's eyes upon him.

"Will they be able to fight their way through?" Prince Phillipos asked.

DiVega's shoulders lifted. "How can I tell? It depends on how—"

"Sire!" Lord Shachio's voice cut across DiVega's. "A formal message from Lord Jagat!"

As he spoke, he was pulling ink and pen and parchment from his robe, his eyes blank, unseeing. All knew that across the kingdom, empty-eyed Seers were reaching for quills.

Shachio's eyes closed. His voice was deep and hollow. "I, Jagat, True Prince of Manjipor by right of male descent, declare full and formal defiance of Chondos, called King of Tarencia."

The Seer's pen moved swift and sure, writing the words as he spoke, although his eyes remained closed.

"I declare him unfit to rule, and claim his crown and land as my own. I call upon the Lords and people of this kingdom to rise against this unjust and unlawful tyrant, and drive him from the throne. Then, when he has been cast down, let the Hasturs decide between my claim and all other claims, such as the claim of Phillipos, Prince of Kalascor, Hansio, Prince of Mahapor, and any other claim." Sharp gasps sounded around the chamber. "So say I, Jagat, Prince of Manjipé and Manjipor, on this seventh day of the month Deyma, called Ashna in the old Takkarian reckoning, in this nine thousand, three hundred and fiftieth year of the Age of Strife."

Jodos controlled his face. Shachio opened his eyes on stunned silence. Taticos wrung his hands.

"So much for questions of peace or war!" Zengio's voice cut harshly across the sound of breathing. "I wish I could march with you, Lord Istvan!"

DiVega's eyebrows rose. He drew a deep breath, held it. "Have I your permission to go, Lord King?" he asked. "I have orders to give, and if I am to march in the morning, I must have some sleep."

"We must all go to our duties," Prince Phillipos said, rising. His face was pale and set; his eyes smouldered.

"Yes," said Jodos, waving a hand. "Go to your duties and your beds."

Jodos kept his face solemn as they filed from the room, and while his servants lighted him to his bed. But when he was alone at last, he let his lips shape the savage smile that he'd hidden for so long. Soon all these lives would be his!

He lay down, and his mind hunted through the castle. DiVega's mind was hidden by the fire of his sword; other

Lords lay awake, troubled. He savoured the jealousy between Zengio and his son, and smiled. He would haunt their dreams this night.

Something still cringed far back in his mind, however, as though he had stood this night before the Master. Yet he knew that even the weak residue of power about the palace, as well as the nearness of DiVega's sword, would baffle any true sending. Perhaps, he thought, his brother had wakened, and been brought before the Master in the flesh.

Inagar was far enough from the Border that a few birds sang at dawn.

"Martos, of *course* I love you!" said Kumari.

Martos, still sour and sluggish from sleep, gazed at her, worshipping her eyes and lips and fragrant hair; his memory stared through her robes at small brown breasts and slender thighs, and he wet his lips, fighting his stammer, forcing himself to speak.

"Then tell your uncle. Now. Today. Tell him you are—you will marry me. Tell him we are going."

Wide dark eyes filled with tears, and she looked at him as though he had struck her. "Martos, I *can't* go now! I am all he has left! Can't you see that? And our baby is Uncle's heir!"

She had said it. He had known she would, but denied it to himself again and again.

"The heir of Damenco!" His voice was bitter. Bleakness filled him. "Heir to miles of poisoned dust! I don't *want* my son to inherit Damenco! Or my daughter! Whichever it is! I want to take you somewhere where—" His throat froze. He could not speak of that fear. He bit his lip, stammered, and finally burst out, "All I want my baby to be is *alive!* Healthy! I want it away from the Dark Things, where they can't—" He stammered again, and swallowed. His tongue was dead again.

"Oh, Martos!" Tears ran down her face. "You don't understand. This is something our women have faced for a thousand years. More than that! Even before Rashnagar fell, the Shadow had been pushing us back. My mother went through it, and her mother, and Uncle's mother. It's safer now than it has ever been! While Pirthio was alive, I had some choice!" Her voice broke in a sudden sob. "Now this baby is all that—" Sobbing took away the words. She buried her face in her hands.

"I will *not* have my child born this close to the Border!" Martos shouted, brutally, his body trembling.

Her face rose from her hands. Her eyes narrowed; she breathed in rapid, angry gasps. *Your* child!" she spat. "Shall I take him from my womb and *hand* him to you? It's *my* baby!"

Martos stared. She seemed transformed, unhuman; and his tongue was a lump in his mouth.

"My child! *My* heir!" She went on. *"I'm* the one to worry about child-bearing, not you! *I'll* be there, whether *you* are or not! *You* don't want *your* child born near the Border? *You* don't have much say about it!"

No woman had ever spoken to him like this. He didn't like it.

"I *won't* run away form the Border! I *won't* leave Uncle without an heir! Our men go out and die fighting the Dark Ones to hold the land. It they can face that, we women can risk children! If everyone ran away, how far north would the Border be now? Most women do run away from the Border, Martos, but I won't be like them, do you hear me! I *won't* run!"

The shrillness of her voice pierced his nerves. He could stand no more: anger gave him back his tongue. "So the baby doesn't matter to you, only your own stupid pride!" he shouted, heedless of who might hear. "You don't care what happens to my baby as long as you have another little Borderman to sacrifice to the land! You don't care about *me!"*

"I have a duty to my people, Martos." Her voice was low, dangerous. "I was ready to give it up for you once, but not anymore! I can't leave Uncle now! Let me alone, Martos!"

"You *will* leave! No child should ever be born in this place!" His voice trembled. "Any sane woman *would* run away! You promised to come with me! There's more to the world than this wasteland! You say Jagat needs an heir, but if the Dark Things curse him before he's born, he can't inherit anything! What then? Just forget, and start over?"

She closed her eyes, and nodded, suddenly pale.

"Well you can start over with someone else! I'm not going to spend my life getting children just to see them die!"

Her eyes snapped open. "Nobody asked you to! Find someone else? Gladly!"

They stared at each other, suddenly mute. When she spoke

again, her voice had calmed. "My people have names for the—for women who run away with foreigners to escape the Border. I'd be called all those things." Her eyes stared at tight-clasped hands in her lap.

"What would that matter?" He tried to keep his voice gentle, to heal the breach he felt yawning between them. "Names can't hurt you. And you wouldn't hear them in Kadar."

"No!" Her lips twisted and her dark eyes flared. "Names don't hurt, if you don't hear them. But I would hear them, because I'd be using them on myself, knowing I'd lost my honour and disgraced my kin! *I was ready to do that for you!* But then I wasn't stealing my uncle's heir!"

"Honour!" he snarled, his attempt to make peace lost in a wave of red fury. "If you cared about honour, you'd think about what was best for the baby!"

She glared past his shoulder. "Go away, Suktio!" she said. "This is private!"

A sword slammed home into its scabbard. Martos whirled. Suktio bowed, his fingers still tight on his sword-hilt, and turned away. Martos watched him go, noting the rage in the tension of the muscles under the loose cloth.

"I could have handled him!" he muttered.

Her lip curled. "I know! You could kill him blindfolded!" she snarled. "Why do you think I stopped him? I don't want *gentlemen* to throw their lives away for me! If he'd had a chance, I might not have stopped him!"

The world was suddenly a hostile place, and he did not understand it. How could this have happened? He closed his eyes, fighting back tears, swaying on his feet, between anger and despair. His mouth was no good to him, had never been any good to him . . . He heard her voice murmur something under her breath. There was a faint rustle of cloth, and her fingers touched his arm.

He opened his eyes. Her hand was on his arm; her face was wet with tears. He wanted to take her in his arms and kiss her. Instead, he watched himself shake his arm free and turn away. He did not understand his own actions. Part of him seemed to stand aside, too detached or lazy to interfere, while another part moved body and tongue.

"Martos." Her voice was shaken, breathless. "I'm sorry— I—"

"*Sorry!*" he heard his own voice sneer, haughtily. He saw the pain in her face. *Good enough for her*, he thought.

"What do I have to do . . . ?"

"Come away with me!"

"*I can't!*" Her voice was breaking.

He found himself looking at her coldly, scornfully. "Are you chained to the ground?"

"Martos!" Her voice was sharp, pained. "We—we've discussed that!"

"What have we to talk about, then?" he heard himself saying. *Why did I say that?*

"Nothing!" she said. "Nothing at all, you self-righteous, pompous, overbearing . . ."

Her voice grew shriller and shriller. It did strange things inside him. Why was he standing here, being shouted at? He walked away, numbness filling him.

All the garden danced, and Istvan DiVega with it. Wings rose and fell as birds dipped and darted, singing. The morning breeze stirred grass blades and shook the tips of branches. Keen and high whistled the steel, flashing as sunbeams burst through morning mist. His feet moved with sure precision over the ground, caught up in the harmony of nature.

His blade skimmed out at waist level, slicing the air, then soared to rest on his left shoulder as he spun, suddenly flying free in a long lunge. A bough swayed and rocked as a bird alighted. Istvan's knees bent and straightened; heel and toe shifted as pivots while he wheeled, left and right, his back always moving—for this was the Whirling Dance that taught a man to fight when enemies surrounded him.

The bird's wings flapped as he settled. Istvan's hands crossed, uncrossed, sweeping the air at throat level with sharp steel. Leaves rustled. In the calm stillness that knew not death, the sword lifted to the scabbard's mouth, then lashed out again in a whirling cut, the last cut of the dance. Exultation disturbed ecstasy: he had forgotten his fear of death!

Easy not to fear in a peaceful garden! he taunted himself. *Try it in battle!* Besides, forgetting death was not the same as accepting death. Yet he felt some victory had been made, some step along the path to his goal.

He left the beauty of the garden, perhaps for the last time.

Bustling down the hallway he heard Lord Shachio call his name. "A message from Manjipor," the old Seer said as he came up. "Lord Maldeo, Chondos' Vicar in the city, has defied Lord Jagat, and denies him the title of Prince. He says he will hold the city for the King—or rather, for the True Prince, which comes to the same thing."

"Has Jagat replied?" Istvan asked, quickly.

Shachio nodded. "Lord Jagat says he will enter *his* city of Manjipor tomorrow, and that Lord Maldeo had better open the gates." Shachio smiled. "Todar—Maldeo's Seer—says that his Lord is preparing for a siege."

"What word from D'Oleve? Where are the companies now?"

"Almost due north of Manjipor."

"How far?" In Istvan's mind, men trudged over Demon-dung dust, while destruction thronged the road from Inagar.

"Just a moment. I'll ask." The Seer's eyes closed in trance. Istvan's mind raced. Manjipor, from Ojaini, horses and men, carrying food . . .

"Less than a day's ride," said Shachio, opening his eyes.

Istvan rubbed the bridge of his nose, calculating. Sparse grass at best. Plenty of water, if it didn't rain; too much if it did. Hay and grain in wagons. The Bordermen's own country. He tugged his beard and sighed.

"Tell them to turn and march straight to Manjipor. Tell them—" He paused, then shook his head. "No. That's all, just to get to Manjipor as fast as they can, and place themselves under Lord Maldeo's command."

Jodos woke, shivering with memory of a dream in which he had stood before the Master—but he had been Chondos! And, as Chondos, he had pitted his will against the Master's. He cringed at the thought.

Someday, of course, he must. But would he ever be strong enough to eat the Great Ones? Or was that only a false hope, a lie to make him serve them? When he had completed his mission, and the Great Ones drew the Shadow over the sky, then he could feast upon the lives of the people, and grow and grow until he could eat the Master . . .

He shied from that thought. He belonged to the Master, until the Master chose to eat him—if the Master did not condemn him to some lesser fate. He cowered in terror. Surely the Master would reserve him for himself, would not feed him to any lesser being! He'd served loyally . . .

That was why he must not fail. If he succeeded, he might in time grow strong enough to devour Uoght himself, the Great Ones' deputy. Then, when the Great Ones returned, to reclaim the world that had been stolen from them, he would be strong enough to challenge them, perhaps even to eat them all! Then *he* would be the Survivor, the last being, alone and sufficient unto himself throughout all eternity, hub and center of the Universe!

He must live, and grow strong on blood and lives, until the Universe of Light was swept away. And even if he could not grow that strong, he must at least grow to make himself strong food for the Survivor. He would become part of whoever ate him.

But he must not let himself be eaten by anyone small. He must accomplish his present mission. Otherwise, the flesh torn slowly from his bones would be eaten by dozens of creatures, goblins and ghouls and trolls, and the Survivor would not remember him at all.

You can't march on an empty stomach, Istvan thought, but he did not feel hungry. Thoughts of war, plans and memories, cascaded through his mind. He had forced himself to swallow a few mouthfuls when he saw Lord Shachio striding purposefully towards him. *More bad news, I suppose.*

"Esrith Gunnar wants to talk with you," said Shachio, sitting down beside him. "He is with one of the guild's Seers, in Portona, and asks if you will permit mind-touch."

"Mind-touch," Istvan agreed, with a nod. He took a quick bite of the hot bread, and felt Shachio's mind against the outer fringes of his own. The Seer's face went blank, and the voice that spilled from his mouth was altered—deeper, rougher—the voice of Esrith Gunnar:

"DiVega? Asbiorn Kung is here with me. We just got a message from Ironfist, in Manjipor. He says they'll be under siege by tomorrow night. You know about the situation there?"

"Yes," said Istvan. He saw Shachio's lips move with his own, and knew that his own voice would be coming from the lips of the Seer in Portona. He closed his eyes and relaxed his mind, allowing himself to "see" Gunnar's face—an unstable image, with muddy colouring. But the expression was there, and the lips moved:

"Aurel Ciavedes rode out last night—riding south, he said. Am I correct in assuming that you will march on Manjipor to lift the siege?"

"Probably," said Istvan, with a quiet smile. "But I thought you didn't want to get embroiled in a civil war?"

"Ironfist is an old friend," Gunnar said. "That makes things different. You're Commander of Mercenaries. You can order us south."

"We can't wait for you," Istvan warned. "You're nearly a day's march away, and we move out within the hour."

"So we follow a day's march behind you." The image in the Seer's mind shrugged. "We can join you at Ojaini."

"Very good," said Istvan. The Carrodian Axemen were considered the finest infantry in the world. They would stiffen Phillipos' pike-line. "Consider yourselves ordered to Ojaini. How soon can you move out?"

"Twenty minutes!"

"Take your time!" Istvan laughed. "An hour will do admirably! We meet at Ojaini!"

"At Ojaini!" Shachio's head jerked in a sharp nod, and his eyes opened. Istvan felt the contact fade.

Jagat's men were already on the march, sweating as the day grew hot. Pitiless sunlight seared the plain. Fine grit billowed up in choking brown clouds. A sheen of lacquer gleamed in the harsh hot light over the homemade armour that the Bordermen wore. Dark skirts flapped above their steady striding feet. The sword-wheel banner they carried swayed against a steel-blue sky.

Martos wanted to race back to Inagar, to kneel before Kumari and beg forgiveness. Instead he cursed the heat and helped herd the horses. The Kadarins were roasting in their ovens of steel: breastplate, backplate, and helmet, all were burning hot. As the Twin Suns climbed, even the Jumpers lowered their bony heads and plodded dully along. But the Farshooters, from N'lantia, south beyond Shadow and desert, joked about the fine cool weather.

The pulse of feet hammered in Martos' ears as the long

grim lines of men from Inagar marched beside his little mounted company, sturdily striding along, breathing through fine gauze scarves. Bordermen on ponies jogged in little groups. Even Hamir, though rich for a Borderman, Lord of miles of undevastated grazing land, could afford to mount only a very few of his fighting men. The rest walked, leather shields bobbing above their packs, the crude lacquered armour over their threadbare clothes coated with fine grime from the kicked-up dirt, their faces veiled with rough cloth.

Vultures followed, soaring in the glare, but no other birds, not this close to the Border. No trees grew on the broad brown plain, only endless sparse seared grass. Far in the south, a black line thickened. All that day, the Border rose before them as they marched, first like a smoky haze on the horizon, then like a distant storm.

Chondos woke shivering in dim grey light, among scraps of wood and cloth that were the ruins of an ancient couch. He rolled over slowly and sat up. A keening icy wind blew through his thin robe.

There was a sudden scuttling sound from the door. Something small and twisted darted down a long echoing corridor as he turned his head. He climbed to his feet, coughing harshly. His throat was bone-dry; his stomach burned and rumbled as though he had not eaten for days. That was nonsense, of course: he had stuffed himself at the banquet only the night before! But he felt weak and dizzy, and his head hurt. He staggered, staring. Horror swept over him as he recognised chairs, half-buried in ancient tatters of rotted cloth, as he remembered table and chest and walls and floor . . .

He was not dreaming. And he had not been dreaming last night either. *Rajinagara,* the black-robed thing had said.

He turned to face the arch in the stone, the cold wind and grey light. Through it he could see only slate-grey blankness, like a sky covered with thick storm clouds—except that there was no movement of clouds. Perhaps the arch was covered with grey-black glass.

He tried to step towards the window, and reeled as he staggered up against a wall. His hands met rough stone, and his feet floundered in rotting scraps of ancient cloth. Dust rose around him, and he sneezed, again and again. The cloth, he thought, had once been as warm and thick as an Alferridan carpet. He reached down, seized a piece, and pulled. Old threads tore, and he staggered back, a long strip in his hands.

Half-blinded, choked by billowing clouds of dust, he wrapped the cracking cloth around his shoulders. The fabric itself was cold, and he shivered more violently. He needed a fire, and something hot to drink. Trying to convince himself that he felt warmer, he hugged the makeshift cloak more tightly around him, and turned again to the window. Now he could make out great, looming, shadowy buildings.

He lurched towards the archway. His eyes were becoming more used to the dim light. Jagged knives of glass projected from the edge of the arch. He saw a webwork of black lines lacing the window. After a moment he realised that they were fragments of the lead that had once held together panes of glass. More glass lay broken on the floor. He tried to pick a safe path through the splinters, but had to desist. He looked at the fragments of the couch, and wondered if there was a piece he could use as a broom. Or perhaps he could bind scraps of cloth to his feet.

He could see now the ground between the buildings, littered with stones from the crumbling walls. A thousand years, it had been, if this was truly Rajinagara. *A man may always die*, the Bordermen said. And it was better to die, they said, than to be a captive among the Night Things.

Something moved on the ground far below. His hand groped at his hip, seeking the sword-hilt that should have been there. A long thin arm had reached up out of a pile of earth, and a pointed, corpse-pale face glared about with bulging eyes. A second spindly arm was followed by a round, bloated body. It heaved itself out of the ground and shambled away from its hole on crooked spindly legs; a second creature followed, shaped the same but covered with dirty grey fur. The two scuttled down the street and vanished.

Chondos shuddered, and peered through the crumbling ruins. A great fortified citadel towered above nearby ruins: doubtless the famed inner hold of Antapor, he thought, and shuddered again. It *was* Rashnagar! As a boy he had studied old paintings avidly, hungry for ancient glory, and the crumbling outlines of that fortress were familiar, though blurred by time.

He was in Rashnagar, in Rajinagara, trapped in the Shadow, with no escape except those blades of glass. *A man may always die . . .*

That thought steadied him, and he straightened defiantly. No escape? Had not Pertap been trapped within the Shadow—though not as deep—and had he not ridden to the light?

> *Then up and spoke bold young Pertap,*
> *A man may die in hope or fear.*
> *I'll risk the death that's worse than death*
> *If it will save my comrades here!*

The old song thrilled through his mind. He glared at the crumbling walls of Antapor. But Pertap had had a silver sword, and a torch, to fight the Dark Things. Chondos had nothing, not even a sword of common steel. He looked at the crumbling cloth, and thought how quickly it would burn; but he had no way of starting a fire.

He turned and stared out into the shadows of the building. Somewhere there must be a way out. But even if he found it unguarded, what hope was there in flight through Demon-haunted mountains, unarmed, barefoot, and with neither food nor water? Might there yet be weapons lying in corners of the deserted building? Or perhaps some tattered scraps of ancient clothing which might help protect him from the chill?

He staggered to the door, and hesitated. The long passage seemed deserted, but he remembered the half-seen shape that had scuttled away as he woke. He forced himself into dimness that deepened steadily as it left the pallid daylight behind. His sword-hand fidgeted nervously, aware of its emptiness. Rooms opened off the corridor. If he could find so much as a sharp knife . . .

He turned to the nearest door, and steeled himself to enter the deeper darkness behind it. He held his breath and listened, but all he heard was the beating of his own heart. Nothing breathed in the room, but many of the Dark Things did not breathe. His empty hand ached for a sword-hilt to close around, even though anything that laired in the room was as likely as not something that steel could not kill.

He stepped into the dark. His bare foot struck something hard that clattered across the floor, and he stood still, his heart pounding. After a moment's groping in the darkness, he was about to turn back when his questing fingers encountered dry scratchy cloth that tore as he touched it. Light glared in his eyes. He pulled forcefully, and tiny leaded panes of unbroken glass, clouded and dull, stared at him.

Turning, he saw the tracks of his feet in thick dust. He glimpsed a fireplace, and an ancient chest, scarred with sword strokes. In the dust of the floor was a jumble of litter: tiny bits of jewelry, broken jars and boxes, scraps of wood—and bones. A skull stared from a corner, bare teeth resting in the dust. After a moment he breathed again, and shrugged. He should have expected as much, in this place.

He rummaged through the jumble on the floor. Even a broken blade would serve! Earrings, an odd-shaped cup, a tiny statue, little jars whose bottoms were smeared with dried stuff that might once have been perfume, medicine, or ink—nothing he could use. Tubular packets of black cloth turned out to hold ancient candles, brittle and flaking, but looking as though they would still burn—if only he could light them! He smiled ironically. A slender chain loomed in ovals over a small box, open and empty.

His fingers touched metal in the dust, and suddenly he was staring, unable to believe his luck, at a slender length of flexible steel, coiled around itself so that one end scraped across a tightly set stone. He pressed the steel across. A spark leaped, and went out in the dust.

He reached for the chain he had found before, and threading it through a twist in the steel, hung it carefully around his neck, concealed beneath the cloth. He stood taller now. With this he could cook food, keep warm, and drive away the Night Things! With this he had hope indeed!

He began to search again, looking for some forgotten blade. A sound jerked his head up. He tensed, breathing slowly and silently. Voices, and faint footsteps. And one voice eerily familiar . . .

He moved to the door. Flickering reddish light reflected from the walls. He hesitated, wondering if he should hide here. But there was only one door to the room, and they would find him quickly enough.

He slipped into the corridor, and moved soft-footed back towards the room in which he had first wakened. Then, through the arched window, he saw that the sky was no longer blank greyness, but great alternating bands of light and dark. He stared, his mind racing. This must be sunset, and those bands of black the shadows of the mountains. And they must run east and west. There was a way to tell direction in the Shadow!

The room bloomed with ruddy light about him, and a harsh voice hissed behind him. "Do you like evening, King Chondos? Be glad, then, I allow you to wake! You have asked for clothing and a torch; here they are. And we have arranged for more suitable quarters."

"I thank you for your thoughtfulness," said Chondos, with an ironic smile, but he did not turn. He watched the grey bars fading from the sky. *East,* he thought. *Then north will be that way.*

"We have brought you food and drink."

His throat was dry as dust, his stomach agony. Memories of pastries and roast meats and fine wine leaped, maddening, into his mind. Turning, he saw, behind the black-robed shape, men with the aquiline features of Bordermen, clad in heavy fur and leather. Two wore ancient shirts of rusty mail, and swords jutted at their hips. But the rest were unarmed. One held out an ewer and a goblet, and rasping thirst in Chondos's throat drove all else from his mind. He had emptied it three times before he noticed the goblet was dirty.

"Last night, Lord King," the hissing voice mocked, "you asked why you had not heard your subjects cheering. Listen now!"

Blackness outside the window trembled with sudden screams, howls, moans, and roars. The men in the room shouted too, but they looked pale and frightened, and their voices were lost in the horrid chorus from outside. There had been no signal that Chondos could see. What this mummery might mean he did not know. Did the thing in the black robe think he would believe this a cheer of welcome? Or was it merely mocking, or trying to frighten him? The minds of the Dark Things were not like the minds of men.

The voices in the night slowly faded, until at last a single voice roared alone, somewhere in the echoing ruins. That, too, stopped. Eerie silence ached in his ears. Cloth rustled, and a man stepped forward with bundles of clothing. Another held a platter of food.

Chondos fought down the crying of his stomach. Not knowing what that food was. Or what spells might be on it, to place him in their power. He studied the men, trying to keep his mind away from hunger. Legend said that there were five tribes in the Black Kingdoms south of the mountains, raiding and slavery their only contact with the outer world. The Dark Lords had allowed them to retain the shape of men, but rumour said their minds were twisted to the likeness of their rulers. He had only seen such men before as blurred figures in the flurry of battle, or as corpses.

"Your subjects, Lord King," the hissing voice purred. "These are men of the Pure-in-Blood: of the Ancient Race, true breed of Old Takkaria, unmixed and unchanged. They do not suffer the bastards they get of their slaves to live, and so they are as they were a thousand years ago."

The man holding the garments dumped them on the floor. Chondos bent to look. Spoils of raids, here—those breeches were Messantian or even Devonian, and that long tunic, surely, was Alferridan. He pulled a warm cloak quickly from the pile, letting the scrap of rotting tapestry fall.

"Now, King of Takkaria," the robed figure said, "you have clothing, though not mine, and here is food, and a torch to light your way to better quarters, more fitting for a King in Rajinagara. Come! Your faithful subjects wait to escort you!"

Chondos felt himself swaying. The agony in his belly grew, gnawing at him. How long had it been since the banquet, then? He would be too weak to escape if he did not have food, and soon . . .

"You think to escape!" the hissing voice snarled, "but you will not! You will leave here as one of us, or not at all. We offer you great power if you aid us willingly—but you *will* aid us, one way or another."

Here at last was the core behind all this mummery.

"And who are *you?*" Chondos sneered. "Another of my subjects? My chief Councillor, perhaps? If I am King here, will *you* come fawning when I call your name. You *have* a name, have you not?"

"My name?" Shrill, unpleasant laughter was muffled by the cloth. "I am called many things. 'Lord' I am to the Faithful, and 'Master' among the Pure-in-Blood. There are other names. If you need one other than these, call me Taratos!" Mocking inhuman laughter echoed from stone walls. "Yes, Taratos will do nicely."

Something like an insect walking on the skin of his mind made Chondos shudder. The creature tainted his thoughts with its loathly touch, so different from the mind of Miron Hastur . . . And with that thought his memory awoke, and chanted the spell Miron had taught him.

Taratos shrieked. The Pure-in-Blood cowered. Chondos smiled, triumphantly, and stepped to the man who held the platter. He could no longer deny the agony of his stomach.

"Fool!" Taratos snarled behind him. "You think you have done well, guarding your thoughts against me! But you cannot hold that guard forever!"

Chondos lifted a bowl of gruel to his lips. The thin, tasteless stuff could at least fill his belly and build up strength for his escape. He looked at the meat warily, wondering if it was human flesh, or the flesh of some loathsome creature of the darkness.

"If I need to know what is in your mind," Taratos said, "I can break your foolish spell easily enough. Pulling out some of your fingernails would do it!"

Sniffing, Chondos brought his nose close to the platter. Venison! He smiled. The outside was burned, the inside raw. But there was another smell that penetrated his stuffed nose, too, and that made him feel less like eating.

"I am the Master," Taratos said. "You will learn what it means to defy me. You will learn!"

Chapter Twelve

In the white crystal glow of the Otherworld sky, the black stars hung above Carcosa. Miron Hastur stared into endless light, trying to wrap his mind around its vastness. Plane above plane, Carcosa rose around him, hub and centre of the Universe Hastur had reclaimed from the dark. Its towers rose beyond the moons; its stairways led from world to world.

In the Universe of Light, a stirring disturbed him. Shadows of this reality would become the events of his world: he saw some great danger gathering. He turned away from the glowing heavens and sorrowfully descended the long stair to the topmost pinnacle of the Tower of Carcosa, and there he found his body lying, bathed in healing light. With a last glance at that glittering sky, he entered the flesh once more, and opened his eyes. His mind cut off the flow of healing rays as he rose and stretched. The spear-wound in his back had healed without a scar.

With a swift glance at the door none may pass in the body, which led upward from the tower's top into the World of Light, he turned to leave the chamber. He passed by the door that would have led to the base of the tower upon the moon Lirdan; he passed the sealed door that once had opened beside the Lake of Hali, and went down the long stair that would bring him to the base of the Tower of Carcosa in the land of Seynyor. Through an arched window the Twin Suns' light glittered on the snowfields of the Mountains of the Clouds; far below, the tiny houses of the mortal city clustered at the mountain's foot.

He stiffened. Loud to his mind came a call, an alarm. His mind looked across the continent to the Shadow's edge: a black tower reared where the tower of his kin had stood only days

before, and rings of deadly power rippled out from it. Fire-clad
Hasturs vanished to escape the ripple's touch, and reappeared,
hurling streams of raging need-fire. Dark ripples absorbed the
flame: the ebon tower stood untouched. The Shadow deepened
and spread, blotting out the sunlight.

Even as Miron prepared to join that conflict, a thought
reached him from his cousin Elnar in Idelbonn, far in the
south. In an instant Miron had appeared at his side, and two
minds joined to move one of the ancient weapons from its
sealed cavern under Idelbonn to a hillside thousands of miles to
the north. There, spreading ripples of death broke on a barrier
of silver fire; but Miron could feel it weakening as each new
wave smashed upon it, and knew it could not be long before it
broke and death poured over the farms and villages that lay
beyond.

Elnar knelt by the ancient web of many-coloured rods,
pulsing with undying fire, that had lain for ages sealed in
stone. Miron joined him, shaping his mind to complex patterns
of energy, swirling through the interlocking crystal rods.

In the air above the dark tower, a spark formed, a tiny pearl
of power. Glowing, it hung growing. Then it fell from the air,
onto the tower. Darkness met it, swallowed it. The fabric of
the tower shuddered, but held.

Again rainbow energies seethed through the crystal lattice.
Again a spark fell upon the ebon tower. Again the blackness
swallowed it. Despair changed to hope as Miron felt the
ancient, powerful mind of Kandol Hastur-Lord join with his
own, flowing strength and wisdom into his mind and Elnar's.

Purple and white flames boiled through the web of rods;
once more a pearl of light condensed above the Dark Things'
citadel. It hung, waiting, at Kandol's command. Over the wide
plains of Kathor and Orovia, the Twin Suns flickered.

A beam of blinding flame burned through the Shadow's
roof, and focussed upon the hanging spark. For a second only,
the spark gathered power, floating in the air, and then it fell,
not upon the dark tower, but on the stone beneath. Light spread
and grew; rock melted. A widening pool of liquid fire washed
the tower's base. The ground glowed and melted.

The dark tower shuddered in a lake of flame, and flashing
sparks drifted slowly through the glassy darkness. The waves

of dark energy ceased; the last deadly ring shattered against the silver shield.

Hasturs gathered about the fiery lake, glowing like stars in the gloom, and bolts of need-fire streamed from their blades and their hands. Crystals red and green blazed up; blue fire and purple fire surged restlessly under Kandol's guiding hands. Light leaped from the molten lake, and the tower was wrapped in a sphere of crackling silver fire. The silver globe shrank and brightened as the Hasturs who ringed the glowing pool pressed it in. The dark tower glowed dull red.

Joined minds felt the fabric of space buckle, as the dwellers in the tower were hurled back to their own place. The tower vanished in a sun-bright flash. Through veiling murk, the Hasturs sensed a whimpering and scurrying as the creatures of the night quailed from the blinding light and fled to their lairs.

Still the glowing lake grew, eating away the stone, a menace in its own way as great as the dark rings had been. Again the three Hasturs bent above the crystal rods. Muted tones pulsed rhythmically; deep lights throbbed. Above the spreading lake of fire, a new mote appeared, a dull red teardrop that faded as it fell. Flame splashed and the pool's raging glitter muted.

Kandol gathered up steam and vapour, and massed them into clouds. The pool's edge faded to a dull, sluggish red, and a black crust began to form. Kandol piled cloud upon cloud. Great black storm clouds grew.

As the ground's light dimmed, there was a stirring in the Shadow. Uoght moved, vast as a mountain, and driven before his terror a loathsome horde poured in a dread wave towards the Border. Rain burst from Kandol's clouds; steam hissed up from cooling lava. In the centre of the pool, weary Hasturs whirled up walls of molten stone, hastily rearing a new tower around themselves. On the far side, Hasturs vanished, leaving the dark screaming victimless at the edge of the lava.

At Miron's side, Elnar swayed and almost fell. Kandol and Miron supported him between them, fed his fading vitality with their own. When he could stand again, he vanished—by Kandol's command—to rest and gather strength until he was needed again.

Kandol returned the crystal lattice to its resting place beneath the halls of Idelbonn, and sealed its ancient chamber.

Then he spoke, his voice loud in the minds of all the Hasturs. His battle-weary kin vanished, taking up watches in the quiet parts of the world, and others who had spent that day resting in Y'Gora, Norbath, or Tarencia appeared in their place, rested for the struggle before them. Then Kandol, too, vanished into the endless mazes of the Tower of Carcosa.

Miron stood, still strong from the healing rays. Over the still-hot lava came now monstrous things, invisible to mortal men, but sickeningly clear to Miron's vision: Dholes summoned from the dark land by the power of Uoght. Wielding deathly power, they rushed upon the half-finished tower. In a crackling of blue-white flame, Miron appeared before them, and bolt after bolt flashed from the sword in his hand.

"Open the gates!" the Herald demanded in a voice like thunder. "Open the gates for the Prince of Manjipor!"

Martos strained his ears to hear the reply. Heralds' voices were strong, but it was the voice of the mind they depended on.

"To Chondos, Prince of Manjipor, King of Tarencia, these gates are never closed," the voice called back from the wall above the gate. "But where is he? My master sees him not! Let the Prince of Manjipor, Chondos of Tarencia, stand forth, and the gates will open!"

Jagat sat his horse like a statue.

"Jagat, Prince of Manjipor, stands here before his army!" the Herald shouted. "Open the gates for Prince Jagat!"

Martos watched the men on the gate. The Herald spoke to another for a moment: Lord Maldeo himself, he guessed.

"To Jagat, Lord of Damenco, these gates have never been closed in the past," the strong voice sang from the gate. "But we know only one Prince of Manjipor, and he is named Chondos, not Jagat! To any who come bearing this title falsely, these gates are shut. My master defies this self-styled Prince as usurper and felon, and bids him leave this place!"

Lord Jagat stirred, and sighed. "Earth must be fed. Bid him send out his women and children. War, red war, and so on." He shook his head. "A pity for such loyalty to be wasted on a fool. Commend Maldeo for me, upon his loyalty . . ."

The Herald straightened, expanding as he drew breath.

"Then war, red war, must be between us, Maldeo of Isudom! So says my master! He commends you upon your loyalty, though he sorrows it is wasted on an unworthy Lord, and he bids you send out your women and children."

Martos stirred, impatient to be done with ritual and to go on with the business of war. Jagat's dark face was sombre beneath his white hair.

"Our women and children are happy enough!" Maldeo's Herald called from the gate. "My Lord thanks you for your commendation, Lord Jagat, but says, in honour there is no choice."

Jagat snapped straight in the saddle. Martos' breath hissed through his teeth. At least half the women and most of the children in the province lived in the city, it was said. Maldeo must be confident of a swift end to the siege, for the Law of Hastur allowed no excuses. If the children in the citadel became hungry, the Hasturs themselves would force Maldeo to surrender. The Rules of War were firm: only warriors could suffer. In its way it was a master stroke, for it limited the kinds of attack that could be made against the city; to avoid endangering women and children, they would be forced into a long slow siege.

Martos studied the gate before them, the main gate that faced the Shadow. It was strong. Atop the long sloping ramp that led up the mound, it was like bared teeth. All around the edge of the mound he could see portions of half-buried walls. Above them newer walls frowned ponderously down.

Many houses in the city, he knew, were sunk in the earth: windows in basement rooms choked with packed soil. There were sculptured walls where stone dancers writhed half-hidden in grass, their shapely legs long buried, and warriors shook bows and spears as they urged on steeds whose bellies barely cleared the ground in which their hooves were rooted.

The ritual courtesies of the Heralds ended. Martos was glad enough to wheel his horse and follow Jagat back to the slowly growing camp. He felt out of place; though he knew a little of siegecraft, nearly all his training had been in open cavalry fighting.

Paidros and the rest of the men had come up from Damenco, and he could at last let poor Warflame rest and ride Thunderhead. The big white horse seemed to be thriving despite the lack of fresh forage. The Borderers fed their horses mostly on grain and ground nuts; they imported vast amounts of hay to supplement the sparse grazing in the ruined lands. But with the war, Martos thought, hay might be hard to get.

Rumours raced through the camp: some said there was fighting in the city; others, that Maldeo had already expelled Jagat's partisans before the army's arrival. Some said Maldeo had no more than three hundred, or a thousand, or three thousand men; some said that ten thousand Seynyoreans had appeared at the gate the night before, and now manned the walls. Maldeo had food stored to last for three days, or three weeks, or three months, or three years. There were a thousand stories, and most, Martos remarked to Valiros, based on some drunkard's wild guesses.

Horns blew. The troops began to move in ordered bodies. Martos led men and horses into a position opposite the gate, and waited. His orders were to hold himself ready, a reserve, against a sortie. He doubted there would be one. The massive doors of the gate looked immovable as the walls, and opened, he remembered, onto a long, arched tunnel, lined with arrow-slits, and only another gate at the end.

Yet men with rams laboured up the causeway, and swarms of arrows flew from the wall. Soon there were bodies lying on the slope, looking as though they were lying down to rest in the heat, except for the stains on the ground. Other men scrambled to the wall with ladders. The Twin Suns glared down, and the heat grew worse. Martos envied the loose robes of the Borderers; the tight-fitting Kadarin clothing clung suffocatingly to the skin, and the steel armour was too hot to touch.

Ladders rose against the wall, and were hurled down. Arrows flew. A framework roofed with hides was set up to protect the ram at the gate. A rhythmic booming came from below. Martos leaned on his dwarf-forged sword, his hands, at the centre of his chest, cupping the pommel. His clothing was soaked with sweat; his breastplate burned the back of his hands if he let them touch it.

"Are we just going to stand here through this whole stinking war?" Paidros snarled angrily.

"What *should* we do, little man? Ride our horses straight up the wall? Or can the Jumpers just bounce over it?"

"Well," said Paidros, gingerly pulling off his hot morion and scratching his sweat-drenched hair, "if we have to stand here and roast, we might at least have a little target practise, like those fellows are having."

He jerked a thumb toward a hillock behind them, where the Farshooters stood, their swollen arms and shoulders rippling as they sent constant streams of arrows from their terrible N'lantian bows. They could shoot nearly twice as far as ordinary men, and even at this range their arrows could pierce mail and all but the finest plate. What few shafts came back from the walls were nearly spent.

Martos frowned, and measured the distance with his eyes. They were just out of bowshot now.

"*What's that?*" Valiros yelled, pointing.

Martos followed the line of his arm, and stared. Horsemen were sweeping around the curve of the mound. Painful pinpricks of light leaped from their armour; their bows wrought havoc among the clustering men in their path. Confused Bordermen stumbled out of their way as they dashed for the foot of the causeway.

"The sortie!" Martos stammered.

Paidros' voice rose, giving the order that Martos' numbed tongue was trying to find: "Mount! Mount and ride!"

Then they were all scrambling onto their horses, and racing towards the walls. Martos realised he was waving the big sword, and ramming it into its sheath, reached for his bow. Already the Farshooters were taking their toll of the enemy horsemen. He saw an armoured figure lifted out of its saddle; saw a horse roll forward, the rider flying over its mane.

Then his bow was drawn, and he was looking down the polished shaft. Over the arrowhead, bobbing as Thunderhead jolted under him, he saw a figure in earth-brown armour: a Borderman, riding among the Seynyoreans. The waxed string slipped through his fingers, and the Borderman threw up his arms and went over his horse's tail. Already Martos' fingers were groping among feathers, plucking out another arrow and fitting it to the string. At the foot of the causeway the horsemen checked, swords flashing.

Paidros shouted and cursed at the men as they formed a line. *I should resign the command*, Martos thought. *I should have long ago.*

A mass of men on foot were suddenly in front, between them and the fighting at the foot of the causeway. The booming ram stopped as the men manning it turned to meet the menace of the horsemen. The gates gaped wide, swords poured out from the city, and there was fighting at both ends of the causeway.

Martos drew a deep breath, willing his tongue to obey, and stretched his bow-hand towards the sky, with a shout of *"Halt!"* In perfect order, the company drew up just outside the boiling mass of Jagat's men that blocked them from the causeway.

Across the sea of milling heads, Martos saw the hide-roofed framework that had shielded the rammers lurch forward and vanish into the arched maw of the gate. Horsemen were surging up the ramp, swords smeared crimson in the hot dry light. The path was choked with fighting: steel waved like branches in a storm. At the causeway's foot, horses dashed back through the waves of footmen rushing to the aid of their companions above. Martos counted. Thirty skilled horsemen had thrown an army into confusion, and now held thousands at bay.

"Paidros," he said, his voice steady, "take twenty men. Harass the Seynyoreans holding the bottom of the ramp. The rest, follow me!"

Paidros quickly picked out twenty men, and Martos turned right and began pushing through the crowd. He wanted to see where those horsemen had come from. On the slope, men died. Swords rose and fell, and the ground was soaked with blood. Paidros and his men pushed their horses through the packed ranks, but they would be too late, Martos saw. Once Jagat's men had been cleared from the ramp, the Seynyoreans would wheel and gallop up the causeway, and slam the gates again.

The crowd thinned before them, and with a shout Martos cleared a path and thundered around the curve. Trampled earth left a clear enough trail. He glimpsed startled faces above the parapets. The sides of the mound rose sheer on his left, unscalable. A sudden arrow quivered in the ground a foot from Thunderhead's hoof. Martos reached for the shield that should have been hanging at his saddle, but it was not there. He had left it behind in the confusion.

Martos saw the track he followed curving into what seemed a little gully, and spurred the horse towards it. He tucked his chin tight against the burning steel of his gorget, and hoped the molded helmet would deflect anything falling at his face. He huddled his arms tight against his body. Walls of grass and bare earth blurred by; then he reined the horse in by a wall of bleached, weathered stone.

He threw himself from the saddle and pressed the horse up against the stones. Valiros and a dozen men had followed him into the cleft. The others raced their horses back and forth outside, shooting up at the walls with their short bows.

No arrows fell into the cleft. Martos blinked in the shade, his eyes still used to the glaring light outside. To his right dull copper—or was it brass?—blocked an arch in the stone. The stonework around it was old and worn, but the metal door looked new and strong. It was wide enough so that two horsemen could ride abreast through it.

As Martos looked, the left-hand gate swung open a little, and a face peered through. He hurled himself at the door, and bruised his shoulder against hard metal as it slammed. He heard a confused mutter of voices, and then the grate and thump of a bar being set in place.

A flicker of ruddy light drew his eye to the thin crack between the halves of the gate. Thought kindled. He pressed his eye to the crack. Torchlight, and moving shadow. He bent, light sliding past his eye as he moved it down the crack. Red light reflected from a flat plane against the door, and only shadow below. The bar. He put his fingers against the door to mark it, and rose.

Valiros' voice murmured a question. Martos hissed for silence. His sword was heavy as he slid it awkwardly from its sheath, one hand still resting on the cool metal of the door.

"Hounos!" he snapped. "Rodericos! Ride to Lord Jagat for more men. Find somebody who knows the city. I want to know what we've found! Valiros, be ready to call the others in! Cavalry came out of this place, so cavalry can get in! Now, *stand back!*"

He raised the blade over his head, fingers still on the door. He brought his left hand up to the hilt at last, and stepped back, measuring the distance carefully. Dwarf-forged, and able to cut trolls' flesh. Bronze should be like butter. He'd cut through thicker wooden bars. But if the bar was iron? The back edge of his sword clicked against the steel between his shoulder blades. The line of the crack seemed very thin.

Air screamed under his edge. Bronze whined, jarring his wrists. A long ribbon of torn metal curled away from the crack. His sword was grasped and pinched. He ripped it free, heaved it high, lashed it down again, with muscle clenching in chest and shoulders. He felt the bar breaking. Muffled voices shouted. The doors shuddered. He levered one open with a twist of his blade, and leaped through.

A whistle in the air clanged on his blade as he snapped an arrow aside. A dark figure lunged, steel-tipped in dim light. Martos sidestepped, long blade keening down. A man's voice screamed.

A sword flew at his face. His blade twisted free and up: edges clashed before his eyes. He felt his return cut spring back from steel; then the wheeling dwarf-sword's tip scraped stone and swooped up to quiver as it cut into bone.

A last wild arrow shattered on the stone by Martos' shoulder, and then the bowman ran to the left and vanished in the wall. Square black shadows blotted torchlight from the room. Martos hurled his weight against the closing door. Suddenly Valiros was beside him, and three others. The door fell open, and men rushed at them out of pulsing torchlight, drawn swords flashing into vision and vanishing again. Martos' blade looped out, and headless figures fell. Belling metal echoed from the walls. Feet pounded in the corridor; Kadarins poured in.

At the end of the passage was a stone wall. Men turned there, running to the right where wide doors gaped, and vanished with their torches behind slamming wood. In flickering darkness, a fallen torch glinted on steel that stabbed up from the floor. Martos dodged back. A bleeding man pushed himself up from the stone and lurched against the wall, his sword jutting like a thorn, defiant eyes glaring.

"Surrender!" Martos said. "You are alone and wounded. Killing you will not even delay us."

Wet teeth gleamed in a dark face. Fire mirrored on steel was lightning rippling towards Martos' throat. Martos' shoulders swung. His heavy blade clashed the other aside, setting echoes clanging, and the man sprawled. Martos' hand spun the hilt of his sword, so that it was the flat that smashed down on the outstretched arm. The Borderman gasped, and his sword flew from his hand. He jerked a dagger from his belt, but Martos stepped on his wrist and kicked the knife away.

"Well done, Martos!"

Jagat came striding through the crowding Kadarins, Huonos at his side. Valiros and Thiondos pulled the wounded Borderman to his feet. He struggled futilely, and almost fell, but when he saw Jagat before him he drew himself up, scowling defiance.

"You fought bravely," Jagat said. "It is no disgrace to fall captive to the Hero of Ukarakia."

"I should have set my back to the door," the wounded man snarled, "and died there!"

Jagat shook his head. "A man may always die," he said, "and you would have died, but for the mercy of Lord Martos. But he could have spared you as easily if you had gone on leaning against the door."

Jagat gestured for them to take the prisoner away, and turned to Martos. "Your man said you wanted someone who knew the city. I was born here. You want to know where you are? This is called the Stable Gate, because it leads to the Buried Stables. Do you know about them?" Martos shook his head.

"They're under the mound now, but they were once old stables, abandoned thousands of years ago." Jagat smiled tolerantly at the look Martos gave him. "Some say they go back to the Age of Terror, or even the Age of Peace. There are jokes about what they were buried in. But they must have been royal or military stables, built of stone. They stood abandoned for ages, while the earth rose around them, and new houses were built on top. They were forgotten until my grandfather's time.

"The last time Manjipor was reclaimed from the Shadow, there was a nest of goblins here, and the men who hunted them down found this place. Old Prince Jal had it cleaned out and repaired, to be a monument to the age and glory of Manjipor. Then, when Olansos married Princess Tarani, they hired builders from the north to turn the goblins' old tunnel into this maze gate. It's a stable again, now." He gestured at the door.

"It's not the gate I would have chosen to attack, but there's only one door left after this one, and you'll be in the stables. There's a ramp that leads up, with an iron grate to cover it, but if we can get through that . . ." Jagat shrugged. "We'll be in a courtyard, with archers shooting at us, but there's only a simple gate to hammer down, and we'll be in the streets."

"We need axes," Martos said as he studied the door before them. Iron straps crossed the old wood. He heaved up his heavy sword and hewed. The point scratched deep; the door drummed mockingly. Without edge or corner to strike, a sword was useless.

Dimly, Martos heard Jagat give orders behind him, but his mind was beating at the door. He stabbed angrily. His point pierced through. He worked the blade from side to side, listening to the old wood crack. He ripped the blade free and stabbed again. Valiros and others joined him, their points pecking away at the wood between the iron strips. Wood shredded: long splinters littered the floor. Wood clattered loudly on the far side of the door.

Martos stared dully at the widening hole, where a long strip of wood had ripped away. Then he waved the others back, and with both hands raised the heavy blade above his head. He measured the gap with his eye. The poised blade shifted in his hands. He struck. The point whirled through the space; the edge sank deep into wood. He felt the hilt twist in his hand as the blade turned to follow the grain. He wrenched, and a wide strip of wood split away.

Through a gap a handspan across he could see clearly the three heavy bars that held the doors. Without thought he slashed at the highest bar. It buckled, pinching his blade, sheared halfway through. He jerked the blade up and the bar came too, clattering into the corridor beyond.

An arrow sprang through the gap and glanced off Martos' breastplate. His head cleared. Feeling suddenly foolish, he pushed his point under the second bar and lifted with the flat till the bar fell away. Another arrow flipped out of the hole sideways, and fell harmlessly to the floor. Valiros pushed Martos aside and, crouching behind his shield, reached through the door and heaved the last bar loose.

Torchlight flared dim behind the opening doors, and arrows came humming in a swarm. Men with shields crowded past Martos. Arrows battered shields and armour. One man fell, his thigh pierced, but the rest rushed on.

Doors slammed far down the corridor, and the torchlight was gone. The Kadarins charged into darkness. Mysterious muffled thumping and clattering sounded from the dark. Someone brought a torch, and they saw stout wood doors. There was no final turn here to baffle entry. Swords began to score the old wood.

"Save your steel for men!" Lord Jagat's voice boomed from the stone of the walls. "The axes are here!"

Six Bordermen with single-bitted axes came pushing through the crowd. Kadarins fell back to give them room. Hammering axes hit thick wood. Chips flew. Jagged planks peeled from the door. Even through the crashing of axes, there was still a muffled thumping from behind the door. Martos rested, leaning his weary arms on his sword. It seemed like hours before the first jagged hole appeared.

Beyond the Yukota, the song of birds ended in a startled hush. Wings fluttered into the forest, and the underbrush was filled with small scurrying sounds. Hooves clattered like rain on a roof. But they could not drown out another sound that came from far behind: the relentless tramp of two thousand feet.

Bird and beast had fled, but the solemn, towering trees of the Kantara had seen armies before. Armies, and other things: royal processions and Kings fleeing into exile; ascetics and lovers; robbers and refugees. Ancient trees, which had stood hundreds of years, arched spreading antlers above the Ojaini road, shutting off the sky with masses of leaves, so that Istvan and his men rode in a vast green hall. Creepers covered ponderous boles.

Hoofbeats drummed through the earth. Dust rose swirling past the whithers of horse after horse, brown, black, grey: Seynyorean war-horses, big-boned, long-legged, gaunt. Far above the ground, their riders' mail and helms were dull in the filtered green dimness. The air was still and hot.

Small parties of outriders could ride through turf-floored, green-pillared rooms at the sides of the road, but the thick brush packed most of the horsemen, ten abreast, onto the road. The persistent stamping of a thousand men almost drowned out the distant patter of the horsemen at the rear.

Tall on his horse, swaying with its rhythmic stride, Istvan DiVega searched the branches overhead for some sign of the Twin Suns, some hint of time. Dark green and light green; these were the colours of the world. Here and there a gnarled black bole would stand stark against the green, but most trees were veiled in vines and moss. Where the shade was too deep for grass to grow, thick green moss spread over the ground.

"My grandfather told me once," Prince Phillipos said at Istvan's side, "that when he was a boy, there were still trees growing here that went back to the days of the Takkarian Empire."

Istvan blinked at him. He had dropped back to ride beside the young man at the head of the long line of Kalascorean foot. The constant crashing of feet behind him had set an old Creolandean marching song beating in his head.

"Some of them are very old," said Istvan. *Older than I am, at least,* he thought, wryly. "But a thousand years is a long time."

"It hadn't been quite that long when grandfather was a boy."

Istvan wondered if it had even occurred to the younger man that Istvan might ever have been a little boy, with a grandfather of his own . . .

In sudden, vivid memory, he *was* that small boy, sitting by the fire, looking up at the massive, white-bearded frame of his own grandfather, listening to marvel-filled tales of distant wars and valiant deeds. He had been no famous warrior then, breathless at Grandfather's feet; long years would pass before any fool harper would sing nonsense about "Istvan the Archer." Soon his hair would be as white as his grandfather's had been, and already he was "Grandfather" to little Rupiros and the girls. Yet, inside, he was still that same small boy.

Out of the far past, he heard the old man's voice: *When I was a boy, my grandfather told me* . . . Again he felt childish wonder at the thought. *Grandfather* a boy? With a grandfather of his own? Awed, he felt himself a part of a chain of living flesh that reached back through the countless ages, grandfather before grandfather . . .

"Lord DiVega!" a voice shouted, through the thunder of Kalascorean feet. Istvan turned. Behind him, footmen marched four abreast, pikes and halberds bristling in the centre, between two rows of long brazen shields.

Down the line a rider came racing, and spurred to Istvan's side. It was the Seer DiChezari, and Istvan pulled his horse to the side of the road.

"Word from D'Oleve in Manjipor. Fighting has begun in earnest. A major assault on the south gate has just been thrown back. Rupiros D'Esnola led a sortie that captured the enemy ram."

Istvan nodded in acknowledgement, and stared into the forest, while the crashing feet marched past. How many of these men, he wondered, were marching to their deaths? He remembered a young man asking that, and his own voice, calm and self-assured, answering: *All men are marching to their deaths, always, from the time they are born.* He curled his lip in self-contempt. Words! Yet that young man had been comforted. No doubt, all in that endless chain of grandfathers and little boys stretching back to the dawn of time had feared death in their turn. Some had died well, and some had died miserably, but they had all died.

Up and down the marching feet drummed on the road. Long pikes sloping to avoid the tangled roof, shields swaying with the swing of their stride, the armoured ranks swept past, marching to Ojaini and then west to Manjipor.

"There's something on the other side!" one of the Bordermen shouted, above the rhythmic crashing of axes.

Sharp echoes ached in Martos' ears. Jagged chunks of wood had to be kicked aside as they fell and piled on the floor. The Borderman's treasure, Martos thought, wryly, and then shuddered, realising firewood might indeed be a treasure tonight. Unless they took the city before nightfall, they would be sleeping in the open. They would need all the firewood they could get when darkness fell and vampires came creeping from the cover of the Shadow to feast on their blood in the dark.

All around him was the musty smell of earth, but as the hole in the door widened, he was startled by other smells: the sweet, grassy odour of fresh-cut hay, the rich pungency of manure, the good, living smell of horses.

He heard gasps from the Bordermen. Torchlight showed the hole still blocked. Echoing axes stilled: the axemen slipped back, away from the door as a heavy bar of wood tipped out at them. Martos heard shouting, and a rush of feet and hooves.

Wood belled on stone. Through the hole in the door, Martos saw a jumble of lumber. Sticking out of the pile he glimpsed a broken wheel and the side of a wagon, the tines of a pitchfork, the corner of a crate. They had buried the door behind piled-up wood. Chinks in the stack were streaks of light.

A Borderman heaved, and the doors pulled back. Martos rushed with his men to push and tug at the pile. At the top a crate swayed and fell away. Bright light glowed where it had been, and out of the light an arrow came darting, to sink into Huonos' throat. Huonos pitched back, blood gurgling as he tried to scream. Another arrow smashed against a wall, and a third skittered from the brim of Valiros' helmet as he bent over Huonos. Men ducked.

Martos set his shoulder to the buried wagon's side. Lumber was piled on top and stacked between its wheels. Valiros and others joined him. He felt the wagon lurch. Wood clattered loud as it fell. Martos hooked his fingers under the wagon and heaved. The wagon swayed away, boards clamouring as they cascaded to the floor. Feathered shafts whispered. The wagon tilted out and fell.

A square of daylight dazzled him. Across a wide floor, a golden block of sunlight crouched on a ramp of rich brown earth, up which men rushed horses. Above the waist-high lumber he saw the far wall, lined with bowmen who launched a cloud of arrows.

Valiros threw his shield before his face and scrambled up onto the piled lumber. Martos, shieldless, pressed his chin to his breastplate as he heaved himself onto the wagon, hoping no arrow glanced down across his face. Wood rolled underfoot as a wave of Kadarins climbed the heap of Borderman's treasure. Some fell with arrows in their legs, some with twisted ankles.

Men were waiting for them with shields and drawn swords. Martos jumped from a toppling crate over scattered boards to land, staggering, with a sword-edge screaming at his eyes. He got his own blade up barely in time: deafening steel clamoured beside his ear.

Regaining his balance, he ducked, slashing at a knee as a sword hummed over his head. His blade bounced from a quickly dropping shield. Enemy steel whirled round again. He straightened and turned the keel of his breastplate to the blow. Ringing armour rocked against his shoulders, as he cut at the frail bones of the elbow exposed by the swing. Mail parted: bones snapped; blood spurted.

Seynyoreans and Bordermen were all around him now. He dodged and whirled in the middle of a thicket of lashing blades. He glimpsed Valiros fighting nearby; then blinding sparks burned his eyes as his helmet rocked on his head. His point caught in a man's throat, and the flat of a sword brushed his armoured shoulder. He whirled his blade and a head bounced on the stone.

The men around him began to fall back. His troops came swarming into the room, followed by the warriors of Lord Jagat. He glimpsed men clearing a path through the lumber, heaving wood aside. His blade whisked above the edge of a lifted shield and looped down to shear mail-rings above a knee.

The last horse was led up the ramp. There was a shout, and Seynyoreans and Bordermen were running back, towards the doors of the ramp. Martos sprang after them. They raced into the square of sunlight, and the enemy began to heave great doors across the daylight. Martos hurled himself at the closing doors, pushed his leg and shoulder between them and pushed, as swords banged on the steel of his armour and his blade.

"Up the ramp!" a strong voice shouted. "Block it from the top!"

The door fell open. Martos staggered as his men came racing up. A man in Seynyorean gear leaped from between the doors. His broadsword lashed at Martos' face. Off-balance,

Martos had to guard. The Seynyorean's shield swept out, pressing the dwarf-sword back, while the Seynyorean blade soared free.

But Martos knew that move. Bent legs straightened: the sword-point hissed through empty air as he sprang out of range. Both hands heaved his hilt above his head. Poised, the Seynyorean paused. Martos saw in his movements the mark of the School of Three Swords—and skill that matched his own.

One of the clustered Kadarins sprang past swinging, and the Seynyorean's steel shield gonged. Martos opened his mouth to shout, but already the Seynyorean's sword had scythed through the cutting arm with a crack of chopped bone.

Martos lunged, his long blade sweeping low. The shield dropped and boomed; the Seynyorean's elbow twitched, but he did not cut. He knew Martos was beyond his shorter sword's reach. He advanced: Martos danced back, blade poised above his head, safe from the shield.

Six men slid between the doors, kicking them shut. Two Bordermen charged. Sharp swords hammered as they met Martos' men. Four Seynyoreans set their backs to the door.

Martos' foe sprang left; Martos, circling away, backed into Valiros. The Seynyorean's edge flew for his eyes. The dwarf-sword met it, then the shield thrust out to drive it aside, while the other blade lashed at Martos' defenceless left.

Martos spun the hilt in his palms, dragging the flat across the shield's face, and let his left knee buckle.

His knee struck stone as his point cleared the shield-edge. Steel thrummed between his hands, his ears ached with the clashing of metal. He twisted on his knees, dipping his point to stab blindly around the shield, knowing that to miss was to die.

Blood squirted down his blade. Steel falling from a dead hand glanced from his helm.

Three Seynyoreans still were fighting, their backs against the doors, Kadarins battering at their shields. The two Bordermen had died, throwing themselves on their foemen's weapons. Their swords were red, and four of Martos' men shared with them the blood-smeared floor.

Martos' left hand lifted the dead man's sword while his right wrenched his own free from the corpse. He wondered who it was he had killed, and if the man had won the fame his skill merited. A sword in each hand, he strode towards the fighting. His men made way for him, and as they fell back, each Seynyorean glanced quickly over his shoulder at the doors, as though expecting aid.

"Surrender!" Martos' voice echoed from the vaulted stone. "There are too many of us. Why die needlessly?" He raised the dwarf-sword high, and poised the shorter blade before him.

"All in good time, Kadarin," one of the men by the door replied. "When our task here is done. Then we'll see how needless it was."

"As you will," said Martos, and cursed under his breath. These were brave men!

He sprang, the dead man's sword thrusting at the nearest foe's eyes. As the shield rose, the dwarf-blade soaring above his head wheeled to dive under its edge, shearing through mail to bite deep into bone. He heard feet behind him and the whir of a sword, and let the force of his cut spin him around, whipping up his left-hand blade to meet falling steel, while the dwarf-sword swirled out to thunder on the shield.

Steel crashed and echoed on his right as Valiros leaped in front of the third Seynyorean as he tried to rush to his comrade's aid. Both swords slashing high and low, Martos danced in, forcing the Seynyorean to guard with sword and shield alike, giving him no time to cut. Mail-rings shattered under Martos' edge, and he felt the soft flesh part. He leaped past the falling man and hurled the stout doors wide.

A square of blue sky high above blinded him. Distant voices shouted in the glare. He blinked the blindness away, staring up the packed brown ramp. Something black edged into the square of sky, tipped, and fell. He sprang back with a wordless shout.

A wagon fell, on end, twisting on its tongue, and slewed towards them, spewing black gobs of manure, spattering their armour. A block of stone followed, splintering one of the wagon's wheels and ploughing down the ramp towards them. A huge wooden beam dug into the packed earth. Martos and his men dodged back through the door they had fought so hard to gain, and watched rubble fall to fill the passage.

Jagat joined them in the doorway. "Even if we could clear it out," he said, "the grate that they cover it with is of iron, and built for archers to shoot down between the bars."

Chapter Thirteen

Jodos clasped the corpse's clammy hand. The message must be quick. Although the Blue-robes could not read the dark channel to the mountains, they might yet sense it, and follow it back to him. He did not want to think of the fiery death that would follow. Instead he let boil up the grim delight he had hidden that morning when the news had come. Manjipor beseiged!

Now war would rage on the Border: it made no difference who won. Whether he summoned back a victorious army, or the Borderers marched north to attack the city, they would leave behind them a ruined, defenceless land. The Master need only wait a little . . .

Through the dead hand that held his own came the answer, a mocking reminder of the tortures awaiting failure, and the feasting that would follow success. Chondos' ghost shuddered in the depths of his mind.

"News from the city, Lord DiVega. From Manjipor."

Istvan nodded to show that he had heard, then stood in his stirrups and gestured with his arm, shouting, "Halt! Dismount! Walk your horses!" A trumpeter passed the signal down the line.

Istvan slid from the saddle, longing for sleep. But they must cover a certain amount of ground that day; they could not stop because one old man was tired. Trees loomed endlessly, aisle after aisle of pillared wilderness. What were they doing here, Istvan wondered, troubling the vast cathedral silence of the ancient forest with the foolish panoply of war?

"What is the news?" he asked, turning to the Seer.

"A party of Kadarins fought their way into the Buried Stables and captured them," DiChezari said. "They killed Nurin Kimerosa."

"Kimerosa?" Istvan's eyebrows rose. Cousin Raquel's best student! He'd barely known the man, except by reputation, but they had practised together, once, and the boy had given him a workout such as he'd not had in years.

"He stayed behind in the Buried Stables, to hold the ramp, with a handful of men," the Seer went on. "Most of his men were killed, too, though a couple have been reported by the Healers. But Kimerosa was killed. There were just too many Kadarins."

"Fewer by the time they got him, I imagine," said Istvan absently, picturing the handful of men holding back crowding enemies. A little thrill of glory ran through him, like the thrill he had felt as a boy listening to the old hero-tales.

He stiffened, angry with himself. This was no time to start dreaming like some slack-jawed poet. This wasn't one of the old tales: Kimerosa had been a real man, cut down fighting a mob of cowards afraid to fight him singly. No glory there, just a nasty death.

"They captured the stables, you said?"

"It won't do them much good, Todar says," answered DiChezari. "There is only the one shaft leading up to the city, and that's filled in. There is a whole company set to guard that courtyard, and the place is a deathtrap. Even if they do dig their way out, they can't break into the city."

"That will draw men from the walls," Istvan mused. He reached back and patted his horse absentmindedly, trying to remember details of the courtyard. It had been ten years since he had seen Manjipor. "How long do you think they can hold out?"

"At least a month or more, Lord," the Seer replied. "D'Oleve says the city can last as long as the stores do. He doesn't think that Manjipor can be taken by storm."

They'd said that the fortress at Belarri couldn't be taken, once: that had been one of the deeds that had made his name the plaything of every stinking minstrel south of the Ice Desert.

"I want you to contact Ojaini," Istvan said, "and order Enchanton DiVega and"—he paused a moment, thinking—"D'Olafos and DiSezrotti to march their companies out at once, and to make camp along the Yukota. Tell them to be as obtrusive as possible, to blow their trumpets a lot. They should send scouts across the river, and be prepared to cross at a moment's notice. And tell every company at Ojaini to be ready to march!"

The Seer nodded, and closed his eyes. Istvan fell silent, his ears filled with the clopping of hooves and the jingle of trappings. He stared down the long aisles of solemn trees, and suddenly remembered another forest, far away, in Y'Gora beyond the sea.

Branches bent and swayed in his memory now, opening a path before him, while he clung in wonder to the back of the mysterious white elf-horse, whose hooves barely seemed to touch the ground, that had borne him over many days' journey in a day and a night, through the Forest of Demons to Rath Tintallain. He remembered Rath Tintallain's graceful towers, and the deep dwarf-halls beneath; he remembered the flame of the swords of the gathering of heroes, and the silver swallows that had come to their aid from the stars.

That had been far away, though, and there were none of the elvish horses here. Were his army mounted thus, they could ride to Manjipor in a single night's gallop, passing the birds in their flight. But these were only mortal horses: too swift or strong a pace would kill them, and it was a long ride to Manjipor, through the barren dust where Demons had walked. With the rainy season coming on, too. He remembered a campaign he had fought, in rain that had turned all this land to mud. And the dust, in time, grew even worse . . .

The clatter of hooves battered his ears. He rode on, at the head of the long line of horses. Gritty clouds swirled higher and higher as more hooves disturbed the ground. The column of foot walked in thick brown mist. Two thousand feet rose and fell in steady rhythm. The happy irregular patter of the horses of the rear-guard set the cloud swirling still higher, to hang in the air long after the last horse had passed, a· the hoofbeats faded to a distant sound like rain. Boughs of ancient trees rustled mournfully. The song of a returning bird piped through the gloom, as the dim green light faded into darkness.

Chondos murmured the Hastur's spell every night when he went to sleep, and again when he woke. Once each night, the black-robed figure appeared outside the door of the new quarters they had given him, but always went away again.

Sometimes there were strange sounds of conflict in the hall beyond the broken door: horrid moans and shrieks, and once the voice of Teratos hissing strange words, while the Pure-in-Blood grovelled, whimpering with terror. They were strange, frightened people, and Chondos quickly gave up trying to talk to them. They seemed more afraid of their surroundings than he: miserable people, silent and furtive, who acted only out of fear. Armed, he could easily overawe them; had they been his only guards, escape would be simple.

Armed guards slept in some other chamber, taking turns to watch his door. His "servants" kept a fire going constantly, feeding it with broken scraps of furniture and with larger logs. Night was like tar outside the tiny barred window, and Chondos wrapped a chair leg with scraps of rotten cloth, and slept beside the fire, starting up at each sound in the night. By day he kept himself awake, amused at the annoyance of his guards. For them, he soon saw, daytime was a safe time, a time to sleep; at night they huddled fearfully, awaiting some unavoidable doom.

Each day he saved grain from his meal, and in a small box he began to save tinder. But was there a real hope of escape, he asked himself angrily, or was it only a game he played, to keep hope alive, when there was no hope?

He stalked angrily across the room, and turned again to watch the guard at the door. If it were not for the others, the unarmed "servants," he might be able to wrest the man's sword from him—then woe to any man, or any creature of flesh, that stood in his way! But many of the Dark Things were not of flesh, and swords were useless against them. It did not matter, he told himself angrily. He must continue to hope. It was his only weapon.

He scratched the black stubble that covered his chin and cheeks, and amused himself with the thought of fighting his way out with a razor. The firelight pulsed from the hearth. He turned to the tiny clouded window, a handspan across, his shadow blocking the firelight away. A red glow persisted in the dirty glass between the bars.

Something leaped in his heart. He pressed his face against

the bars, and reached his fingers between them to brush away the furring of dust. He saw a dim red glow moving in the sky: growing, coming towards Rashnagar. Faint screams and howls sounded from beyond, as though the Dark Things themselves were afraid. Hope of rescue flared and soared.

Through the murk, the red light began to take shape. Vast wings glowed red-hot in the darkness. Tiny between them glimmered a slender, serpentine body. A distant mountain-peak was blackly outlined between the wide wings as the creature passed behind it, and he gasped at the size thus revealed.

Dragon! Ages had passed since the last had been seen on the continent, but their wonder and terror had come down in story: flesh of molten stone, breath of lightning; the ancient terror that could smash a castle with a blow of its wing, or crush a city beneath its bulk.

Mountains appeared out of darkness, reddened by rushing wings. Wailing and shrieking sounded through the night, but above them a high-pitched whistle rose, growing louder as the glowing wings neared.

It had always been said that at least one of the great dragons still lived beneath the Shadow, yet few believed it. Not even the Hasturs could unravel the tangled web of legend that told how the Dark Ones controlled these monstrous fire-beings, impervious by nature to the fire of Hastur.

The whistle grew to a roaring wind. Nearby mountains reflected flame; then the ruined city was revealed in sullen light. The snaky body grew, dwarfing crumbling towers as it glided overhead, blotting out the sky with forge-red wings. Floor and walls shook around him, and the glowing wings vanished. Chondos turned, ears aching. He saw the Pure-in-Blood huddled, cowering, near the fire.

A red glow came from across the room. Chondos strode towards it, and found another tiny window. Through it, he saw the huge form shrink as it swept toward the crags. Its great wings dippped. The mountains burned a brilliant red.

The dragon vanished from the sky. Stark black mountains stood outlined by rosy light that slowly dimmed and died.

"Do you tremble, King Chondos?" a mocking voice hissed.

Chondos whirled, his hand groping at his belt for the sword

that was not there; he blinked dragon-light from his eyes. Faint through plugged nostrils came a hideous, familiar stench.

"Now you may see our power," the hateful voice went on. "Yarkaroth has come from his cavern in the north, and awaits my command to carry death across the Border. Nor is he the mightiest of those gathered here. Powers summoned from Outside wait in deep caverns, ready to shatter the towers, and with them broken, the land will lie helpless before us. Already Takkar slays Takkar on the walls of Manjipor, and Istvan the Archer marches to crush the Border rebels, following *your* commands, King Chondos!"

"*My* commands?" Startled, Chondos spoke before he could stop himself.

A mirthless chuckle sounded in the dark. "Who do you think now wears your crown, signs orders with your seal, and sits on your throne in the city of Tarencia?" A log crackled in the fire; a small burst of flame flashed on black cloth. "Who could walk into your palace, into your very bedchamber, and spirit you away with none the wiser? Only he whose face cannot be told from your own—or have you forgotten your twin brother, Jodos, the Lost Prince?"

Shock shivered through Chondos. He had in truth forgotten the brother he had never seen, the twin who was as much a legend to him as the Black Dragon that slew Fendol, or Thale the False Hastur, or Pertap. If they did not know he was gone . . .

"The Hasturs will know!" His voice was a trumpet, echoing. "They will see the difference and be warned!"

"By now the Blue-robes will have forgotten that your little kingdom ever existed. Servants of Uoght in Kadar and Orovia give them no time to think of petty kingdoms in the south, where the Border is quiet—for not one of my servants sets foot beyond the Shadow there."

Chondos listened, silent, his mind racing.

"At my word, powers far greater than those the Blue-robes fight in the north will carry the Shadow all the way to the sea," the Master hissed. "The Phantom Fleet that even legend has forgotten shall sail from Portona Mouth, and our galleys shall rule the Sea of Ardren. Your people shall be our food and our slaves, and sacrifices for the Great Ones from Outside. But by *my* will, you may be King again."

Scornful words seethed at Chondos' lips—but he held them back, perhaps for the first time in his life.

"If you submit to me, serve me, I will set you on your throne again, King as before, and give you better support than ever the Blue-robes did. And you will gain this ancient kingdom of your fathers, and I will make you ruler of the Pure-in-Blood. As you can see, they are good and docile servants. Far better than the Tarencians who now rebel against you!"

"What is it you wish to do?" Chondos asked. Rage made his voice tremble.

"When the time comes, you must cross the Border with the men of the Pure-in-Blood. The Border castles will open their gates at your command. And you can give false orders to the army that fights against us. When the Takkars have fallen, the rest of the land will be easy prey, and we will set you on your throne again, and make the people obey you."

Chondos could only stare. They said the Dark Things did not think like men . . .

Suddenly the anger burst out of his throat. He heard his own voice shouting, "You dare think I would betray my own people!" He clamped his mouth shut, knotting his fists.

"Of course you will," said the Master. "You have no choice. You cannot argue away your only hope of life! And dead or alive, you will do my bidding. Certain fortresses would be closed to you, as to us, if you were dead. That is the only reason we have kept you alive this long. Think well! Your death will not serve your masters, and there will be no glory. No one will ever know what happens here. Remember, too, that however well you serve the Blue-robes, they will let you age and die. If you serve us, you may live forever,"

"Must I answer you tonight?" Chondos asked, fists still clenched. He was tempted to pretend to agree, and wait to escape until they sent him across the Border, but that would be too late. And might not such a lie only put him further in their power? He could feel the Master's mind battering against Miron's mind-shield.

"You are a fool if you do not!" the deep voice snarled. "There is but the one answer! Do you hope to escape, or think that your former masters will rescue you? They will never know that you are gone! And even if the Children of the

Nameless knew you were here, they could not help you. You must give me your answer when Jodos sends us word."

The Children of the Nameless, Chondos thought. Was that legend true, then, after all, that the Dark Things feared the name of Hastur, so that it was a weapon against them? He had no other weapon. Proud words of refusal pressed on his tight-locked lips. If he spoke, he wondered, would they kill him out of hand? Or would they hold him, hoping they could break his will?

One of the Pure-in-Blood threw wood on the orange coals glowing on the hearth. Yellow flames showed the black robe turning away; a single long stride took it to the door. It was not like a man's step, Chondos thought. More like a rooster, or some long-legged marsh bird.

"Think well, O King." The black cloth turned to glare at him from the door. "Remember, you will die unless you obey me. You are mine, now."

Death-fires burned on the plain around Manjipor, under a sky bright with stars and tiny moons. But west, south, and east, slim stalks of light glowed dimly against vast starless blankness that men watched nervously, fingers stroking their hilts. Horses snorted at the smoke of burnt flesh and hair that hung over the camp. Yet, despite the stench and heat, the Bordermen huddled close to the fires. More than once, Martos heard repeated the line men had sung earlier above the pyres of their comrades: *Save us, O Fire Immortal!*

"Lord Kaitsio will bring a thousand," Lord Saladio was saying, "but he cannot be here for three days."

Martos saw men look longingly at the lights and safety beyond the city walls. The voices of Jagat's other commanders became a meaningless buzzing as he looked up at the bright stars and wondered if Kumari, too, was looking at them, and if she thought of him. Or was she sleeping now, with his child growing within her? Tears blurred the stars, and he blinked them away.

"Ekakin!" an indignant voice shouted nearby. "They dared to say whoever was Prince of Manjipor, or King of Tarencia, they could be sure that the Border was guarded, and the men of Ekakin true to their trust!"

Ekakin . . . That was a small fort, Martos remembered, far in the west, near the Shadow. Kumari had told him, once, that its name meant "loneliness."

"No!" Jagat shouted above angry murmurs. "No, they are *right!*" Other voices stilled, and Jagat's, tired but firm, went on: "They are right, and we are wrong. But . . ." His voice trailed off in a sigh. He shook his head, and straightened. "Another two hundred came in an hour ago. Whose men are they?"

"Mine, Lord," said Bajio of Kasthapor. "Lord Kumbo with his men, Mahadio and his vassals from Kirtama, and men from Mandapa, Inprakar, and Janida. They follow Lord Kurran, but he won't be here until tomorrow."

A puff of wind rolled smoke in Martos' face, and he moved away, sickened. He felt alien and alone among these men, in their skirted robes and homemade armour, huddling near their dead comrades' pyres for protection from the dark. *Save us, O Fire Immortal!*

Red-robed Healers bustled busily by. All that afternoon they had carried screaming, dying men into camp; men whose bodies fueled the fires all about . . . *Nurin Kimerosa.* That had been the name of the man he had killed in the Buried Stables. A swordsman of his own school.

Across the plain he saw tiny lights under the walls of Manjipor, and knew that Healers still searched there—and women. He remembered seeing a vulture land above the gate. But Suktio had said that the birds would not stay long. Even for them, the Shadow was too close. And the Border had its own scavengers. He shuddered, suddenly realising how far he was from the fire. He turned and started back.

Jagat sat on a low stool as if it were a throne. Wide skirts fell in graceful folds around his bowed legs. Firelight glittered on ancient mail-rings in the opening of the flaring-shouldered vest he wore over his armour. He rubbed his bushy white eyebrows.

". . . at least two thousand Seynyoreans," he was saying as Martos came up. "Lord Maldeo's personal following, counting the Carrodians, must add up to another thousand. Probably five or six thousand men, all told."

"Six hundred, more likely!" barked Lord Saladio.

"With Chondos' personal troops?" asked Jagat. "Come now. There are four thousand that we know for sure. Might be more."

"I'll stake my life there are only a few hundred willing to fight for Maldeo!" Martos saw Saladio's eyes and teeth flash firelight.

"We are all staking our lives," said Jagat gently.

In one of the rich chambers of the palace that had grown up around Roger of Aqilla's robber hold, there was music and dancing and mirth. It was the first court function since the old King had died. Candles burned in multitudes; they hurt Jodos' eyes. If any thought the King acted strangely, they paid no heed. The strain of war, they thought.

There could be no better opportunity to exploit the petty weaknesses and jealousies between the men of the court. As evening wore on, wine opened their minds to Jodos, and happily he steered their thoughts. Hatred, jealousy, envy: these were easy tools to understand and use. But much of the thought he touched was alien, and horrifying. The simple greed of eating and drinking was familiar: the Pure-in-Blood and even the goblins had their own feasts and revelry. But there was another element here, so disturbing that it drove him at last away from the lights and crowding and music, into the relative darkness and quiet of the night.

Glaring pinpricks of light filled the sky, but he could look away from them. There were shadows where one could escape light altogether—but these were occupied by young men and young women, and what they had come for was connected to that which occupied so many minds.

Little laughs, low whisperings, and sighs sounded all around him. He shrank back against the wall, and closed his eyes against the brilliance of the moons. He withdrew into himself, away from these creatures and their unstable thoughts. Just as his panic began to subside, a woman's voice shattered his calm.

"Out for a fresh breath, Lord King? It is stuffy in there!"

His eyes snapped open, to see a slender, blond girl, her white dress, like many worn that night, open in a long V from throat to navel, barely covering her little breasts.

"What a glorious night!" She looked up at the sky, and opened a gaily coloured fan. "Not a cloud in the sky, and the moons and stars so bright." She smiled up at him. "You haven't spoken to me all evening. Not since the Coronation. Now that you're King, I suppose, you're too good to speak to me?"

"Why, yes, of course, that's it," he stammered, then realised, belatedly, that that was not what he would be expected to say.

She laughed, then pouted. "You always say horrible things. I think you delight in torturing us poor women, batting your beautiful eyes at us, and making us swoon with your broad shoulders. I know I'm not the only one who has had the honour of pleasing you, and I know you've been troubled and occupied, but tonight, at least you might have smiled at me."

Jodos ransacked Chondos' mind, trying to remember who this woman was, and why she was acting this way. Most of Chondos' memories of women he had set aside. They were disturbing, and irrelevant, and he could not understand these strange creatures who let their females run around unchained and did not use them for food.

She leaned closer, and he pressed back against the wall. Somehow she had shrugged the opening of her bodice further apart, and the rounded cone of one breast stared at him. His confusion grew. Did the little fool *want* to be eaten? He remembered her now: the daughter of a cousin of Lord Zengio, who held some minor post at court. She was called Melissa.

She kept moving closer. He felt himself trembling with a rage of need: he wanted to bite, to tear, to taste this meat and blood so temptingly offered.

"You know my mouth and breasts are yours, Lord, whenever you want them," she whispered, and actually pushed her body up against his. "You could be kind to me, a little. You know I worship you."

How dared this slave, this creature, make demands on *him?* He shuddered with horror at the sudden realisation of what Chondos had done with this girl and others. The pulsing that racked his body confused him even more as he viewed it through the haze of Chondos' memory.

His hand closed on her breast. She gasped with pain. His

head swam; he could barely keep himself from leaning down to tear out her throat. He became aware of a tremendous pressure on a part of his body he had been taught strenuously to disregard.

"My King!" she gasped. "Sweet King and Lord—of me!"

He could not eat her without betraying himself. But he must do *something!* Not what Chondos had done, what she doubtless expected. No food-thing would eat of *him!* The thought sickened him. Chondos had not only allowed it, he had insisted on it. He understood the reasons in a dim way, though it would have been so much simpler just to kill her. But the Blue-robes would not allow that, of course.

She was touching him now, and her gown had slipped back from her shoulders to bare her breasts. Chondos' memory told him what she really wanted, and this made him so curious that he dived into her mind to see if it could be true.

He withdrew from her swirling emotions with a fastidious shudder. It was true. She wanted to create another one. And she would not even eat it! Some of the creature's motives were sensible enough; the new thing would be a tool of power, both for Melissa and for her master—her father. But mixed with this was that furious passion, almost like a feeding frenzy, but in these humans it was different. Among the Pure-in-Blood . . .

Suddenly he smiled. The Pure-in-Blood did this, to fatten their victims before they ate them. If he gave her what she wanted, it would make her better eating later, in seven or eight months. By that time he would be the master here, and his main problem would be to keep this delectable morsel for himself, to be sure no other robbed him of his feast when the city was overrun.

His mouth watered, and his body pulsed. He thought of the screams of others he had eaten, and licked his lips. He tightened his grip on her breasts, and her mouth gaped. Nearby he saw a low wall that was just the right height. Leading her there, he lifted her onto it and began pulling up her long skirt. Eagerly, she helped him.

He pinched one of her soft, meaty thighs. They would be tasty. She forced a giggle and began to make some jesting remark, but fell silent as she saw him fumble with his own clothes and realised what was about to happen. He hesitated.

He had never done this except to slaves already partly eaten and dying. He saw fear mingle with triumph in her eyes.

"In my womb," she whispered, her eyes wide and frightened. "You want my womb! Oh, be gentle . . ."

With a laugh he tore her brutally open, delighting in her pain. The smell and feel of blood excited him still more. She bit her lip, tears running down her face, fighting a scream.

He licked blood from her mouth. After a moment he could no longer hold back from the breast bouncing so close. His teeth met in her nipple, and he sucked her blood furiously, holding himself back from taking another bite, and then another, and another.

When he had finished, he sneered at the way she tried to keep loathing from her eyes as she gathered her clothes around her and ran off into the dark. He supposed he would have to do it again, in order to ensure his feast. Excitement at the thought helped drown the shame and disgust he felt at seeing a victim walk away from him, still alive.

When Martos closed his weary eyes, he saw torchlight glimmer on steel blades that vanished and reappeared like a lace of lightning. He shook himself awake. His body ached. Had it only been one day? He felt as though he had been fighting forever.

Jagat and his men still talked, but only occasional words reached him now. He kept trying to listen, dutifully, but his mind wandered. *Nurin Kimerosa*, he thought. One of Raquel DiVega's students. He found himself smiling, and shame filled him. How could he feel anything but sorrow at the death of such a man? Was it pride in the proof of his skill? Or, worse, a merchant's delight in the fame that would bring students flocking to his school?

His school. Would he ever have a school now? Did it matter? Longing rose, painful in a swelling of pulsebeats. What madness had made him walk away? What did fame matter now? What use to be a great Swordsmaster, if not for Kumari's sake?

He looked into her eyes, and his hands felt the softness of her breasts. But the steel flickered in torchlight behind his eyelids. He saw scavenger birds roosting on the walls of

Manjipor, siege ladders tipping back, desperate men clinging frantically. Falling men screamed . . .

He felt himself falling, and jerked awake. He shook his head, angrily.

". . . know how many men *we* have!" Jagat was saying. "How can I tell about the force inside the city? But I would guess around six thousand men, not counting children or those too old to fight."

Martos wondered how old a Borderman had to be, to be thought *too old to fight*. And this would be the heritage of his child! He shuddered. If the child lived, if the Dark Things did not reach into the warmth of her womb to destroy it . . .

He huddled into himself. Why could she not understand that all he wanted was the child's safety and health? And now that had come between them, and she had not even said good-bye to him, and he had ridden away to war, perhaps to death, without a kiss or a touch.

"We need the horses!" Saladio was shouting. Martos looked up, startled.

". . . Orissians? Merchants and farmers! Bid them declare themselves, and warn them we will fall on them if they will not join us. Why, one Takkarian is worth ten of these soft-gutted midlanders!"

Jagat shook his head sadly, but said nothing. Pity wrenched Martos. How changed the old man was! Before Pirthio died, Saladio would never have dared speak in such a tone. He saw Pirthio's face, heard his voice saying: *Saladio has hated the Prince ever since Chondos made Maldeo his Vicar*.

". . . not much more than the number of men in all the Seynyorean companies. All the fighting men of Manjipé, even with Ekakin and Manjipor on our side, would come to no more than fifteen thousand men. I have no doubt that Kalascor can field twice that many. Unless Prince Hansio comes to our aid—"

"Is there any word from Mahapor?" someone asked.

Jagat shook his head. "Hansio is gathering his men. But where will he lead them, and when, and against whom? Who can say what the Fox will do?"

Several voices spoke at once, and Martos stopped trying to listen. He yawned, and rubbed his eyes. Would they go on all night? He rose, feeling the stiffness in his legs, and walked to look out across the camp. He eyed his tent with longing. There were few tents: most of the Bordermen slept on the ground. His own men had them, and the Massadessans, and some of the great Lords like Hamir and Bajio. He heard Ironfist's name, and listened.

". . . Ojakota and took every man to defend the city," a voice was saying. "Those axes cut steel like butter, men say."

Martos looked out across the plain. Yes, Ojakota was dark, hidden in the distance; he should have been able to see its lights from here.

Behind him he could hear arguing about various gates, and where to make the main assault. Then, suddenly, all the men were rising, and Jagat was bowing, bidding them good night. *It must be past midnight*, he thought. *About time*. He had begun to walk towards his own camp, when he heard Jagat call his name. He turned back. In the dim glow of a failing fire he saw the tired old eyes in the swarthy face.

"Martos, tell me." Jagat's voice was almost a sob. "Am I right? Or am I only deluding myself, destroying my own people for vengeance?"

Martos could only stare at him, shocked to see Jagat broken—Jagat who had always been so strong.

"All my children are dead now. Only a little time ago, and my knee was the horse he rode—but now my son is dead. No children of my body are left. You and Kumari must be my children." A smile came over the old face, as Martos started. "Did you think I could help knowing what is between you? Stay with us, Martos! Wed Kumari, with my blessing, and stay to be Lord of Damenco when I die. Or Prince of Manjipor, or even King of Tarencia! I have not long to live; let me see her happy before I die. She has taken the place of the daughter who died. Let me see her children, and know my blood has not died out!"

Martos' mouth was frozen. Lord of Damenco—Lord of a dying race, clinging desperately to this last scrap of what had been an Empire, greater than Kadar in its day. But was it not too late? Angry words re-echoed in his memory; he saw that hateful look defile her eyes.

What answer could he give this broken old man, begging

some hope against a desolate future? Would she have him, even if he could accept her, and the land that came with her? Suddenly, he knew what to say.

"Be happy, my Lord," he said, very quietly. "You will see a child of ours, soon."

And that, at least, was true enough.

Chapter Fourteen

Chondos remembered—but it might have been a dream—the Master's voice chuckling evilly in the night: "Yarkaroth sleeps. He will wake at my command. Be grateful; were he awake he would hunger, and all of you would not fill his belly!"

The voice gloated on, but the words lost their meaning and blended with uncomfortable dreams—dreams still preferable to the reality outside his shielded mind. Then he found himself waking; the dismal, pallid light of day was struggling through grimy windows.

He pushed himself up and rubbed his eyes, sniffling, wishing his nose would clear, although he supposed that if it did, the smells of the place would doubtless make him wish it speedily plugged again. Perhaps the ancient dust was a blessing, despite all discomfort. He yearned, futilely, for a bath, and wondered if his captors thought this luxury.

The guard at the door seemed far more concerned with what might lurk in the corridor than with anything that might happen inside the little room. Chondos toyed again with the idea of throwing himself on the guard and trying to wrest his sword away. The man probably had orders not to kill him, but others would wake up, of course, and they would all be on him.

Around him, sleeping forms lay rolled in blankets. One was missing, his blankets piled in a heap. That was odd; at this hour his "servants" were usually all asleep. Perhaps he had gone to gather more wood?

Chondos rolled to a sitting position. The fire blazed merrily; it would be allowed to burn down to a few embers during the day, but never to go out. Again Chondos muttered the little spell that kept his mind closed, and as quietly as he could, slid out of his blankets and came to his feet, the fire-striker chafing his back as it swung.

The guard never looked around. No sleeper stirred. Chondos had set himself to practise quiet movement. Softly he crept over the carpet and through the thick piles of dust beyond. There was a little alcove behind the fireplace, almost a separate room, that he wanted to investigate away from prying eyes.

There was black soot underneath the ancient dust. It was dark, but he could see irregular lumps on the back of the chimney. A little iron door was set into the brick, and it was hot. He folded the fabric of his sleeve across his palm and jerked it open. A blast of hot air reached him, and bending, he looked into the interior of what was surely an oven.

He started to shut the door, but then something clinked softly as his foot moved. It sounded like metal! Instantly he was kneeling, searching through the dust. Then he was lifting something long and black and cold. A knife—a dull knife. Something about the weight and the peculiar blackness caught his attention, and then, because he had nothing else, he carefully worked the fire-striker around, and scratched the black surface.

Silver. In a moment he was sure. A blunt-edged thing with only a hint of a point. But the Dark Things feared silver, or so he had always heard. Men said that the magical swords of the Hasturs and the elves were made with silver somehow interwoven with the steel.

It was not much, but it was a weapon. He cast about for somewhere to hide it, fearing that the Master might be able to sense the potent metal. Almost immediately his eyes fastened on a small oblong niche set into the stones of the other wall. He reached out and pushed the knife in.

It clinked against something, and he wondered if there might not be more of them, if this perhaps had been a storage cupboard, or something of the kind. He moved to look closer, and his foot came down on a brittle surface that gave with a loud crack. Suddenly he was grasping desperately at the wall as he teetered on one leg at the edge of the dark hole that had appeared in the floor.

Below him he heard a sound of sliding earth. A soft cry escaped his throat. Sounds came from the room, sleepy voices muttering, and the voice of the guard, harsh and commanding: "What was that noise?" There was a note of fear in the words. "What are you doing there?"

For a second he thought of seizing the knife and diving through the hole from which he had just so narrowly saved himself. But he knew he would not get away with the whole pack after him.

"Just an old piece of wood that broke when I stepped on it," Chondos said, and walked around the chimney into the room.

The guard was halfway down the stairs, his rusted sword half-drawn. He snorted, and rammed the curved blade back. "I thought it was the ceiling." He gestured towards the dark, bowed beams. "I always fear something will be walking up there, and will fall through and eat up the lot of us."

He went back up the stairs. Chondos' eyes followed the sword hungrily. But no—he must escape with what he had, and run.

For now, however, he must wait. All around him, his "servants" were getting up and rubbing their eyes. Little chance of escape without detection tonight. Tomorrow, when it was light . . .

Istvan DiVega's shield leaped before his eyes, and his blade whirled through the air where a man's thigh would have been. A perfect dancelike step carried him to the side, and his sword flickered like lightning above the falling shield as it dropped.

A sizable ring of men had gathered, veteran warriors and youths yet untried, and on their faces awe and wonder mingled with admiration. He was dimly aware of the crowd that watched, open-mouthed; a faint irritant that did not jar his concentration. But Istvan was puzzled. It must be the reputation, he decided, the ridiculous, overblown reputation.

His left side ached, as he finished. He had not worked with shield as often as he should have during the past few weeks. The all-important muscles under his shoulder had weakened while he had babied himself after that silly scratch. That could get him killed.

He became aware of the growing murmur of appreciation

that swelled around him, and glanced up, embarrassed and annoyed that he had been observed, ashamed at the thought that others had seen him when he was so badly out of training.

It was time to eat, and after that, to mount and ride. They were making good time: tomorrow evening they should reach Ojaini. And then across the Yukota, and on to Manjipor. And then his shield-arm had better be in shape!

Murmurs were running among the men. He frowned to hear the name "Istvan the Archer" among the voices. He cursed all poets, and especially the one who had coined that hated name. Then, worst of all, after he had fastened his shield in its place on the saddlebow, and set himself down to eat, he heard the sound of a harp, and a man singing that very song, the song that glorified his first famous deed and his deepest shame.

He closed his eyes, remembering. He had been seventeen, away from Seynyor for the first time, on his first service with old Bernarrho Elduayen: seventeen, his head full of dreams of fame, and proud of his skill with the bow.

It was a trifling war, another in the long series between Arnor and Daria over who collected the rents from a few mountain valleys that hardly seemed worth the trouble. Barren, rocky country, a land of steep cliffs where the wind blew always. Perhaps it had been simply to get him out of the way that Elduayen had ordered him to watch a narrow defile at the army's rear.

He remembered the sun-baked, yellow-brown stone walls, and the huge amphitheatre where the cut opened out, forming a great circle. He had taken his post atop a tall rock which overlooked the circular hollow. He had been given a horn to sound the alarm, but he had brought plenty of extra arrows, his childish dreams prophesying events to come. He had sat on the rock, filled alternately with pride and irritation as his mind swung between the responsibility of guarding against a flank attack, and the suspicion that Elduayen might have sent him there to keep him out of the fighting.

Bored with watching, he had fallen into daydreams of old tales. He had been running over in his mind one of the songs about his great ancestor, Adwarho DiVega, when a movement in the shadows caught his eye. For a second all he could see was a white horse's head hanging in darkness. His ears caught the jingle of armour, and the sounds of feet. Then the horse emerged from the cleft, and dazzling points of sunlight leaped from the armour of the man on its back.

Following came five more, mounted, and then men on foot; Carrodian mercenaries swarmed out from between the walls. Behind him in the distance, Istvan heard the clash of arms. The battle had begun while he sat dreaming. The signal horn was ready to his hand; in an instant it could have risen to his lips to sound the warning.

Instead he had reached for his bow and nocked an arrow. With good reason, he had been proud of his skill with the bow. Arrow after arrow hissed through the air, picking off the last men in line. Half a dozen had fallen behind their comrades' backs before those in front realised that anything was wrong, and turned to see corpses bleeding on the dust. Istvan put an arrow through the leader's throat.

As the men in the hollow milled in confusion, he picked off the mounted men, and frightened horses ran madly about. He saw one man trampled under the hooves. Some broke for the shelter of the cleft from which they had come, but none reached it. Others rushed on, hoping to come to grips, but they too went down before unerring shafts. Not for nothing had Istvan practised so long and tirelessly. Each arrow took a life. Then something like pity for the trapped men began to rise through the boy's excitement.

"Throw down your weapons!" he shouted.

One of the footmen, a black-haired, scarred man, features twisted with hatred, glared up at the boy on the rock, and his lips writhed in a sneer as he shouted back: "Throw down our weapons? What difference does it make to you whether we have weapons or not, you filthy little coward! We can't reach you!"

Red, murderous rage coloured the boy's vision, and drew the arrow back to his ear. The man's face and the throat below hung before his arrowhead; he sighted down the shaft at the sneering lips . . .

But the truth of the words struck home before the arrow left the string. It was true. He had been in no danger: these men had been helpless, undefended against his attack. And he had murdered more than a dozen of them.

"Surrender!" He heard horror in his own voice. "Throw down your weapons and surrender!"

Then, at last relaxing the bowstring until he could grip the arrow between his fingers and hold the bow one-handed, but still ready, he lifted the signal horn to his lips.

Even now, with his hair grey and his face wrinkled, he could picture clearly the scarred, scornful face, and he could never forget those words: *What difference does it make to you whether we have weapons or not, you filthy little coward? We can't reach you!*

Nor had he ever forgotten the dressing-down Bernarrho Elduayen gave him, for attacking on his own instead of sounding the alarm. He had stood and listened, white-faced, offering no excuse. Yet even then he had heard his secret shame bring praise to men's lips as the story of how he, alone, had captured an enemy force and killed more than a dozen men, spread, and grew in the telling. The minstrels got hold of the tale, and in Carcosa, the City of Poets, men began to sing the first songs about Istvan the Archer.

He threw himself into swordsmanship, and abandoned the use of the bow, trying to expunge the dishonourable glory that had come to him. He sought to prove himself with the sword, and for this he fought the famous duel with the great Amranorean Swordmaster Hoseib Anazak Benelgaron; and the result was another song of the glory of Istvan the Archer.

Recklessly he sought out danger, but it was no use. Istvan the Archer he had become; the Archer he would remain.

And all the time, he was making excuses for himself: it had been his duty to protect the army's flank; there were too many of them to have fought openly, he would only have thrown away his life; it is a warrior's business to stay alive during a battle, a warrior's business to kill.

But the answers to these excuses came with them: his duty had been to sound the signal horn, not to take on the whole force single-handed; the same skill that had put those men so utterly at his mercy could have wounded instead of killed; to stay alive he did not have to kill them; to kill needlessly is the act not of a warrior, but of an assassin. And he had acted as an assassin, a murderer, slaying helpless men from ambush for the sake of glory.

Well, he had received the glory he had sought. And it was worthless. Strange, now, to think back on those fearless, reckless years between the time he was seventeen and the time he was twenty-two. Death had no meaning then; danger was only a way of wiping out the stain on his honour that he alone perceived.

Yet those excuses had had their effect after all. For, as the smart had eased, it was easy to let caution develop, and did it partly excuse his act to accept the philosophy that *staying alive* was the important thing in a battle? To begin to listen and accept the constant lecture from older warriors who called him a fool . . .

It was time to mount and ride, and he had to gulp the rest of the meal hurriedly. His officers were bustling. The army was ready to move, and they must reach Ojaini soon.

A philosophy of cowardice, a philosophy of *success*. And what, after all, he wondered, as he swung himself into the saddle, had it brought him? A few more years of life, perhaps—perhaps not—and those were now spent, and death was never very far away. It could come tomorrow, or the day after. It could come at any time during the long war that stretched ahead, and it could come in a fall from the saddle as easily as a sword-cut.

But now he feared it.

Where was the dividing line, he wondered, between caution and cowardice? Or was there one? Were they simply different words for the same thing? Cowardice had brought him his one great deed of shame—and the praise of men at the same time. The courage for which he had first been praised was a lie. Was all courage a lie?

Orders were called, trumpets blown, the feet of men and horses beat upon the ground as the army swung into motion, down the Ojaini road. The Twin Suns glittered glorious on armour.

Was there another kind of courage, he wondered, a courage based upon familiarity with death rather than ignorance, a courage that was its own reward? If there was, he must find it, make it, within himself.

At the walls of Manjipor, the clamour of the assault filled Martos' ears. The heavy shield rested easily against his shoulder; his long blade waited in his hand. He heard arrows whistle, but this close to the wall it was unlikely that they would strike anywhere but on his helmet or his shoulder-pieces. The sound of splitting stone made his head ache.

Enough men had come in during the night and early morning to enable Jagat to station a small force at each of the gates to the city. Half of Martos' company, with Paidros at its head, was patrolling just out of bowshot from the walls, ready to sweep down as a reserve. There would be no repetition of yesterday's sally.

From the north came a thunderous din. Men worked under a shielding roof of captured timbre from the Buried Stables, beating down the ponderous northern gate. Most of the army still stood before the south gate, and with siege ladders and new rams had mounted a second assault. Yet these attacks were but feints. The real attack was here, at the little postern that was called Tower Gate.

The gate itself was a slab of iron, smooth and handleless, set into the stone of the wall next to the base of the great west tower; it could not be broken or battered down; some said it was the strongest gate of the city. But Lord Jagat had been present when the iron door had been put in place; he knew where the sockets were for the heavy bolts, and how far into the wall they were set. He had come and gone by this gate a thousand times, and years ago had amused himself working out a way in which it *could* be taken.

Under the shelter of an improvised shield of planks taken from stalls in the Buried Stables, sweating men with pickaxes chipped away the weathered stone on both sides of the door. For hours they laboured: already the corners had fallen away, and it could not be long now before the sockets were laid bare.

The planking over their heads was feathered with arrows. Half of Martos' company stood back from the walls with their short bows, and more than one archer had leaned too far over the parapet for the difficult downward shot; their bodies lay scattered at the foot of the tower. Pickaxes rang on, undisturbed. Only a sally from the gate could stop them, and for hours Martos had been ready to spring at the first sound from the door. Red-robed Healers hovered near the wall.

The defenders would be spread thinly. North gate and south gate had claimed their attention, and, in addition, a party of workmen and a large number of wounded had been sent into the Buried Stables: the workmen to remove precious lumber; the wounded to make as much noise as they could in order to simulate an attack through the blocked-up stable gate, forcing the enemy to station extra men there.

A shout from one of the workmen brought Lord Saladio running up. He looked at the shattered stone and laughed. "Good work, lads! Not much longer now!" He came trotting to Martos' side, an exultant smile on his lips. "The middle bar is bare. A little longer and we'll be able to start prying it open. Then Maldeo will see whose city it is!" He grimaced fiercely, then turned to the Bordermen who crouched against the walls, waiting, and his voice was loud and cheery. "Be ready, men! Not long now!"

Martos closed his eyes, trying to picture in his mind the inner parts of the gate that would be revealed when the door went down. There was a long steep stair, they had told him, and then a landing, wider than the stair, with a blank wall of solid stone facing them, and a narrow door to the right. The landing was large enough to swing a short battering-ram, but also large enough to hold a fair-sized party of defenders. And once that door was down, there was another stair to climb, a wall with arrow-slits behind it, with a door leading into a narrow alcove to the left.

They would have to block up the arrow-slits and take down the door with axes, while standing on the stairs—there was no landing there, unless the door to the alcove was open—and the right side of the alcove was a narrow opening into the tower itself. A fairly simple gate-maze, all told, but impressive all the same. This section of the wall must surely be no less than four hundred years old, and this was a very efficient gate-maze by the standards of the time. The north gate, which was fairly new, was as good as anything in Kadar, by all accounts.

Martos looked unhappily at the shield on his arm. His generation, born and rised in an era of peace, had grown up to think of the sword as a duelling weapon, a part of daily dress. A duel in the street would be fought with sword alone, with neither shield nor armour, and thus the study of the shield, used only in war, had become unimportant in Kadar. There were those, indeed, who maintained that a shield only encumbered a horse-archer and had no place in modern war; and even a few who scorned the use of the shield as cowardly, and denied that it gave any practical advantage in combat. But Martos knew better: Birthran had trained his shield-arm well. Yet the habits of his background persisted. It was hard to remember that fighting in a battle was different from a duel or a street fight.

Picks crashed on stone, swinging in a rhythm that made them answer like echoes of each other.

"Here comes Lord Jagat!" called one of the men.

Three horses came pelting towards the wall: Jagat, with Suktio and another of his vassals, Todaro. The Kadarins bent their bows, ready to let fly if any archer tried to pick off the horsemen; but the enemy soldiers were keeping their heads down. Martos sheathed his sword and went with Saladio to meet Jagat. The old man swung down from his horse, and stepped quickly under the planking.

"Careful!" Jagat said, stopping just outside the swing of the picks. "Let me see . . ." The workers stopped; he stepped in and bent to examine their work. "Good!" He turned to Saladio and Martos while the picks began again.

"They're almost through over the bolts—two of them are clear already," he said, shouting over the regular crashing of the picks, "and its only a matter of minutes for the other. The hinges don't seem as close, but I'd wager they'll tear out if we put enough pressure on the bars. The sooner we get the door down, the better."

There came a shout from the archers behind and a hum of bowstrings, and at the same moment there was a splintering of wood as an arrow tore entirely through one of the thick planks and drove into the ground next to the feet of one of the workmen.

A cry from behind made Martos wheel, and she saw Rinaldo stagger and fall, an arrow driven through the heavy steel of his breastplate. He leaped away from the shadow of the wall, pulling his arm out of the harness to let his shield hang loose from his neck. He ran to the fallen man, snatched up the short bow, and grabbed hastily for an arrow. He ducked as another arrow drove towards him.

A red-robed Healer ran out from the wall, to kneel at

Rinaldo's side. Gazing along the shaft Martos recognised the slender, dark-haired figure, the broad, oversized shoulders. He let fly, saw the heavy bow move to sweep the arrow aside, and felt almost glad. The figure ducked back behind the wall as a dozen more arrows hissed up.

"I thought all the N'lantians were on *our* side!" exclaimed Thiondagos.

"They are," said Martos. "That was Alar Arac, Ironfist's son. Ironfist's mother was N'lantian."

And that meant, he realised, that the Carrodians must be guarding this section of the wall. Ironfist and his men would be waiting beyond that door. He looked down at the Healer as other Red-robes came running up with a litter. The Healer shook his head.

"Pierced lung," he said. "We might save him. We might not. We'll try."

Martos grabbed up the quiver that the Healer had stripped from Rinaldo, and drew an arrow to provide cover. No man would shoot a Healer deliberately, of course, but there were always accidents.

"What kind of a man would marry a N'lantian woman?" asked Romulos.

"A strong man," said Martos. "Ironfist's father was—"

A shout from the door cut him off. The workmen had stopped, and now Jagat ran to examine the exposed bolts. After a moment some of the men began to pry at them with iron bars. Jagat ran to his horse and grabbed a large coil of rope from his saddlebow. Suktio and Todaro had brought rope as well, and men clustered around the door, straining to lever it open, while Jagat fussed with the rope.

Every time Martos moved, his shield banged against his thigh. He allowed his arrow to slide halfway down, locked it with his finger and thumb, and let go the string to reach up and unbuckle the strap that held the shield at his neck. He pulled hard at the strap, and after a considerable struggle managed to settle the shield between his shoulders. Lord Saladio's voice reached his ears:

"Lord Jagat, I claim the right to lead this assault! Is it not my right to be the first man to set foot inside Manjipor?"

Glancing up quickly, Martos saw Jagat's eyebrow twitch,

but Jagat's voice was controlled. "Very well. I should show myself at north gate in any case." The old man swung himself onto his horse, and began backing it away until the rope was taut. Todaro and Suktio did the same.

Martos raised the bow just as another archer leaned over the wall to aim at Lord Jagat. A volley of arrows swept the parapet, and the bowman vanished, though whether he was wounded or had only ducked Martos could not guess.

"Now!" shouted Lord Jagat, and the three horses strained at the ropes while the men around the door drew back.

Martos watched, unable to believe that those slender, quivering ropes could budge that massive slab of steel. Surely the ropes would break, the horses lame themselves under the strain . . . ?

There was a hellish scream of tortured metal; the door swayed, tipped outward, and toppled to the ground with a booming crash. Jagat and the others threw off their ropes. Saladio shouted and, waving his sword, jumped on top of the fallen door and plunged into the darkness of the opening. Bordermen swarmed into the entrance. Martos threw down his bow and ran, drawing his sword.

"I'll order in your horsemen, Martos!" shouted Jagat, pounding past him, with Suktio and Todaro riding hard behind.

Then the portal was before Martos, and steps that rose steeply out of sight. Bordermen crowded on the narrow stair. Loud shouts echoed, and the sound of steel. Torches lit the landing, and in their light Carrodian axes flashed. Martos saw Lord Saladio's body hurled back, staggering the rank behind, blood and brains oozing from his crumpled helm.

Bordermen were shouting as they leaped up the stairs, three abreast; the great axes lashed out, smashing through helms, hooking shield-rims aside, throwing broken bodies in their comrades' faces.

Martos saw one Borderer clap his shield in front of his face, thrusting up under it into a mailed belly. The Carrodian staggered, but the blow fell unchecked. The Borderer reeled back, shield nailed to helm. Martos saw another whirl his blade down in a great semicircular cut that glanced harmlessly from heavily armoured shoulders. Then the Borderman was hurled back down the stairs to lie cursing, his bone and leather target cracked and the arm behind it broken.

But most of those who reached the top of the stairs died before they could aim a blow. Blood flowed sluggish down the stairs, men slipped in it as bodies were hurled down upon them by crushing axe-strokes. The impetus of the Bordermen's charge was shattered, and even a Borderman might well pause before the keen-edged death waiting on the landing.

Martos pushed his way through the crowding Bordermen. He could see the Carrodians clearly now: big-boned, bulky men in mailshirts that reached to the knee, fair hair flowing from under their conical steel caps. The mail-rings that covered their shoulders and arms were visibly heavier than normal. Two stood at the edge of the landing, feet braced wide apart, deadly axes raised to strike; behind them, others gathered. Huge among them loomed the towering figure of Ironfist Arac, his monstrous gnarled shoulders marking him even among his own breed.

Bordermen hesitated; then, as the crowding below them increased, swarmed again up the slippery stairs, clambering over the bodies of those who had gone before. Down swept the great axes. Flimsy shields buckled, helms split, fragments of mail-rings were driven deep into deadly gashes.

Martos pressed up the stairs. Bordermen could not stand up to Carrodians! He alone had the training necessary. He must reach the top. Then he was stumbling over sprawled corpses. He raised his heavy blade in both hands. An axe lashed towards his head. Twisting his shoulders, he batted it aside and lunged up three steps, driving the long sword like a spear into a throat. He pulled it free as the axeman toppled. He leaped to the landing, his blade brandished above his head, and at his left the other axeman whirled to strike. Martos stepped back. The flat of the dwarf-blade brushed the axe-shaft, diverting the stroke, his left hand let go, and he whirled the heavy blade around, slicing into temple beneath the helmet's rim.

Another axeman leaped at him as he tore the blade free. Martos dodged away, and as the heavy axe fell, he heaved up the long blade in both hands and struck. The Carrodian whipped his hands apart, pulling the axe-shaft through his right hand to meet the blow with the shaft solidly braced between widespread hands. An ordinary sword would have bounced from the tough wood, or cut partway through and stuck. The dwarf-blade sheared through the shaft and struck the helm with enough force to send the man staggering, blood pouring from his nose. And Martos turned—to face the hero of his childhood.

Ironfist must die. The pain of that thought threatened for a moment to blind him. Martos knew Ironfist was no match for him. And the Carrodian, too, must know.

Ironfist stood braced on wide-spaced feet, his left knee bent and forward, axe raised high and gripped firmly below the head and at the butt, which pointed at Martos. Framed in the angle of his elbow, fierce eyes glared above the wild beard. His whole left side seemed exposed. Martos snapped his blade high as he leaped in, then whipped it down in a long swooping cut aimed to land just below the lowest rib.

The great axe lashed down, the head hurled forward as the Carrodian's right hand slid smoothly down the shaft, and the dwarf-blade rang like a bell as the falling axe drove it to the floor. And the axe was circling around, and Martos saw the terrible edge whirl towards him.

A desperate sweep with the flat of his blade diverted the axe stroke and brought the dwarf-sword back by his left shoulder. He seemed to have a clear cut at the temple, but as the long blade lashed out again, he saw the shaft sliding in Ironfist's hands, saw his own edge glance harmlessly along the suddenly lifted shaft as Ironfist ducked under the blow with a slight bend of his knees; and then the axe was whirling once more towards his eyes.

Again he whipped his blade across his body, smashing with the flat to catch the shaft just below the head, leaping back frantically. His rear foot groped in empty air, and he reeled back to find himself balancing precariously, one foot on the landing, one on the steps, with Bordermen about him. Belatedly, he remembered that Ironfist's reputation had not been made with the sword but with the axe.

The Carrodian charged, and the great axe was driving towards Martos' right shoulder. Left to right, Martos swept with the flat of his blade, hard, and once again the double-edged axe missed its mark. He felt his hilt tug between his hands. The axe blade had hooked over his sword, and Ironfist had been pulled just a little off-balance.

He whirled the long blade back, its edge singing in a perfect line for the Carrodian's throat. Ironfist stepped back, spinning on his right foot, and the blade whipped harmlessly past.

Martos hurled himself after him, his sword whirling around to cut down at the face. Once again that terrible axe flew, glanced ringing against the flat of Martos' blade, driving it to the floor, and whirled up.

Martos looked up to see the axe-head rising again, circling around for his head. Acutely aware of the edge of the landing behind him, he jerked the heavy sword up over his head in a strong two-handed guard—and realised, too late, that though it was the perfect guard for a sword stroke, it could not stop that terrible, pile-driver blow.

Sharp stinging pain in wrist and palms: he felt his arms driven down as a crashing blow to his head took away his sight. He thought of his mother and tried to picture Kumari's face, but only a few sparkles of light stirred the sudden darkness. He felt himself flying, and was aware of the smell of blood clogging his nostrils. Then the last glittering sparks left him, and silence closed in.

All through the day, Chondos had trembled with the fear that the hole in the floor would be discovered. He repeated the formula of his spell over and over in his mind, lest his guard should slip and all his plans be revealed to his captors.

He hovered near that corner of the room, watching to make sure none of the Pure-in-Blood blundered upon his secret, and trying to decide what to do if one did. But his "servants" appeared to have other things on their minds. The terror that seemed their perpetual state was even more marked today.

The man whose absence he had noticed that morning had not returned, and at last, his curiosity roused, he asked about it. Only empty, frightened stares answered him.

"Where is the other man who was here yesterday?" he asked again. "The man with the crooked nose?"

Again those mute, fearful looks.

"One of the Great Ones—summoned him," one muttered, in a low voice. A suspicion formed in the young King's mind.

"And when will he return?"

Once more they exchanged furtive, frightened glances among themselves.

"That is for the Great One to decide." The voice was a low mumble. The speaker would not meet Chondos' eyes. But they always avoided his eyes.

The answers seemed evasive enough to confirm his suspicion. Later, when the pallid grey light began to fail, he heard the low voices of those who had gone to fetch wood.

". . . plenty of meat," one of them was muttering.

"Ha! And do you think any of us will be left by then?" snarled another.

"Some of us, at least, among the Blood-drinkers?"

"Too much longer, and even the Blood-drinkers will go into the bellies of their masters," the oldest of them muttered. "No immortality there."

The voices dropped still lower, and Chondos could only make out a few words. Their dialect was strange and hoarse—archaic, he suspected—and he found the few words he could pick out difficult to interpret.

What would happen to them, he wondered, after he escaped? Perhaps they would not dare to report it, but would flee themselves. That would give him more time. He pitied the wretched creatures, yet he had heard enough to be convinced that they could be as cruel as their masters to those weaker than they.

Among the miscellaneous piled clothes they had brought him there was a pair of stout boots that fit him—more or less. They would have to do. There were no warm clothes as such, but he found two fairly thick cloaks, and decided that if he wrapped himself in both of them he could survive the cold of the mountains.

He picked a long robe of the kind the Bordermen wore, with the loose, sacklike sleeves in which one could carry a number of things; he took a sash and a pair of Border-style skirted trousers as well. He concealed his tinderbox in one of the sleeves, and hid the box in which he had begun collecting food in the pile.

He wished desperately for a bath; he itched, and the accumulating dust was maddening. But the change of clothing would help a little. After some thought he picked out a long Alferridan tunic that could serve as an underrobe. He set the pile near the space behind the chimney; he could change there in the morning while the others slept. Nightfall streaked the sky with grey and black, and the meal was cooking. He thought of the pitiful supply of food in his box, and wondered how long he could make it last.

When at last the food was dished out—a generous helping, as always, and envious stares from the others—he moved quietly back to his corner to eat, and managed to scoop it quietly into the box. Along with the perpetual grain, there was an odd paste that tasted like fish, some flabby stuff that apparently came from a sort of giant mushroom they grew, and some meat that he finally decided must be wild boar, though it did not taste quite right. He managed to shovel it into the box unnoticed, after taking only a few bites of the meat, and a little of the fungus.

He was hungry, but he would be hungrier tomorrow. And the day after. He tried again to guess the distance to the Border, and how long the journey would take on foot. Tomorrow! When the long night had come to an end and the invisible suns turned the opaque skies to dingy grey, while the Night Things slept he would dare the darkness under the floor.

Escape! Away into the half-light of the Shadow, alone and on foot, ill-armed and with little food . . .

There were so many things that might go wrong! The thought of escaping was as frightening as the thought of remaining. If he remained, he would at least be able to delay, to stave off death a day at a time.

He recognised panic growing in his mind and fended it off with an effort. He realised that he was trembling, and forced himself to look down at the floor, examine the cracks between the stones, and the thick dust. He went to the woodpile, and began picking up the odd scraps of old wood, examining them. Imagination could unman him at this point. His resolve was all he had.

A broken chest had been brought, and pulling out the drawers with idle curiosity, he found them filled with jewelry. He smiled. *The treasure of Rashnagar!* He pushed the drawer closed again. He was steadier now, trying to keep his thoughts away from tomorrow.

Suddenly he pulled the drawer open again, and looked more closely at the baubles within. The rings . . . The gold ones were no use to him. But the others, black with tarnish—a fist loaded with silver was a weapon not to be despised. And that bracelet, surely . . . He began pulling out the rings, laying them on the floor. He would have to try them on, find those that fit him.

The soft, hissing voice of the Master made his heart pound horribly, and sent a deluge of icy shivers pouring down his spine.

"Do the jewels of Rashnagar please you, O King? Shall I have treasures gathered for you from the deep vaults? Do you wish the wealth of your forefathers? The treasure of the Takkarian Kings is yours!"

Chondos felt a strange sensation, a curious sense of *pressure* upon the fringes of his mind, a faint electrical prickling that made his head swim and ache as though a hand were squeezing at his temples. Memories of the mind of Miron Hastur rose into consciousness, and with a sudden thankfulness he began repeating once again the formula of defence.

"You seem comfortable enough in these quarters," hissed the Master. Chondos looked up now, and saw the black-robed figure stride towards him, while his human minions slunk cringing from his path. "Have you become reconciled to your position here? Have you abandoned your foolish attempts to resist my power? Are you ready now to serve us and to take up your rightful place, Lord of Rajinagara, King of Takkaria by the will of the Dark Lords from Outside, and Uoght their servant?"

Chondos thought, *Why not say yes? It will not matter. Tomorrow I will be far away.* And perhaps to agree would make his captors less suspicious, give him a better chance for escape.

Almost he had opened his mouth to agree, but then something deep within him revolted at the lie, and all he said was, "I seem to have little choice."

"Choice is not for such as you, Small King," hissed the poisonous, mocking voice. "There is willing obedience, free from pain, and there is forced obedience. You will serve us, one way or the other. Emicos will know how to persuade you. You will do as you are bid, never fear."

The strangeness of the mind that could speak thus caught his attention once more. They said that humans who served the Dark Ones went mad.

"Who is Emicos?" he found himself asking.

"Emicos is one who has learned the advantages of serving the Lords from Outside. He was a wizard, serving the Blue-robes with such powers as they would allow him to acquire. Then he turned to us for knowledge. He is immortal now, and wields greater powers over life and death than his former masters would have allowed. You should be grateful to Emicos, Little King, for it was he who brought your brother to us. He is a Lord now, over the Kingdom of the Real Men. Such a great Lord as you can be, and he will never die or age. He has served himself well by turning to us, and you may do the same. Emicos eats well, and none dare oppose his will."

Chondos remained silent. If what men said about the Dark Things was true, the less he listened to the Master's words, and the less he tried to understand them, the better.

"I am sure that if we removed enough of the skin from your legs you would see the wisdom of cooperating," said the Master. "We could remove an inch every day. That would be most instructive. It could easily be done where it would not show. Or we might remove some of your more useless human appendages. They are only a distraction anyway."

Chondos wondered if he could kill the creature before the guards interfered, and what would happen if he did.

"We shall see," said the Master. "I shall have to think about the matter carefully. I am sure that you will serve us well when the time comes. As you say, you have no choice." The black cloth that covered the face was impassive. The warped figure turned, and strode away. Chondos watched cloth billow out, and realised again how long the hidden legs must be.

Chondos shuddered. He must sleep tonight, must sleep soon, in order to rise early in the day. But how did one sleep after a discussion like that? His skin crawled. He began nervously pulling out the silver rings and trying them on. He should find at least one for each finger.

Chapter Fifteen

Two suns sank in the swirling opal sea west of the Shadow, beyond the narrow triangle of the kingdom of Norbath, trapped between the ocean and the hidden, haunted mountains. Towers of the Hastur-kin glowed reassuringly against the blankness that blotted out the eastern stars, and would hide tomorrow's dawn. North in Kathor and Orovia, new towers guarded the Border. A thousand miles to the east, by the Lake of Hali, weary Hasturs watched dimly sensed forces gather in the ruins of dead Thendara.

But deep under the earth, the men of the Black Ravens, the elite soldiers of Norbath who patrol the network of cavern and tunnel that runs beneath the Border, depending more on sharpened smell and hearing than on fickle torchlight, heard from the far reaches of distant caves the rustle of many feet. While the Hasturs prepared for attack a thousand miles away, the Shadow moved on the undermanned Towers of Norbath.

The tower that guarded the narrow road south to Araja flared once and crumbled, and the Shadow poured down to the sea. A vast terror from beyond the world reared dark and cold above the Tower of Tharna, and shattered it to white-hot fragments. Blackness swept over the neighboring Tower of Falthru, blotting it from sight and aid. Above the narrow road that ran north to Kathor along the barren coast, shielding flames flickered around the Tower of Dwarthon, and Dark Things crouched on the road itself.

Demons flew like fleshless bats from the Shadow, blotting out stars with their wings. Bells rang in Norbath: men rushed from their beds; warrior, wizard and tradesman alike hurried to aid the Hasturs, arming themselves with fire and silver and steel.

Kandol Hastur-Lord crossed the continent in the blink of an eye, gathering his kinsmen around him. Miron was one of those who joined him outside the boiling darkness that covered the light of Falthru, where Herstes Hastur was trapped alone.

Need-fire sprayed against the darkness. The will of Kandol rippled a thought through massed minds, and the white spray tightened to a cone of light, boring into blackness. Underground, the Black Ravens battled by the light of the need-fire on their swords, as scuttling goblin hordes poured through the tunnels.

The brilliant cone lengthened, burning until it touched the tower's wall. Then Kandol's thought once more moved the linked minds, and blinding spray stripped the dark shroud to tatters. Falthru gleamed forth, for a moment. The darkness closed again, but in that brief blink of time a dozen Hasturs appeared inside the tower.

Angiro Hastur met the shrieking Demon that swooped down on the city of Jarnath: buildings trembled with deafening thunder, and the streets were lit as though by daylight.

Falthru's fire glowed through its pall as Herstes and those with him hurled power outward. Mortal men saw darkness turn lurid red. Falthru gleamed forth triumphant.

Fluttering Demons still flocked in the sky. Fire-arrows rose to meet them, and Demons vanished in flame. A net of crackling power leaped between Falthru and the neighboring Tower of Varlthon.

Kandol flickered into the dark inferno where Tharna had stood. Need-fire flared around him, driving back the hordes of Dark Things that surged to meet him. Others of his kin appeared, and need-fire streamed from their swords as they made themselves room to stand. A beam of power lanced from Falthru. Kandol caught it, and hurled it on to the tower beyond, sealing the gap. The molten walls of a new tower swirled up around him.

In the mind of every Hastur rang a cry of alarm. North in Kathor, dragon-headed Uoght reared above the towers, the legions of the Shadow around him. Even as Miron Hastur leaped five hundred miles to the north, the Hasturs who watched by the Lake of Hali cried the alarm.

Now the whole northern third of the Shadow was rimmed

with need-fire, and alarm bells pealed in six kingdoms. From mind to mind the question flowed: *Is this the true attack at last?* The calm thoughts of Kandol answered: *Be thankful! But for Prince Tahion there would not be enough here to man the towers; two-thirds of us would be fighting the Sabuath in Y'Gora.*

All that night the Border flamed. Mortal men fought Demons with silver and steel. Hard-pressed, weary Hasturs looked to the ocean, calling to the sea-elves for aid. Mortal and Immortal alike wished for the dawn.

Martos lay in dark silence that pulsed with red. Bursts of brilliance flashed. *I must be dead,* he thought—and laughed.

Bone ached in his head. He found he had eyelids of flesh, and opened them. Dim figures moved in pulsing light. A giant's face swam into view. Firelight glowed on red cloth.

Martos blinked, and tried to move stiff, dry lips. "I'm alive?" he whispered.

"Alive, yes," an old man's thin voice said. "Your helm turned the blow. But you must rest. We'll have you back on your feet soon enough."

For a moment, it almost seemed better to be safely dead, with nothing to fear, ever again. That seemed terribly funny, and he began to laugh again, although his head throbbed unbearably.

"Here now! Calm down!" the Healer said in his fussy voice, and that made Martos laugh all the more.

"Well, you're no more mad than any man your age!" Cool fingers touched Martos' temples and the Healer chuckled. "For a moment I thought your head was hurt worse than I realised! Rest now. Let your head quiet down."

He moved away. Out in the darkness Martos heard now a sound of singing. The Healer returned, and lifting Martos, pushed something against his lips. "Drink this."

Martos sipped, then swallowed greedily, something thick like cream with the taste of strawberries. Out in the dark, deep voices were chanting, and now he recognised the words of the Borderman's Litany for the Dead:

> *The Blood of Life turn to rain*
> *And the Soul return to the Womb!*
> *The bone into Mother Earth*
> *And Her child return to Her Womb!*

"Rest now," said the Healer. Obedient, Martos closed his eyes, and when he opened them, it was dawn.

Chondos' eyes opened on pallid daylight. Despite all determination, despite his hatred and fear of his captors, terror swept through him as he thought of the desolate miles between Rashnagar and the Border. He was afraid to go, and afraid to stay. The hole down which he must blindly crawl, unarmed except for a few bits of silver, might lead to a Demon's lair or a goblin-tunnel—or simply a cellar with no way out. He lay fighting panic, while his "servants" snored around him. He knew that if he let fear rule him now, he would never escape.

Dreadful to go—but worse to remain, he thought. If he gave up now, his will would be slowly ground away. He faced terror against terror, and rolled out of his blankets with practised stealth.

He knelt a moment, listening to the sleepers around him, and glanced quickly at the door. As usual, the guard's back was turned, as he gazed into the corridor. Chondos came silently to his feet. The guard never moved, and again Chondos toyed with the thought of creeping up behind him, overpowering him or seizing the sword from his belt. But a single shout would bring them all around him, smothering him with numbers, and then they would surely tie him up, and all hope of escape would be gone.

The pounding of his heart seemed to echo from the walls as he put on the garments he'd laid out the night before. He crept towards the alcove, tying his sash, barely breathing. His hands clumsy with the weight of rings, he groped in the dark niche, fearing the heavy silver would scrape noisily across the stone.

His fingers found dust on the smoothness of a plate. He pulled it towards him, peering through darkness. The dull silver blade was there, and beneath it dim shapes were furred with dust. Hope blazing high, he blew the dust away. His hand closed on a hilt of ancient wood or ivory, smooth and comforting to his palm, and lifted a curved, single-edged knife.

The sword is the weapon for a gentleman, his father's voice said in the back of his mind, *but, at need, a warrior must make do with whatever is at hand: a whip, a staff, a carving knife.* In the dark, his trained wrist swayed like a serpent, the curved edge cutting through despair. He remembered his father, towering dark-bearded over him: *It is the man who is dangerous, not the weapon.*

He tucked the knife into his sash, and the silver blade as well, then lifted the two-tined fork that had lain beside it. The sharp tines were spaced like a man's eyes. He tucked that into his belt, too, and turned to stare at the gaping hole in the floor.

The knife seemed suddenly so puny a weapon! With the familiar weight of a sword at his hip, he thought, that hole would hold no terrors. A shiver racked him, and the thought of close-in fighting against creatures he would never see . . .

A good swordsman uses his ears as much as his eyes, he heard his father say. *A great one, more.*

But there might be only a sealed storage room below. Or he might find himself drowning in the waters of an ancient cistern. Or it might be the lair of some creature of the darkness who had not the Master's need to keep him alive.

Death is the Bride of the Warrior, the Bordermen said. Surely, he thought, whatever might lie below, death was still only death. But no. That was not true. The verse from the "Ballad of Pertap's Ride" sang in his head.

> *You will but die upon the road,*
> *While cold your undead corpse returns*
> *To seek the blood of your sweetheart dear,*
> *Who for her young Pertap still yearns.*

Yet, doubtless, if he remained, the same fate waited. He licked dry lips. He could not just cast himself in blindly, not even knowing how far he had to drop! He might break both legs, and have to lie there helpless, waiting for them to haul him out. He forced himself to remember the sound of sliding earth that had followed the trapdoor's fall. It could not be far, and soft earth would soothe his landing.

He kept himself from turning back, to light a torch at the fireplace. They would surely see him then. He made himself kneel at the edge and swing his legs out until his feet dangled over emptiness. Still he delayed. His torch was tucked in his sash with the knives; tinderbox and food were in his sleeves. Had he forgotten anything? Could he live with what he had? He must force himself, now, to the quick blind leap, or he would never go at all.

Earth is the Bride of the Warrior.

He closed his eyes, his fists clenched on the edge, and pushed himself into space.

His feet struck loose earth and slid from under him; only a swordsman's reflexes kept him from cracking his skull on the rim. He slid on his back, smelling old dirt clouding around him. His robe dragged at his neck; his fingers thrust into earth.

When the shifting dirt was still beneath him, he opened his eyes to see a dim grey square, before stinging grit fogged his eyes with tears. He closed them, and pushed himself up. The soft earth ramp beneath him, he guessed, must once have supported wooden steps now long rotted. He groped his way down, useless eyes still shut.

Suddenly, his foot lurched across a hard, level surface, his bootsole scuffing sharply. He stood on stone, listening. Faint sounds came from the floor above, but the hollow dark around him seemed empty and still. Groping before him, he took a few uneasy steps forward, his feet scraping over the floor. His outstretched hand touched stone. His eyes flew open, and strained in indistinct greyness.

A glance over his shoulder showed the grey square high above. His fingers fumbled over rough stone, and folded suddenly around a corner. A door? A tunnel? A recess in the wall? His eyes stared, aching, into blindness until he closed them again, and inched his way around the corner. The soft shuffle of his feet echoed faintly. An outflung elbow struck stone. He was in a tunnel. Opening his eyes again, he looked back. Even the grey square was gone.

Trembling, he pulled the torch from his sash and groped for

the fire-striker under his robe. He was startled by the loudness of rasping flint and steel: jumping sparks burned his eyes. He blew as tiny glowing worms crawled on the tinder, until blossoming light blinded him.

He looked away into darkness that suddenly turned into brick and crumbled mortar, flashing and fading as the torch flame danced. Smoke stung his nose, and then rose to the arched bricks above. Far ahead, something moved with a scuttling sound in the dark corridor beyond the torchlight.

His heart thrashing wildly, Chondos pulled the steel knife from his sash. Cursing himself for the stupidity of making the light, he moved on towards the sound, his knife-hand cocked at his side, the torch high over his head. The arched brick tunnel flickered, empty, out of darkness. He heard the sound again— fainter this time, as though whatever made it was fleeing from the light.

The tunnel ended. A forest of thick stone pillars stretched away into darkness. Then a whistling moan of wind and moving air touched his face. Flames wavered wildly on his torch. He turned with the breeze in his face, and moved out among the pillars, breathing deeply of cold, outdoor air. He had almost become used to the scent and taste of ancient dust.

Darkness leaped grotesquely around the tiny, wavering light. Blocks of stone lay fallen on the floor, and he saw places where wooden beams had long ago rotted away. He began to sweat at the thought of the thousands of tons of stone suspended over his head, and quickened his pace.

The breeze blew away the ancient dust scuffed up by his feet. The pillars seemed endless. At last darkness ceased to flee his torch, and turned into a black stone wall. A staircase flickered into the light, and faded. He held his breath until he saw it again, and knew it was really there.

The flame danced more wildly; the breeze grew. Atop the stairs he saw in the darkness a dim grey arch. But as he rushed forward, he heard again that scuttling, scraping sound, but now it was behind him.

He whirled, thrusting out the torch, drawing back the knife to stab. Down a long row of pillars, great sickle-shaped eyes threw back the light. They blinked, and vanished. He heard feet scurry in the dark. Chondos sprinted up the stairs. If the thing had gone to fetch more of its kind—or the Master . . .

Wind whistled through the door, cold and clean. He looked out into a long ruin of a hall, littered with rubble, one wall fallen in to show the grey sky above the crumbling roofs of ancient Rashnagar. He clamped his lips over a cry of joy.

He raced through the hall, hurdling piles of fallen stones; ancient bones crumbled under his feet. A kicked golden goblet went rolling away. Then he was through the crumbled wall and looking down the deserted street. He clambered down the ruin of an ancient stairway, and stood at last on solid earth, with the cold wind raging around him and pulling at his garments.

High on its hill, the ancient citadel of Antapor brooded over the city it had failed to guard. He remembered its glory in old paintings and tapestries. And he remembered the great arch in the wall at the end of the street on his left, the great north gate of the city.

He pressed his burning torch into ashy soil to put it out, and ran, his boots clamouring on hard stone. Looming shells of ancient buildings watched him with glaring windows. Earth-rimmed mouths opened along the flagstones, entrances of goblin-tunnels which might at any moment vomit forth shaggy, misshapen hordes.

The gate gaped before him. He ran through aching night-mare darkness, waiting for some guardian horror to spring. And then the dim grey sky was above him once more, and before him the broad highway of the ancient Kings wound down the mountain, vanishing into vague shadowy vastness beyond the shrouding grey.

Outside his hot tent, Martos, still sick and dizzy from the axe blow, could hear the distant sound of battle on the walls. Someone had picked up his helmet and brought it back, but that useless piece of steel might as well be thrown away. One whole side was crushed in: a paper-thin shaving of steel hung above a wide gouge where the terrible axe had scraped it away. The carefully sculpted curves had turned the edge, as the maker had intended, but only barely. To look at it now was to wonder that a man's head could ever have fit inside. Vivid in his mind he saw Ironfist's axe flying down . . .

And yet death had not seemed terrible when he had awakened in darkness, not knowing that he was alive. What was it Atrion has said? *We fear death, yet we know not why. For all we know, Death may be the King of pleasures.* And there was always the famous line from Eldir that the House of Fendol had taken for a motto: *Death is kind to the man who meets him in following a just cause.*

Atrion's conception was the nobler, he thought. *Better to die without fear than, fearing death, to live on.* Or was that someone else? What was it the Bordermen said? *Death is the Bride of the Warrior.*

Through the canvas he could hear men shouting, and a chorus of horns. His troops were fighting and dying now. He pushed himself up, and tried to walk, but the world swayed and dipped around him.

The ashen land was empty and desolate. Breathing hard, Chondos turned and looked up: impregnable Rashnagar brooded above him, the abandoned crown of the Takkarian Peaks still commanding the great road over the mountain pass.

To rule as King in Rashnagar . . . For a moment, then, the old dream swept over him, veiling in glory the ruined shells of ancient houses. Then his eyes glared at the barren land, the wind-bared rocks and poisoned ash, and his dry and dusty throat banished dream and nightmare alike. His ears fixed on a dim whisper of sound. Somewhere among the rocks off to his left, water was trickling.

Someday he might return with an army to reclaim these blasted lands—but first he must escape the Shadow alive. Drawn by the harsh itching of his throat, he turned from the road, and was soon scrambling in the slippery dust between the boulders.

Martos felt searing heat strike his face, as Paidros helped him out of the tent. The ground seemed to sway and swirl underfoot. He staggered against the little man, and then he was in the shade, and Paidros was helping him down.

"I told you!" Paidros snorted. "And later I'll have to carry you back in again. Should have brought a derrick!" He wiped sweat from his face.

Martos pushed himself up, and tried to look at the city. Everything was blurred. His head ached, and his mind wandered. His hands imagined the curves of Kumari's hips, and his lips tried to shape themselves around her nipples.

". . . a foothold on the walls," Paidros was saying, somewhere in the confused mist of the world around him, "but they were driven back. Hamir wasn't wounded seriously, but he lost a lot of his men. Lord Jagat is still making a show of force at the south gate, but the real attack now is at the tower gate, where you were hurt. They've got a siege tower up against the wall, and they're trying to get at Ironfist from both sides at once—through the gate and over the wall."

Martos' vision slowly cleared. He could just see the tower gate past the curve of the wall. The battlements swarmed with the tiny figures of men, their mail-rings jewelled with painful sparks of sunlight. Their double-bitted axes rose and fell, bloodying the drabber leather-armoured Bordermen whose distant swords were like pins.

Was that not Ironfist himself, his axe rose-hued with blood, sweeping back the men who leaped from the siege tower to the wall? Distant shouts and screams were ghostly and dreamlike: men looked like fighting dolls.

Hoofbeats pounded up. A man in Kadarin armour threw himself from the saddle and came running over. "Lord Jagat wishes to speak with all the commanders, sir," the saluting man said. "At once. He plans an assault on the length of the wall."

Paidros swore. "You remember that that Healer told you to *rest!*" he snapped at Martos, then dashed to his horse and rode away, still cursing.

Martos stared at the distant fighting; his head throbbed with drums of pain. Tiny dolls in sun-jewelled armour killed and died upon the wall. Sudden trumpets blowing through the camp lifted a wave of Jagat's men up against the city. Swarming arrows skimmed the ramparts, and siege-ladders lurched against the wall. Inside the city, Martos saw men run to their posts. He heard distant chiming music hammered out of steel. Among drab-armoured Bordermen in flowing ragged robes, his own men shone in armour-mirrored sunlight over tight-fitting cloth.

The tide of men rolled back from the wall; the maddened chiming faded. Arrows raked defenders who stood waiting for a second assault that never came. Only at the tower gate did the angry iron music continue: Martos knew Jagat had planned the assault to keep aid from reaching the Carrodians.

But Martos, far across the fields hallowed by the ashes of the dead, could see what Jagat could not: Ironfist needed no aid. A wall of leather-armoured bodies piled up, like dismembered mannequins, beneath the bloody axes, as man after man leaped, thin swords agleam, from the siege tower to the wall.

The Twin Suns sailed serenely through the sky, while men died in blood on the walls of Manjipor. Helpless, Martos watched the slaughter, his head buzzing, his eyes aching from the prickles of sunlight that leaped from distant mail, until at last Jagat realised he was only wasting lives.

Then horns called: men fell back, and in sudden aching stillness, armies stared at each other across bloodstained stone. Glittering in mail, the Carrodians leaned on dark-smeared axes. Dismembered figures stirred, and far across the plains Martos heard distance-muted moaning.

The pain in Martos' head grew worse. He tried to stand and walk back into the tent, but the earth rolled under him and he sat down again. His mind wandered. He dreamed Kumari sat between his knees, kissing and caressing him.

Chondos scrambled over bare rock, his hands torn and bleeding, his dry lips chapped. The sweet gurgle of water grew louder. Faint dampness touched his skin. He staggered into a little ravine, threw himself on his belly, his face in swift-flowing water, and drank and drank and drank. When at last his throat stopped itching and he raised his dripping head, he stared uncomprehending at the pallid, sickly stems at the water's edge. His fingers were sunk in brown mud. Brown soil, instead of the poisoned ash. Live grass. There was life, then, still, in the mountains. He gazed at the sparse, whitish stalks as tenderly as if they were flowers.

The stream, barely a stride across, fell down the mountain-side over a stairway of ledges, then vanished, growling, over a sudden cliff. Beyond, grey earth and grey sky blended in a blur. He dipped bloodied hands in the water, and the urgent current darkened, tugging at his palms. He watched the swirling grime and blood wash away, then, climbing wearily to his feet, followed the splashing water over slick black rock.

A cup-shaped hollow made a stone-rimmed pool at the top of the falls. Chondos circled it to look over the edge. Beyond the crashing water, he saw in wonder, treetops spread broad, pallid leaves. Stunted bushes grew in clusters, and between them, greyish-brown, flabby stalks.

A flicker of movement made his heart lurch, and he crouched against the rock. For a moment it seemed like tiny trees tilting, with a grey shape moving under them. Then the blurred shape cleared: an antlered stag stood, ash-grey fur blending ghostlike with the shadow-mist around it. Half-forgotten legends stirred in his mind, tales of the ghost-deer, wary and invisible, that had survived the Dark Things' coming.

The beast threw up its head, tasting the wind, and sprang high in the air, sailing across the stream. Two more soared out of the bushes, following the first, and in a moment they had melted into the greyness. Chondos crouched closer to the rock, and moistened a finger in his mouth. Chill air from below told him that it could not have been his scent that had startled the beasts.

A shout took his eyes to the road he had left. Above the corner of a crumbling boulder he could see the gates of Rashnagar. Tiny figures swarmed down the road. Some were men—his "servants," no doubt—but around them, stunted goblin figures ran stooping, faces pressed to the ground like hounds on a scent.

They were tracking him! The rocks around him seemed a trap. He leaned out over the waterfall, surveying the cracks and tiny knobs of rock that could take him down the weathered cliff. It was no worse than the north face of the Rock of Tarencia, he decided, and he had been up and down that many times. He fought down the claws of panic, and slid his legs over the edge.

The great North Road sweeps suddenly up out of the endless cathedral of the forest, and the traveller from the north finds Ojaini Hill towering above him as though its steep wooded slopes were suspended from the air, while behind it, the foul blotch of the Shadow stains the southern sky.

To Istvan DiVega it was all an old story, and he had drawn his first gasp at the sight of Ojaini Hill forty years before. Even so, the sight chained his eyes and did something to the centre of his chest: for a second his youth had come back, and he was the same wide-eyed young idiot who had ridden here with Raquel and Olansos, and had thought the whole mountain was going to tip over on top of them. It was all a trick of the eyes, of course, part of the curious angle of the road, and the sudden exposure to open sky after the long ride through the leaf-roofed wood.

He ordered the trumpets blown. Shrill ringing rose from the host, and echoed merrily from the mountainside. Prince Phillipos spurred up on his fine white horse, and leaving the army to its own pace, the two rode shoulder-to-shoulder up the steep mountain road. Above them, Ojaini Hill reared like a curling wave, its crest bright with the domes and pinnacles of the citadel.

They rode past ancient watch towers, and the crumbling cenotaph that praised famous deeds of the Hero-Prince Orlando. Beyond, the gates were open, but choked with wagons laden with provisions for Istvan's army. His captains had been busy gathering food for men and horses: mostly hay and grain from Orissia. Once across the Yukota there would be scant forage for such an army, and none at all in the grey waste of poisoned dust that surrounded Manjipor.

Beyond the gates, trees grew up the slope, hiding the houses, and Istvan found himself homesick for Carcosa. He knew, now, why so many Seynyoreans had settled here, to marry Kantaran women and live in the forest city. As a boy, fresh from the City of Poets, with little knowledge of the world, he had not seen how similar the two cities were, but even then he had felt Ojaini comfortable and homelike.

He glanced at the western sky, where the colours of sunset were gathering. He had not expected to reach the city until after sunset. Now there would be time to hear reports, to think and plan. Perhaps even a few scant moments to relax. He felt a great longing for rest, here in Ojaini. But the siege must be lifted. As soon as his army was in order, he must march, across the Yukota, and on to Manjipor.

A knob of rock broke in Chondos' hand; he let it go and it fell. He heard it splash in water below as he clung with bleeding palms to the rock. He wondered how deep the pool below him was. Soon it would be dark. Already bands of blackness shot across the sky: the shadows of jagged mountain peaks. Soon the very rock he clawed would vanish in the starless dark.

His fingers and the knotted muscles in his shoulders ached as he groped his way from one fragile hold to another over the worn, smoothed stone. Spray from the waterfall chilled his face and hands, and beaded his cloak with tiny drops. He scrambled down as fast as he dared.

He dropped the last few feet, into ankle-deep water at the edge of the pool, and remembered the stories of the things that lurked in the waters of the Shadow. That was why the Hastur-towers always stood beside the rivers that crossed the Border, why the water was screened with need-fire. He raced around the edge of the pool, and ran splashing in the shallow water of the stream.

Moans and screams sounded as the grey streaks faded from the sky. He crouched, and leaped high in the air, trying to cross as broad a space of the bank as he could, trying to reach a thick clump of bushes he could see in the fading light. He bruised his shoulders as he hit the ground and rolled. In a moment he was wriggling through thorny branches. A chorus of shrieks rose above the sound of falling water, followed by splashing and scrambling sounds.

He lay still, huddled into the thicket, clutching his fire-striker. His heart pounded furiously. He felt a now-familiar fumbling at the borders of his mind. He closed his eyes, repeating over and over the symbol Miron Hastur had taught him, and felt armour close around his brain.

He opened his eyes on glaring torchlight. Men splashed noisily in the stream, wavering torches gilding the water. Dimmer forms prowled in the darkness, lamplike eyes throwing back the light. He crouched, barely breathing, the hard metal of the fire-striker cutting into his palm, as the splashing and shouting drew nearer. Firelight outlined the leaves. Twisted shadows moved between him and the water as they came abreast of him—passed him.

The torches and shouting grew fainter, going away down the stream. His breathing slowly eased. A man screamed. Chondos glimpsed a struggling figure, and heard violent slashing. A torch went out in the water, and others scattered away from the stream, running and vanishing in the darkness. Shouting faded. He lay shivering under the bushes, staring into blindness, listening to rippling water and the cries of the Dark Things as they hunted each other in the distance.

He was cold. He had folded his spare cloak into a bundle, and it was hard work unwrapping it by touch and spreading it around him. There was no point in keeping his eyes open. He could see just as well with them shut. After a time, exhaustion claimed him, and he slept.

Chapter Sixteen

"It must be soon, Small Prince!" the dead man's harsh voice croaked.

"No!" Jodos stuttered. "You must wait—"

"Not forever may Uoght war in the north, without the Blue-robes guessing that our main force is here." It was the Master who spoke through the dead guard's mouth. "And then they may come to visit you!"

"But to strike now will ruin all!" Jodos exclaimed, fighting his panic. "Mortal armies move slowly. They have hardly fought at all! They will unite at the first sign of trouble on the Border, and combined they can resist us while the Blue-robes gather!"

"It is you who will suffer if the plan fails."

"That is why I must have more time!" Not since childhood had the panic that had shaped his life so distorted his voice. "They are still strong! They must have time to kill each other!"

The dead man stood, ominously silent, while fish-scented wind blew snatches of drunken song up from the wharves. Unfamiliar stars burned Jodos' eyes.

"Very well," the dead voice said at last. "I will await your signal. Do not dare to fail. You are nothing, only the instrument of my will. Do what you were sent to do, I bid you by the terror of Uoght!"

Cold clenched Jodos' heart: thousands of miles to the north, dragon-headed death answered the Name of Power with eyes of ice. "I will not fail!" he cried.

The corpse blinked. Jodos felt its link with the Master drop away. Hatred and relief rushed through him. The spider was in his power now! He would make it suffer for what the Master had made it say.

"When next I summon you," he said, smiling cruelly, "you will bring Hotar and the others to the palace."

He tasted the creature's fear. Savouring his malice, he dismissed it with a wave of his hand. It would suffer in the palace, burning with the remnant of the Blue-robes' spell. He watched his victim stagger away. It would need a new body soon; the corpse of the guard Tonios would not pass much longer—certainly not by day, and it might not have passed at night if Jodos had left his guards' minds free. He reached back into their minds now, deep into the crucible of wordless chaos where thought arises, and the roots of action. There would be no memories of this night to start more rumours of his mysterious meetings.

He would not be safe until he had seized the minds of all about him. The court's Healers and Seers he had contrived to send south with the army, save for old Shachio, and now the minds of men were his. It was for this he had been trained, for this the Master had driven him across the Border. It would not take long for envy and suspicion to break the strange bond that bound the officers of the court together, and isolate each man from all others.

But this work had dangers of its own: the human minds were corrupting. His brother's memories lurked in his head, a pattern for human thought, mocking him with similarities between these creatures and himself. Worst of all, these strange emotions seemed to touch some answering chord in himself that made the vague glories of the Great Ones' minds seem ever more remote.

Chondos woke, hearing loud breathing and the rattle of leaves in the black beyond his feet. He pulled the long knife from his sash, smelling something rank and bestial.

Bushes moved, and two round amber moons glared above his feet. They bobbed, and a snuffling sound came, louder and faster. He blinked once, then stared straight into the burning orbs. They dipped, and he felt a hairy hand seize his ankle.

He writhed up. His knife slashed empty air. His free foot flailed into flesh, and the grip on his ankle fell away. Something snarled. He rolled to his knees, thorns tearing his cheek. The creature growled menacingly. Its stink was all around him. But the glowing eyes, only a little higher than his own, held a purpose and menace that was more than merely animal.

He heard a shuffle and a snarl, and the eyes lunged towards him. He rose on his knees to meet it, stabbing furiously. Sticky wetness poured over his hand. The snarl changed to a shriek. Glowing eyes faded and were suddenly dull, and a small hairy body fell into his arms. He pushed it away with a shudder of disgust, sensing something very foul in the texture of its fur, and the smell of its blood.

It must have been alone: the only sounds were distant ones. He groped his way to the stream, and let the rushing water lave the blood from his arm. He groped his way to another thicket, knowing that somewhere in the blackness around him the hungry Night Things prowled. He huddled under the bushes, waiting for the dawn.

Beyond the Shadow, the Twin Suns lifted into a sky that was unnaturally clear, feverishly bright. Birds sang joyously in the Kantara; flowers glowed ecstatically brilliant.

To Istvan DiVega, surrounded by the whisper of his dancing sword, there was something ominous about that pale, brilliant sky, and part of his mind worried at it, until at last a scene from his youth slid out of memory: such a sky heralded the coming of the rains. All along the Border, weather-wise old men would be nodding sagely. Soon clouds would cover the sky, and the winter rains sweep over the land. As the day wore on, the brilliance would turn to pitiless, searing heat, as though to do the most damage before the rains arrived.

Dizziness reminded Martos that the Healer had told him to rest two days before returning to the heavy work of war. From the comfort of his tent, Martos could see the walls of Manjipor waver and shimmer. All the stony plain writhed, danced, unsubstantial in the heat. Only the Shadow loomed solid and immovable.

It was too hot to fight. Across the burning stones of the wall, two armies watched each other in the glare, panting in breathless heat. On each side were men who knew that a brother, a cousin, or a beloved comrade-in-arms waited, somewhere on the other side of that wall.

And Martos was haunted by Kumari's eyes. If Jagat won, if Jagat's claim to the throne was accepted by the Hasturs, Kumari's child would be Jagat's heir. *My child,* Martos thought: his love, growing in her womb, embodied in flesh that was both his and hers. Heir to a throne. That was something to fight for.

No, that was wrong. *The true warrior, the Self-Judged Man, must be detached and free from the temptation of gain or loss,* Atrion had written. *Ill deeds are done by those desiring to win, or fearing to lose.* To fight for gain—even for his child instead of himself . . . His thoughts swirled in chaos. A throne for his child—would that make him love his enemies less? Perhaps it would have been better to have been on the other side.

Give all, even your life, in detachment, concerned only with honour . . .

Piled-up clouds gathered above the Sea of Ardren, but the white-walled merchant city of Poidia baked under the blazing eyes of the suns. In the coolness of the Shippers' Guildhall, the Duke of Ipazema sat fuming, frowning at the Seer before him.

"Six days!" Prince Hansio's voice tumbled from the Seer's lips. "I do not fight to lose! Wait the six days, and fight with my aid, or fight now without it!"

"Why?" the Duke asked. "What difference will six days make? In six days we may lose our advantage!" He kept his voice calm and fought his anger down. All the coast was ripe for action, Lutazema bound to his cause, his vassals gathering, and cities as far south as Orontopol ready to rise.

"Seven thousand Seynyoreans are sitting on the west side of the Atvanadi," Prince Hansio's voice said. "They'll be on my flanks if I move now. Six days from now they'll be busy in Manjipé! Then, I take Thantakar, and we'll have Kalascor between us. But if you strike now, I'll laugh while they crush you!"

The Duke's fist knotted, and he shook with anger and wished he could smash his fist into the Seer's face. "But if I attack," he said, keeping his voice calm, knowing that Hansio's Seer in Manapol spoke with every nuance of his voice, "will not the Seynyoreans—"

"Do not be a fool!" Hansio interrupted. "You cannot take

Kalascor without my aid! They'll expect me to move, and they'll crush you quickly! DiVega will leave Manjipor to fend for itself, and ruin all my plans! Wait for me, and you will have the whole province at your mercy!"

"Six days, then." The Duke licked his lips, hating to agree, but knowing that he must. "And the signal to move will be your attack on Thantakar?"

"My *capture* of Thantakar!" Hansio's proud voice corrected. "Then you must strike hard and fast, while they are still confused. You will be on your own for ten days after that, or more. I will have other business to attend to."

Chondos was awakened by a loud crashing and crunching. His eyes snapped open. A ghost-grey deer was stripping great chunks from the fleshy, grey-brown plants, shapeless and leafless, that grew between the bushes. Chondos' stomach gnawed with hunger, and he stared at the deer with thoughts of venison.

As though it had sensed the thought, the ghostly stag wheeled and bounded away. Chondos crawled from under the bushes, straining his eyes to follow the tiny shape, already far up the slope, as it blurred against greyness. A jutting overhang made a patch of night-black shadow across its path. Something huge and fearful moved in the darkness. The deer swerved, and a massive arm lunged clawing towards it from the dark.

The deer bounded aside, and a deep, moaning roar reached Chondos' ears. The ghost-deer faded into the greyness. Chondos blinked at the shape in the shade, then looked up. The sky was silver: a bright irregular patch hurt his eyes. He looked back up the slope at the thing under the overhang. It was manlike, but gigantic. Chondos nodded to himself. A troll.

It clawed the darkness, like some misshapen figure of rough clay, filled with malice. Its rumbling bellow came like thunder down the slope, but it kept itself well out of the light. The troll glared after the vanished deer, then slowly turned and slunk back to the cliff face, to vanish into some hidden crevice in the rock. If even this much light kept the Dark Things underground or cowering in the shade, then Chondos could cover much ground during the day.

Chondos looked around, and saw the body of the thing he

had killed in the night, lying sprawled in the bushes a little way off. He stepped over to look at it, and shuddered at the pallid goblin face, with bulbous eyes and sharp-toothed gash of a mouth open in death. Its rotund body and long sprawled limbs were matted with dirty whitish fur.

He started, and bent down. The white shin bone of one long leg showed through where *something* had gnawed away the flesh. In the bone were marks of tiny pointed teeth. He glanced up at the overhang—but no, the troll would have carried the body away, and that huge bulk would have crushed and flattened the bushes all around.

He knelt, looking for tracks, and quickly found them. But all his skill as a hunter could make nothing of these. Whatever it had been, it was quite small, no larger than a rat. The distance between fore- and hind-paws suggested a long body, like a weasel or a ferret. But the prints themselves were like the marks of tiny hands.

He shuddered and stood up. He must get away quickly. He had been lucky that the troll had not come down. He looked again over his shoulder at the overhang. Against that ponderous mass of living stone, his pitiful armament would be worse than useless. He longed for a sword, or a spear.

A spear. The thought drew his eye to a nearby tree, to a branch that was almost straight. Such a makeshift weapon would be of no use against the troll, of course. But there were other things to fear.

The desire for a weapon was an aching need. He drew his heavy knife and stepped towards the tree. It occurred to him that these trees were likely the most wholesome living things within miles, and as he set steel to bark, he breathed a plea of forgiveness from this cousin, the tree.

A dozen voices were raised at once. Istvan pounded the table with his fist, and the shouts muted to a mutter, then died away.

"Now," he said, turning to Rafael Vega, who had been speaking when the argument broke out, "O overlooked survivor of my ancestors' wrath; what were you saying?"

Smiles and chuckles sprang up around the table. The old feud between the houses of Vega and DiVega had long ago become a matter of jest, although two hundred years before it had been deadly enough.

"We are outnumbered, Emilio," Rafael Vega muttered to the only other Vega in the room, with a twitch of bristling moustaches. Then he sobered. "I was saying that Hansio is gathering his men at Udapor, so that he can march along the Oda to Tarencia. That's the same route his grandfather used a century ago. The men gathering at Mahapor will move north, but he's stripping his southern forts, and Mahapor is central. That's what I think."

"Thank you, Lord Vega," Istvan said, smoothly. "Now, Robardin"—a slim, dark man looked up—"tell us why you disagreed so violently?"

"Hansio knows we're here," Alon Robardin said, with a shrug. "I have heard many things of Prince Hansio, but I have never heard that he is a fool. He knows we'll be on him if he tries to attack along the Oda; and he knows that if he takes that route, he winds up on that narrow spit of land where the rivers meet, with hostile territory on either side, and only the frailest wedge—even if he invests Iskoda and Thantakar to guard his flanks—between us and the forces of Kalascor."

Istvan saw Prince Phillipos nod sharp agreement.

"So," Robardin went on, "the force from Mahapor will move west, cross the Atvanadi—probably at Kanianadi Mouth—and work to cut off the city from the rest of the province. I think he'll march to the Yukota and link up with the Massadessans. He can control the northern area of the province in two days."

"While we sit here?" The Lord of Ojaini's voice was scornful. "Lord Rinmull?"

"I could not help but wonder," Rinmull of Ojaini said with a shrug, "what the esteemed Lord"—he inclined his head courteously at Robardin—"thinks we will be doing while Prince Hansio is stringing his men out between rivers? I do not believe Prince Hansio will leave us so far out of his calculations as you have, my Lord."

Prince Phillipos stirred, as though to speak, but Istvan had been watching one of the younger Bordermen, whose frown had grown constantly deeper as he listened. It was important that the Bordermen speak; it was their country, after all.

"You, my Lord—I do not know your name, forgive me . . ."

"Ajeysio of Kantakin!" The proud voice was like a trumpet, and the handsome dark face was familiar. As the sullen eyes met his own, Istvan felt suddenly sure it had been a mistake to call on this man.

"You have an opinion on this matter, Lord Ajeysio?"

"I?" An expression of mock surprise crossed the dark features. "I know of nothing Prince Hansio is doing, other than mourning his son and heir, slain by some Seynyorean blade." The boy turned to the Lord of Ojaini. "You were there, Rinmull! You and I were drinking with Tunno and Pirthio the night they died! You know as well as I that the attack on the Guildhall was no more than a prank, with no treason and no malice!

"Prince Hansio and his people, and Lord Jagat, are our own kind, of the blood of Old Takkaria! Why do we sit here, while these foreigners try to involve us in a war against our own blood—a war which they began?"

Istvan fought back angry replies, justification, excuse, and explanation that swarmed to his tongue. But old Palos DiFlacca, who had brooded long hours over the fight in the Guildhall, had grown redder and redder as the boy spoke. Suddenly his fist smashed down on the table, and his voice boomed from the walls.

"Which *we* began! Oh, our guilt! Our shame! Because some of my men were too stupid to keep from defending themselves when they saw men coming at them with swords!"

"DiFlacca!" Istvan snapped, gesturing for silence; but DiFlacca's voice poured on, heedless.

"*We* began it! Your own feuds and hatreds had nothing to do with it—or did we start those, too? And I am to blame, because one of my men dropped a spark in this tinder-pile! We began it? Oh, aye, and we'll finish it, too—" His eyes focussed on Istvan's wildly waving hand, his face went pale, and he closed his mouth.

Ajeysio of Kantakin's voice was in the air before Istvan could speak, or even think of anything to say. "*You* shall finish it? Well then, what need for me, or for any of my kindred, at this Council?" Ajeysio rose, and stalked from the hall. Others among the Borderers rose to follow.

While Istvan searched his mind for words, Rinmull of

Ojaini's rang out, saying what no foreigner might say: "Enough! Are my vassals grown so tender that they must flee the room if two men raise their voices, like children running from a family quarrel? Run, then! But remember that it was *your* Prince, Chondos of Tarencia, and his father and grandfather before him, who brought these men to be our allies! Remember, too, that without Seynyoreans fighting at our side, the Shadow would cover this city now! Their ashes have sanctified our land!"

Men hesitated. One followed Ajeysio through the door; the rest sank sheepishly into their seats. But Istvan saw hostile glances aimed at him.

"Send one after Lord Ajeysio," Rinmull was saying. "Remind him that, whatever men may debate, whatever his private opinion, Kantakin stands guard over the road from Mahapor, and the fords of the Atvanadi. His duty is to look to his walls."

Chondos made not one spear, but two. One he tipped with the silver knife. That would serve against some of the less material creatures of the Shadow; but it was too dull, and he saw another branch, on a second tree.

After the laborious cutting of the limb, he stumbled over another: straighter, still green. Old troll tracks showed how its split end had been ripped from the trunk. He forced the fork handle into the split and unravelled thread from his robe to bind it.

Dirt scuffed. He looked up. Something rat-sized and brown darted back into the brush. Probably the thing that had gnawed the goblin's shin, or another of the same breed. He finished binding the fork to the wood, and trimmed the stubs of twigs from the staff. He frowned over his work, then, with rocks for hammer and anvil, began to pound down the tines.

The echo of his second stroke was drowned in a roar from the slope. He came to his feet, useless spear levelled, and saw the troll lunge out of the shade of the cliff. It staggered back, its bellows frenzied. Safe in the shade, it glared and roared, its eyes burning sparks. Chills swept Chondos' spine. If the light should dim . . .

He hammered the tines until they met. Strips of cloth torn

from the hem of his robe made rough slings, so he could keep his hands free, or fight with either spear without abandoning the other. He slung both over his shoulder, and looked up at the troll, roaring at the edge of the light.

When night came—or if the light dimmed—it would be after him. He should get as far away as possible. He snatched up the other stick he had cut, frowning, uncertain of what to do with it. Using it as a staff, he began to pick his way down the slope, following the stream.

Martos licked dry lips, and thought of the heir to Damenco, his child, growing now in Kumari's womb. Soon her belly would swell. By this time next year, it would be born, and drinking milk from those perfect breasts. But they would be larger, of course, swollen with milk.

How could he achieve detachment as she intruded into his mind? She and the child—his child. *Shall I take him from my womb and hand him to you?* He shuddered. Such a useless quarrel. The child was no safer, and now . . .

He should have known—had known—that she would never leave. She came of a warrior breed; her dolls had been cradled in helmets. He remembered old stories she had told him: of men who killed themselves when their honour was questioned; of women who had leaped living on their husbands' pyres; of men and women refusing to flee cities where the Dark Things hunted at night.

He watched the ancient city's stones twist and ripple in the haze. Manjipor had been under the Shadow not once but many times. Again and again her ancestors had reclaimed it. And he had shouted at her, insulted her, because she would not flee with him! And now he could not kiss her lips or take her hand, could not stroke her thigh or cup her breast in his palm.

His head was throbbing, and he did not know whether it was the wound, or whether the heat and glare would have made his head hurt anyway. He staggered into his tent and gulped mouthfuls of water that changed suddenly from sweet and cool to warm and brackish. Then he pulled off his sweat-stinking clothes, and lay naked on the blankets. How could men live in such heat! No wonder the Bordermen—and their women— were all mad!

* * *

"Cousin Enjanton," said Istvan, "has there been any sign of forces gathering to oppose the crossing of the Yukota?"

Enjanton shook his head. "We've seen a few horsemen—scouts, I would guess—but no sign of any large force. And that's all flat country."

"Good." Istvan studied the younger man: a typical DiVega, slender, dark, aquiline. "As soon as we finish here, you and DiSezrotti go back to your men, and get them across the river before night. Make camp within sight of the river—pick your spot before you cross."

One of the men who had come in with Enjanton, short, red-haired and long-nosed, looked up. This, then, must be Pression D'Olafos, Istvan thought. He had never met the man, but his reputation as a commander was formidable.

"What of my men, Lord DiVega? Are we to march out also?"

"Your men will stay on this side of the river tonight, and march in the morning, along with . . ." He paused, scanning the faces of his commanders. "Hmmm . . . DiBrais, your men must be tired of sitting on their tails in Ojaini by now. Think they'd like a change?"

"Indeed yes!" Aimon DiBrais laughed, with a flash of white teeth and a twinkle of pale blue eyes. He was red-haired and freckled and lean; his people came from near Heyleu, Istvan recalled, and there was supposed to be Nydorean blood in the family.

"March your men out tonight, then," Istvan said. "Camp next to Lord D'Olafos. You will both cross the Yukota at dawn." He turned back to Enjanton, adding, "And you will march at dawn, Cousin, you and DiSezrotti, for Manjipor, at a pace that will allow DiBrais and D'Olafos to remain in sight. If attacked, you will fall back until they have joined you, unless I give other orders or there is a clear strategic necessity for holding your ground." He hesitated. He had to assign command on some basis, but did not know which of these men was the most able. "You will be in charge of the vanguard, Cousin, and if—"

"Lord Istvan!" One of the Bordermen was on his feet, a muscular little man, tall for a Borderman, whose face was crossed by a narrow moustache. Istvan blinked at him mildly.

"I am Ballo of Kotulmer, of the blood of the Omdavans, and I claim the privilege of leading the vanguard! It is my right!"

And several of the Bordermen murmured, *"It is his right!"*

Istvan stared.

"It is true, Lord Istvan," Rinmull of Ojaini said. "The Omdavans of Kotulmer have led the vanguard of the Kantara for centuries. Their right was confirmed by Prince Rinaldo."

Silently, Istvan cursed behind his mask of calm. "How many men have you?" he asked, playing for time. There might be no way around this. He knew Border pride.

"Thirty men wait for my word to march from Kotulmer," the man said proudly. "Twenty more wait outside, with their horses. We will ride ahead of Lord DiVega, your cousin, and Lord DaiSeor . . ." He paused, struggling with the foreign name. "DaiSeezorti!"

You will, will you, thought Istvan, his face expressionless. He did not like it: Bordermen were brave, but lacked the polish and discipline of northern troops. Yet they were tough warriors; their hardiness might well make up for their lack of size or weight.

"You must get your men across the Yukota tonight, then," he said, "and camp with Enjanton's men. You're under his command, Cousin. But"—his grey eyes met Lord Ballo's black ones—"if you fall back to join D'Olafos' company, you will be under *his* command. Do you understand that?"

The Borderman hesitated, then nodded. Istvan forced himself to smile, although he felt bleak foreboding that this Borderman's pride and rashness could cost dearly.

Chondos stumbled down the widening ravine, while the stream chattered over stone at his left. The brush had thinned, but the flat branching plants like flabby grey antlers were all around.

A scurrying behind him brought his head around, to see a tiny brownish blur vanish behind one of the huge boulders jutting from the ashy soil. Another one! Or was the one he had seen before following him? He remembered the toothmarks on the goblin's shin, and shuddered.

The walls of the little valley were growing steadily steeper as they emerged out of the grey blur that ended his vision. His eyes moved constantly in the uncertain light, and he listened intently, cursing the rushing water. An odd sound from the sky made him look up. Batlike shadows moved in the greyness. He threw himself behind one of the boulders.

Three winged things flapped down, and landed on manlike legs on a finger of stone. They looked horribly like children pretending their cloaks were wings. Hooked beaks jutted under bulging golden eyes. Sudden chills poured down his back. There was something different about one of them, something strange—as though some other creature was looking out through those great gold eyes.

He felt pressure on the edge of his mind, and cowered behind the rock, chanting the Hastur-spell. He slid one of the spears off his shoulder. *It knows I'm here!* he thought, shuddering. His hand trembled on the spear-shaft.

Raucous croaking ripped at his nerves. Two of the winged things launched themselves into the air with a frenzied beating of wings, and sailed over the stream and the cliff beyond, but the third still stared at Chondos' hiding place, as though the gold eyes could see through stone. The silver sky was blotted away as something vast and solid covered the gorge from wall to wall. It drifted like a cloud, but was not a cloud.

Chondos thought of a huge fish swimming above a crack where tiny water-creatures hid in terror. Festoons of ropy tendrils dropped out of the sky, and dragged writhing across the ground. With a slapping of wings the bat-thing leaped from its perch, but too late. A coiling tendril wrapped around it, and drew it into the sky.

Chondos crouched down, watching the tendrils grope across the valley's floor, furrowing the ground as they twisted and looped, tearing the grey plants up by the roots. They drifted on, slowly, over the crack of sky, and slid past the cliffs. Chondos stared at the moving roof until at last an end appeared, dangling masses of tentacles.

Once one of the writhing ropes came within a yard of the rock where he was hiding. He tried to make himself get up and run, but his legs would not move, and then the tendril dragged away again.

The monster drifted to the cliffs, drawing its tendrils through the water. Things that struggled and fought were caught in them. Then they dragged up the cliff, and were gone. The grey sky was clear.

It was a long time before Chondos could get his shaky feet under him. In all tangled Border legendry, he had heard no whisper of a thing like that. He staggered down the slope towards the winding, twisting furrows where living ropes as thick as a man's wrist had swept the ground, dangling from that sky-filling horror. He ran.

A terrible sound brought his eyes up to the dreadful sky. A shape lurched from the edge with flopping wings, and half flew, half fell down the cliff. Wings fluttered madly. It leveled, and flew over the stream towards him. He saw it clearly then.

It was the winged thing he had seen pulled up into the sky, but it was smaller now, because its legs were gone. Blood poured from tatters of chewed flesh that hung from its hips. The golden eyes met his own, and he screamed. His spear was still gripped in his hand. He pushed it out to keep the thing away. He felt something snap, and the glaring eyes were suddenly dead globes of flesh. With a last flopping of wings, it crashed to the ground at his feet.

He stared at the spear in his hand. There was no blood on the blunt silver point. The thing had been dead when it came at him; it must have bled to death before it fell down the cliff. But *what* had looked at him out of those eyes? He bent towards the corpse—

A curious ripple in the air sent him lunging back, and a figure appeared above the corpse. Its eyes were slits of glowing black. Fangs in massive doglike jaws dripped slime.

The landscape moved about it as though it walked in ooze. It flickered, and suddenly was within arm's reach, the talons at the end of its long fingers reaching for his throat. The gargoyle face grinned into his own.

He was falling into the pits of its eyes! The wood of the spear-shaft passed through it harmlessly. He hurled his ring-encrusted fist at the gaping jaws. Sparks leaped from the silver, and shocking pain ran down his arm. For a moment he seemed to gaze into another place, where a black tower rose above shifting ooze and mist that was thronged with ghoulish forms. And then the air before him was empty. He began to

run again, the spear gripped in his hand, while the other shafts
swung and banged painfully against his back.

Throbbing in his veins, Istvan felt the thrill of war: the brief,
pitiful, drunken glory, which made men pour their lives out red
upon the ground.

The Carrodians marched singing into the city. In the light of
the westering suns, double-bitted axeheads glowed above their
shoulders like stars. Istvan pitied them their sore feet. They
would get little rest. Tomorrow they must wade Yukota's ford,
and some would not wade back.

"Lord DiVega?" He turned from the window. In the dim
corridor, a boy in flowing Border robe and wide-skirted
trousers bowed from the waist, in the old way that had come
down from the court of the Takkarian Kings. Black hair fell to
his waist from the silver ring that gathered it atop his head. "I
am called Arjun of Chagor, but in your country my name
would be Arjun DiFlacca. My father was Lucarrho, your
cousin."

Lucarrho! Aunt Estalita's boy! Memories lifted above the
years, smiling at small boys playing in winter snow, in
Carcosa, at well as at this young man in the hot south.

His smile died. "Your father?"

"He is part of the land now," the boy said. "Three years ago.
He led a charge against a big raiding party, right into the
middle of them. Something tore his throat out." *Lucarrho!
Another gone.*

"I'm sorry," said Istvan. "Your father was a good friend to
me."

"Earth must be fed," said Arjun.

Three years . . . but Istvan's mind had flown back ten,
remembering Lucarrho's home here, the ancient castle
renewed by his work; the slender dark bride, all frail bones,
nursing Lucarrho's baby while her wide brown eyes followed
the older child—six or seven, surely this same boy—with the
haunted look with which all Bordermen watched their few
surviving children.

"And . . ." Memory fumbled vainly for her name. "Your
mother?"

"She is well," said the boy, "but I fear she would not be

pleased to hear me talk to you. The traditions of her kin are very dear to her. She is the last of the Omdavans of Chagor. And the pride of the Omdavans is the command of the vanguard." He paused. "But I owe something to my father's kin as well."

Tiny wrinkles twisted frowning brows. "Never think that I dislike my kinsman, Ballo of Kotulmer, or that I do not respect him. There is no braver or more honourable man on the Border. Yet my father told me a little about how civilised wars are fought. My cousin is not accustomed to taking orders. I fear he will take them lightly, and either forget them quickly or hear them badly. He is more brave than wise."

Men said, *Bordermen always run the wrong way*, Istvan remembered, suppressing a smile. "What can I do?" he asked aloud.

"I do not know." Arjun shook his head. "Even in the days of the Empire, they say, the Omdavans led the armies of the Kantara. There is a story that, after the fall of Rashnagar, the survivors of the Kompawut Clan, who had led the vanguard of the Imperial Army, settled in the Kantara, and, when Mahavara revolted, attempted to claim the privilege here; but the Omdavans disputed their right, and the two clans quarrelled. The Last King, to settle the matter, decreed that whoever had the first man inside the walls of Agopor—that was a small fort across the Atvanadi, under the Shadow now—would lead the vanguard forever. The Omdavan chief —the Lord of Kotulmer—died at the top of a siege-ladder, but his brother caught the body before it could fall, and heaved it over the parapet, so that it fell inside, and was thus the first man in the fort."

Stroking his beard thoughtfully, Istvan watched the pride glow through the boy's face.

"Only once after that," Arjun said, "was their right challenged—in Prince Orlando's time. The Prince had never heard the story, but when he did—well, he too had an enemy fort he wanted taken, so he called for a new trial. Omdavan elephants smashed through the gates while the northerners raised their siege-ladders."

"I am no Prince of Tarencia," said Istvan, thoughtfully, "and once this campaign is over, the command of the vanguard will be no concern of mine. So I can hardly order another fortress taken for a third trial! But I see no other way to deny Lord Ballo, and I cannot afford to offend the Lords of the Kantara. Have you any influence with your cousin? If you ride with him, can you keep him from rash actions?"

Arjun shook his head. "He is six years older than I. In his eyes, I am still a child."

"Then we must hope Ballo will learn wisdom," said Istvan. "But I thank you for your warning, Cousin DiFlacca. Since I am so unfamiliar with your ways, and since it seems that many of the Kantara Lords insist on riding with me, perhaps, then, I should have someone to advise me. Will you ride with me, Cousin?" The boy gaped at him.

DiFlacca. Something stirred in the back of Istvan's mind. *Lucarrho . . .*

"I am—I am honoured, Lord!" Arjun bowed, and then bowed again and again, bobbing up and down until Istvan was forced to fight laughter. "I am not worthy of such honour. Indeed, Lord, I have but ten men under my banner, and I must leave some of them to protect my lands and my Lady Mother."

"Leave them all," said Istvan gruffly. "The Kantara will be nearly stripped of men as it is. Lord Rinmull has been far more generous than I desired. With the rains coming, I fear the Dark Things may yet end this war for us."

"I hope that you are wrong, Lord," said Arjun. "I have longed all my life for a real war! I hate this Border butchery!"

Martos woke from fevered dreams of Kumari, his hand groping for his sword. There was someone in the tent. Then a creamy, leathery scent made him pause: the scent of a woman's flesh, a woman's sweat, and in the dim tent his sleep-blurred eyes found a slender, willowy figure, long dark hair hanging down her back.

His lips moved to sound *her* name, but his dry throat made no sound. Finally he gasped, "Who is there?"

"Mirrha, dear Lord."

Mirrha! Was her mistress here with her? He sat up, blinking sleep away. "Where is your mistress?"

"At Inagar," she answered. "She sent me away because—"

She paused. "She sent me to comfort you, Lord. She does not want you to be alone."

Her frail body seemed all bones, but his memory saw through the faded green robe to the angular, adolescent body, the cones of budding breasts.

"Is she well? And my—and our—"

"The baby?" she laughed, teasing. "They're both fine. There isn't much baby yet. Nobody else knows." She giggled.

He became aware of his nakedness, and of the throbbing manhood his dreams had brought him—dreams, and now this soft flesh so close to his own. "There's more than you've told me. Why did she really send you away?"

She sighed, and knelt on the blanket beside him. Her soft hand touched his shoulder; her voice was low and sad. "Because—she does still love you, but—she kept saying things I knew she did not mean, and we quarrelled." He listened with closed eyes, picturing Kumari's rage, and Mirrha defending him. "She *does* love you, Lord, but she is hurt and angry. She said that if—that I should come, and stay with you." He felt her hesitant hand touch his chest, and then stroke gently down. It was Kumari he wanted, but he must not hurt Mirrha.

He felt her warm mouth engulf him. He tried to pretend it was Kumari. He heard the rustle of her robe as it slid from her skin.

"Besides," Mirrha laughed, "she said I needed stretching!" He felt her body press against his own.

Twice Chondos slipped and fell, running under the haunted grey sky from which thick live ropes might drop at any moment. The second fall jarred the breath from him. He lay, fighting his panic until he could move again, then dragged himself to the stream.

A bitter undertaste in the water sickened him, but it was wet and cold. He splashed some across his face. That helped. He fought to get his breathing under control, and the sick, helpless panic slowly ebbed.

The apparition had looked like a ghoul, but ghouls were flesh and blood, and did not vanish and reappear like that. An illusion? But then why had the silver affected it at all?

Still shaking, he followed the stream. Eventually it would

flow across the Border, and there would be one of the towers, its net of light cleansing the river. The Hasturs would read his mind, and save his kingdom. And there would be a bath, and real food, and a soft bed, and people to talk to.

The slant of the slope grew steeper underfoot, and he dug his staff deep to keep from falling. Areas of poisoned grey dust were slippery, and he had to fight for footing.

A low, growling, droning sound startled him. He stopped and waited, then slowly crept towards it. It did not cease or change, and at last he recognised the crash of falling water. The walls of the gorge had grown higher on either hand. Suddenly he saw them end ahead, as though cut by a knife. Warned by that, and by the rising roar of the falls, he slowed and watched the ground cautiously, though the thought of the sky brought prickles of fear.

The ground ended. The stream fell. Wind blew spray in his face. He stepped to the edge and looked down. A flat floor stretched below him. He blinked, wondering if he was dreaming, or mad. He looked again. He was standing in a crack in a perfectly smooth wall, looking down at a flat, polished plane of stone, through which water ran in a straight-walled trough.

He felt like an insect looking into a room. He could not tell whether he looked from a great height onto a broad stone plain, or at a narrow ledge close at hand. The far edge of the floor blurred into grey vagueness. He stared at falling water until perspective returned. Kneeling at the edge, he reached to touch the wall. It was smooth as glass. He lay carefully on his belly and stretched down his staff. With his arm stretched full-length, he felt the tip of the staff touch stone.

No more than ten feet, then! He let the staff clatter to the bottom, and slid the spears from his shoulder. Leaning out, he tried to scan the sky, but the dust was slippery, and he drew himself quickly back. His spears and spare cloak and the food went down. Then he wriggled cautiously over the edge. Only where the waterfall had gnawed the stone was there any kind of hold.

His foot blundered into falling water, and the stream plucked him from the cliff. He twisted in the air, and landed rolling as he had learned to do when thrown from his horse.

Greyness spun. Hard stone bruised his arm, but then he rolled to his knees, sucked in a deep breath, and scanned the vague sky. The silver patch that marked the suns was low. Running half-bent, he quickly gathered up his spears and food and cloak.

He found himself staring at the angle where wall met floor in a perfect corner, and shivered. What force could have cut this squared gap in the mountain's side—and *why?*

Off to his right was a dim triangular wedge—another wall, he supposed. He set off across the polished stone, following the cut channel in which the stream ran. Near the cliff, its squared edges were chipped and cracked by the force of falling water. In time there would be a pool there. It made no sense. His mind whirled.

Then, looking over his shoulder, he saw the thing in the sky. It looked like a fish indeed at this distance. It hung somewhere in the vagueness beyond the triangle, floating in the grey haze.

He began to run. Stone hurt his heels. Ahead, he saw an edge. What lay below? Had the whole mountain been terraced into a giant staircase?

He heard water falling ahead, and slowed, lest he run over another cliff. Then, through the vagueness, he glimpsed branching shapes, and sighed with relief. At the end of the trough, the water foamed into a wide pool. Below, the hillside slanted down, with clumps of fungus and a few pale-leafed trees rising here and there on a boulder-strewn slope.

Scanning the sky, he made out a dim mountain below the hanging fishlike shape. The creature was searching the hillside with its tentacles. A glance in the other direction showed both suns, visible as pallid balls of flame, low in the sky.

He had to swing wide, skirting the pool, but the loose soil under his feet was a welcome change from the stone of the fish-thing's table. The stream poured down a steep ravine. He followed it, keeping to the thickest of the trees and fungi, as though they could help if those tendrils dropped from the sky.

Then, glancing over his shoulder, he saw a flash of colour in the greyness. Something small and brown was running across the stone. He stared a moment, then ran. He could think of no reason for such a creature to cross the tableland, except to follow him.

Between two pillars, Istvan caught a glimpse of Esrith Gunnar, beard bristling silver and gold, and heard the

Carrodian's harsh voice growling among echoes: ". . . so we're anxious to get our orders and move on."

"He should be here soon," Rinmull of Ojaini's clear voice rang in answer. "From what he was saying at the Council, I suspect you'll be marching out at dawn, with the rest of us."

Another voice, softer and lighter—Asbiorn Kung's, Istvan guessed—added something, but Istvan could not make out the words. *Dawn.* He pictured this army flooding over the Yukota, into the grey wastes of Manjipé. Rounding a pillar, he caught sight of the little group of men: Asbiorn and Esrith Gunnar, Rinmull of Ojaini, old Palos DiFlacca . . .

DiFlacca! Suddenly the thought that had worried the back of his mind since Arjun had mentioned his father's name broke free. *Lucarrho*—Lucarrho D'Esterras, of Palos DiFlacca's company, the man who had carried the message to Jagat that had started this. He'd meant to take D'Esterras to Lord Shachio, and find out why he had delivered the message despite Istvan's orders. The bustle of war had pushed it from his mind.

But DiFlacca's men were here, and there were Seers in plenty. He'd have D'Esterras examined, and then they'd know—

What? He shook his head. Probably nothing of any use.

He had increased his pace: his boots, normally silent, slapped the floor. He could hear their voices, but only a few words came clearly, until Esrith Gunnar's voice rose above the rest.

"They'll have a new song about Ironfist before this war is over! 'The Song of the Walls of Manjipor,' or something like that. Lord Todar said that at the tower gate, he was holding the stairs alone, and he killed the Kadarin captain, Martos of Antecca, or whatever his name was."

"What!" Istvan's heart lurched, and he rushed towards them. "Martos of Onantuga? Dead?" The depth of his shock surprised him: he had never met the boy, that he remembered. Poor Birthran! From the pride in his voice you would have thought Martos his son.

His mind reeled back eight years to the news of his own son's death. He shook his head, angrily. Men died in war; you could not mourn them all, though you flooded the land with tears!

Birthran—he remembered sterile mountainslopes under the grey Shadow: feet slipping in grey ash, when he and Birthran had gone together into the Shadow, nearly twenty years ago, to search for the Lost Prince.

"Tell me about it," he heard himself say.

"Well, Ironfist was commander at the tower gate." Gunnar's voice was puzzled. "You remember it—rather complicated maze? Ironfist was holding the first section, the stairway, with a few men. All the others were cut down, and he met the Kadarin leader in combat and killed him. I didn't know he was a friend of yours. Sorry to have to tell you."

"I didn't . . ." Istvan blinked, felt foolish, letting his voice die away. He hadn't known the boy—and Ironfist was an old friend. He should be happy Ironfist was alive.

When heroes meet, no victory . . .

"DiFlacca!" he said, turning his mind to business. "I want to talk to D'Esterras—Lucarrho D'Esterras, the one who took the message to Jagat."

"D'Esterras?" DiFlacca stared at him. "Didn't you know? He's dead." Istvan stared. "He was one of the men riding with DiGarsa. He was killed in that first fight, on the Marunka."

Jodos could feel strange tensions rippling through the minds of the people of the court and city of Tarencia, as subtle changes in the air affected the fluids of their bodies. Great masses of cloud were gathering above the Sea of Ardren, mountains of vapour that loomed above the shore.

Fastidiously, he moved among the courtiers' minds, flinching from their alien thoughts as he hunted for the tiny seeds of hatred that would tear the city apart. Then, through the web of minds, he sensed the approach of that victim he had marked as his own special prey. He licked his lips and his strong teeth, anticipating her screams and the taste of her blood.

Only her father's orders had driven Melissa to return. Her own greed, unsupported, would not have brought her back for more of the precious royal seed—not, at least, until she was sure she would need it. "Chondos'" callous brutality had hurt and frightened her, but she feared her father more.

Fascinated, Jodos studied her mind, amazed at the obedience and fright the old man had caused with such silly, harmless threats. He touched her mind delicately, guiding her. He must be very careful. It would be so easy to spoil everything, after such a long time without real food!

He would put a compulsion on her that would keep her coming back, whatever he did to her. He examined the fears swarming in her mind, and smiled malignly as he compared them with his real plans. It would be amusing to do the things she pictured, just as she imagined them. That could keep him amused until his mission was safely over, and he need fear the Blue-robes no longer. Then she would learn—they would all learn—what fear really was!

Mirrha's hands stroked Martos' chest, and he remembered Kumari, touching him the same way and laughingly saying that she had never before had a lover whose ribs she could not count. And now she was far from him, even as his seed grew in her womb!

Mirrha snuggled against his shoulder. It was not fair! Why could he not love her as she deserved? He stiffened. He had just poured his living seed into her body. What if she, too—

"Martos?" Valiros' voice sounded outside the tent. "Lord Jagat wishes to speak to you."

Martos sat up. Sudden pain made him dizzy. "I'll be right out!" He groped for his clothes. Mirrha wrapped her robe about her and began to help him dress.

"May I enter?" It was Jagat's voice. Martos started.

"A moment!" He did not want Jagat to find Mirrha in his tent, even though a calmer part of his mind told him it did not matter.

"As you wish," the courteous old voice said.

Slipping on his boots, Martos staggered from the tent, buckling his sword-belt around his hips. Jagat looked bent and old. His voice was sad and tired.

"I hear you've kept to your tent all day," said Jagat. "Wise, in this heat. If I'd known the day would be like this"—a strange agony crept into the old voice—"I'd have taken my boy home, to Suknia. The field is plowed and ready. I sit here staring at the walls, and my boy is not yet with the land!" He shook his fist at the city. "I could have gone! I could even have gotten back by now! But Kumari—it would have been too far for her." He sighed, and shook his head. "I suppose the dead from this war will reclaim miles of the land." His voice was bitter. He shook himself. "Earth must be fed."

Turning to Martos, he added: "The Seynyoreans are crossing the Yukota. Word just came in from the watch we left at Kajpor. Do you think you're healed enough to ride against them?"

"Yes," Martos lied.

"Good. My men are brave, but we know nothing here of how wars are fought in the rest of the world. Fighting the night-haunts teaches nothing of strategy. You are the only one I can trust to ride against the Seynyoreans."

Against Istvan DiVega, Martos thought. He, the youngest son of a younger son of the House of Raquio, to face the greatest swordsman among living warriors! The wonder and the glory stilled his tongue.

Chapter Seventeen

Chondos huddled in a thicket, drifting in and out of dream—dreams fed by the screams and roars that filled the night. A voice called his name.

He started from sleep, looking round him, then settled back down. Another dream. A troll bellowed upriver; beneath its distant moaning came another sound: a shrill squeaking that had almost the sound of human words, like a tiny voice that cried "Flee! Flee!"

He lay back down, closing his eyes against the night. What else would a voice cry, here?

Suddenly his eyes opened again and he sat up. Silver shimmered on the water that murmured to his right; black branches moved against a sky. He could *see!* The night was not the usual blindness, but a dimness like starlight, though there were no stars.

He heard a crashing on the stone above, and a fresh burst of roaring from the troll. It sounded nearer. He shook his head, stupid with the need for sleep. Something else shrieked, far across the hills. He could see the river shimmer on the mountainside above him. The troll's roaring sank to a kind of snarling moan. He had heard a troll moan like that once before, when he had stayed with Pirthio and Jagat at one of the Border castles. Jagat had said it was following a trail, hunting by scent.

Something scampered through the bushes—something small. He started, as the squealing broke out anew. *"Run!"* it shrilled, somewhere near him, the words unmistakable. *"Run! A troll! A troll is coming!"*

Icy worms wriggled in his spine. Stones clattered above him on the slope. He sprang to his feet looking up. Beside the dim stream, a giant, manlike shape rode an avalanche of stones and loose dirt.

"*Run!*" the shrill voice shrieked beside him. "*King Chondos! Run!*"

And he did run, bursting in a cold sweat from his covert. *It knew his name!*

Below, between black cliffs, pallid radiance, dimmer than starlight, filled the cleft, glimmering on water. Hope flared. Was it the glow of the Border? A furious bellow thundered behind him. Red eyes were tiny sparks.

Both spears were gripped in his hand, but they were useless against that mountain of stony flesh. Only the eyes would be soft enough, and his spears were too short to reach them without coming into range of those crushing hands.

Slippery ash shifted under his feet. Canyon and river veered left. The dim glow brightened. He heard water plunge in a sudden fall. Then, beyond the ground before his feet, he saw a ring of blue fire surrounded by stars. He checked a moment at the edge of the sudden steep, then ran down, half running, half sliding. Below, stone glowed.

Long ago, a Hastur-tower had stood here, cleansing the water as it flowed out from the Shadow. Dark magic had shattered it, but the fire of its builders still burned in its foundations.

He slid and ran and fell through powdery ash. Stones from the nearing avalanche bounded past him; the troll's bellows drowned the sounding stream. The slope curved out to a level, and he floundered in a bank of deep dust, then found his feet and ran. Breath scraped his raw throat. Suddenly he stumbled from slippery dust to bruising stone. Here, the earth had been stripped away, scoured down to bedrock. Scattered tiny shards flamed like stars about his feet.

The troll fell, bellowing, thrashing in the deep dust piled at the slope's foot. Between its bellows, crushed dust-grains squeaked, terrifyingly soft, beneath its rising weight.

Chondos paused before the low, gleaming wall, jagged like broken glass, and turned, his spear raised. The troll was closing fast, reaching out with arms longer than Chondos' body. He hurled the steel-tipped spear at one red eye. The point glanced across the stony cheek and fell, harmless. Whirling,

Chondos set his hand to the least jagged part of the wall, and vaulted over. Pain lashed his hand; his palm was wet.

His feet came down on a softness that was not the softness of the powdery ash. His heart lurched. Pulling the knife from his sash, he hurled himself frantically back, looking down to see what horror had lain waiting in the ruined tower. In the blue glow he saw, beneath his feet, a wide mat of thick bristles like fur or . . .

Grass. The drawn knife fell from a shaking hand; his knees folded under him. Frightened hands roamed gingerly over the ground; he breathed deep a welcome, unexpected scent. The floor of the ruin was carpeted with living grass.

For a moment he almost forgot the troll, until a roar brought his eyes up to see, looming above the glowing stone that barely came to its waist, the great red eyes glaring at him. A huge, taloned hand reached across the wall.

Stone flared white. The troll stumbled back as though singed, clapping its hands to its eyes. Chondos scooped up one of the glowing fragments of stone from the grass and hurled it over the wall. It struck the massive shoulder, and flamed white. The troll bellowed with pain.

The wall dimmed to pallid blue once more. Chondos knelt on the grass, smelling it, feeling it under his palms as he ran his fingers through blades and matted roots. The troll moaned beyond the glowing stone, but Chondos did not look up. He stretched himself out, wrapping his cloak tightly around him, and fell asleep, breathing the scent of grass.

Jodos waited at the head of the stairway up which Melissa must climb. His mind intercepted others that might come this way, and turned them back, changing their plans. He would not be disturbed.

He licked his lips, thinking of her blood and her screams. But not yet. Not until the city was his, and the Blue-robes driven away. And not until his spawn had ripened within her. Before it ripened enough, he would have been Master here for a while, gorging himself on blood and flesh. He would make her watch, so that there would be plenty of time for her to realise what was going to happen to her.

She reached the foot of the stairs. He stepped back,

watching. The pulsing need within him was disturbingly similar to that he had sensed in the young men of the court. But it was *not* the same, he told himself angrily, fighting off his shame. It was not as though he were going to let her live, or his spawn! It was only the feeding frenzy that he felt! And the Pure-in-Blood did the same thing to fatten their slaves before they ate them.

His brother's ghost sniggered in the back of his mind. He waited, watching her thoughts as she climbed the stairs slowly, hesitantly, afraid to go on, afraid to go back. He smiled. She would keep him fed and entertained for a long time, if he was careful, and cauterised often, to make sure she—or the thing inside her—did not die too soon.

When she was almost at the top of the stairs he made her look up, and savoured her fear as she stood, staring at him. His eyes caught hers, and dragged her to him, step by unwilling step. His teeth glittered white. He reached deep into her mind, setting the compulsion that would keep her coming back.

Pounding tension surged through him, and he fought the urge to take off one of her breasts *now,* to tear soft flesh and taste warm blood. Angrily, he forced himself instead to look inside her mind, at the fears he meant to play with tonight.

He clamped down with his mind to keep her from screaming, as his hand clenched on her breast.

Towards dawn, the towering clouds piled above the Sea of Ardren slowly toppled, drifting south in a vast armada.

In the transparent night sky, Istvan DiVega saw the first outriders sail into the northern sky, where Tressil glowed like an ominous red coal. His sword, kindled by the nearness of the Shadow, flashed in its own light as it whistled about him.

The rising Twins gilded with dawn the floating mass of white and grey that rolled slowly south, ponderous with winter rains, covering the sky above Portona and the royal city.

Along the Border, the skies were still blue, and in the Shadow itself the filtered light was still so clear that the troll who had prowled nightlong around the burning ring of the fallen tower hugged the deep shade of the gorge's eastern bank as he fled back to his lair.

* * *

On the east bank of the Yukota, trees reared like a sudden green wall against the barren grey lands to the west. Giant trees marched to the water's edge; long snaky roots wove thirstily into the broad shallow water. Today no birds sang, and the beasts had long fled from their familiar green-dappled haunts. Small rocks splashed water over themselves, water yellowed by the constant churning of hooves.

Istvan DiVega's saddle rocked and swayed under him. Water splashed into his boots. He slitted his eyes against the glare of sun-gilded water. Above the trees, the Twin Suns poured golden light through the narrow strip of blue between the advancing mass of cloud drifting down from the north and the immovable, glassy murk to the south, in which the dim, ghostly shapes of sunless mountains could be barely seen.

Tiny in the north, he saw a distant flock of geese, or swans, perhaps, wheel suddenly back towards the north, frightened by the flood of men that filled the Yukota. Or was it the nearness of the Shadow? He wondered if the swans that wintered here were the same that flew up from the south in the spring, white wings wafting them above Carcosa and the Mountains of the Clouds on their way to the Bay of Heyleu and the wide swamps of Gersalt.

His wife had always asked for tales of the lands where the swans flew in the winter . . . But that brought up memories of sickbeds and tombs, and other things he did not want to remember. Again he buried her, and escaped into this present, with cold water dripping into his boots, and the rhythmic splashing of horses and men in his ears; with the ancient forest green behind them, and the drab, barren land of the Manjipé shore drawing ever nearer, nearer.

Wagons creaked and rattled on the narrow, sunken causeway at the centre of the ford: wagons of food for horses and men, and for the cattle that drew them. Istvan spurred his grey mare through shallow water, and rode dripping up the bank. At the top he wheeled his horse smartly. Below, black against light-gilded water, thousands of men and horses flowed constantly from under the leaf-clouded branches, filling the broad stream as far as the eye could see.

The last wagon rocked clumsily up the bank, and now the footmen appeared, Prince Phillipos gorgeous at their head on his big white horse, white plumes waving above his helmet, the steel of his armour polished and glittering.

The Kalascoreans marched in a narrow column, for they, too, must keep to the old causeway, wading first knee-deep and then waist-deep in the swirling yellow water. Feeling their way with lance butt and halberd shaft, swords and wide bronze shields swaying, strapped high on their backs, the marching men mirrored sunlight from polished breastplates and helmets.

Horsemen swam and waded all about them, rippling the glare-coated water with tiny, muddy waves that splashed like surf on steel breastplates. On the bank, the companies gathered and spread out into the planned marching order. Off to the right, sunlit Kadarin-style plate armour glowed above sombre clothing as Erwan DiBolyar's company rode their gaunt, long-legged horses up the bank. Behind them came DiCalvados' men, conservative in close-linked ring-mail like Istvan's own. In ten or fifteen years, he supposed, everyone would have switched to the Kadarin style.

Wet horses dripped on the sparse brown grass and the thin strip of green at the water's edge, already grazed by the vanguard. Here and there a pitiful young sapling, cast across the river by the wind, struggled with the starveling soil. Yet even this would seem lush compared to the leagues of reclaimed land they must cross now.

This corner of Manjipé had never been under the Shadow. Around the castles that lay on their line of march would be miles of dust, and bare rock where the dust had been scoured away with wind and rain by the Hastur-kin: waiting for transported soil, for manure and sand; waiting for the plow and the planting and the ashes of the dead.

But worst of all would be the miles of poisoned dust surrounding Manjipor. And with the rainy season coming on . . . He scowled at the clouds he could see in the north.

A messenger came spurring up, saluted, and announced: "Kajpor is abandoned, sir, but our scouts found signs that men ate there yesterday morning, and tracks of horses that might suggest men left it just about the time the vanguard crossed the river. Commander DiBrais wishes to know if he should leave a detachment to garrison the castle."

"Ride to Lord Rinmull," Istvan said. "Tell him to leave a garrison to hold it."

The man saluted and rode away. Istvan looked across the river, at the vast green wall of the forest, and then south, at the even vaster wall of darkness that hid the southern sky. Shaking his head, he rode to join Prince Phillipos as the fine white horse came dripping from the water.

When Chondos had opened his eyes that morning, with the thick softness of living grass beneath him, he had thought himself waking from evil dreams, on some hunt with his father. The memory of that waking, and the disappointment with which he had seen the glowing wall, the grey sterile dust beyond, was with him now as he moved cautiously down-river, stumbling in the hateful grey dust.

With the dim daylight, the need-fire that had burned in the broken tower wall had faded to a pale bluish glimmer. All around the tower had lain chips of the glassy stone, some blackened and dead, some still burning with pallid light. Several of those now made a comforting weight in the pockets of his sleeves, and one piece, a slender, dagger-shaped splinter, rode the end of the branch that had served him as a staff, wedged into a split made by his knife and bound there tightly with thread taken from the hem of his robe.

He had recovered the spear he'd thrown at the troll, and both the steel and silver-tipped spears now hung from his shoulder, but it was the new spear, tipped with glowing stone, that he gripped ready in his hand.

Suddenly he stopped, every nerve shrieking. Ahead was only the grey ash, with no plants or trees where an enemy could hide. Yet the sense of sudden danger was so strong that he brought his spear up, ready to fight, and saw the point blazing with bright blue flame.

He stared at it, wondering, then drew his left arm into the sleeve and groped in the dangling pocket until he found one of the larger shards of glowing stone. Sliding his arm free of the sleeve, he tossed the stone out, onto the dust ahead.

White flame seared his eyes: the stone burst into blackened fragments, and a sharp whine hurt his ears. The grey ash was suddenly stained with black. Transparent darkness oozed out from the dust, howling in a shrill, humming whistle.

Chondos stumbled back, spear-point raised. In the dim light of day, the Demon screamed, and oozed quickly to the shade of the cliff. A Demon powerful enough to shatter the stone and survive—and that chip had been larger than the splinter that tipped his spear. The pallid light of the Shadow would not hold it long. But all he had were a few chips of stone, and the silver—and his fire-striker . . .

He fumbled in his sash for tinderbox and torch, working in furious haste. Sparks leaped, and then, as he sat blowing the tiny crawling sparks, numbness washed through his brain.

What was he doing? He stared through the brightness around him. There was too much light. He would go lie down, in the shade under the cliff. He started to climb to his feet. He looked dully at the thing in his hand. A stick. And on its end . . .

Burning!

His eyes focussed on the flaming blue stone, and then he was chanting the spell Miron Hastur had planted in his brain. Barriers closed around his mind. He bent over the tinderbox, driving horror and relief alike from his mind. A ribbon of blackness curled out of the shade of the cliff. It swayed like a snake, and vanished in the dust.

Chondos thrust his torch into the burning tinder, fuming as urgency grew. He pictured himself walking onto that patch of dust. His bones would be part of that dust now, if he had gone on. The Demon would have risen around his legs, dissolving them as he walked; it would have risen from under the dust . . .

Under the dust!

He tipped the tinderbox out in front of him. He suddenly *knew* that that black tendril was groping towards him in darkness underground. Then he *felt* it hesitate at the barrier of fire, and dive deeper into the ground, then reach around the coals for the flesh of the feet.

He emptied the stones from his sleeve, and snatching one up, hurled it at the shade where the Demon hid. The stone fell short, landing in dim light at the edge of the shade, and burst into flaring fragments. Again the shrill scream tore his ears, and a black curl writhed out of the dust almost at his feet. He lunged with the torch, shouting Hastur's name. And blackness burned.

The shade of the cliff was a sudden pool of flame, writhing and crackling. He covered his ears against the thing's shrill scream. Hungry flames writhed in air before the cliff . . .

And were gone.

He shuddered. It had been close. It would be a long time before he'd rid himself of the vision of the tide of darkness rising around his feet; of looking down to see the flesh dissolve and the bones begin to crumble.

He stared down the river. Was that a dim glow on the mountain, another of the broken towers? Every time the Border had been driven back over the last thousand years, a new tower had been raised beside the stream to purify the water. If he could reach the next one by nightfall, he could sleep safely. And at least he now had a weapon against the Shadow. He looked at the flaming tip of his spear—now faded again to a dim blue glow—and remembered a verse from "Pertap's Ride":

> Lend to me your silver sword,
> And kindle me a torch of flame:
> I shall ride forth from Kudrapor,
> To call for aid in Hastur's name.

A rustling sound made him look back. Something small and brown darted behind a rock.

Martos and all his men kept their eyes to the north, where the flat, barren land, spread out under the vastness of the sky, with piled clouds drifting slowly through blue distances, held a kind of ruined, sombre beauty. None liked to look behind, where the Shadow, looming like a wall of dirty obsidian, seemed to draw the sky down to a low ceiling, cramping the soul.

Across the grey and barren land, the Kadarins rode flaming. The light of the Twin Suns leaped in silver splendour from the polished steel of cuirass and morian; the powerful, deep-chested war-horses towered above the stubby, rough-coated Border ponies. Metallic dust shifted under the horses' feet, barely stirring. The Bordermen's faces were veiled against the poison of the dust, but Martos did not bother—it didn't puff above his horse's knees.

Far behind now lay the newly fertile reclaimed fields of

Manjipor, each acre bearing the name of the man whose ashes had hallowed the soil. For miles before them lay only leaden dust and bare stone, with the rare patches of unblasted soil covered by sparse, sun-dried grass.

Where once unclean things had crawled under a sunless sky, clouds of purple, green, and crimson rippled beneath the banner of the sword-wheel, with Martos' personal standard—the silver ghost-wolf of his ancestors joined with a winged blade—fluttering from the same staff. The sleek coats of the Kadarin horses—roan, palomino, bay—glowed in the morning light. Warflame blazed like a sunset.

Martos' borrowed helmet sat on his saddlebow, and his brown hair gleamed pure gold. Gloomily, he eyed the nearing clouds, and wondered if he would be forced to eat raw fish. Once the rains came, he knew, the Bordermen, with no sunlight for their cooking mirrors, ate uncooked food all winter. "Fisheaters," men called them, and said they killed the flavour with strange sauces.

But nothing could blunt the glory of this campaign: somewhere beyond this ashen desert, Istvan the Archer marched with his army. Martos remembered long nights planning with Paidros and Valiros, finding ways to equip his little force by hard work instead of the money that they lacked. With hard work, high-placed kin, and Birthran's prestige, they had succeeded, and now it was time to take this fine, hand-ground weapon and test it against the finest known.

Horseshoes squeaked on powdery dust; armour creaked and rattled, both leather and steel. Yet the leaden ash swallowed the sound of hooves, and the deathly stillness preyed on men's nerves, until Martos ordered the trumpets sounded to break the birdless silence.

The last time he had ridden this way, he'd commanded Kumari's tiny escort, with her womb barely beginning to swell with his child. What mattered this glory, without her eyes on him, without her waiting for him to come back?

Merchant! he mocked himself. *So that is where your profit lies now? What price for the Self-Judged Man? Will you sell your honour for the light in a lady's eyes?*

Kumari's eyes, and leaden dust stretching out mile on mile ahead, without a bird, without a tree, and Istvan the Archer somewhere on the other side . . . Somewhere beyond the dust were six thousand Seynyoreans, or more, with Istvan the Archer at their head. The glory of that thrilled through him.

Grey dust rolled away under horses' hooves. Bugles beat back the birdless silence; bright colours and polished steel defied the bleakness of the ruined land. Gleaming they rode, their eyes turned always to the sunlit north, away from the dark southern sky, where the Border brooded above them like a wave about to fall.

End of Volume One.
To be continued in Volume Two:
KING CHONDOS' RIDE

Discover New Worlds
with books of Fantasy
by Berkley

____	***FAITH OF TAROT*** Piers Anthony	07037-9/$2.95
____	***COLLECTED FANTASIES,*** ***AVRAM DAVIDSON*** Edited by John Silbersack	05081-5/$2.50
____	***PEREGRINE: SECUNDUS*** Avram Davidson	04829-2/$2.25
____	***A GLOW OF CANDLES & other stories*** Charles L. Grant	05145-5/$2.25
____	***THE WORLD AND THORINN*** Damon Knight	05193-5/$2.50
____	***THE SAILOR ON THE SEAS OF FATE*** Michael Moorcock	06158-2/$2.50
____	***BENEATH AN OPAL MOON*** Eric Van Lustbader	07040-9/$2.75
____	***THE NORTHERN GIRL*** Elizabeth A. Lynn	06387-9/$2.75
____	***THE SWORDS TRILOGY*** Michael Moorcock	06389-5/$2.95
____	***PEACE*** Gene Wolfe	04644-3/$2.25
____	***DREAM MAKERS, The Uncommon*** ***People Who Write Science Fiction*** Edited by Charles Platt	04668-0/$2.75

Prices may be slightly higher in Canada.

Available at your local bookstore or return this form to:

BERKLEY
Book Mailing Service
P.O. Box 690, Rockville Centre, NY 11571

Please send me the titles checked above. I enclose _____. Include 75¢ for postage and handling if one book is ordered; 25¢ per book for two or more not to exceed $1.75. California, Illinois, New York and Tennessee residents please add sales tax.

NAME_____

ADDRESS_____

CITY_____ STATE/ZIP_____

(allow six weeks for delivery)   **76M**